The Mule

a novel by
Barry Lee Davies

PublishAmerica
Baltimore

First printing

All characters in this book are fictitious, and any resemblance to real persons, living or dead, is coincidental.

PublishAmerica has allowed this work to remain exactly as the author intended, verbatim, without editorial input.

ISBN: 1-60474-870-2
PUBLISHED BY PUBLISHAMERICA, LLLP
www.publishamerica.com
Baltimore

Printed in the United States of America

Other Novels by the Author:

Chasing the Truth

Dedication

Patience, encouragement, love, and faith usually promote the will to succeed. I know it is true in my case.

For my wife and partner in life:
Shirley Donna Davies

Mule:

- The sterile hybrid offspring of a male donkey and a female horse, characterized by long ears and a short mane.

- A sterile hybrid, as between a canary and other birds or between certain plants.

- A stubborn person.

- A spinning machine that makes thread or yarn from fibers; also called a *spinning mule*.

- A small, usually electric tractor or locomotive used for hauling over short distances.

- *A person who serves as a courier of illegal drugs.*

Drugs are a reality.

Crime is a reality

Victims are a reality

The fact that you could unwittingly become a "mule"…

Is a reality!

The Mule

CHAPTER ONE

Tam Hy walked through the dimly lit tunnel towards the barn, his slight frame standing erect without having to worry about overhead obstacles. He was thinking about the large crop and the time consuming harvest yet to come. He had heard others call it hemp, weed, Mary Jane, dope, cannabis, magic smoke, crazy weed, and grass; but at the end of the day, it was just a crop.

This crop had a reputation on the street for being very potent, as well as for being the best in the world. The THC or tetrahydrocannabinol concentration is about the highest in North America. Just mention the name, *BC Bud*, and there are no questions asked. Demand is high, but then, so are the stakes.

The six-foot plants were nearing the ninety-day cycle and close to being harvested. Growers referred to them as monster plants. The lush, dark green vegetation gave off an intoxicating aroma that hung in the air like something physical and just breathing the air assaulted the senses.

Even though the old chicken barn was well off the road and hidden from view, on certain days the heady scent from the marijuana plants drifted across the countryside and turned more than a few heads. The old chicken barn was two hundred feet long but had not seen a baby chick in six years. It had been a home to pigeons until the new renters took over.

Now the barn seemed alive as the huge fans moved the heated air in and around the massive 430-watt hydroponics' bulbs and reflectors suspended over the plants. Timers controlled the lights as well as the flow of water that trickled through tubes to each plant. Now that the plants were mature, the timers reduced the lights from eighteen hours to twelve hours.

It was a sophisticated operation. The walls of the barn were made of inch thick planking and a crew had filled the cracks between the planks with expandable foam insulation to keep the heat in, and prying eyes out. Highly reflective insulation maximized the effect of the heat bulbs. The temperature was a constant 82 degrees, kept that way by exhaust fans near the roof, and intake fans lower down; airflow was one of the secrets to a good grow.

Tiny sensors set into boarded-over windows, would activate an alarm in the main house if anyone tried to gain entry. There were six cameras: one in each of the four corners, and two swivel-mounted cameras halfway down the main run. Monitors were set up in the old farmhouse as well as the barn. The dogs roamed freely within their boundaries and provided an additional level of security.

There were no doors in the barn for the curious to enter, or for the police, or for those seeking free samples. A trap door in the floor led to a tunnel. From the bottom of the ladder, walking west, it led to the basement of the house, the opposite direction led to an underground room with two huge generators.

Exhaust pipes extended out of the ground amongst bales of hay to help muffle the noise. It was all very expensive, but too many electrical bypasses in the past had introduced the authorities to profitable operations.

The trap door moved up rapidly and slammed back down onto the floor; dust erupted and swirled back onto itself as Tam Hy climbed off the ladder and into the barn. Looking quickly around the interior he was satisfied that all was as it should be and started his journey to the other end of the barn.

Hy was a quiet man and rarely offered his opinion on anything, unless of course it had to do with raising a crop. His family's very existence used to depend on his skills as a farmer in Viet Nam. Now, years after leaving his country, he found himself employed as a caretaker farmer and artfully involved in the cultivation of cannabis.

The Mule

Although never arrested he had no illusions as to what would happen if the police were to arrive at his door. He knew very little about the law but he depended on his *employer* to look after him.

Authorities had hauled away others like him but they were all back and tending to business two days later so he was not concerned all that much. Although he spoke in broken English, and understood it well enough, he always played dumb with strangers.

Hy began to inspect the twenty-three hundred plants currently in the last stages of growth. It was a massive crop. They were very heavy with buds and he knew everyone would be pleased. This would mean a bonus for him. It was going to take a lot of work to cut, separate, and package before he was able to start the process all over again. He would need many cuttings for cloning. The cloning assured female plants only. That was important.

Hy heard footsteps behind him and turned as a large broad-shouldered man walked towards him through the dense foliage. He was about six feet tall, balding across the top of his head, and displayed a large gold ring in his left ear. He always had a continuous scowl on his face and a perpetual three-day growth of beard that rubbed up against the inside of the collar of his dirty shirt. His name was Mike Sigger, and because he appeared to be miserable most of the time others sarcastically called him 'Happy', but only behind his back of course.

Tam Hy was always offended when he looked at the unkempt man. The other man always had an unclean smell about him and he was always in a nasty mood. Hy smiled and bowed slightly as Mike Sigger walked towards him and he was again sickened by the man's large stomach and his disgusting appearance, although it never showed on his face.

It was times like this that Tam Hy thought of working for the East Indian gangs that were taking over. "Ho, looking good. Soon we cut."

"No shit," Sigger sneered, watching as Tam Hy walked away without a comment. His bloodshot eyes squinted with disgust and he did not hide his dislike for Orientals,

Turning, Sigger walked further into the grow-op, wishing not for the first time that it belonged to him. He was looking at twenty-three hundred female plants yielding about one pound of buds per plant, and at up to five thousand dollars per pound on the street that was worth fighting for. Sigger also knew it could sell for eight thousand dollars a pound in New York City.

Site security was one of Mike Sigger's functions. Given the dollars and the time and equipment involved he had to make sure everything went as planned. It was no time for a screw up and he was always nervous just before a harvest. He shifted his shotgun to the other hand and started his rounds.

Just before starting down the ladder, Sigger glanced at a different set of monitors. Each one provided a different view of the outside grounds and the cameras penetrated the darkness with ease.

He could see that it was clear at the front and south side of the barn. The other camera displayed the rear and the north side and it showed no activity. The third camera watched the long driveway that gave access from the roadway. He was well aware that the dogs would grab onto anyone prowling outside. Still, he did not take anything for granted. The moment you did that you ended up in jail or dead.

Sigger moved along the dirt-walled tunnel. The light bulbs that were strung and attached to roots in the dirt wall stuck out at odd angles. The floor was covered with planks and squeaked when he walked.

There was no heat in the house but the generators provided any needed electricity. However unlike the barn the house had a lived in appearance from the outside. Timers allowed lights to shine onto the closed and dirty curtains, and the carport contained an old and unused vehicle. Neighbors were far enough away that they were not curious.

As he walked up from the basement of the house, Sigger kicked aside the mounting debris on the floor and moved into the kitchen. He backhanded an empty pizza box off of the counter and into the corner, watching as the box landed on top of other garbage. He selected a take out sandwich from a box and a can of beer from a cooler and ignoring the monitors exited the rear door.

The night air was a little on the damp side. The old farm was located in a bit of a depression in relation to the surrounding area and was not too far from the river. The farm was on the municipal border of Langley and

The Mule

Abbotsford, British Columbia. It was also only ten miles to the wide-open Canadian and U.S. border.

The frogs croaked constantly now, stopping only when they became aware of a dangerous presence. Sigger set down his items on an outside rail while he placed the night-vision binoculars onto his head. He adjusted the straps and looked into the darkest area at the rear of the house. The dark and moonless night blossomed suddenly into an eerie florescent-green landscape that resembled a planet in some science fiction movie. What had been in total darkness a moment before now exposed every bush, rock, and movement.

Leaning against the railing, Sigger took a bite of his sandwich, his shotgun sitting comfortably close by. He enjoyed this time, with nothing to think about but the night and what moved around in the darkness. He adjusted the old 9mm semi-auto Browning that was sticking into his back and took a swig of his beer. It was almost time to move into position.

The dogs brushed up against his leg. He hadn't heard them approach. Their eyes sparkled evilly and looking into the bottomless green florescent marbles made him shiver involuntarily. It was like looking into the eyes of the devil. He was glad he didn't have to face them in the darkness.

Trained not to bark, they moved silently wherever they roamed, moving in on a person like silent phantoms. Now they just stood there, quivering with restrained power, waiting for his command.

Sigger let out a soft belch and picked up the shotgun, moving off the back porch and into the darkness beyond. The Dobermans padded softly ahead, crisscrossing from side to side. They seemed eager, looking back at Sigger in what seemed like anticipation. Again, their marble green eyes looked like something from hell.

One hundred feet beyond the chicken barn the dogs scooted under a split rail wooden fence and disappeared into a neighboring cornfield. Sigger climbed over quickly and walked through the corn a short distance. He reappeared at the fence and stopped.

He desperately wanted a cigarette after the food and the beer, but he quickly put it out of his mind as he settled back for the wait. The frogs started up again, the sound soothing to Sigger's ears.

Twenty minutes later the frogs stopped croaking and the dogs appeared suddenly at his side. They were sniffing the air and looking intently into the darkness towards the east. There was a bit of ground fog and it drifted in lime-colored, effervescent waves on the small breeze.

Three men stepped out into the open. They were all dressed in dark clothing. They stood there, looking for any signs of danger.

So, Sigger thought, *the information I was given was right.* Sigger strained to get a closer look at their faces. *Please, don't let them be kids.*

Sigger wasn't worried whether they were young punks at all, but he wanted them much older so at least one would be able to carry the message back to the right people. He wanted everyone to know that it could be an ugly scene, and dangerous, to fuck with Sigger.

The three men crouched down and ran to the side of the barn. Not finding what they wanted they came towards the end where Sigger was standing.

"Shit!" one man said. "Where's the fucking door?"

"It must be down the other end," another one answered.

"From what I heard this place is loaded," the third one said in a loud whisper.

"Yeah, well let's find a way in first. If it's like you say and there's only one old Chinaman, we'll rake off a load."

Sigger walked quietly over the grassy ground in complete darkness. Now he could see them clearly. They were all in their late twenties or early thirties and it looked like they meant business. One carried a baseball bat, the second man appeared empty handed while the third carried what looked like a machete.

Sigger had no intention of allowing them to snoop. "Can I help you, boys?"

They all whirled in unison as they looked for the source of the voice in the night. One turned as if to run while the empty-handed one stepped forward, sure in his mind that they could handle this lone farmer standing alone in the dark.

"We were looking for a telephone. You got one we can use… Can't see you, where are you?"

Sigger smiled as he watched the man. The brave one had removed a six-inch knife from a sheath on his belt as he searched for Sigger with his eyes. The other two were standing with legs apart, ready for battle.

"You're trespassing," Sigger said, deliberately exposing his position.

All eyes turned towards Sigger, but they were not sure what they were looking at. The night was too dark. The brave one took a step forward and his two companions followed suit. He held his right hand down close to his leg, the blade partly covered by his clothing.

"You boys move out, and don't come back," Sigger instructed. He felt one of the dogs quiver beside him. "I won't tell you again."

The one to the right of the brave one brought his baseball bat up in a fiendish, yellow-green pantomime and the sweat on his face glistened as if it was alive. They all felt they were immune.

Sigger snapped his thumb and third finger together. That was all that was required. The two dogs shot out from behind Sigger and launched themselves into the air. They never made a sound and the three men never saw them coming.

Each dog had picked his mark and their eyes locked in on the target area they loved best: the throat. They hit with a brutal ferocity, their speed and weight knocking their quarry to the ground.

Sigger just stood and watched. The shock value was very pleasing to watch. The third man was still standing in place, not even sure of what was happening. He soon found out.

Once the dogs locked on, their suppressed freedom bloomed into a primitive rage. The guttural sounds sent shivers up Sigger's back as they went to work. They twisted and dragged and were further enraged by the taste of blood.

The third man woke up from his daze. His friends were in trouble. He raised his machete in a menacing stance, looking for the animal that was ripping apart his nearest friend.

Sigger walked ahead in the darkness and struck the man violently in the face with the butt of the shotgun. He went down hard and did not move.

Sigger turned towards the two other men. They were screaming for mercy, the agony apparent in the horrible sounds that escaped from their torn bodies. Sigger stepped forward and issued a command. Both dogs immediately backed off.

Both victims were lucky, lucky not to be dead. One dog had grabbed onto the right shoulder muscle just beside the neck of the brave one. He had missed his mark but had held on. The wound was horrific. Blood ran like a lime-green river and soaked into the man's torn clothing.

The second man's wound was around the jaw and the lower part of the face. Sigger took a closer look and felt a little chill, but not because of the wound, but because of the power of the dogs. He would need major surgical work.

Both men were moaning constantly now, the pain beyond endurance. Sigger walked up to each man and drove the butt of the shotgun against their heads, knocking them unconscious. *Hell, I did them a favor*, he reasoned.

Shit, he thought, *three unconscious assholes to lug*. He went to the male with the machete and bent over him; his nose appeared squashed against his face. Sigger propped him against the barn wall and threw water at him from a rain barrel. He moaned and became aware of his surroundings.

"Listen to me, asshole," Sigger said, looking at his greenish complexion. "You have a car close by. Where is it?"

The man just looked stupid for a moment, and then pointed towards the cornfield. "At duh udder end of duh field," his broken nose making it difficult to talk.

"You have a choice, asshole. You can go get your car and bring it to the end of the driveway so we can load your buddies into it, or I can bury you in the back forty. What's it to be?"

"I… I'll ged id. I don't have duh keys. Glen has dem." The man stood, shivering against the wall as Sigger retrieved the keys.

Sigger helped the man move in the right direction. "I advise you not to be too long. Your buddies need medical attention."

Ten minutes later, an old van pulled up to the end of the driveway where Sigger had dragged the inert bodies. He opened the sliding side door and called to the driver. "Get your sorry ass out here and help load these guys inside."

The man stumbled to Sigger's side and helped to lift one, then the other into the van. He started to turn away when Sigger grabbed him by the back of his neck.

"Did you learn anything…what's your name?"

"Bruce," the man stammered in pain.

"Did you learn anything tonight, Bruce?"

"Ye…ye…yeb," he shivered.

"What did you learn, Bruce?" Sigger demanded.

"No… Not to cub around here?"

"Very good, now get these two to a hospital." The man opened the driver's door. "Oh, one more thing," Sigger slammed his fist into the side of the driver's face. "I don't want to see you or your friends, or any police nosing around here in the future. I do and you are one dead mother. Tell the hospital anything you want, but it had better not have anything to do with this place."

"Don'd worry. I won'd say anything," the man said, starting the engine with obvious relief.

"Oh, I'm not worried, Bruce" Sigger smiled. "But you had better be. I know who you are."

The van drove away slowly as Sigger walked back towards the house. The two dogs seemed calm as they walked slowly beside him, their heads hanging slightly. They too were coming down from an adrenaline rush.

He grabbed another beer and sat down on the porch step as the frogs started up again. The dogs were resting close by. He took a swig of the beer, lit a cigarette, and sighed. He would have to tell the Tully brothers about the visit when it got light. They were due to harvest soon and they might want to move up the schedule.

Maybe he shouldn't have let the assholes leave, but it was far too late to worry about that now. The word would spread on the street and in the bars fast enough though. That was important also.

He switched his mind to the next phase of the operation. This was the worst part. This was when all their work could go up in smoke—literally. After the goods were packaged, transportation became a major hurdle to overcome and it was mostly his responsibility.

When he found out how the goods were to be moved he would probably do the escort and go along to make sure a rip-off did not occur, riding shotgun to the contact point in Washington State. But not too close to the stuff. He was not that stupid.

Picking up his cellular, Sigger hesitated hitting the speed dial. He knew he could not wait on this. There was too much of a chance that one of the assholes would crack under pressure or want revenge.

Which one of the Tully brothers should he contact? Frank was the one that was more level headed but Roy had more contacts to run interference. Right now he needed to know if they wanted an immediate start on the harvest. If so, he needed to make some calls.

He punched Frank Tully's phone number. *This is going to be interesting,* he thought.

"Yeah," a sleepy voice said in his ear.

"It's me," Sigger said without any introduction. "I thought you should know. I had some visitors tonight."

"Anyone we know?" Frank Tully asked back.

"No, they're locals. They won't be back. The dogs got hungry."

"Serious?"

"Yeah, somewhat… I gave the driver a serious talking to, but you never know. What do you want to do about the cut?"

The line was quiet for a moment then Frank Tully gave his instructions. "Start moving on it." He hung up.

Sigger closed the flap of his phone and listened to the sound of the frogs for a few moments. He raised the can of beer to the barn in a mock salute and said aloud, "Here we go again."

CHAPTER TWO

The humidity was brutal. There was no relief from the oppressive heat, and the recent rain had turned the well-used trail to ankle deep mud that sucked and then seized at every step. Vines clawed at the face and the insects crawled down the neck to drink the salty rivulets of sweat.

Jesus Eduardo Patino was tired. He had been up since dawn and had left Peurto Ospina, Ecuador and the Putamayo River far behind. He needed to rest soon, as did the mules, but he was in an area that was patrolled far too often by the Colombia National Police. Trained and assisted by the American 7th Special Forces Group and sixty of their Black Hawk helicopters and Hewey-2 gun-ships, they had created havoc in a usually uncontrolled area.

He shivered in the heat as he remembered. Twenty-six labs, twenty-four hundred kilos of coca paste, and 170 kilos of refined Cocaine had gone up in thunder and smoke in a very short time. If they were not hunting, they were spraying the crops. The guerrillas were always in an ugly mood but now they were even uglier what with the gradual crop shrinkage.

Jesus Patino stopped and walked back to his train of mules. The coca leaves from the Erythroxylon Coca plants were piled high and tightly compacted and he needed to check the bindings and the welfare of the animals. They would require water soon.

Patino was a tiny man. He had radiant looking skin and large brown eyes and when he smiled, as he did often, his face took on the innocence of a little boy. He was not a little boy however; he was twenty-nine years old.

Patino hated the jungle, preferring instead the wide-open spaces like the well cultivated lands around Monteria. He liked the feel of the wind and he liked to be able to see towards the horizon. Now however, he could not see more than five feet as the trail turned this way and that through thick foliage, tangled roots, and hanging vines. No matter, he would soon be at the compound. He would then be able to get something to eat and get some rest before starting back.

It was not a pleasant way to make a living, but at least he was making a living. Never mind that the FARC rebels crossed the river from Ecuador and relieved him of part of his income every three months.

The FARC, or the Revolutionary Armed Forces of Colombia, were considered the best-trained and equipped, and most effective insurgent group in Colombia. Extremely violent, they used bombs, landmines, extortion, as well as conventional military action against their enemies to inspire fear and submission amongst the population. Jesus Patino knew he would soon have to move on to something else.

The barking dogs alerted the compound to Jesus Patino's arrival. He walked out of the dense jungle into a clearing that showed a rough wooden hut with coca leaves piled near by. He could not see a living sole, but knew they had all scattered into the jungle fearing an attack. The dogs ran up to greet him as he made his way to the hut.

"Ah, there you are my little amigos. They have all run away again and you are left to fend for yourself. But you knew it was me all along, didn't you?"

The dogs barked with excitement, glad of a change from the monotony of jungle living. Chickens, and one pig, moved lazily around a second structure across the clearing. This was where the workers slept, ate, and spent their evenings.

One man, then two more, emerged from the jungle. They walked towards Jesus Patino, crossing a six-inch deep creek up-stream from the coca hut.

Jesus waved to them. "Amigos, it is only me, the jungle fighter. You are safe now."

The Mule

The first man scoffed and waved his hand towards Patino. "Always with the jokes, you must spend the whole day on the trail thinking up things to say." He stopped in front of Patino, a worried look on his face. "I tell you, you stay here all day out in the open and listen to all of the sounds out there and you will become jittery too."

Jesus Patino placed his hand on the other man's shoulder and smiled in amusement. "You are a brave man, Jorge, but all your talk is not helping my hunger or thirst. You must have some of that good tequila."

"It is the only thing that keeps us from going loco. It also helps to wash down the shit we call food."

Jesus untied the bundles and watched them drop to the ground. The mules wandered off towards the stream for water. Taking off his hat, he wiped his forehead and stretched, moaning with pleasure at being able to see the sky once more.

Jorge led him towards the shack of a house, just a glad as the dogs to have different company for a change. "The paste is finished. They will be coming for it tonight."

Jorge was talking about the first step of turning the coca leaves into Cocaine. Jorge knew exactly what that process entailed and he was still amazed after all this time that any sane person would actually put the stuff in their body.

It took about four hundred liters of sulphuric acid to turn the leaves to paste. Acetylene alcohol, quicklime, sulfuric acid, ethyl ether, acetone, hydrochloric acid and kerosene were some of the chemicals used in the process of the coca leaves. Eventually, all of these chemicals ended up back into the polluted earth and waterways of Colombia.

"I should leave here," Jesus Patino stated. "Sooner or later I will end up killed. I am thinking of going to work on the coffee plantations or maybe even into the city."

Jorge leaned ahead, a look of alarm on his face. "You must be careful of your mouth, my friend. Do not talk openly like this. You surely will end up killed. If you are going to do this then just sneak away into the night with the shirt on your back and go. The FARC will not let you go when you have so much knowledge of their business. You will become food for some animal in the jungle."

"Gracias, Jorge," Jesus smiled. "I will remember what you say. Now where is that drink and fine food you were talking about?"

* * *

The coca paste moved northward through the mountains along the Pan American Highway towards the city of Cali. The two sleepy looking men inside the old delivery truck stared out into the night with little enthusiasm. The highway could be treacherous and it didn't help to have a truck that was in very poor condition with worn brakes, bad tires, and one headlight that shone ineffectively out into the unknown.

They were grateful they did not have to go all the way to Cali. The laboratory was set up in a hidden location, well guarded, and far from probing eyes. In an hour they would unload the paste and leave. Their part would be complete. It was the job of others to transform the paste into Cocaine hydrochloride, the white crystalline powder so readily known to users.

The Cali Region, in the Valle Del Cauca Region, and the Caribbean North Coast is the starting point for the largest production and distribution of Cocaine in the world. About eighty percent of the world's Cocaine comes from Colombia and Colombian traffickers really have the best of both worlds as far as growing and distribution. Connected to that little slip of land called Panama, Columbian traffickers have a choice of distributing to both sides of the continent.

The Caribbean Sea offers many routes, including a quick flight of only two and a half hours to Miami.

The Cali traffickers however are close to the Pacific Ocean. They also have a very short trip north and their counterparts in Mexico are the recipients of tons of Cocaine for shipments bound for the United States.

Although a lot of it stays in Mexico and moves into the hands of treacherous gangs such as the Zetas, the deserters from the Mexican Special Air Mobile Force Group, the big market and money lay in the United States. The Cocaine moves north by any and every means possible.

The Mule

It was the third day on station and Diego Montega felt impatient and irritable as he bobbed in the rough swollen seas in sight of the fleet. He did not like the looks of the sky and he was anxious to get it over with. They were taking forever.

He could see at least ten fishing boats and they appeared to be riding low in the water. *Why the fuck are they not heading in?* He asked himself for the tenth time that day. The fish in his hold were starting to stink. He wanted to get rid of them.

Diego Montego was a barrel-chested, wide shouldered man and he commanded attention. He had a reputation for quickly punishing any crew member that thought they had a say in the running of things. His black eyes missed nothing as they squinted above his stinking cigar, his bushy mustache failing to hide his bad teeth.

He wiped his face on the sleeve of his dirty sweater as he turned and looked at his crew. They were mulling about, reading magazines and listening to the radio from the United States mainland. *What a pack of mongrels*, Montega silently criticized. *If there was any trouble they would leave you to rot rather than lend a hand.*

Montega could not contain his bad mood any longer. "Get up off your lazy backsides. Look at the equipment. Try to look like fucking fishermen."

They got up slowly, resentful at having to even move. They had become lazy and did not take orders easily. Montega knew he would have to dump this bunch very soon.

Listening to the radio and the banter that went back and forth between the fishing boats he knew that they had not become suspicious of him. When the time came he would slip among them and head for port.

The next day Diego Montego got his wish. He watched as the boats turned towards the Continental United States. He set the pace of the boat so that he would not be the first, or the last, to enter Gray's harbor on the coast of Washington State.

He let the fleet gradually out-distance him as they headed for their wharfs for unloading. Turning south, Montega entered the quiet waters behind a small island and moved slowly into the waters of a small town south-west of Aberdeen. He tied up to a deserted dock and let his crew depart for the local tavern while he waited for his contact.

Four men arrived twenty minutes later, two in a large refrigerator truck, and two following in a pickup truck. A man jumped down from the truck; "Not bad, huh? It has only been an hour since you called us from this stinking boat."

Montega looked at him without interest. The man was young and eager and appeared to think his job was important. He was dressed for work however and Montega could not find fault with that. "Yes, you did very well, amigo. Now all you have to do is unload the precious fish. I'm afraid you will find that the ice has melted somewhat and they do not smell quite as sweet as when I started."

"They will be back in the fucking ocean soon enough," the young man laughed as he jumped aboard followed by the others.

The men began to fill square plastic tubs with fish, placing the tubs on rollers and pulling them upwards with hook and rope to the dock and the truck. They were fast and efficient and it was apparent that they did not want to linger too long.

The truck started up and the young man waved goodbye as Diego Montega headed for the tavern. This was probably the last time he would have to drink with these vermin. When he got back home it would be good riddance.

Further down the coast at a deserted beach the seagulls were becoming frantic and their shrill clamor alerted still more birds. The feast seemed to be endless and they gorged themselves until they could not fly. There would soon be no evidence of the dead fish that the men had dumped.

The truck continued non-stop to Seattle, finally coming to a stop well after dark at the rear of a radiator shop. The men exchanged few words as they transferred the brick shaped bundles of Cocaine into the unlit shop. One of the men closed the doors and turned on a small light. Three men stood looking at the shipment.

"Shee-it, they have got to find another way of shipping this stuff. Fuck, it stinks," one man stated.

"Never mind, Conway, we'll clean it up nice and pretty for you before you have to deliver it," the one standing next to him said sarcastically.

Ted Conway made a face, screwing it up against the smell. "You have to do *something* with it, man. This shit smells dead."

The Mule

Jairo Herrera-Sanchez sniffed the air and agreed. "You're right. We can't store it like this. Slit it open and package it in new bags. We will burn the old ones. And I don't want to catch any of you chippin'!" Herrera-Sanchez scowled and pointed to one of the men and barked an order. "Bring the scales."

Herrera-Sanchez did none of the work; soiling his clothes was unthinkable. He liked fine tailor-made suits and he liked the look of success. He also liked to establish the fact that he was a cut well above the hired help.

Born to Mexican parents, he was still conscious of how poor all of his relatives were. Fortunately for him he was born north of the Mexican border on a day his mother just happened to be visiting.

"Jairo, this is going to take a long time," Conway offered. "Maybe we should get us something to eat and some beer."

Jairo Herrera-Sanchez looked at Ted Conway and shook his head and thought: *They always want somethin' for nothin'.* Conway would only look at him for a few seconds at a time and his eyes were always flitting away from direct contact. He did not like the little prick but he carried out essential work.

"It's only a suggestion," Conway explained as he smoothed back his long, black oily hair on the side of his head.

"You just do some friggin' work before you worry about a friggin' break," Herrera-Sanchez said in rebuke.

Jairo watched as the men put on latex gloves and slit open the Cocaine bricks. The Cocaine was piled high in the center of a table that had a three-inch siding all the way around, then the bags were carefully checked for residue before they were put into the burn pile.

Jairo Herrera-Sanchez watched carefully because even though the organization was unforgiving in matters of rip-offs and punishment was swift and harsh he did not trust any one these men.

There were several cells in the Seattle area and Jairo Herrera-Sanchez was in charge of one of them. Each cell leader was either related by blood or had been closely associated for years. It was almost impossible to penetrate or infiltrate into the inner operation; if you were not born to it, you were probably the enemy.

Although he collaborated with his peers, Jairo reported and was responsible to only one person at the top who had personal contact with the drug lords in Colombia in regards to shipments, payments, security, marketing, and wholesale prices. All on highly state of the art encryption devices that turned communications into garble.

"Conway!" Jairo called. "I want to talk to you."

Ted Conway slipped off the rubber gloves and sauntered over to where Herrera-Sanchez was standing. "We are almost finished."

"I can see that. Get rid of the other two when you are finished and we will store it away."

"No problem," Conway replied.

"You know we have a shipment scheduled to Canada."

"Yeah, we have a possible mule set up. It looks like a go."

"Good. They have been on time with their payments and I do not want any delay. They've also been increasin' their demand with almost every shipment."

"I'll move it over to the garage tomorrow during the day. It's too risky at night. It'll be in place by the time the mule makes the run."

"We are all finished here," one of the other men called from the dimly lit work area.

Conway left the side of Jairo and walked back to the men. He looked at the fresh wrapping on the Cocaine and then towards the men. "Okay, take off. I'll see you tomorrow," he instructed them as he handed them each two one hundred dollar bills.

The men moved to the doorway and waited until Conway shut out the light. When they had gone Conway turned the light on and moved towards a side shelf that was stacked with anti-freeze, hoses, radiator cores, and clamps.

Lifting up an old radiator laying on the shelf, he reached underneath and pulled a chain that ran back to the rear wall. The shelf swung outwards on well-oiled rollers revealing a staircase that dropped into the floor towards a basement storage area.

A thick metal door blocked the way at the bottom of the stairs and a huge padlock hung from a thick metal bar. Conway reached up and turned a small light bulb illuminating the entranceway at the bottom of the stairs.

The Mule

Herrera-Sanchez followed Conway down the stairs, opened the huge padlock, and unlocked the deadbolt set into the doorframe. Lifting the metal bar he opened the door into a twelve-by-twelve concrete room and flicked on a light.

Bundles of Cocaine were stacked neatly on wooden shelves along the walls as well as on shelves running down the center of the room. The bundles were labeled by the date and the weight; the information would be removed before the bundles left the room.

"Let's get busy, it's gettin' late," Jairo directed.

They worked for forty minutes, hauling, stacking, and labeling. With the shelf back in position the only evidence that remained was the foul smelling wrapping from the fish.

"Can you take those with you and burn them somewhere?" Jairo Herrera-Sanchez asked.

"Sure. I will see you in the morning."

Jairo locked the door and set the alarm. The alarm went directly to a house one block over and not to any alarm company. God help any intruder who picked that particular building for a night excursion.

Ted Conway drove back into the radiator shop in the early morning. He met Jairo Herrera-Sanchez, collected the appropriate number of bricks, and loaded them into the hidden panel in the bottom of the coffee truck.

He was late for his rounds and had several legitimate stops to make before he could get rid of this load. He drove onto the main thoroughfare and drove north for ten minutes in light rain before pulling into the construction site.

"You're late," a short well-muscled man said as he walked up to the truck, "I'm dying for a coffee. Give me one of those things there—the stuff with the icing inside."

Conway spent ten minutes at the site then worked his way to a small canoe manufacturing plant. Trips to small businesses in a new industrial complex and a stop at a clothing manufacturer went rather quickly considering the traffic. He finally pulled into the auto service center in Kirkland during the noon hour.

A longhaired male stuck his face up to the service bay window, his pale ghostly complexion covered in acne scars. His blue eyes were perpetually bloodshot and they somehow seemed misaligned on his thin face. Conway nodded to him as the staff walked towards the coffee truck.

It was a full fifteen minutes before he was able to drive around to the rear of the service center and park next to a van with a sliding door on the side. He opened a rear door on the coffee truck to shelter the area in between the two vehicles.

The youth walked up to Conway five minutes later. "You ready to unload?"

"Yeah, Sheldon, and you had better be on top of things until it leaves. When do you expect it to head north?"

"Tomorrow sometime, at least that's what I heard. You see that big motorhome in the bay? It's being serviced and the owner is supposed to pick it up in the morning."

"Is he the mule?" Conway asked, starting to hand the packages over to the scraggly worker to slide into the van.

"He's the one. He doesn't know it," he laughed, "but he's the one."

"How are you going to hide the stuff so it can be retrieved?" Conway asked, looking at the long RV.

"That's the great part," Sheldon enthused. "Unless he looks way under his rig he won't see a thing. Each bundle is attached to a magnetized plate and it snaps onto the side of the frame near the rear. It fits in as neat as can be. Somebody better know where the guy's heading and what border he crosses. That's a lot of shit to get lost."

"Nothing to worry about," Conway said. "This guy will think he inherited a new family. There's no way they'll lose this sucker."

CHAPTER THREE

Dan Haggard looked over his shoulder and smiled as the sound of laughter reached him from the patio. He picked up the plate of sausage rolls Connie had instructed him to bring out and then put it back down and placed a round dish of dipping sauce on the plate in the middle of the food. Juggling three beers in his other hand he wandered in a leisurely manner towards the sound of further laughter.

Connie was sitting at the round table under the umbrella. Her back was to the house and her shoulders were still hunched in laughter. "What's so damn funny?" Dan asked.

Connie turned to him as he set the food and beer down on the table. "Amber was just telling me about her brother. He's a computer freak and he looks exactly like a nerd you'd see in the movies. He has thick glasses, doesn't know how to dress, has no imagination, and the other day he brought his date around. Amber said she almost fell out of her chair. The girl is drop dead gorgeous and falls all over her brother's every word."

"He must have some hidden attributes I'm sure not aware of," Amber smiled.

"Either that or he's hung like a horse," Connie replied.

Dan looked over at Amber and smiled. She was beautiful. Her white teeth were perfect and her face glowed beneath dark eyes that shone with happiness. Although she was black she said she got her name from her complexion. She always looked like she had a perfect tan and her dark hair was just the right length to compliment her face. She had lost her husband in an industrial accident two years previously.

"You women," Dan said in mock disgust. "You want a guy to respect you for your intelligence and your mind but here you are with your mind in the gutter. Do you think the woman might actually want the guy for his intellect?"

Amber laughed, "You mean a guy's brains aren't in his crotch?"

Both women went into hysterics again, the effects of an afternoon of watching golf on TV and drinking wine, and now beer.

Connie looked over at Dan and down at his lap. "You must be pretty smart."

Amber laughed and then looked into Dan's eyes. "I like a smart man."

"Watch it, Daniel," Connie said. "She likes you and you are a weak person."

The easy banter went on for another hour as the lazy afternoon sun moved across the sky before touching the edge of the rooftops and producing pockets of shade.

Connie and Amber had been exceptionally good friends long before Dan had entered the picture. She worked at a local law firm and had a degree in business and was working her way towards a law degree. She was a smart cookie with absolutely no hang-ups at all. She loved people and got along well with everyone. She was also still in love with her dead husband.

"So, you guys are taking off tomorrow," Amber stated.

"You bet," Dan pronounced as he reached for a sausage roll. "First thing in the morning I pick up the rig and we are gone."

"Lucky people," she smiled. A small flicker of sorrow still touched her features. "You guys make sure you call me when you get back."

"Hey, we're not leaving for a year you know," Connie said after swallowing a mouthful of beer.

They said their goodbyes an hour later, lingering and hugging at the front door and then again at her car. Amber slid effortlessly into Dan's arms and hugged him again. He could feel the firmness of her breasts against his chest. She looked at him with a twinkle in her eye. "Now don't you go getting too brainy on me."

Dan felt a little flush and gave her another hug. "Get your beautiful butt out of here. You're trying to get me into trouble."

Connie turned to Dan as Amber drove off. "Beautiful butt?"

"Hey, it's just an expression."

"I'd believe you...if your brains weren't in your crotch."

They both laughed and walked towards the house to finish getting ready for the trip. Walking with their arms around each other they felt more relaxed then they had for months.

* * *

Dan still felt relaxed and contented as he wheeled the Sunbird into the service lot. He parked in the customer service area and stepped out into brilliant sunshine and crisp clean air. The light breeze ruffled his short sandy colored hair as he adjusted his sunglasses and looked around the lot for his motorhome.

"Hey, Dan," a cheerful voice called from across the lot.

Haggard turned and saw the owner. Richard Zeron waved and moved in his direction. Zeron never stopped smiling and he treated his customers very well.

As the overweight owner came closer Dan smiled and indicated the parking lot. "You rent out my motorhome?"

"Hell no," Zeron chuckled. "I gave it to my wife. She's always wanted one of those things." His laugh and booming voice easily carried across the lot. "It's long enough too. She can ride in the back."

Dan laughed along with him, finding the man very easy and pleasant to talk with. Zeron had quite a huge beer belly and it was kept in place by a large belt and wide suspenders. His unruly hair and large, sparkling white teeth reminded Haggard of the old actor, Andy Devine.

"Your rig will be out in a few minutes. I had the boy clean the windows for you."

Dan was pleasantly surprised. "Hey, that's what I call service. Thanks. Find anything wrong?"

"Nope," the owner smiled back. "We fixed the electrical problem like we discussed and checked the oil all the fluid levels like you wanted. The tires are all okay and you're ready to fly.

Dan handed the keys for the Sunbird to Zeron. "Thanks for the loaner. It made it easier than trying to juggle vehicles."

"No problem. We can settle up inside."

Haggard started towards the building, watching as a bay door opened. A guy of about twenty years of age was wiping down the front of his big diesel motorhome. He had greasy looking unwashed hair and a demeanor that Haggard recognized immediately. He did not like him around the motorhome.

Richard Zeron saw Dan's look and whispered to him as they neared the door. "Hey, don't worry about him. I didn't let him near anything. I have a hell of a time hiring anyone for detailing. Sometimes I have to take on these flunkies. Hell," Zeron chuckled, "I almost have to do a tool count every night myself."

Dan laughed along with the owner and poured a coffee while Zeron printed out the bill.

He watched the guy outside wipe the headlights. Watching the guy brought back memories. It was as if they came out of a mold or were cloned. Every one of them thought of themselves as clever, and every one of them was so readily recognizable for what they were: rejects. They were always plotting ways to screw their fellow man. He could spot them a mile away.

His five years in the Denver Police had not lessened his dislike and his distain for these vermin and he still felt the helpless frustration whenever he saw them. Maybe it was his Marine training. They taught you to deal with assholes not mollycoddle them. It seemed that no matter what they did, after they were arrested they were free within hours.

The Department was right, he thought, *I would have ended up killing one of the bastards.*

"She's already, Dan," the owner smiled. "You want to drive her out of the shop?"

Dan brought himself back to the present and sighed. He was better off now anyway and he didn't have to bother with the scum anymore. "Yes. Thanks, the rig looks great."

The Mule

The guy who was the detailer was wiping off the front bumper as Dan opened the door.

"All prettied up for you, Sir. Sure is a nice boat you got here."

Haggard looked at the guy, taking in his pock marked skin and oily hair, noticing with satisfaction that the guy looked away as soon as he looked at him. The guy was trying to con him for some reason. He nodded and stepped inside.

A visual check of the interior showed everything was in place. The large slides were firmly locked and the counter was clear of items that could fly off. He really liked the motorhome. He and Connie had waited a long time and had spent many weekends looking for what they had wanted.

Inside, the forty-foot diesel-pusher was pure luxury. The wide windows, plush carpets, leather seats, and tile floors truly made the interior a home away from home and Dan felt a surge of pleasure as he drove off of the lot and headed for home to finish the loading.

It had been a grueling ten years, but he finally had a good manager to run the auto parts business he had built up. Now he could afford to enjoy some pleasures in life while keeping an eye on the business either by phone or by the Internet.

Haggard had been a Marine; a well-trained hard-hitting decorated Marine. He had loved the Marines, and he had loved his job in the Combat Development Command and the Urban Warrior program at Quantico. He was an expert in hand-to-hand combat, small arms, and a specialist in infiltrating and commando tactics. He still missed the challenges of that life.

Kuwait, Bosnia, and other places in the world had been an experience that he wished he could do over again. However it had been the downfall of his first marriage. His first wife had given him a choice: stay in the Marines, or keep their marriage. He had resigned from the Marines and joined the Denver Police. A year and a half later she left him.

He had often wondered if the failure of his marriage had something to do with his attitude while he was a cop. He had hated dealing with the assholes and had not taken any shit from them. He was not sure if it was his Marine training, his own attitude, or society's lack of dealing with them that had landed him in trouble repeatedly.

The jerks on the street knew exactly how far they could push and exactly what they could get away with. They often pushed too far and Officer Dan Haggard found himself dealing with them the old fashion way.

Haggard rarely had repeat problems with any of them but the Department had asked him to resign rather than face further public enquiries in regards to complaints against him.

It had been a bit of a blow to his ego because he had never failed at anything. Later on he finally realized that police work had not been for him and he came to realize that his resignation had been for the best. If he hadn't resigned he wouldn't have a thriving business that he continued to build. It was funny how things worked out.

* * *

The motorhome rumbled contentedly along Interstate-5 towards Bellingham, Washington. The cobalt-blue sky paraded huge clouds towards the mountains to the North and East like puffed up feathered comforters.

"Are you relaxed yet?" Connie asked, her eyes sparkling mischievously.

Dan looked over at her sitting in the huge passenger seat. Knitted purple and pink slippers jutted out from the bottom of her jeans and she had one foot tucked up under her. "Why do you say that? Do I look tense or something?"

"You didn't look any too relaxed when we started out," she remarked. "You worried about leaving the business?"

"No, not at all," Dan answered, watching the traffic through the huge eight foot wide windshield. "I can keep in touch every day if need be."

"Well I hope you're not going to do that," Connie stated. "You can't get away from it if you take it with you."

"The only thing on my mind right now is camping and fishing," Dan said, smiling over at her.

Connie was a good companion. It seemed no matter what he enjoyed, she liked it too. She stuck out the long hours of fishing in companionable

The Mule

silence and enjoyed the quiet lap of water against the side of a boat the same as he did.

She enjoyed the long and challenging hikes along old trails and the smell of the earth rising from the forest floor. She was a sun worshipper. She loved the wind blowing through her hair as it rose from the valley floor and soared across the top of the crest, bringing tears to her eyes with its strength. She loved to play games with the huge breakers crashing in from the Pacific, trying to outrun the fast moving water as it surged rapidly across the sandy beach.

Connie Hutton had walked into his business about five years previous, picking up a part for the trucking firm she worked with. He had been impressed with her looks, and over time, with her knowledge of the trucking business. He had asked her out.

They both knew that they suited each other and they had just naturally graduated to going steady. It was not long before Haggard had dropped his apartment and had moved in with her at her place in Kirkland, Washington. It also was not long before he stole her from the trucking company. She was an important part of Haggard's business.

Neither had discussed marriage and Connie, having been married before, did not seem in a rush to jump into anything permanent. Haggard had a feeling that if he asked her to marry him she would say yes. He already thought of her as his wife and he knew he had to do something about it soon.

He looked over at her. A strand of her sandy brown hair had fallen onto her forehead; the rest was pulled back into a small ponytail. It suited her. Her dark skin complimented her blue eyes and when she smiled her white teeth lit up a face that glowed with a natural radiance that needed no make-up.

She was fiddling with a tiny gold locket he had given her. The delicate chain twinkled in the sunlight and the diamonds in the double heart shaped locket glittered with a fierce whiteness.

They were into the mountains now, having left the flatlands of Skagit County behind. The freeway had split and the southbound lanes were further down the mountain and a little further to the West. Haggard watched the white line on the edge of the road scroll by in his right concave mirror.

Connie turned in her seat, the shoulder harness stretching back to the wall as she tried to see further down the mountain. "It's been a long time since I've come this way. The highway is pretty good."

"Not bad," Haggard answered. "Better than the pounding cracks we hit a while back."

A few moments later they rounded a curve in the road and found themselves cutting through the center of Bellingham. The traffic tripled in volume and Haggard found himself tensing as cars cut in front and large trucks passed with what seemed to be only inches to spare.

"You handle this thing very well," Connie remarked.

"Thanks but the lanes are bloody narrow," he answered as he swept the traffic, mirrors and the backup monitor.

"You're doing great. I'm not the least bit nervous."

"Yeah?" Haggard smiled. "Then wait until you drive it."

"Me?" Connie exclaimed. "Not on your life. I'm quite happy where I am, thank you."

Dan smiled, pointing through the windshield. "Here's our exit towards the border, only twenty-five more miles to go."

The big diesel rumbled quietly as it rolled through dairy country. Rivers and creeks crisscrossed the rich farms and a lake, framed with large homes, sparkled as it flew by.

CANADA CUSTOMS: FIVE MILES

Haggard glanced at the monitor and the towed Honda CRV. The camera at the rear of the motorhome worked fairly well and Dan could adjust the angle if necessary. Everything looked fine as he slowed for the small line-up at the border.

He drove the wide-bodied unit into one of the ports, easing slowly by the cameras and crash-bars before stopping gently next to the customs booth. He slid open the driver's window.

"Where are you folks from?"

"Seattle."

The Mule

"What's the purpose of your visit?"

Haggard smiled and leaned further out of the window, handing their identification to the man. "A vacation; we're coming up to see if you have any fish up here."

The customs officer glanced at his computer screen and seemed to be satisfied with what he saw there. He punched a few more keys before turning back to Haggard. "How many people are in the coach?"

"There's just the two of us."

"I'm going to ask you if you have any firearms. If you have and you tell me now, there will not be a problem but they may be confiscated. If you say you don't and I decide to search and I find any, you will be liable to a fine and seizure procedures. Do you have any firearms or ammunition?"

"No, sir," Haggard answered looking the man in the eye. "I've been this way before. You won't find any guns."

The customs man looked at Dan for a moment and then nodded giving the ID back. "Enjoy your stay in Canada," he smiled.

"Thank you." Haggard smiled back and drove slowly ahead. A large Canadian flag announced their arrival, rippling in the currents of the warm westerly breeze.

"Welcome to British Columbia," Haggard said.

"Oh I forgot," Connie pointed. "They changed miles to kilometers up here."

"Yeah, I know. I read that most Canadians hate the metric system. At least the older generation does. Now all I have to do is figure out how fast I can go."

Connie laughed and pointed out the large windshield. "It's fishing time! Put the pedal to the metal and let's roll."

* * *

The provincial park offered everything they could ask for. They found a sunny spot big enough to allow the Honda to park behind the motorhome. A fresh water tap was close by for refilling the tanks on the motorhome and a woodpile offered wood if you split it yourself.

Harrison Lake loomed to their right, the sun highlighting the brilliant

41

green of the opposite shoreline as it met the slate-blue of the water. The sparkling water unleashed an occasional eye searing brightness as a larger wave caught the sun at just the right angle.

"Ahh, peace and quiet," Connie said as she stood and stretched. She took in a deep breath and turned her face towards the sun.

"I say how about a piece and then quiet?" Haggard leered. "Looking at you makes me raunchy."

"You're always raunchy," Connie scolded. Her face took on a mischievous look. "Maybe later, when we get things squared away. You go and register and I'll fix us a drink. Besides, I want to walk along the lake. It's so nice out."

"Why do you women always have to be so orderly? Can't you simply do something when it's supposed to be done?" He started walking towards the registration station. "It'll be all old and shriveled by the time we get to it."

Connie laughed and called after him, "Mumble, mumble, mumble, the sooner you get back the sooner..." Connie looked around, other campers were busy tending fires and relaxing in the sun. She decided not to finish what she was about to say.

A motorboat swept by twenty yards from shore. The wake brought frothy turbulence to the sandy beach in the silence that followed. Connie could hardly wait to set up a chair and sit back with a drink and a magazine.

The afternoon turned out exactly as it should be with a walk, a couple of drinks and laid-back conversations. The warmth of the sun and the lull and smell of the water allowed Haggard to put aside any reservations he had about leaving the business. A Canadian couple stopped by to say hello as they were walking the beach and they ended up inviting them over for a happy hour at the other camp site.

"Names Oliver," the man said. "This is my wife, Vicki. Have a chair."

They spent an enjoyable hour and a half sitting outside of their host's large fifth wheel. Oliver and Vicki told them about the camping areas available, the fishing, and some of the sights they would find interesting. It was soon time to stroll home for supper. They thanked the two people and left.

The Mule

"That was nice," Connie said. "Are you real hungry?"

"Not really, but if I put a steak on and open a bottle of wine my stomach will probably get the idea."

"Okay," Connie said stepping up into the motorhome. "I'll start a small salad."

Haggard walked around the motorhome and noted the dirty windows on the Honda CRV. He was debating whether to clean them when a couple walked by. He turned to nod a hello to them and noticed a dirty van and a small pickup in a camp space further up the road. He did not notice the men sitting drinking beer at a picnic table on the other side of the vehicles. If he had he would have recognized the type. He would have realized that they were definitely out of their element.

Haggard shut out the light and settled under the covers. Wrapping his arm around Connie's waist he pulled her closer and nibbled on her ear lobe.

"Didn't you get enough supper?"

"You're my dessert," he said as he felt the silky smoothness of Connie's breast fill his hand.

Connie turned towards him and he ran his hand down the small of her back and onto the firmness of her buttocks as they lay facing each other. He pulled her even closer his interest turning to a sudden need as he kissed her.

"Mmm…you're not fooling around, are you?" Connie murmured.

"You're damn right I'm not. Damn, you feel good."

There was a scrape and a small clang that reverberated throughout the bedroom of the motorhome. Connie pulled herself away and sat up. "What was that?"

"I wish I knew. Stay here." Getting up from the bed Dan walked naked in the darkness towards the front of the coach.

He turned the key in the ignition and waited for the backup camera to illuminate. The hazy ghost of the Honda came into view just as the shadow of a man moved in front of it.

"What the hell?" Haggard whispered aloud. He quickly returned to the bedroom and gathered his pants.

"You're not going out there are you?" Connie asked.

"It's okay, I'll be right back. I'm going to turn on the alarm to shake up anyone who's out there. Turn it off for me after I get outside."

Haggard pulled on a pair of running shoes and just before opening the door he hit the bright security lights on both sides of the motorhome and activated the alarm. Flashing lights, air horns and sirens erupted into the still night. Jumping to the ground he raced to the rear where someone was obviously tampering with the Honda. A man ran off into the night and Haggard gave chase.

A van started up and took off into the night as the man Haggard was chasing jumped into a small blue pickup. The pickup started moving forward as Haggard yanked open the passenger door and jumped into the interior.

"Get out of my truck!" the man yelled.

He hit the driver alongside the head and the truck swerved and hit a tree. Thrown forward, Haggard thudded into the dash and fell partially onto the floor amongst the litter. By the time he pulled himself clear the man had disappeared into the night.

"Shit!" Haggard spat in frustration as Connie silenced the alarm. "Keep running you damned no-mind."

He was about to walk back to the motorhome but turned back to the small pickup instead and rummaged through the glove box. He removed the registration papers and put them in his jacket pocket. He could turn them over to the police later.

Connie, shaken by the night intruders, did not want Haggard to turn off the outside lights. It took quite a while to calm her down and ease her worries. Several campers had gathered around, some knocking on the door to find out what had happened and to offer assistance.

"It was only some punk looking to steal the Honda or whatever else was lying around," he told them with thanks.

"What was that bang?" Connie wanted to know.

"They probably thought they could disconnect the tow bar but it's locked on. Look, this isn't going to ruin our holidays. I know you won't sleep or feel comfortable staying here now so let's just put things away and go further up country."

"I know it shouldn't bother me but I'd feel better."

"Then it's settled. Let's get busy. You do the inside and I'll put stuff away outside. We'll listen to the radio and have a nice relaxing drive."

"You can be so thoughtful. Thank you."

Despite having to move further north to the Coquihalla Canyon Provincial Park they had a wonderful time. The fishing was good and the days were long and hot. They spent time walking, relaxing, creating great and simple meals, and making love. The days went too fast however, and it was soon time to head home.

Connie was wiping the pine needles off of the tablecloth on the picnic table when she heard a thump. She walked around to the rear of the motorhome and Haggard was standing looking at the Honda. "What happened?"

"I forgot about the damn stump. I bent the tow bar receiver. We won't be able to tow this thing home." Dan explained.

"Oh wonderful, you mean we have to go home in separate vehicles?"

"You know of another way?" Dan asked, angry with himself for not paying attention.

The drive to the border crossing at Sumas, Washington was not that far. Connie drove through first and waited at the edge of the road for Dan to clear customs.

"Pull your motorhome into the lane on your right, sir," the customs agent instructed.

"What's going on?" Dan asked. He saw that he was being directed towards a group of men wearing coveralls with various insignia displayed on the outside of the garments.

"It's just a routine check. Pull ahead please."

Haggard pulled forward and stopped the rig when instructed and shut down the engine. As he stepped out of the doorway a red haired man met him wearing a ball cap with U.S. Department of Homeland Security—United States Customs—Border Protection—emblazoned across the front.

"Stand over there for a moment please. We're doing random checks and it shouldn't take long."

Haggard watched as a small golden Labrador padded silently around the front of his motorhome and worked his way to the rear. The dog stopped, sniffed, then turned to his master and sat down.

"We've got something here guys. Take a look."

As the men started forward Haggard started to move as well, curious as to what was happening. A hand fell onto his shoulder and another gripped his elbow. "Stay put fella. If it's nothing you'll be out of here soon."

One of the men dropped onto a mechanic's roller and pushed himself under the rear of the motorhome overhang. A few moments later he emerged with two wrapped bundles. He handed one to one of the other men who made a small incision in the package.

"It looks like we got a runner here. There's a lot more underneath."

"What do you mean, 'We've got a runner'?" Haggard asked, alarms going off in his brain. "What are you talking about?"

The man got to his feet and looked at Dan Haggard with hard eyes. There was a look of contempt on his face. "What are we talking about? We're talking about Cocaine, lots of Cocaine. We're talking about smuggling drugs into the United States. You are under arrest under Section twenty-one, subsection nine fifty-one, of the United States Customs Act for transporting an illegal controlled substance. This motorhome is hereby seized by the Government of the United States."

Haggard could not find any words. They were there in his head but he could not put them together.

As Dan was led towards a small office a uniformed officer gave him a contemptuous look and turned towards his colleague. "I thought we would come up with a load of pot, not coke."

The officer indicated a chair to Dan as they walked into the office. The officer closed the door before Haggard found his voice. "I know you won't believe me but I didn't know that stuff was under there."

"Sure," the Customs Officer said. "Save it! Your lawyer will believe you. They're paid to."

Dan remembered the man at the campground. The guy must have stashed the Cocaine there. He had not been interested in the Honda at all. He'd been set up. Haggard felt his anger start to float to the surface until he thought he would not be able to contain it.

It was all a blur after that. Connie, allowed into the office, found out what was happening and she went ballistic. He convinced her to go home until he could get bail. He told her what he suspected and how someone had tried to use them to smuggle dope across the border. He told her he would call her as soon as possible and left her with a 'please don't worry.' It was all a nightmarish blur.

A man finally came into the room and sat at the table. He had dark hair that fell down onto his forehead. His complexion was dark as were his eyes. A permanent five o'clock shadow made him look scruffy although he was well dressed. "Mr. Haggard my name is Anthony Rosza. I'm with the Drug Enforcement Administration, commonly known as the DEA. You my friend are in very serious trouble."

"I didn't know about those drugs," Haggard said lamely.

"No? That is your motorhome and you drove it into the United States. There was one hell of a lot of crap hidden under there. If you didn't put it there then who did?"

Haggard looked at the man, his anger turning his stomach into a twisted knot. "I don't know. Whatever name I could come up with wouldn't do me much good anyway, would it? Whoever it is, he isn't about to share it with me either."

CHAPTER FOUR

Mike Sigger and Vince Rizzo stepped out of the car and stood in the darkness outside of Frank Tully's home. The air was suddenly damp and cool, their light summer shirts providing little warmth. Dew was forming on the freshly cut grass on either side of the bricked sidewalk as they walked towards the door.

"Frank's brother is here," Rizzo said quietly, pointing to the black Mercedes in the horseshoe shaped driveway.

Sigger nodded absentmindedly as he walked into inky darkness beneath a large cedar tree. He knew he should not have phoned ahead. "You better brace yourself, Vince baby. They are not going to like this."

Rizzo followed Sigger to the side of the house and walked past rhododendron bushes heavily laden with dark red flowers. The entrance to the basement peeked out from the brick wall. Sigger walked down four steps. Small lights set in the concrete lit his way to the polished mahogany door.

"Shit, I don't look forward to this," Vince Rizzo muttered.

"Don't sweat it," Sigger said as he tapped on the door before entering. "He can only kill you."

The warmth of the basement entranceway engulfed them immediately. The brick colored ceramic tiles set in the entranceway led the way to the dark, wide-planked flooring of the games room and entertainment area. Sigger by-passed the pool table and walked down two steps into a small lushly carpeted bar area. There were two men in the room: Frank and Roy Tully.

The Mule

Frank Tully turned as Sigger and Rizzo came to a halt by the bar. Roy Tully took a sip of his drink and quietly put it back onto the bar top. Neither man said anything as they looked at Sigger, then at Rizzo. Rizzo became fidgety and his discomfort was evident to everyone.

Frank Tully sighed and turned to Sigger. "Okay, what the fuck happened?"

Sigger looked at Roy Tully, the slim and dark haired man before him. He was glad that Frank Tully was the man who had spoken first because he was the more levelheaded of the two brothers.

Frank was about five foot ten and kept his frame in good condition. He did not use drugs and he did not allow anyone else in the business to use them either. Sigger knew that Frank kept his wife and his marriage separate from any dealings and that his wife thought that their success came from the piddling motorcycle business that Frank used as a front in the Vancouver area.

"I'm not about to make any excuses, Frank, but all hell broke loose. One minute Vince here was getting the stuff and the next minute an alarm went off. We had to leave for the time being."

Rizzo spoke up now, eager to explain. "The guy had the whole fucking thing wired. It was like the forth of fucking July. He had fucking air horns and sirens and..."

"We get the idea," Roy Tully broke in. "By the looks of your face you ran into one of those sirens."

Rizzo did not like the quiet manner of Roy Tully. He was a miserable prick ninety-nine percent of the time. Turning his face away Rizzo touched the sore spot. "I had to fight the guy off. He was a big mother..."

"If he was a big mother-fucker," Roy bellowed suddenly, "you wouldn't be standing here. It was probably an old guy of fucking eighty who yelled at you, you snot nose." Roy Tully continued to stare at Rizzo in disgust as Frank raised his hand for quiet.

Roy was bigger than Frank, and harder, but he needed and respected his older brother and trusted him with his life. He was the only family he had left. However when it came to discipline Frank left it all to the younger man. Wasting someone did not bother Roy Tully either, not if it was business and benefited him.

He moved in different social circles. He had an appetite for the big bucks. He would not allow anything or anyone to interfere with his income. Divorced, he took his women and sex when he wanted it and dumped them just as fast. The women that he dumped were lucky; he had a vicious temper. When he got angry his already bulbous eyes bulged out even further on his narrow face. His thin lips became nothing but a gash in his face.

"Where's the junk now?" Frank asked. "What campground?"

"Harrison," Sigger replied.

"You have any idea what that shit cost?" Frank asked. "We need it and we need it soon."

"You're damn right we need it," Roy fumed. "Send a pussy foot to deal with some camper and he runs away because of a fucking car alarm! That's brilliant just fucking brilliant. Would you mind telling us what plan you have to get the stuff back?"

Sigger spoke up, moving closer to the bar. "I'm going in myself about an hour before dawn. If he shows his face again I'll nail him."

Frank got up and walked behind the bar. He placed two glasses on the surface and poured a stiff drink for each man and then slid the glasses towards them.

Sigger picked his up and downed it in one swallow, nodding his appreciation. Vince Rizzo stammered his thanks and drank with a shaking hand.

"You get your ass back to the farm and get busy with the last of the harvest," Roy Tully ordered Rizzo.

Rizzo gulped the last of his drink. "Right away," he mumbled as he headed for the door.

Roy called after him. "If we don't get that shit tonight, Rizzo, I'm going to have to give you some boxing lessons so you don't have to run away in the future." The door closed and Roy turned to Mike Sigger.

Sigger looked directly back at the younger Tully. "It's my fault. There's no sense taking it out on him. I should have moved in to cover him but he was right, it happened very fast."

"I don't give a rat's ass, Mike," Roy snarled. "Quit wasting time here and just get the goods. You better hope the guy's still there because it's your responsibility."

Sigger sighed quietly, and then nodded. "I'm on my way. I'll keep in touch either way. I'll need some wheels."

"Why?" Frank asked.

"Vince wrapped the pick-up around a tree."

Roy threw his hands up in the air. "Brilliant! The guy is fucking brilliant! Get the fuck out of here, Sigger."

Frank threw a set of keys to Sigger. "There's an old red Ford pick-up behind the garage, take that." Sigger snatched the keys out of the air and turned to go; Frank's voice stopped him. "We're counting on you to bring the load back. Not only did we have to pay for something we now don't have, we are getting low at the street level."

Sigger swallowed back his inner frustration and anger as he looked at the two brothers. "I told you. I'll get it if he's still there. If he isn't I'll look around. He may have headed back into the States."

"Well you best get your ass moving then," Roy said sarcastically, mocking Sigger for his foul-up. Sigger walked towards the door, Roy's taunting voice following him. "You call us. I want to hear from you first thing in the morning either way. You hear? You fucking hear me?"

Sigger closed the door quietly and stepped out into the damp night air. His face was tight with anger as he made his way to the truck. The stinging words from Roy Tully still echoed humiliatingly in his head. "Fucking cockroach, wasn't for me doing all your work you would starve," he muttered.

Getting into the cab he moved the seat back and away from his large stomach and started the truck; he floored the gas pedal without waiting for the engine to settle. Blue smoke erupted and hung in the damp, still air as he turned onto the street. *I hope you are still there you prick! Alarm or no alarm, you're dead meat if you so much as look out the door!* Sigger screamed in his brain.

The telephone rang once before Frank snatched it up into his eager hand. The bright sun swept around the edge of the bedroom blind, alerting him of the fact that he had overslept. "Yeah, who is it?"

"It's me. They've disappeared from the campground. I've checked every place I can think of and made some phone calls but I think they've high-tailed it back into the States. There are no other local places to check, Frank."

Tully laid his head back onto the pillow. The other side of the bed was empty. "What time is it?"

There was a slight pause on the line as Sigger looked at his watch. "It's a little past eight-thirty. Look... I'm sorry, Frank. You know that. I'll keep looking."

Tully unconsciously shook his head from side to side on the pillow as he spoke into the mouthpiece. "No. No sense wasting anymore time. Get back to the farm and pack everything into the house ready to go. The last thing we need is more problems."

"Okay. If I hear anything I'll get right on it."

"You do that." Tully hung up and got out of bed and started to head for the bathroom. The phone rang again.

"Well? What's the word, Brother?" Roy Tully asked.

Frank sat down on the edge of the bed and rubbed his face vigorously with his free hand, attempting to bring himself fully awake. *These late nights are killing me*, he thought.

"I take it the news is not good," Roy said when he did not get an immediate answer.

"No, so far it's not good. Sigger went back but the motorhome has taken off. He did a search but didn't come up with anything. He thinks they went back to the U.S. and I'm inclined to agree with him."

"Great. That's just fucking great. We're out of pocket big time here, Frank. Besides that, we gotta phone and pay for another shipment. I was going to have Rizzo start delivering the load we lost, later today or tonight."

Frank scratched the top of his head. He needed a coffee and some time to think. "Look, Roy, come on over and we'll make a call. Who knows, maybe we can do a deal with Seattle."

"I'm on my way," Roy replied and hung up.

Three quarters of an hour later Roy Tully walked into Frank's kitchen and sat down at the table. Small bags, like shrunken prunes, were noticeable under his tired bloodshot eyes.

"You look like shit," Frank remarked. "If you want a coffee grab a cup."

"I was up most of the night. I stopped in to make sure the cut was going okay at the farm."

"That explains your bloodshot eyes. That stuff doesn't agree with you."

Roy poured a coffee and carried the black liquid back to the table. He took a sip and wrapped his hands around the mug. "The only time it bothers me is when we do a cut. Must be the shit floating around. What about the call, did you make it yet?"

"No," Frank answered. "I was waiting for you."

"Then let's do it. We've got nothing to lose."

Frank picked up the cordless phone and punched in two digits. It was ringing by the time he put it to his ear.

"Yes," a male voice answered.

"Let me speak to him. It's Frank."

"Frank? Oh, Frank. Hold on a moment."

The telephone rattled against Frank's ear; he heard the sound of a slamming door as he waited.

"What are you going to tell him?" Roy asked.

"I'll just tell him we didn't receive the shipment. Maybe he'll give us…"

"Yeah, how you doin', Frank?" the voice said into his ear.

"Fine, hope I'm not taking you away from anything."

"No problem. I got your next shipment ready anytime you say. You guys are really movin' up there."

"That's why I'm calling. We didn't get the shipment."

"What happened, did the cops grab it?"

Frank sat back in the kitchen chair and forced himself to relax. He kept his voice casual and friendly and tried not to sound too concerned. "Not that we are aware of. You said it was coming up on a motorhome. We didn't get it."

"Well, what the hell…? Didn't you guys have it covered, or what? My man says it crossed over just fine."

Shit, Frank thought. He was hoping they had not bothered to follow the Cocaine to the border. "My guy went to collect and he says it wasn't there," Frank lied. "Either it fell off in transit, or it was the wrong motorhome."

53

"It never fell off on our side I'll tell you that much," the irritated voice said. "From what I was told the owner never stopped either. You guys must have frigged up somewhere along the way."

"Well we never got the shipment. I was hoping maybe we could come to some sort of an agreement on…"

"Now you Canucks know the rules. It gets lost on our side we absorb the loss. If it disappears on your side you take the hit. That's business. We can't be responsible for what happens up there."

"That's what I thought you would say," Frank chuckled, looking across the table at Roy and shaking his head from side to side.

"That's just the way it is, Frank."

Frank sat forward in his chair and got down to business. He had no choice but to accept the decision. "Okay, listen. We need another shipment right away to cover the loss. I mean fast because we're short."

"I don't know. I have other regulars to look after and…"

"I have some prime *Bud* and I'm willing to sweeten the deal if you move fast on what we need. We'll pay in the usual way for the next buy."

"How sweet a deal are you talkin'?" the man asked.

"I'll throw in some Ecstasy. I'm cash shy right now."

There was a silence on the line as the man calculated the transaction in his mind. Frank heard the rustle of paper before the voice returned.

"Okay. You're talkin' a few dollars here. So that's payment for the goods plus the sweetener, is that right?"

Frank took a deep breath and agreed. "That's right. Do you agree?"

"On two conditions," Seattle came back. "You deliver the weed to us at the same time you pick up the shipment. There will be no delivery this time and no pick-up. You bring the weed. After that we continue as before."

Frank knew this was a major inconvenience and dangerous; the loss of the marijuana would be disastrous. "Why do we have to do that?"

"Because you guys have frigged up and I don't know who's looking over your shoulder. I'm not getting involved until I know."

Frank Tully sat and fumed. Again, he had no choice.

"What's it to be, Frank," the voice prodded.

"You have a deal," Frank acknowledged. "We'll set it up real quick. I'll be in touch."

"Just remember, the deal is complete when we get it here in our hands in Seattle and not before."

"Well that was a waste of time," Roy said when Frank rang off. "So they won't help with our loss."

"No they won't…and they're right. We can't afford to piss off our supplier. You heard the offer I made. The only way we come out of this is to give a little something to them."

"More profit down the drain," Roy Tully grumbled.

"Not only that, we have to deliver this time—and pick up."

Roy sat and smoldered in his anger, his thoughts turning to Sigger and Rizzo. He saw his money disappearing because of someone else's foul up. "Fucking brilliant," he muttered.

"No use dwelling on this, Roy. Get busy and have the men prepare the parcels. Call and arrange for the container and the semi-trailer and for God's sake hide it well. We cannot afford to lose this. They check just about every truck entering the States since 911."

"You know, I was just thinking," Roy said as he got up to go. "We can do a come up. If we step on the coke a lot more we can get our money back."

"We'll see," Frank nodded. "Not a bad idea."

"It's fucking brilliant and you know it. I feel better already. See you later," Roy said as he waved goodbye and started for the door. "Yeah, I'm fucking brilliant."

Frank just smiled and shook his head.

* * *

The farm looked deserted from the roadway except for the permanently parked car in the carport with the dim yellow light dangling above its roof. The large dog stood guard at the end of the driveway as the harvest and packaging moved into full swing.

Cut systematically row-by-row, the men placed the plants on specially set up tables. Others were busy separating the marijuana buds from the large healthy plants, moving the buds to a separate pile for packaging. Another man took the marijuana stocks and leaves and placed them in a corner for later processing.

When the pile got too high with *BC Bud* the pickers changed jobs and started the task of reducing the heaping mass. Rizzo had supplied scales, cellophane bags and tape for the packagers. Soon the tower of marijuana became bundles for transport.

The aromatic and pungent bouquet from the plants soaked into the clothing and the pores of the men and the strong secretion would be with them for a long time. A change of clothing would be required before they could venture out into the populace.

"Com'on you guys, you're slacking off," Rizzo said as he stepped off the ladder from the tunnel. "We've got a long way to go and this shit has to be ready, and I mean ready, to move out at moments notice."

Some of the men looked at Rizzo, their faces weary with exhaustion and their eyes rebelling with allergenic reactions from long exposure to the marijuana juices and plants.

"It would help if you did some fucking work," one of the men said. "We've been going nonstop and I need to quit for a drink and a breath of fresh air."

Rizzo turned on the man. "You've got the rest of your life to frigging breath." Rizzo looked at the work already accomplished and relented slightly. "I'll get you guys a cold beer. Take five until I get back." Rizzo disappeared back down the ladder.

"How generous," the guy muttered. "Take five he says, like he's a drill-sergeant or something."

Rizzo entered the house from the tunnel as Sigger entered from the outside. They looked at each other for a moment, both remembering the meeting at Frank Tully's house.

"How'd the meeting go after I left?" Rizzo was a little nervous being around Sigger again.

"How the hell do you think it went?" he snapped back. "I didn't find the motorhome. It was gone when I went back. They are some pissed at us I'll tell you that."

"Maybe it'll turn up," Rizzo offered lamely.

The Mule

Sigger just looked at him. His face and eyes were empty of any expression, almost a look of contempt. Turning and surveying the small stockpile of prepared bundles his face became animated. "What the hell have you been doing? Is this all you got done?"

Rizzo stepped away from the cooler with beer in his hand, shaking his head in way of an explanation. "No... No, there's a hell of a lot done. I was taking the guys a beer and then I was going to start to truck it through. It'll be ready to ship. We're well over half finished."

"For your sake you better be on time." Sigger said with menace in his voice. "He picked up the shotgun, yanked a beer out of Rizzo's hand and headed for the door. "I'm going to look around. If I was you I wouldn't stick your head out the..." Sigger's cell phone rang, interrupting him in mid-sentence. "Yeah," he answered in a surly tone.

'I've got an urgent job for you."

Sigger recognized Roy Tully's voice. "What is it? We're trying to wrap up here."

"You said you thought the guy in the RV went into the States didn't you? Well I want you to pay him a visit at his pad. Wrap it up there and take shit-head along with you. I'll have an address for you by the end of the week or on the weekend."

"That's fine but that means getting back across the border with it," Sigger reminded him.

"You just do what has to be done. There's a lot of money involved and if there is a chance to get it, I want it."

"Does Frank know about this?" Sigger asked suspiciously.

"Don't you question me you son-of-a-bitch," Roy Tully yelled.

"Okay, okay," Sigger said as he resigned himself to the trip. Then he thought of the campground and the missed motorhome and his misgivings turned to anticipation. "I guess it's time to break a few balls."

"You find it, Sigger. I don't give a shit how. You hear me?"

"I hear you just fine, Roy. I hear you just fine."

CHAPTER FIVE

Dan Haggard walked out onto the wet street in Bellingham. The stench from the nearby mill seemed to coat the back of his throat as he turned and looked back at the courthouse. He had almost missed making bail. The prosecutor had seemed obsessed at the need for his incarceration but he had been able to prove his place of residence and his length of time in business in the Seattle area. The look on the judge's face conveyed the message that he granted bail grudgingly.

He had never been locked up in a cell before and he'd had a hard time dealing with it. The constant noise almost drove him nuts and it was almost impossible to think straight with people constantly yelling back and forth between cells and with metal doors clanging.

He had been tired and battle hardened or not, he had not been able to put his head down on the filthy mattress. He could see traces of old feces and urine around the toilet in the corner of the cell.

He had finally been called to sign the papers for his bail and was led down a hallway. Dark gray concrete block walls rose on both sides and he felt hemmed in. He was told of the legality of what he was signing and was given his personal effects, stuffing them into his pockets without the usual thought of where each item belonged. He was temporarily free. He kept mentally kicking himself for not checking the motorhome after chasing the guy away at the campground.

Three quarters of an hour later he dropped behind the wheel of a rental car and directed the nose towards Interstate-5. He increased the speed of the small car until he was fifteen miles an hour over the speed limit. He felt impatient, irritated, and didn't give a shit.

The sluggish bureaucratic pace had kept him behind bars too long. Now that he was out of jail his fatigue hit him. The anger, worry, frustration, lack of privacy and unanswered questions had robbed him of any thought of sleep but now he moved as if he was in a trance. He had to concentrate on the road to ensure he would not fall asleep.

Passing through Mt. Vernon he turned his exhausted thoughts inward and the same scenes played repeatedly in his mind. He saw himself pulled over at the border and searched, the stacked packages of drugs, his arrest, and the taking of the motorhome. *They took the motorhome!* He still could not believe it. He had busted his ass to get that thing and it was gone in a blink.

The anger faded, he was just too tired to be angry. He needed to talk to Connie to assure her that he was not involved in anything. She had seemed even more stunned than he had been when events had unfolded at the border. The last thing he needed was for her to think he was a drug runner. He had not been able to talk to her. She would be frantic with worry.

As he rolled to a stop and gently applied the brakes he saw that Connie had parked the Honda CRV on his side of the driveway. He turned off the key and sat rubbing his tired eyes, looking forward to a shower and some sleep. First he and Connie needed to talk.

Getting out of the car he stretched and then walked slowly towards the front door on the short walkway. He was about to open the door when he noticed the damaged lock. Pushing the door all the way open he stepped into what looked like the aftermath of a storm.

The first thing he noticed was the large television. It was on its back with an end table jammed into the center of the screen. Someone had destroyed the rest of the living room in the same manner with pictures punctured, chairs and couches slashed, and ornaments smashed. A large mirror was broken and lying in front of the fireplace grate. Haggard just stood there. He was too tired and dumbfounded to feel anything.

"What the hell?" he whispered to himself. He walked towards the kitchen stepping over broken furniture and felt his heart starting to beat faster, his tiredness forgotten in a surge of adrenaline.

The refrigerator door stood open. Open jars lay on the floor, the contents strewn across the walls and cabinets with dried raw eggs thrown on top of the mess for good measure. Haggard stood there surveying the mess and then woke up from his trance and moved rapidly throughout the house.

"Connie? Connie, are you here?" Running down the hallway and into the bedroom he was greeted by a further shambles. His search of the main floor got worse with each room. "Where the hell is she?" Haggard wondered, feeling anxiety erupt when she didn't answer. He looked into his ransacked office and saw his computer monitor visible on the floor.

"Connie?" He called down the stairs towards the basement.

A voice from the front door spun Haggard around and he moved rapidly in that direction, stepping over and around broken items. It was the neighbor from across the street. Haggard was glad he had someone to talk to. "Hi, George, do you have any idea what happened here?"

George was about fifty-five years old. He always wore faded jeans and some sort of a western shirt. Today it was red, yellow, and black. His ball cap was perched slightly back from his forehead. "Oh, Dan it's awful. I didn't know where you were. God, the police was here early this mornun along with the ambulance; God, it's bloody awful."

"What? What the hell happened, George? Where's Connie?"

The other man was busy looking at the mess in the house. "She went in the ambulance, Dan," George said turning back to look at him. "Oh I'm sorry, Dan. She is very, very bad. Somebody broke in and beat the hell out of her during the night. The police say they ripped out the phone lines along the outside of the house probably so's the alarm wouldn't work. "What the hell was they lookun for?"

Haggard immediately thought of the drugs. "I ran into some trouble at the border. The same people that did this probably put some drugs under our motorhome."

George looked stunned. "God, why did they do that?"

Haggard did not want to stand and answer questions; he needed answers. "I appreciate your help, George. Where did they take her?"

"As far as I know just to the local emergency; I tell you whoever did that must be some kind of animal."

The Mule

Haggard put his hand onto George's shoulder and steered him towards the doorway as he thanked him for the information. "I've got to run up to the hospital. Keep an eye out for me will you? Call the police if you see anyone else nosing around the place."

"Oh, I forgot. I got a police business card here. Says you are to get in touch with them. It's got the cops name on it."

Dan took the business card, noted the name, and put it in his pocket. He pulled the door shut and started walking towards the car with George trailing along beside him.

"Don't you worry none I'll look after the place. You want me to call a locksmith for you so you can lock it up?"

"That would be great. You're a good guy, George. I won't forget your help." George was still talking and waving goodbye as he backed out of the driveway.

Twenty-five minutes later Haggard walked into Connie's hospital room. He looked at the small body lying on the bed and did not recognize her. Her eyes blended in with her puffed and bloated cheeks. Small cuts, surgical stitches and some sort of reddish disinfectant covered her face and head. Tubes were running out of her nose and mouth and her left arm. Her right arm was in a cast.

Haggard's eyes grew moist and his breathing felt restricted within his chest. He knew he was scared. It was not often that he felt helpless but this was one of those times. Pulling a chair closer to the bed he sat down quietly but knowing that it was unlikely that he would disturb her. He watched her chest rise and fall in a steady rhythm as he gently took her hand in his.

He sat there for a long time and forgot all the disasters that had burst into his life. He watched her and willed her to fight.

Leaning forward, he whispered quietly. "You're a tough broad, you know?" He stopped talking for a moment to stop from choking up. "You'll be out of here in no time." He sat and watched, helpless and scared.

Dan felt the presence of someone and turned and saw a man standing at the base of the bed. He was dressed in a white smock with a picture ID attached to the upper left pocket. "Are you Mr. Haggard?"

He got up and took the doctor's offered hand and looked into steady brown eyes that were topped by grayish eyebrows. Reading glasses were perched on the top of short and thinning gray hair. Tiny, tiny wrinkles radiated outwards around his eyes. Haggard was not sure if they were laugh-lines or from years of working under harsh lights and conditions that required concentration and precision.

"She looks pretty bad, doctor."

The other man took Haggard's elbow and turned towards the door. "Let's talk out in the hallway."

The door closed softly on a pneumatic shock absorber, the silence of the private room replaced by the busy corridor. Haggard moved against a wall as a high trolley filled with dirty dishes rolled past him.

"How bad is she? What injuries?" Haggard asked right away. His stomach was doing silly little things. It felt like little rats running around inside.

"Well besides what is obvious, she has a concussion and severe trauma to the head. She has a broken forearm from some blunt weapon, bruising to the kidneys, and a ruptured ear drum. I'm concerned about her eyesight but we will have to wait on that. Her teeth have some damage also but that will have to wait. She was stabbed in the stomach…"

"What!" Haggard barked, turning white and unable to contain his shock.

"We have looked after that. That is under control. She will be in a lot of pain for a while and a lot of what you see will heal rather quickly. It's a little too soon to say what the long term will be. She took quite a beating. She was not sexually molested; perhaps she put up too good a fight. I am very concerned about the injuries to her head and bleeding or swelling within the cranial cavity."

"Do you have any idea when she will wake up, doctor?"

"I have her heavily sedated. I intend on keeping her that way for a while to give the body a chance to get over the trauma. You can stay if you want but you look like you need some rest yourself."

Haggard knew the doctor was right. He was running on empty and he had trouble thinking straight. The constant throbbing up and behind the eyes could only be relieved by sleep. "Okay. Do you have my number?

No, wait, the phone is out you'll have to call my cell." Haggard offered him his card but the doctor suggested he leave it at the nurse's station.

The cell phone brought him out of some deep dark hole and he had a hard time climbing back to where the light was. When he finally opened his eyes to reality the phone had stopped warbling. He looked at his watch and quickly calculated that he had slept nine and a half hours. He looked around the small hotel room and put his head back on the pillow. He felt like hell.

He lay there going over what he had to do during the coming day. Besides checking on Connie he had to contact the police to find out what they knew. He would need to go back to the house. He also had to get in touch with the insurance company. Thinking of it all he felt a smoldering anger building deep within. Someone had seriously invaded his life.

Haggard could not remember experiencing such deep-rooted rage and frustration. He could not let them get away with this. The scum had come out of the woodwork to make him a victim and by God he was *not* going to be a victim. The rage was intensified because he didn't know who *they* were.

Dan called the hospital and found that there was no change in Connie. She was 'resting as well as could be expected.' He made sure the nurse had his cell number and headed for the shower, feeling the pangs of hunger as he undressed.

The police did not offer any new information, nothing that he had not already seen with his own eyes. They had found Connie on the floor after receiving a 911 call from a neighbor. They had no motive and they had no suspects.

'*Well I know what they want!* Haggard thought. *They think I still have their drugs.*'

Calling his insurance broker and reporting the loss and then making an appointment for the following day gave him something to do. Going to the house he started to straighten up the destruction but gave up, trying instead to reconstruct what had taken place instead.

Most of the damage was simply malicious, an intimidating or hostile message meant to make you cower and feel insecure. He could see where most of the struggle or beating had taken place in the front room. The coffee table had one broken leg with blood smeared all over the top of the table. Haggard looked at the leg and saw that it had been dusted for prints; dark blood was splattered on the end. *Why did the police not take it for evidence?* He asked himself.

Connie must have fallen backwards onto the table then someone beat her with the wooden table leg. That would explain her broken forearm. The guy would not believe she didn't know about the drugs and would keep beating her. When she kept fighting he probably got mad and stabbed her.

Thinking of her laying there suffering while they ransacked and destroyed the rest of the house brought the fury back. The feeling that they were 'getting away' was a physical thing and he felt the need to jump up and run out of the house after them. He fought back against the fear and anger.

"Hi, Dan," George called from the front door.

Haggard turned and gave George a weak smile of welcome. "Pull up a chair. That's if you can find one in one piece."

"Naw, I can't stay. I just wanted to let you know that nobody was lookun over the place. The lock guy got here a little late but he worked fast enough." George handed Dan the key and smiled self-consciously. "I told the guy to leave the house unlocked for you. He said he would bill you. How's Connie?"

"Just like you said. She's pretty bad." Haggard nodded his thanks and took the key.

"This doesn't look like they were just lookun for somethun," George said as he indicated the room. "I mean look at this place. They was just plain mean."

"They were trying to send me a message. I think I got it."

"Shit, some message," George muttered.

"I appreciate your help," Haggard said as he bent and picked up a broken picture frame containing a photograph of Connie and him at a local restaurant.

"It's no big deal. I feel awful about Connie. The wife says she will go up and visit when she is able to have visitors."

"That's going to be a while, George. I'm thinking of sending her to her mom's place when she gets out." Connie's mother had just popped into his mind. "I haven't even told her mother yet and I'm not looking forward to the call."

George took off the blue baseball cap and scratched the thinning hair underneath. He fiddled with the cap. 'New York—Never Forget' was inscribed in gold letters across the front. "That sounds like a pretty good idea to me. You're go'un to need help and I can't see Connie comun back to this."

"Yeah, I know. I'd better phone her mother right away," Dan sighed. "I'm moving into a motel for now."

It took a lot of convincing to stop Connie's mother from leaving Wenatchee and showing up on the doorstep. He had tried to break it to her gently but he found that she was having none of that and wanted to know everything. She was a no sugarcoating, get to the facts kind of woman. After a lot of talking she finally agreed to stay put until he could deliver Connie to her doorstep. She realized there really wasn't anything she could do for the moment but she wanted to be there. She gave in. Right or wrong it was a load off his mind.

Five more days went by. He spent long hours visiting Connie and talking on the phone to her mother. He would hold the phone to Connie's ear so her mother could talk to her. He bumped into Amber many times in the hallway as she waited for news also. She was having a hard time dealing with what happened. He felt better having a friend of Connie's close by and they sat for long periods in the waiting room—waiting for an improvement.

Haggard turned in the forgotten rental car and attended to his auto parts business. He received numerous invitations to supper and offers of help from friends, neighbors, and business associates but he turned them all politely down as he gradually straightened up the house. He tried to keep busy and he tried not to think. When he did think, a mounting fury built inside, a kind of wildness with nowhere to go.

The doctor had been right. Connie's outward wounds healed rapidly and he noticed changes and improvement every time that he saw her. As he walked down the hall towards her room he felt awkward carrying the bright yellow flowers. He tried to adjust his mood so she would sense him being in a cheerful and upbeat mood. He needed to keep her spirits up even though he was having trouble enough dealing with his own emotions, emotions he was keeping buried.

"Hello, Mr. Haggard."

Haggard turned. Connie's doctor was walking towards him. He was moving slowly and without his usual bounce and energy. His hospital greens were soiled and he looked like he had not slept for hours. "Hello, doctor. I'm just heading in to see Connie."

"Come and sit down, Dan. We need to talk."

Haggard did not like the look in the man's eyes. "Why? What's up?"

Led by the elbow he allowed the doctor to escort him to a small waiting room. Four brown imitation leather chairs with wooden arms were crammed into the room. A couple of end tables littered with last year's magazines greeted him as he sat down across from the doctor. The light from the window bothered him and he moved to a different chair. The doctor's expression appeared grim as he settled into the chair.

Mr. Haggard... Dan, I...

Haggard felt a huge knot form in his chest like his heart had stopped. A great feeling of dread welled up in his chest and surged upward into his head as he watched the doctor try to deal with what he had to say. But the man did not have to say another word. Haggard knew from the look on the doctor's face that his world had stopped.

"Dan, something happened. An hour ago Connie's condition took a rapid turn downward. Her blood pressure plunged and we worked hard and fast to contain the problem."

"She's gone. Hasn't she?" Haggard heard himself ask from far away.

"She fought very hard. It was as I expected. Her brain could not withstand the horrific damage inflicted upon it. We could not stop the swelling. I'm very sorry, Dan."

Haggard wanted to cry out. He wanted to scream, 'No-o-o-o, and to walk into her room and hold her hand. He could *see* her smile and he could *hear* her laugh, and her eyes *sparkled* within his own mind. An involuntary moan escaped from his lips.

"Believe me, Dan; we tried very hard for her. She really deserved a better break than she got. It may not mean much but all the nurses and staff in here went the extra mile. We wanted to send her home. I'm very sorry we lost her."

Dan could not hold it in any longer. All the emotions that he had held in for so long erupted and spewed forth in a deep cry from the center of his soul. He heard a horrible deep cry and gut-wrenching wail, the sound of a wounded and wild animal, and he realized with a shock that it came from inside his twisted and agonized mind, tearing itself loose from someone else's body.

It couldn't be true. It happened to other people not to him and Connie. They were so suited to each other and had so many plans for the future. He was sure that if he got up and walked down the hall she would be in her room and nothing would have changed.

"I'm going to administer something to help you, Dan. It's too much of a shock to handle alone."

Haggard looked at the doctor without hearing, thinking only of the total void that Connie had left in his life. Her smiling face and mischievous eyes played across his mind. The tinkle of her laugh still echoed in his ears. How could his life have been altered so rapidly?

Then he remembered her as she was in the hospital bed, her eyes swollen shut and her pain and suffering very, very evident. He remembered the ugly beating that had been administered. Something shifted inside. He blinked and sat up straight. He saw the doctor sitting across from him quietly, and Haggard shook his head. "I have a lot to do."

As he walked out of the hospital under clear blue skies he wondered if he was in the same world. How can everything outside be sunny and bright while everything inside felt black and empty? He stood next to a tree, the wind caressing his face as he thought of Connie. He heard himself whispering into her ear as she lay unconscious. '*You're a tough broad, you know? We'll have you out of here in no time.*'

He had failed her. He had not kept his promise and he had not been there when she needed him. God, he loved her. She had always been there for him. She was part of him and she was *right* for him. He had to fight down that shriek from within, that wail of despair that threatened to engulf him. Again there was that sudden shift inside and the deadness came and pushed aside the agony. It was replaced by something else.

Haggard immediately took time off from the business. He left to see Connie's mother in Wenatchee; he simply could not tell her the news over a telephone.

He drove mechanically. The images of Connie performed in living color in front of his eyes, superimposed on the windshield like some heads-up screen. He saw her head thrown back one moment in spontaneous laughter, her eyes full of life and merriment. There she was with her hands on her hips and a flash of anger dancing in her eyes. Her voice rang out clearly: '*Oh, is that a fact? Well, listen to me buster.*'

He saw tears running silently down her cheek when she was upset and he could see her far away look when she was sitting quietly and did not know he was watching. Little things he had long forgotten became so lifelike and real.

His mind played new and different images over and over, sometimes bringing a smile, but often making him blink away the dampness that accumulated suddenly behind his eyelids. So strong was his memory of her and so strong was his grief he had to pull into a lookout by a lake so as not to cause an accident.

He got out of the car and looked out across the water, the wind gently touching the moisture on his cheeks. The water and the wind that she had loved so much now seemed like an alien landscape. He stood and looked at a beautiful but dead world.

You're not gone! He shouted in his mind. "You're not gone," he screamed aloud, the echo bouncing across the water. The cry that erupted from within startled him and he realized that she would never answer him again. It had just been a cry in the wind.

Eleanor Clark saw it in his eyes when she opened the door. She stood there shaking and then quickly rushed into his arms. They stood like that for a long time, drawing and giving strength to one another.

She put her emotions aside with obvious effort and led him into the house. It was small and welcoming and Haggard felt like he was at home as soon as he stepped inside. He followed her into the kitchen and she placed a stiff glass of whiskey in front of him, and then knowing his needs she quickly had some food on the table.

Haggard went on walks with her and had quiet meals with her. He thought he knew her before but soon learned that she was a special person. He could see a lot of Connie in her. He talked of Connie and what they did together and what they had planned. She was a great listener.

She loved to cook and found an excuse to lose herself at the stove, but he caught her quietly crying on numerous occasions. Eleanor discussed the funeral with him and asked to have Connie sent home. He had no objections.

Eleanor also needed an outlet for her feelings and Haggard listened to stories about Connie that had expanded into a family joke. At other times it would have been funny and although they did laugh at times, now all it brought was a chuckle that was filled with sadness. Still, this one person had affected so many others. It was an amazing thing to have those things to hold on to.

Eleanor needed time alone too and he wondered off on a long walk in the quiet neighborhood to let her grieve alone. The sun was warm and inviting as he walked back and approached the house. He sat on the front step and leaned back to let the sunshine warm his body.

His mind drifted over the events that had taken place. His arrest bothered him and played on his mind as did his coming court appearance. Until now he had not had much time to dwell on his arrest and the drugs they had seized from the motorhome. Thinking about it now he still did not know how they had had time to fasten it under the motorhome. If it were not for the guy banging and making noise he would not have a clue even now.

His mind flashed to his humiliating arrest at the border. The scene played behind his unfocused and unseeing eyes as he sat in the warm sunlight. He saw himself led to the office and the disapproving look of the officer as he walked by. The memory hurt him. Then out of nowhere a voice said: *'I thought we would come up with a load of pot, not coke.'*

Haggard sat up slowly from the warm step. The voice re-played itself again. *What the hell*, he thought as he became aware of the memory. Where had his mind been all this time? He knew that Cocaine flowed northward.

He had been in police work long enough to know that. He knew that it was a little unusual for it to flow out of Canada in any great amount. So what did it mean? He sat for a moment realizing that the junk could have been placed on his rig anywhere.

He had duped himself into thinking that someone had placed the coke under the motorhome in Canada. *Shit! The guy was trying to get at the Cocaine,* Haggard thought, *I took it across the border, twice!*

Haggard spent one more day with Connie's mother and then said goodbye. He left early in the morning, knowing he had left her feeling a lot better. She was grateful of his visit. He was just as grateful for her company and for sharing her memories. He would see her soon for the funeral.

Driving back through the mountains gave him lots of time to think. His court appearance and the need to talk again with his lawyer, the problem of finding a new place to live, and the constant question of who had set him up, all went round and round in his mind. No matter what he considered he could not arrive at a solution as to how the Cocaine got onto the RV. The motorhome had always been stored in a secure location.

"Damn it all to hell," Haggard said aloud to himself as he zipped past a slow moving, low-geared transport truck on the steep downgrade of I-90 heading towards Seattle. *Nobody is going to believe me. I'll be found guilty unless I find the assholes that did this.* He tried to think of who it could be. There were no answers.

The traffic was heavy as he hit the 405, I-90 inter-change and headed north to NE 85th Street. Not for the first time he asked himself why any human being would subject themselves to the crawling ant-like existence of the Seattle area freeways. He was glad that his business was close to home and he did not have to use the freeways often.

Haggard moved the car through the cloverleaf and headed west into the busy business area and towards home. He passed an RV lot displaying trailers and motorhomes; a sign invited everyone to enjoy the good life. It brought back the image of his RV.

He groaned inwardly. In his mind he saw it parked under a tree at the lake. He saw himself polishing it and taking time out for a beer. He saw it sparkling in the sun.

The Mule

Haggard drove another one hundred yards before another image emerged and locked into place. He visualized the dazzling sun flashing off of the wide windshield of the motorhome as he walked towards the building and the service bay. He could see the puke of a guy rubbing it down and he saw the sly face and heard the false words being spoken to him: *"All prettied up for you, Mr. Haggard. Sure is a nice boat you got here."*

He remembered thinking that the guy was trying to con him but he did not know why. His annoyance returned in full as he pictured the man's face in his mind. The puke had all the time in the world to load the Cocaine. He could not think of any other explanation. There was no other place that the RV had been stored where anyone could get at it. The puke could work out of sight with no one to bother him.

Haggard also remembered talking too much about where he was going on vacation. *Yeah, I talked too much,* he thought. *I talked far too much!*

* * *

He lingered in the far corner of the dark parking lot inside the quiet, black interior. The warmth inside of the Honda had cooled long ago and he cracked a window to let out the moisture. A flickering beer sign in a window was partially lighting up a few square feet of the ground in front of the tavern just to the left of his windshield.

'The Puke', as Dan referred to him in his mind, had entered the murky looking building two hours previously after he had followed him from his auto detail job. The guy's car, a fading old Toyota, was parked to Dan's left and three cars over. One and a half hours earlier he had kicked the left rear tail lens out so that a white light would show to the rear. He hoped 'The Puke' would not be much longer and not be totally sloshed out of his mind.

Ten minutes later the door opened and a female came out into the parking lot with 'The Puke' close on her heels. He was talking to the woman but Haggard could not hear due to the angle of the Honda. She stopped and turned on him in an impatient manner and it appeared that she was upset with him.

She walked in Haggard's direction and he realized she was walking to the car parked next to him. He lowered the window a fraction so he could hear and leaned further back down into the interior gloom.

"Come on, babe," the guy was pleading. "Let's make a night of it. You don't need to go home yet."

"I *told* you to leave me alone," she said as she came up to her driver's door. "Go away!"

"What the hell, I bought you a couple of beers and you're all cozy. Now its goodbye time, just like that."

She opened her door and got in but before she could shut it he stepped up between the door and the car frame and held it open. "Tell you what," he said, slurring his speech slightly. "You let me buy you a hamburger and then I'll quit bothering you. Okay?"

There was silence for a few moments and Haggard heard her reply. "Okay, go around and get in the other side."

Haggard groaned inwardly. *More time wasted.* He sure as hell did not want to spend all night with this guy.

The car started up as the guy walk around to the rear of the car towards the other side. The lights came on and the vehicle started to back up.

"Hey! What the fuck? Where you going?" he yelled. "Hey! Open the damn door!"

As she pulled away she leaned out her window and gave him the finger. "Try using some mouth wash. You stink."

Haggard smiled as he watched 'The Puke' run after the receding vehicle. "You slut, you slimy slut, come back here and I'll close that big mouth of yours," he screamed as loud as he could.

The car left the parking lot, scraping the rear undercarriage on the pavement from the sudden drop to the road. The squeal of the tires drowned out 'The Puke's' muttering as he returned to his own car and opened the car door. The car door slammed on his obscenities. "Bloody bit...."

Haggard followed at a discreet distance; the rear white light guided him through the built-up areas and then south onto Lakeview Drive. Four miles later the vehicle moved into a quiet residential area and an older section of 112th Avenue. The Toyota rolled to a stop beside a fence and he watched as the guy got out, stumbling in the dark as he walked towards the backyard.

The Mule

A light came on in a basement window as Haggard walked quietly along the side of the old house. The rusted shell of an unidentifiable car loomed to his right and other obscure objects cluttered the nearby ground. As he bent to look into the window a light breeze carried the scent of the ocean and merged with the damp smell of the earth and old rotting leaves. He could detect the smell of rain in the air.

Haggard looked down onto a small kitchen counter. An open pizza box with old and hard crusts of leftover pizza sat next to a sink full of dirty dishes. Moving back slightly, Haggard saw a cheap wooden kitchen table and two chairs that were once white in color. The table was surprisingly uncluttered and the only thing visible was a set of car keys and a jacket thrown over a chair.

A loud bang made Haggard jump slightly and he realized that the window he was in front of was slightly open. A moment later the head of 'The Puke' came into view and he watched as he sat down at the table with a bottle of beer and something wrapped in cellophane.

Haggard stood up and moved deeper into the night, his eyes trying to adjust to the darkness. An outline of an outside railing and stairway led him down to a doorway and a concrete landing. He stepped quietly to the door and stood there. The sound of a radio or television came to him faintly as it changed from one station to another. He tried the door. The handle turned easily in his hand and the door opened inward.

An old washer and dryer were dimly visible in the small dark room. A tub to his right was full with dirty clothes. Haggard closed the outside door, looking at the narrow beam of light under the door to his left. He moved closer and put his ear close to the door just as the guy on the other side of the door let out a large belch. Haggard turned the knob and the music became louder as light flooded the laundry room.

Haggard stood in the doorway. The other man had leaned his chair back against the kitchen wall. He was digging for something in his nose. A small television had a hard rock music video playing. The characters on the screen pumped their hips backward and forward rapidly as they all tried to see who could stick their tongues out further. 'The Puke' took a long swig of his beer and put the bottle down next to a half eaten sandwich. He gave out another loud belch. His eyes appeared to droop as he tried to watch the screen.

"Don't you excuse yourself?" Haggard asked.

The guy did not react for a full three seconds but then he turned and looked at Haggard stupidly. His eyes then opened wider and his chair came crashing forward onto the floor so fast he almost fell forward onto the floor. "Who the fuck are you?" he yelled as he got to his feet unsteadily. "Get the hell out of here!"

"What, you don't remember me?" Haggard asked quietly.

The guy dropped his belligerent look and gazed at Haggard through bleary eyes. He was trying to make his brain function in its alcoholic haze and was trying to match the face in front of him with any past association. It was not working.

"You do a hell of a good job of shining up motorhomes," Haggard prodded gently.

The eyes just continued to look back, the thought processes outwardly looking like they were in neutral. Then the eyes cleared slightly and focused on Haggard with a new awareness. The face came alive and he stood straighter and looked nervous for the first time.

"Do you remember now?" Haggard asked.

"Ye… Yeah, sure…you're the guy with that big boat on wheels. What…what you doing here?"

"Oh, I think you know why I'm here, ah…what's your name?"

"Sh…Sh…Sheldon."

Dan Haggard watched as Sheldon's eyes flicked about the room. He knew he was looking for a way out or for some method of defending himself if he needed to. That sly look was there, the workings of his brain displayed all over his face. The man was so obvious. "You had better turn down that music, Sheldon. You'll wake up the people upstairs."

"There's nobody up there. It's up for rent," Sheldon blurted, not thinking.

"That's good because you and I are going to have a talk about Cocaine. It can be a short talk or a long talk, it's up to you."

Sheldon made a sudden break for the door. He never saw it coming because he never bothered to look; he hated looking people in the eye.

The Mule

The pain, when it came, was like being hit in the mouth with a hammer. He flew backwards and crashed into the old refrigerator, his head snapping back and thudding into the hard edge of the door. He stood for a few seconds and then slid to the floor.

"Thanks for confirming what I already knew," Haggard sighed as he walked out into the night in search of a tool.

He had a hard time waking up Sheldon, alias The Puke', but ten minutes later he sat beside him on the floor in the laundry room with a belt wrapped around Sheldon's head.

"Alright, alright, oh Jesus, help me. Oh fuck, alright," Sheldon screamed. "All I did was what I was told, man. I didn't know it was you."

"I want names, Sheldon. I want them now."

"No way man…no way. They'll kill me if I say anything."

"Listen to me, Sheldon. It's not them you have to worry about right now. If I do not get the names you will not see the morning sun, ever again." Haggard reached up and twisted the tire iron one more half turn and the belt squeezed even tighter around Sheldon's head.

His screams blended in with the music video perfectly and he kicked hard against the restraints holding him to the clothes dryer. It looked like he was close to blacking out. Haggard loosened it slightly.

"I figure two more turns and you are a dead man. Your head should split like an old dried-out coconut." There was no answer. Haggard reached for the tire iron.

"No! No! I'll tell you. It's in my back pocket, man. God, they'll kill me."

He reached into Sheldon's back pocket and pulled out a flattened notebook. The rifled pages displayed a list of names, addresses and phone numbers. There were quite a few. "This is a pretty stupid thing to carry around, Sheldon. Give me the names."

Sheldon groaned and sobbed out the names: "Carlos. Carlos Neigel and…and Ruddick, I help them out once in a while. Man they'll kill me if you go near them."

"Then you had better leave town or keep your mouth shut, Sheldon. If I run into trouble I'll come looking for you again."

Again the cagey look, quickly agreeing with you and thinking he could con you. "No problem, man."

Haggard remembered all that the punk had put him through. He remembered to control his anger. A brutal upper-cut to the jaw snapped the look off of Sheldon's face. "Remember that, Shel-don."

CHAPTER SIX

The funeral was harder on Haggard than he thought it would be. He thought that he had all of the gut wrenching emotions in hand. If anything, it was harder to deal with and it took a major effort to keep his agony inside and hidden. Not that he was against crying or displaying his grief but it was apparent that Connie's mother needed someone strong to lean on.

"Oh, Dan," Eleanor Clark said through a ragged intake of breath. "What a horrible day. I never would have made it without you. Thank you."

"My goodness, Elly, you don't need to thank me. Connie was the spark and fire in my dull life. I needed you just as much." They were in Eleanor's kitchen, the funeral over with and the gathering of mourners had departed. Amber was the last to go.

"You were pretty strong for me today, Dan. I know what that took to maintain that strength."

"I loved her so much. Elly, I'm sorry I asked you to stay away from the hospital."

"You were trying to spare me and you were doing what you thought was best. Dan... I know how much you are suffering. If you ever need a friend to talk to or a place to visit, you know where I live."

Haggard reached over and squeezed her hand, taking a moment to ensure himself that he would be able to speak. It took longer then he thought.

"I'll tell you, Elly—I have this. . .this huge void sitting inside of me and every time it fills up with a memory or a feeling, this. . .this huge pair of pliers yanks everything out and takes it all away."

Haggard hesitated, a tear escaping involuntarily. "I keep *seeing* her and hearing her voice. I keep thinking she will be there when I turn around.... I'm not very good at this," he said, shaking his head.

"Some men have a hard time expressing themselves," Eleanor smiled. "You're not one of them."

Dan squeezed her hand. "It was a pretty good send off for her, don't you think? She had a lot of love out there today."

Eleanor smiled and then gave a small chuckle for the first time. "My goodness the stories about her; some of them were very funny."

"Amber had a real hard time," Dan said quietly. "But she did pull out some good memories and made everyone laugh. I don't know where she got the strength."

"Yes, Connie sure touched other people and she had a lot of friends."

"And you remember that," he said. "She was a great person and you helped make her that way."

Eleanor Clark smiled gratefully and leaned back tiredly in her chair; "Such a waste. It is such a terrible waste."

"No, Elly, it's not a waste. You and I will carry her here." Dan placed his hand over his chest. "She will be inside the rest of our lives."

"Maybe so, but the pain is so hard to bear isn't it?"

"I have to tell you something else, Eleanor. I have some other feelings. You are family and I want you to know. I. . .I have a problem accepting what has happened. Someone destroyed your daughter and my wife."

"Your wife?" Eleanor smiled.

"You're damn right she was my wife and someone took her from me." He hesitated for a moment. "I have a problem. I can't accept it like some dog that has been kicked into the corner. I want you to know that I cannot let that lie. Someone out there has to answer for it. I have this horrible— *rage* that won't go away."

"I don't want you lost also, Dan. I am aware of your past experiences and training, but God will make them answer for their crimes."

The Mule

"I'm sorry, Eleanor, I can't wait that long and God can't have them. I'm going to do my level best to send them straight to hell."

* * *

The older house was on a piece of property almost underneath I-90 close to 106th Avenue, S.E., in Bellevue. It was a rental set amongst high-end homes with an absentee landlord waiting as property values soared upwards. The steady rumble of heavy traffic drifted down from above.

A single streetlight cast a pitiful light down onto the dark and littered street. For the past two hours, Dan Haggard watched the comings and goings of small groups of people. They slipped in and out of the house quickly.

He was somewhat refreshed after the six-hour sleep he had managed during the latter part of the night and early morning. He had been surprised that he had been able to sleep at all, what with his mind so full of the information that he had tried to absorb from Sheldon's book. He had also been concerned that Sheldon might have run screaming to someone. He could only guess that Sheldon was taking his advice because no one had looked sideways at him as he nosed around.

He did not fool himself into thinking that he was dealing with reasonable people because these people would kill him as soon as look at him. However he needed to find out who was behind the drug set-up and he could not think of any other way but to do it himself.

He was not overly concerned about dealing with this type of crowd; he had dealt with them before. Oh they were dangerous, no doubt about that, but dangerous within the safety of the pack, like hyenas.

There had been deadly adversaries in the past that he'd had to deal with. And those people were better equipped than these people were. At the same time he knew there could be no surprises.

Looking through the binoculars the house leapt into his vision once more. One light showed in the back corner of the house and he figured it was the kitchen. There had been no movement for the last fifty minutes. He had to make a move. It was dangerous to wait in one spot too long. He needed answers and they sure as hell weren't going to come to him.

Haggard double checked the magazine of the Glock and moved the slide back enough to see the brass cartridge in the breach, satisfied that he had a loaded magazine and one up the spout. The weapon was a throwaway from years before. The added green eyes of the Tritium night sights glowed softly in the dark and helped to provide instant target acquisition.

Slipping on the thin black leather kid gloves he stepped out of the vehicle and into the darkness. Except for the distant rumble of the city it was very quiet.

Stopping at the corner of the house he was not sure how he was going to get in. He needed the element of surprise and he needed to know exactly how many were inside. He placed a soft rubber-soled toe onto the landing and lifted himself up without touching the stairs, moving quietly to the front door. There was no sound from inside as he tried to turn the doorknob; it would not turn.

Moving to the rear of the house he studied the back entrance from twenty feet away. Four stairs led up to a small four-foot landing and a windowed door with a closed curtain on it. Light and voices poured out of an open window to the right of the landing and he moved closer until he could hear what they were saying.

"We've been going at this too long now," a deep and gravelly sounding voice drifted out of the window. "I'm bloody beat."

"It won't be much longer now, Stu. We can get this shit weighed and out of the way in fifteen more minutes." The second voice had a higher octave and with a trace of an accent. "Besides, it'll give us a change of scenery tomorrow instead of sticking around here."

Haggard moved to the stairs and placed his right foot onto the very edge of the stair just above the vertical support and gently added his weight to the structure. Satisfied that it was solid and would not squeak he moved steadily upward until he was level with the window. He scanned the backyard to ensure there was nothing back there. The light from the kitchen window vanished into the blackness.

"Its one thing to cut the stuff that Herrera-Sanchez drops on us," the gravelly voice said and wiped his nose across his left sleeve. "It's another thing to have to baby-sit it until we can move it. Mark my words the cops'll be knocking at our door soon."

The Mule

Gravelly voice was sitting with his back towards the window. Long and dense black hair surrounded a bald spot on the top of the man's head. His hair was pulled back into a ponytail that ran down the back of his red long sleeved shirt.

Haggard scanned the room and noticed drug paraphernalia on the counter and what looked like filled freezer-lock bags with tape wrapped around them. He could not see the other man who was hidden behind the first.

"Calm down. Why are you jumpy all of a sudden? Have we had any problems?"

The other man was about to reply when the kitchen door exploded inward on its fragile hinges and thudded against the wall. The entrance was filled with a large male wearing a black windbreaker and carrying a gun. Stuart Ruddick turned quickly around but froze in place. Carlos Neigel made a dive for the counter where a mean-looking black police tactical shotgun was ready for use.

"You're looking for a way to die!" Haggard warned.

Neigel stopped two inches short of the shotgun. Looking over at Haggard he gradually straightened up and sat back in the chair. "Whoever you are, you are a dead man my friend."

Haggard pointed the Glock at the center of the dirty blue t-shirt Neigel was wearing and looked into the eyes set above a narrow nose and thin mustache. Hatred looked back.

"What do you want?" Ruddick asked.

Haggard looked back at an unshaven face divided by a crooked nose. "Put both hands flat on the table and then stand up and push the chairs back. One twitch, one little twitch and you'll wish you hadn't."

He kicked Ruddick's feet apart and backward until his full weight rested on his hands and rammed the barrel of the Glock up behind his testicles. "Move the wrong way and you'll be talking in a higher voice."

He did a thorough search removing a folding knife with a five-inch blade from a rear pocket and a small caliber semi-automatic from a right ankle holster. He placed both items in his jacket and followed the same procedure with Neigel who was shaking with anger. The second man had nothing on him. Haggard pulled the shotgun away from the two men and told them to sit down.

"Okay, hotshot," Neigel said. "What the fuck you want?"

"I want answers, and I want them very quickly," Haggard replied as he took Ruddick's small semi-automatic out of his pocket.

"Answers to what?" Ruddick demanded. "Who the hell are you?"

"You guys set me up," he replied as he backed away to cover the rear door of the house and the entrance to the kitchen.

"What is this guy talking about, Stu? This guy talks in riddles. Don't he talk in riddles?" Neigel asked sarcastically.

Ruddick just nodded in agreement, sitting poised in the chair watching Haggard's every move.

Neigel laughed. "We've never seen you before, man. If I was you I'd get the hell out of here."

"Let me refresh your memory. You loaded my rig with crap. I'm not very happy."

"You're out of your mind," Neigel snarled.

"I lost a motorhome because of the shit you loaded underneath. You bastards are going to tell me who's behind it all."

"You're *really* out of your mind," Ruddick smirked.

"How'd you lose the motorhome," Neigel asked.

"Drug Enforcement took it at the border," Haggard answered reluctantly.

A strange deep sound emanated from Ruddick and it took a few seconds to recognize the sound as it grew out of the man's barrel-like chest. It started soft and deep and grew harsh as it finally broke into a loud mocking laugh. With a smile on his face Ruddick looked at Haggard with hard eyes. "Tough shit!"

Haggard's anger started to fester within as he looked around the kitchen. He realized he had been foolish and really did not have any way to force these two to tell him anything. He spotted an old and dirty telephone on the counter. A thin black book with tattered pages lay open next to it. Moving quickly he picked it up and got an instant reaction from Neigel and Ruddick.

"Leave that the hell alone," Neigel said, starting to get up."

"Hey," Ruddick bellowed in his abrasive voice.

Haggard could see that Ruddick was poised to move and pointed the Glock at him. "Sit back down."

Ruddick sat back in the chair slowly as he moved back and glanced at the book. The pages showed numerous names and phone numbers. The numbers were listed in columns across the pages. "I think I'll just borrow this."

Both men jumped out of their chairs and were only held back from moving any further by the small black hole in the end of the pistol.

"Listen, asshole," Ruddick snarled. "If I were you I would put that back! I'll kill you, man. I swear I'll find you and kill you." Ruddick's threat, delivered in a low and quiet voice sounded very real and very menacing.

"That was just a little talk your fluff got before," Neigel cut in viciously. "Wait until I catch her in some nice dark corner, just her and me...alone. You can count on it."

Haggard looked from one man to the other...and he knew. He saw their faces change from anger to smug knowledge. He knew they meant every word of their threat and would carry it out. From what Neigel had just said they not only knew who he was, they knew all about Connie's beating. He had to get out of thinking like a cop if he wanted to survive.

A picture sprang into his mind. It was a puffy face swollen beyond recognition and a body beaten and stabbed without hesitation. He saw the pain and suffering on that face and he knew he would always see it. Haggard's eyes grew hard with the memory. The loss, the anger, the frustration and the knowledge that these people were involved overwhelmed him and his eyes changed to a deeper hue that Ruddick mistook for weakness.

"Oh look, the prick's going to cry. What an asshole. You and me my friend are going to meet again very soon," Ruddick smiled. "I'm going to find you and your bitch and we'll have some more fun."

Haggard looked down at the small semi-automatic in his hand and back at Ruddick. "I don't think so."

Ruddick finally recognized the look in Haggard's eyes for what it was, and lunged at Haggard.

Haggard watched Ruddick's eyes grow impossibly large just before he shot him in the forehead. The man's head disappeared backwards and bounced backward onto the tabletop. The body dropped like a sack of wet sand onto the floor. Haggard's ears rang from the loud detonation and the smell of cordite filled the room. He quickly swung the sights onto Neigel who was standing with a shocked and stupefied expression on his face as he looked down at the twitching Ruddick.

Neigel came out of his trance and looked into the icy eyes of Dan Haggard. "No! Don't do it, man. Take what you want! I was only joking! I... We... I... I didn't beat her up. It was that Canadian. He was looking for his goods."

"What Canadian?" Haggard demanded, thinking of the little runt at the campsite.

"I...I...I don't know his name. He's a big guy, bald with a ring in his ear. I...I..." Neigel stuttered with fear, realizing that he had seriously misjudged the man in front of him.

"I'm going to ask you once more. What is his name?" Dan steadied his aim.

"Okay, okay. Some guys call him Happy. Honest, I don't know nothing else. It's just rumors, yuh know? Look, I was only joking about the girl." Neigel squirmed and tried to sound convincing.

"The problem is, shit-face, you guys killed her."

"I didn't know!" Neigel screamed. "Man, honest...I was only kidding man...you know?"

"You know what, man? I just don't believe you." Dan squeezed the trigger gently.

A brown satchel sat on the floor by the refrigerator and he picked it up. Green untidy bundles of one hundred dollar bills filled half the case; Haggard threw the black book inside and placed it by the back door.

He tossed the shotgun down next to Neigel and threw the small caliber semi-auto pistol belonging to Ruddick onto the floor next to him. He scattered the remainder of the Cocaine that was on the table all about the room. Two minutes later he was six blocks away and out of the area.

The Mule

*　*　*

Even with the windows cracked open two inches and the defroster blowing a strong gust of air the inside of the windows refused to give up their high concentration of moisture. Anthony Rosza turned his head to the left and then to the right in an experimental fashion before leaning back against the headrest.

"Is your neck still bothering you?" Quiring asked from the driver's seat.

"Yeah, it's the weirdest thing," Rosza answered, rubbing the back of his neck. "I have a hard time turning my head to the right."

"I've got the perfect cure for that."

"Yeah," Rosza asked. "What?"

"Don't turn your head to the right." He laughed as he quickly turned left onto the final stretch of roadway to the crime scene.

Rosza looked to his left and at his partner, taking in the tall and athletic figure decked out in the usual blue jeans and black windbreaker. He was handsome in a craggy sort of way, and his unruly red hair provided the perfect enhancement for his ruddy complexion. They had been partners for three years and they got along like brothers. Although they went out occasionally, Quiring spent most of his time either at the gym or with his long-time girlfriend, Julia.

"Shit! That would mean that I would be looking at you and your ugly face all the time."

Quiring laughed as he pulled to a stop. "Here we are. Looks like quite a crowd."

There were two marked police cruisers, an ambulance and three unmarked units parked in disarray on the lawn and street. A uniformed officer stood by one of the marked cars. The lights blazed from the roof in a rapid brilliance and seemed to singe a person's vision. The officer extended his arm and motioned them to stop.

Lloyd Quiring produced his Drug Enforcement ID as Rosza walked around the car to join him. A tall man with thick salt and pepper hair walked out of the house to greet them as they neared the doorway.

"Hi, Howard," Rosza waved briefly as he approached.

"I saw you coming," Howard Edicott said as he shook hands with them both. He had a narrow and weathered face with deep creases and crevices that looked like an old terrain map. He had been around as long as Rosza and Quiring could remember. Always the consummate professional he maintained an easy and relaxed style on and off the job. As far as they knew he kept his private life separate from his professional life, never mixing the two. Both men had always liked and respected him.

"Your case?" Rosza enquired.

"Two of us are working on it for now. Double murder and looks like an attempted drug rip-off. There's Cocaine all over the place so I thought you might like to take a look."

"Appreciate it," Quiring answered as they walked towards the house.

"These guys had weapons and ammo stashed throughout the house," Edicott continued as he stood in the kitchen entranceway. "It doesn't look like it did them any good though."

"Did they have any clocking paper?" Rosza asked.

"Not a dollar bill in the place." Edicott shook his head in the negative, "Which is odd if you ask me."

"I think we've been here before," Quiring said to Rosza. "Last year?"

Rosza looked at the investigator. "What are their names?"

"Oh you know them I'm sure, Ruddick and Neigel, a couple of sweethearts."

"Oh, yeah, they're a couple of distributors for our friend, Jairo Herrera-Sanchez. Maybe we'll come across some info for you on the hit. You never know," Rosza said.

"Oh they've probably made a few enemies along the way and as usual this will be almost impossible to crack. Believe me, *anything* will be appreciated," Edicott joked as he escorted Rosza and Quiring around the premises. He showed them the Cocaine in the kitchen as well as a small stash hidden under towels and sheets in a hall closet.

"It sure as hell looks gang related to me," Quiring commented. "Maybe the Asians are making a move. I don't think anyone else would be stupid enough to take these guys on."

"Did you find any notes? Something we could use for a paper trail?" Rosza asked, looking at Edicott's rugged face.

"Not a thing, no money and no paper. The place is as clean as hell."

Twenty minutes later Rosza and Quiring thanked Edicott and headed for the door. They stood aside as body bags and gurneys were rolled into the house. "Two less people to spread their poison," Quiring commented.

A misty rain fell from a low depressing sky and the windshield wipers had very little effect as the water reappeared like a greasy blanket. The gloomy sky seemed to drop lower, mixing with the bruised and liver colored formations that were threatening to discharge their hidden cargo.

Both men were silent. They sat and listened to the clunk, thump of the wipers as they thought their own thoughts, the images of the dead still in their minds.

"Man, it's dreary," Quiring muttered for something to say. Rosza and Quiring were not used to the mugginess that clung in the air. "You want to go over and pay Sanchez a visit?"

"No, it would be a waste of time but I think a little visit to his lackey might produce something. Ted Conway is all over the bloody place and the little weasel just might slip up on something."

They sat in the car for almost an hour waiting for Conway to appear in his little coffee truck. Rosza became agitated with the wait and his short over-weight frame became uncomfortable in the confines of the car. He knew he should phone his wife because the neighbors expected them for dinner. He also knew that he had better be on time. He was about to call her on the cell phone when the coffee truck arrived.

It arrived in a slither of mud and a blast of the horn. Both men watched as Ted Conway slipped easily out of the cab and walked to the side of the truck to open up the raised side against the rain. He began dispensing coffee and snacks to the construction men on site. Conway walked to the rear of the truck and after reaching down into a compartment he handed over something to a worker. The man pocketed it immediately and left looking a little ill at ease.

"I bet that's not on the menu," Anthony Rosza offered quietly.

"We better hit him as soon as he leaves the lot, Tony, and shake him up a bit. Let him know we know he's carrying," Quiring suggested.

A few minutes later the truck bounced into the street off of the temporary wooden ramp that was rammed against the curb. Mud shot up and behind in its wake, depositing large chunks of earth and smeared muck onto the pavement as it accelerated away. Half way down the block Lloyd Quiring expertly maneuvered the car to the side of the coffee truck and forced it to the curb.

"Hey, what the hell are you doing, man?" Conway yelled out the window. His face was contorted and flushed with anger. It changed to puzzlement as they both approached the truck.

Rosza held his badge up to Conway's face. "Get out of the truck."

Conway opened the door reluctantly, sliding off the seat and out into the street between the frame and the barely opened door. He nervously scanned the two men before him, shoving his hands into his pockets then out again as rain started to coat his hair and run down his forehead.

Rosza moved slightly to Conway's right to protect his partner and to help ease the pain in his neck. Conway was forced to look back and forth between the two men. "What's up?"

"We've been watching you, Teddy baby. You're pushing crap along your route," Lloyd Quiring snapped as he stepped in a little closer to Conway. "This truck is loaded with shit! Am I right?"

"No way, not on your life, man. I'm just delivering my regular stuff. I'm keeping clean."

"Yeah," Rosza smiled, raising his eyebrows at Conway. "Sure you are. You won't mind then if we open up that back compartment and take a look?"

Conway's face betrayed him immediately. His eyes darted towards the back compartment then back into the eyes of Quiring before sliding off into some distant horizon.

"We want some information, Conway," Quiring continued sternly. "Two of your buddies got blown away last night and we think you can help us pin it down. A little inside track as to who had it in for them."

Conway became alert, looking from Rosza to Quiring in rapid succession. "What? Who got blown away? Who are you talking about, man?"

"Your buddies, Ruddick and Neigel, they took a couple in the head last night," Rosza told him. "It wasn't a pretty sight."

"Holy shit…I…, nobody told me nothing about…" Conway stopped suddenly and looked at the ground. "Ah… Who'd you say? The names don't ring a bell."

"Ah come on, Conway. You're going to make us have to bust you and if I remember right this is your second offence. You're looking at ten years inside, minimum. That's a lot of time. You'd miss all this beautiful sunshine," Quiring said, pointing to the rain swollen clouds.

Conway fidgeted with some coins in his pocket while his brain tried to sort out the best way to get out of the situation. He finally concluded that if he did not offer something he was going to jail. Bullshit worked in the past and he could do it again he reasoned.

"Well?" Rosza prodded.

"Alright, I knew them but this is the first I heard of it. That's the truth, man. Right off I don't know who it could be that done something like that. I haven't heard of any trouble or anything, honest. I'll ask around if you want."

"That's very civic-minded of you, Conway. You can be sure we will be back to see you at a very inconvenient time. Bullshit only goes so far so you better rustle up some answers for us," Rosza instructed him as he leaned very close to Conway's eyes. "Or you are going to be the center of all our attention."

"Yeah…yeah… I'll ask around. Don't worry.

Rosza and Quiring watched the truck leave as they settled into the car. Drying their faces and hair with a clean handkerchief they opened the windows a crack to clear the windows of fog and pulled out into traffic.

"How much you want to bet he's heading to tell Herrera-Sanchez about the hit," Quiring asked.

"Herrera-Sanchez probably already knows. I don't think Conway has a clue about any of this. He was surprised as hell when we told him. Let's get back to the office."

The Drug Enforcement Administration office was located at 400—2nd Avenue West. The two men spent very little time there except for the required paperwork and for the computer queries that assisted them in their investigations. An answer to one of their queries was waiting for them upon their return.

"Hey, take a look at this, Tony," Quiring said, offering several sheets of paper to Rosza.

Rosza took the offered paper and glanced at the bold letters of the heading: Federal Bureau of Investigation. Glancing down at the subject line a name bounced out at him. He glanced at Quiring then scanned the document before sitting on the corner of the desk to read it thoroughly.

"Well? What do you think?" Quiring asked.

Rosza read on for a few moments, holding his hand up to Quiring and silently asking him to wait. He lowered the printouts and turned to his partner. "Well isn't that a twist. He's an ex-police officer and a highly decorated Marine. He's served in the Gulf and Panama. It says here he's a Combat Specialist. What does that mean exactly?"

"It means he can handle himself," Quiring answered dryly.

"Maybe this guy Haggard *was* set up. It sure doesn't add up to smuggling Cocaine for a living what with his record and his business, does it?"

"I've seen stranger things," Quiring stated. "But you're right; it is a little off base what with him owning a successful business and his professional background. It's lucky you were up at the border when he was brought in. We may be able to work some Intel out of this."

Rosza slid off the desk and moved to a wall map while he rubbed his sore neck. "Someone had to work while you took a day off." He scanned the Washington State map, taking in the familiar territory.

Large tracts of Washington State were designated by the Office of the National Drug Control Policy, a component of the Executive Office of the President, as a High Intensity Drug Trafficking Area, or an HIDTA area. It brought fourteen Northwest counties together to synchronize task forces and provide investigative support. A tactical intelligence center in place along the U.S. –Canadian border dealt with the threat of the infiltration of drugs.

Rosza thought of all the agencies in place to combat the scourge that never seemed to end. Besides the DEA, there were the Border Patrol and Customs/Border Protection Agency, State and Local Police, the FBI and the IRS, the Coast Guard, the Postal Service, and even the Department of Defense. It wasn't enough, not by a long shot.

The Mule

Traffickers modeled their operations after international terrorists groups and they had tight control over their soldiers and the highly compartmentalized cell structures. Everything from drug shipments, communications, security, distribution, recruitment, and money laundering ran efficiently and effectively. They spent vast sums on advanced hi-tech equipment to improve communications and they had the best that money could buy. They had their own boats, planes, radar and weapons. Their counterintelligence and transportation networks were something to take very seriously.

Rosza knew that although they had made significant dents in the drug business at times and had seized enough drugs and equipment to impress most people, they were not keeping up. The man-hours rarely produced the desired results. In the case of Dan Haggard, he wondered if this was a case where an innocent guy was going to fall through the cracks. Turning from the map Rosza walked back to where Quiring was sitting and handed the FBI sheets back to him.

Quiring looked at the information again and shrugged. "I wonder what's going through Haggard's mind right now. I mean he's a combat veteran and an ex-police member and if he's innocent like he says it's going to be a hard pill for him to swallow."

"Yeah he's got quite a background." Rosza smiled slightly and sat down across from Quiring.

Quiring leaned forward to throw the paper into a tray and stopped. He noticed another printout lying in the basket. Quickly reading down the paper he realized it was a continuation of the queries. It was an automated reply from another agency. "Dan Haggard's been hit."

Rosza leaned forward quickly. "He's dead?"

"No, sorry, I mean he's a complainant in an assault. His home was hit in a home invasion; the file is out of Kirkland. His girlfriend was badly beaten."

"Drugs involved?" Rosza asked.

Quiring shrugged his shoulders; "It doesn't say. You said that Haggard kept saying over and over again that he didn't know about the Cocaine."

"Yeah, so?" Rosza gave Quiring a questioning look.

"Well maybe he's telling the truth. Someone hit his house and did some real damage. Why?"

"Maybe it's because he lost the drugs?" Rosza yawned.

"I don't know. A decorated Marine and an ex-cop and a well established business man...I just think we should look into it a bit more."

Rosza looked over at Quiring. "Then I think it's time we visited our Mr. Dan Haggard."

CHAPTER SEVEN

Dan Haggard had traveled the emotional roller coaster many times in his life, suffering the abrupt and swift adjustment from anger, frustration, and fear, to sudden jubilation and relief. Nothing quite matched this plunge from pulsating adrenaline to the dead halt of regret and gloom.

There really had not been any choice. He had known it then and he knew it now. He had seen it in their eyes. They would have been the stalker and he would have been the target. It would not have ended. He *knew* all that but it did not make it any easier. He was trained to take out armed aggressors not unarmed men.

He stopped and picked up a bottle of scotch and then because a headache was starting, some painkillers. He chose a motel at random and settled back and waited for the booze or the painkillers to work but neither had the desired effect. His head pounded steadily and the throbbing pain would not go away.

He counted the money in the bag, counting an even one hundred and thirty thousand dollars. He looked through the black book he'd taken from Neigel and Ruddick. The names and numbers meant nothing to him.

His exhausted mind fell into a deep void while he sat propped up against the headboard. The black book still lay open in his hands. He escaped into a world of nothingness and was surprised when he woke up late in the morning to bright sunshine, minus the headache and minus the remorse.

Hunger stabbed into him unexpectedly while he finished showering and there was an urgent need to leave the confines of the room and get out into the open air as soon as possible. He found a restaurant that served a twenty-four hour country-style breakfast and settled back into the booth with a cup of coffee while he waited for his order.

The black book still held his interest and he noted that some names had numerous entries and were abbreviated or entered as a code. However the more he looked it over the more it looked like a simple abbreviation. CW and BK were common entries, the numbers beside their names appearing to be quantity amounts rather than dollar amounts.

Haggard reached into his jacket for a pen so he could underline certain entries and pulled out a piece of paper along with the pen. A bold heading ran across the top of the page: Vehicle Registration—Province of British Columbia. He had forgotten all about it. It was from the truck and the guy he had chased from the back of the motorhome.

He read the name and address to himself, remembering now what Neigel had screamed just before leaving this world. *'I... We... I didn't beat her up. It was that Canadian. He was looking for his goods!'*

His breakfast was placed in front of him. *'It was that Canadian! He was looking for his goods!'* The words echoed in his mind again.

Dan Haggard ate his breakfast with little pleasure. He ate mechanically while his mind dwelled on all the events that had taken place. He thought about the campground disturbance and the information from Neigel that the same men had come looking for their goods.

Sitting in the Honda, Haggard called the store and talked to his manager. It was the press, he said. Business was really bad. Customers were disappearing in droves. He made some decisions so the manager could act upon them and made a mental note to increase the manager's salary if he pulled through this. He felt relieved to have at least one responsibility temporarily off of his back. He had very little time before his next court appearance and he certainly did not have time to think about business.

Punching in another number from a card clipped to the sun visor he waited for the connection. The phone rang twice before the real estate agent answered it. He wanted out of the house as soon as possible even though it was too soon to make important decisions and a little pressure on the real estate salesman did not hurt. He wanted him to put in some effort to sell not just have it sit on the market until someone showed interest.

"Yes, Mr. Haggard, I have a showing this weekend. I know you are anxious to sell and I'm doing what I can."

Haggard gave a sad smile into the phone. "I appreciate your effort. I will be out of town so show it anytime you want. You have my cell number if you get an offer."

As he drove towards the house he made a call to G. Wendell Hawthorne. His lawyer was with a client. Having already gone over the details once with the lawyer he still needed to talk to him a lot more. The criminal lawyer had been recommended to him by Larry Cole, his business lawyer. 'He's very good,' Cole had told him. Haggard hoped so. He set up another appointment for the following week and hung up.

The house was secure and reasonably tidy when he walked through the door. Picking up mail from the floor he did a quick check of all the rooms. Everything was in place although it would require more than a little polish if it was to sell. The cleaning agency had done a reasonably good job. What it really required was a woman's touch. It was not going to happen.

Haggard quickly threw some casual clothes together along with other personal gear. His binoculars and the black book went into an overnight case. He was ready to leave.

Running around and trying to find answers felt a little strange and out of place. And yet it was no different than any other police investigation he had been involved with, he just did not have the badge to back him. When it came down to it the badge was not there to hamper him either. *Nothing is going to change unless you make it happen*, he thought to himself.

Turning off his street and onto a main thoroughfare he aimed the Honda towards the I-5 freeway, quickly finding himself swallowed up in the traffic. He had a way to go but did not particularly care about the time. He needed time to think. He needed time to get his priorities straight and to think of the consequences of his actions.

As Dan Haggard entered the freeway a car pulled quietly into the driveway of his house. DEA Agents Rosza and Quiring walked up to the front door. It was kind of deflating when there was no response. They had more than a few questions for him.

* * *

"I want some friggin' answers!" Jairo Herrera-Sanchez screamed into the phone. "I always have to do everythin'!"

Stepping away from the open doorway of his small cubicle he threw his glass across the radiator shop in a fit of anger and watched it smash against the cinderblock wall.

He turned one way then another, seething as he listened to the man on the other end of the cell phone. "No! It is not good enough! Start puttin' pressure on people. I want answers right friggin' now! Two guys hit, our shit destroyed, one hundred and thirty thou missin' and you want me to sit back and wait? Get some answers!" Herrera-Sanchez slammed his palm against the phone disconnecting the contact.

"Did you hear anything new?" Conway asked as he walked up behind Herrera-Sanchez.

"Will you quit sneakin' up on me?" Herrera-Sanchez snarled as he whirled around. "Always slidin' around like a friggin' snake! What the hell are you doin' here anyway? Get out and nose around. See if you can come up with some answers. Make yourself useful for a change."

Conway left without saying a word, his mood sulky and angry. "Call me a fucking snake. Bloody grease ball."

The weather-beaten old Dodge left a trail of blue smoke in its wake, the left rear spring sagging with age. Conway had no idea where he was supposed to start looking or what he was supposed to even look for. He headed for his favorite tavern. A few beers and some company would take his mind off Herrera-Sanchez and his miserable temper. Maybe he could find himself a chick for the night.

The place stank of stale beer, cigarette smoke, and years of neglect. The floor was filthy and the grimy walls, which were made from some long ago material that looked like pebbled copper, were streaked with long trails of old beer. Feeble fans turned in sync with feeble music that emanated from a corner near an old threadbare pool table.

A handful of people decorated the bar and a few sat at the tiny round tables. Conway recognized Sheldon sitting at one of the tables by himself. He had his chair turned sideways and was leaning backward against the wall. He looked up nervously as Conway approached.

"What the hell's with you? You look like shit," Conway declared frankly as he sat down at the table.

"Nothing," Sheldon mumbled uneasily. "I just got a headache." He looked like he wanted to get up and leave.

"What's bugging you, man? What are you so jumpy about?"

"Nothing, I told you. I got a headache."

Conway shook his head and waved to the waiter for a beer. "I'm the one who should be worked up, frigging Sanchez screaming at me all the time. You hear what went down with Neigel and Ruddick?"

Sheldon's eyes enlarged with a look of shock upon hearing Ruddick and Neigel's names. The question made him come away from the wall and the chair thudded to the floor. "No. What do you mean?"

"Blown away, man," Conway shrugged. "They were just blown away. Can you imagine those two being blown away? There's going to be shit to pay over this. Somebody busted into the house and…"

Sheldon stood up abruptly and after fidgeting for his keys for a few seconds moved towards the door. He stopped and quickly turned back to Conway. He looked sick. The area around his eyes had an ashen look and he was sweating. "I…I gotta go. I…I got a headache."

Conway looked at Sheldon, puzzled by his actions. "What the…"

"I gotta go. I'll see you later."

Conway's eyes narrowed suspiciously. "What the hell's the *matter* with you?" Sheldon just kept moving towards the exit door. "What the hell's *with* you?" Conway yelled at the retreating back.

Sheldon usually liked to sit and gab over two or three beers. *He's nervous as shit*, Conway thought. Sheldon had not been happy to see him at all. In fact the more he thought about it, Sheldon was really scared about something. He had jumped out of the chair as soon as he had mentioned the….

A light went on somewhere inside of Conway's brain. It was not very bright but it was bright enough to see something was out of place.

Conway got his cell phone out. *Fucking snake am I. We'll see,* he thought. *That prick knows something.*

* * *

Once free of Seattle's traffic grip, Haggard was able to sit back and relax. He had the radio tuned to some quiet station, filling the car with music without being distractive.

The scene from the drug-house played repeatedly in his mind. He went over it for the umpteenth time and tried different scenarios to see if he could have handled it differently once entering the house. *Not if I like living,* he finally admitted, already knowing the answer.

At least he would not be short of cash. He had two thousand dollars in his pocket having stashed the other one hundred and twenty-eight up under the flooring in the basement of the house. *Whoever is behind this owes me a hell of a lot more,* he thought grimly. *They can go to hell.*

He arrived at the southern fringe of the greater Vancouver area at an abysmal time. His swift drive through flat, sea level farm country quickly deteriorated to a nerve-wracking struggle. Traffic emerged from all sides as lanes narrowed, disappeared, or changed direction completely.

Haggard emerged unscathed from a tunnel and marveled at the speed in which the other vehicles maneuvered and changed lanes around him in the daily ritual of survival. There seemed to be no traffic enforcement at all.

Driving further north a sign caught his eye as it flashed by: Richmond. It was the area listed on the guy's registration. He was soon to find out that it was a big area to search.

Rugged mountains loomed on the horizon to the north as Haggard eased off the freeway onto a wide street and pulled into a gas station to ask for directions. He got out into a light warm breeze that filled his head with the smells of the sea. A low flying 747 passed overhead and drowned out all other sounds as it dropped lower on its flight path for the Vancouver International Airport. The tail logo stood out boldly against the pale blue sky.

Twenty minutes later he made several passes along a busy street. The registration indicated an address but half the buildings did not display a number and everything appeared to be commercial.

He exited the vehicle and walked casually down the sidewalk. His eyes traveled over the exterior of the buildings as he walked. A small painted number in the corner of a window under a credit card logo on a motorcycle shop caught his eye. It was the number he was looking for.

Dan got back into the Honda and found a parking spot closer to the business. It was set back from the street and had a small display area in front of the shop. Multi-colored motorcycles faced the street, the long front forks on the bikes jutting out at wacky angles and defying gravity.

Three men lounged around an old picnic table off to the side of the building. It was difficult to say if they were employees or guys who just hung out. One man, dressed in blue jeans, black t-shirt, and a black leather vest stood with one boot lodged on the seat of the table and waved a cigar in the air as he talked.

Three hours dragged by. Customers came and went and the men at the picnic table were long gone. Dan needed to eat and he needed to use the washroom and it looked like he would need to find a place to sleep for the night. A sign for a fast food outlet glimmered further on down the street and he finally gave in and drove quickly to the parking lot.

After using the washroom and washing up he ordered the hamburger meal from the limited menu and sat in a booth that gave him a slight view of the motorcycle shop.

The sun moved much further to the west and long shadows played across the ground. Haggard decided to move in closer but a long line of traffic forced him to wait before he could enter onto the roadway.

He was just about to his surveillance point when a small blue pickup approached from the opposite direction. It turned left in front of oncoming traffic in a U-turn and pulled quickly to the curb in front of the motorcycle store. A large man walked from the bike shop and moved to the passenger side of the small truck and got in. Haggard could not see the driver but he sure as hell could see the truck. It was the one from the campground.

The small truck left the curb and forced itself into traffic. Haggard found a gap and was able to accelerate to within three vehicle lengths.

Noting the license plate he quickly compared it to the piece of paper in his jacket. It was the same.

As the vehicle turned the corner the driver looked to his left and displayed his profile to Haggard. He was not sure if it was the same man or not, it had been a brief encounter in the dark.

The truck kept on an easterly heading and Haggard found that he could easily hide in the heavy volume of traffic. He stayed in the same lane as the pickup and well to the rear to ward off any surprises that could occur from driving in a strange city.

Half an hour later the distance between the two vehicles had lengthened considerably. The traffic had thinned dramatically and the risk of being noticed had increased. Dan Haggard was thankful when the small truck pulled to the left and entered a horseshoe shaped driveway that circled behind a huge old cedar tree. The two men had parked behind a black Mercedes and they were in the process of getting out as Dan continued past the large house.

He found a place off the road with a half view of the house and backed up into some trees. Whoever owned the house was well heeled and the two men who had gone inside certainly did not look like they lived there. All he could do now was wait and hope that no one phoned the police to report him as a suspicious person.

"Grab yourselves a beer and sit down." Frank Tully said as the two men entered the room. "We have a lot to discuss."

Mike Sigger sat down next to Roy Tully and nodded a hello to him. Vince Rizzo brought the beer from the refrigerator behind the bar. As usual Roy looked like he was in a dark mood and unhappy about something.

"How did it go in town?" Frank Tully asked.

Sigger nodded to Vince Rizzo as he took the beer and then turned his attention to Frank. "Fine, it's all set up with the downtown-eastside bunch. They want to increase their volume and want to know if you could guarantee a steadier supply."

"Okay, Roy will handle that. I have another job for the two of you."

Sigger nodded and gestured towards Rizzo. "He picked me up. I left my wheels at the shop for an oil change."

Roy Tully interrupted, looking at Rizzo and then at Sigger. "You can go together. Go back to the farm. I got word that the police are setting up an operation. We have to move to a new location.

"Shit, that's a pile of work, Roy," Sigger exclaimed. "And it's risky."

"We don't have a choice," Frank cut in. "We can't take a chance on loosing everything. We have a new spot close to the border. If we move fast the cops will hit an empty barn and besides being close to the border is going to make transporting it across a lot easier anyway."

"We need lots of room," Vince Rizzo offered.

"Don't you worry your sorry ass," Roy Tully said with disdain. "You'll wish it was smaller by the time you move everything and get it set up."

Sigger took a swig of beer and belched softly. He looked at Frank Tully. "I thought you wanted me to follow the shipment to Seattle? I can't do both."

"You didn't do worth a shit on your last trip down there," Roy Tully stated. "In fact it was a complete waste of time. I even gave you the address. What do we get?—Zippo. That was a brilliant job, Sigger, fucking brilliant. You couldn't even get some broad to tell you where the coke was."

Sigger felt his temper heave itself to the surface; his face was unable to hide his desire to hit back. There had been many an occasion that he had wanted to teach this so called tough guy some manners.

Roy Tully saw the affect he had on Sigger and goaded him on. "When you follow the shipment down, see if you can actually find out something this time. Instead of a woman this time, try to locate the *man*. That's if you can handle him."

"Enough!" Frank ordered and turned to Sigger. "Get things moving at the barn! It'll take a couple of days to get the shipment ready for Seattle anyway."

"When are the cops supposed to hit us?" Sigger asked, looking at Frank but fully aware of Roy's presence a few feet away.

"I'm told it won't be for two, maybe three days. You have time."

"Maybe you can redeem yourself," Roy said as he turned towards Rizzo. The message was not lost on Sigger. "I'm leaving a lot of this in your hands. You do this right and I'll forget your last screw-up."

"I…I appreciate your confidence in me," Rizzo stuttered lamely, flushed in the face with the sudden realization that he was going to be in charge.

"Just remember," Roy squinted menacingly. "You will share the rewards if all goes well. You will also share something else if it doesn't."

"Okay, okay," Frank cut in. "Let's get at it. We have a lot to do. I'll have someone drop your vehicle off for you at the farm," Frank continued, looking at Mike Sigger.

Rizzo and Sigger guzzled down the last of their beer and left the house, walking out into the last remnants of daylight. Rizzo turned on the headlights as he turned onto the road and accelerated rapidly away. With his mind dwelling on the job ahead he never bothered to look into the rearview mirror.

Haggard had to use all of his skills to even get a visual on the place. The farm was set in a bit of a hollow and there were no places to pull off and park. The paved two-lane country road was lined with deep, water filled ditches. Trees, fences, and tall swaying crops in the rolling countryside were his only method of concealment other than the darkness and the darkness was both an ally and a threat. With no equipment it was very slow going.

His left pant leg was soaked well above the knee from the water in one of the ditches. The mosquitoes had swarmed and bitten him until he was able to reach dryer ground. A half buried loop of barbed wire caught his leg as he moved inland and away from the ditch leaving him with torn pants and a stinging and irritating abrasion that ran diagonally across his right shin.

He saw the light of the farmhouse further on and moved quickly. He settled down in the tall grass on the far side of the ditch directly across from the driveway. An old yellow light flickered weakly down onto the roadway from a weathered wooden pole.

He was about to move when two sleek shadows moved into the circle of light like black ghosts moving on the wind. The silent and deadly silhouettes made Haggard's hair rise suddenly at the back of his neck. *Dobermans!* If there was anything he hated it was meeting a dog in the darkness of night. Another shiver went down his back. He checked for the feel of the wind and hoped they did not pick up his scent.

A man appeared out of the darkness and approached the road. He appeared to be working the dogs. Haggard realized it was one of the men from the blue truck. The guy was carrying a shotgun and Dan did not even have to guess what was hanging from his neck. He had used them enough himself: night vision gear. Haggard realized how lucky he had been. He could have been spotted easily. The place was guarded well and from all appearances they were serious about keeping people out.

The man moved to the edge of the driveway and put the shotgun on top of a fence post. A moment later he urinated between the fence rails into a cornfield. The dogs were roaming in the darkness along the edge of the property, moving with that quick elasticity that suggested power and energy.

The guy stepped away from the fence and quietly took in the sounds of the night, looking carefully about him before he turned and put the night vision goggles back on his face. A sharp whistle brought the dogs leaping out of the blackness.

Haggard watched the dogs as they bumped and leaned against the big man in a display of affection. They moved back up the driveway and disappeared from sight into the dark hole beyond the house.

He really wanted to know what lay beyond the house and he wanted to talk to the driver of the little pickup truck but it was obvious he could not get onto the property with those dogs roaming around. If he was the same man from the campground then he had answers to some very important questions. He would be the key to finding the man who gave the orders.

And the bastard that paid a visit to Connie could be in there, Dan thought. *The guy who thinks he can cross the border and zip back without facing the consequences.* That man had to learn that sometimes there are no borders.

CHAPTER EIGHT

Sheldon grabbed his jacket off of the back of the kitchen chair and slipped it on, checking for his wallet and keys in the pockets before heading for the door. The door from the kitchen to the laundry room and inner mudroom was open and a large pile of dirty clothes still lay untouched in the large tub attached to the wall.

His eyes moved involuntarily to the spot in the laundry room and Dan Haggard sprang clearly into his mind. He felt the belt twisted excruciatingly around his head again. His head still ached from the ordeal and he shuddered at the memory. He could not wait to get out of the dumpy basement and out of the city. Tomorrow he would hit the road. He had connections in Portland and he didn't need these people.

He opened the door to the outside and almost collided with two men who stood in the dark opening. His heart tripled its beat as he jumped backwards and collided with the washing machine. "Shee-it, you scared the hell out of me!!" His eyes were unaccustomed to the darkness and he could not see who it was. "What do you want?"

The guy on the left answered. "Going somewhere, Sheldon?"

"Yeah, yeah, I'm going for a beer. Is that you, Ted?"

Sheldon reached over and flicked on a light switch. The naked and dim light on the ceiling of the laundry room erupted in a weak glow as the man on the right stepped into the room.

Sheldon remembered seeing him on occasion with Herrera-Sanchez.

He was short but looked powerfully built. He was in his forties and looked like he had seen rough times. Looking to his left he saw Ted Conway.

Conway gave him a funny smile as he leaned against the doorframe. "We need to talk, Sheldon."

They don't know nothing! Sheldon thought quickly to himself. *Play it cool.* "Sure, come on in," he smiled weakly, his lips twitching nervously.

"No. Not here, Sheldon," Conway said.

In these circumstances Conway was—*The Man!* He was the hawk dealing with the mouse. It was times like this that Conway felt the power. He was somebody to reckon with. It never entered his mind that he was only working for—*The Man.* It was times like this that he could inflate his worth; because after all he knew what it was like to be considered the mouse.

"Okay," Sheldon quickly agreed. "We can go get a beer."

"No. No public places. We're having a meeting of all the guys and you need to be there."

"How… How come I wasn't told of this before?" Sheldon asked nervously and with suspicion.

Conway laughed easily, patting Sheldon on the shoulder as he led him outside. "We can't let the whole world know, pal. These are spur-of-the-moment decisions. You want to go up the ladder you have to attend the meetings."

"Look man, I don't feel right about this. I mean I should have been told about any meeting," Sheldon said lamely.

"Hey, I'm buying the beer after the meeting. Quit griping," Conway said good naturedly as he opened the rear door to the older dark maroon Cadillac and jumped in with Sheldon.

Sheldon felt sick. The sick, nauseous feeling of fear gripped him and made breathing difficult. As the car accelerated he sank back into the seat with the forward motion, feelings of dread balling his stomach into a knot. He tried to convince himself that he was just being jumpy but it was not working. Why was Conway riding with him in the back?

The guy driving the car had not said a word and Ted Conway just sat there with a funny smile on his face. The smile disappeared as they pulled up in front of the radiator shop. They entered by a small door at the side of the building.

It was dark in the shop but the floor was illuminated from the light from Jairo Herrera-Sanchez's office. Sheldon started walking towards the light but twisted back nervously at the sound of the bolt shooting home in the door. He stood looking uncertainly at the bolted door until Conway turned and forced him to move ahead.

It was quiet. Sheldon could not hear any voices. The rank smell of rubber hoses, antifreeze and filthy water made him screw up his nose. He walked with his head downcast, stepping around patches of oil, grease and spilt antifreeze that reflected back from the office light. His heart started to hammer within his chest as he got closer to the office. He was nudged into the office from behind. The light in the office made him squint uncomfortably.

Herrera-Sanchez was lounging back in an office chair. He was impeccably dressed in a dark blue suit, gray shirt and a black, blue and tan tie. The air in the room was rank with the stench from a thin cigar in Sanchez's hand. He never said a word as they all moved into the room and stood in a small crowded group.

Sheldon turned to Conway, a question forming in his mind and a look of anxiety upon his face. Conway and the other man looked back with indifferent expressions on their face. He was about to speak when Herrera-Sanchez spoke to Conway.

"Any problems?"

"No, none," Conway replied.

Herrera-Sanchez turned to Sheldon and gave him a look that shriveled any hope that he might have had. Sheldon found some unknown reserve of courage and suffered through the look, holding a wavering and uneasy gaze.

Herrera-Sanchez appeared hard and unsympathetic. "Sit down!" he commanded and Sheldon fell back into a hard chair. Sheldon's courage was plummeting rapidly.

Herrera-Sanchez bent forward and carefully placed the smoldering cigar into a battered ashtray made from an inverted piston-head. He looked at Sheldon through swirls of smoke, aware of the other man's fear. He could see the beads of sweat on the man's upper lip and his breathing was short and rapid. He hated to admit it but it looked like Conway was right. The guy was deathly afraid about something.

"Ah... Ah, I didn't do nothing. Why am I here?" Sheldon stammered.

"Why are you so friggin' nervous?" Herrera-Sanchez asked quietly.

"I...I... It's just that I was brought here for a meeting and...and I don't see no meeting. You know?"

"You're the reason for the friggin' meetin', Sheldon. We think you can help us out with some information."

"I don't know nothing," Sheldon blurted out.

"That's for fucking sure," Conway volunteered from the corner of the room, a smile on his face.

Jairo Herrera-Sanchez turned towards Conway and gave him a murderous look, his dark eyes shimmering like the large diamond ring on the small finger of his left hand. "If you friggin' interrupt me again, I will personally make you sorry for doin' so."

Conway's smile left his face and he shifted uncomfortably from one foot to the other. "Sorry," he mumbled.

Herrera-Sanchez continued to glare at Conway, making him uneasy and aware of his minor position in the scheme of things. He was quickly turning the hawk back into the mouse. He then turned his attention back to Sheldon. "Now, where was I?"

"What kind of information do you want?" Sheldon asked, feeling somewhat better after having the attention diverted from him.

"I'm goin' to ask you one question and then you will tell me what you know."

"Sure... Sure, anything to help," Sheldon said bravely, starting to feel his confidence returning.

"Why did Ruddick and Neigel get hit?" He spoke the words quietly but his tight lips showed a trace of anger at the remembered loss of his goods and the trespass against him. He knew that if he did not move swiftly word would spread that he was an easy mark.

Sheldon jumped visibly at the mention of the two names. He began to sweat profusely and he could not find his voice. His breathing came in irregular gulps.

"Well!" Jairo barked at him.

Sheldon jumped again but managed to blurt out a weak answer. "I...I heard about that. Conway told me."

"You knew about the hit before Conway told you, didn't you?"

"No, no. No, I didn't. I... How would I know that?"

"You tell me. I lost two men, one hundred and thirty thousand dollars, and a friggin' load of coke. I can tell that you know somethin'. You are goin' to tell me about the hit or I am goin' to get upset."

Sheldon was shaking visibly. He had no talent for hiding his thoughts and his reactions were almost laughable when asked a question. He was on the verge of breaking down and crying out in anguish, and no one had laid a hand on him yet.

He tried desperately to come up with something to please the man in front of him. *My fucking brain won't work,* he screamed to himself. How could he tell them about Haggard? How would he even know about something like that? He had to come up with something to make them happy. He had to come up with something so he could walk out of the place!

Herrera-Sanchez picked up his cigar and drew on it until the end of the cigar was a fiery red. He turned it around and studied the end, watching as the smoke curled slowly towards the ceiling. He looked through the smoke at Sheldon. Sheldon was watching the end of the cigar with a terrified look on his face. It was obvious to Sanchez that the man had an imagination.

"Please, I don't know how they were killed."

"Then you tell me *who* made the hit, Sheldon. I think you know who did this to me. You are either with me on this or you are protectin' someone."

"No, I'm not protecting him, I..." Sheldon froze in mid-sentence. He realized his blunder and tried to correct it. "No, I'm not protecting anyone. You are getting' me all confused."

"You see that guy over there, Sheldon?" Jairo Herrera-Sanchez pointed to the other man with Conway. "He is what I call a consultant. I consult with him whenever I need to know somethin'. He is very good at talkin' to people. I bet you he could take this friggin' cigar, for example, and get almost the whole length up your ass before you pass out."

Sheldon jumped out of the chair and looked for a path out of the room. His heart raced so fast it felt like it would burst. He backed up against the wall knocking a cheap frame containing a city business license onto the floor. "You stay away from me! I didn't do nothing! It was that Haggard guy. He fucking *tortured* me!"

Herrera-Sanchez turned to Conway. "Do we know someone by the name of Haggard? Who the hell is this Haggard?"

Conway shrugged his shoulders. "It doesn't ring a bell."

"He… He's the guy you wanted for the run to Canada. He's the one with the motorhome. You… I…we loaded his rig with the coke," Sheldon managed to get out.

Herrera-Sanchez smiled. "Ah… Now I see. He is the guy with the lost Canadian Cocaine." His smile faded from his face as he turned back to Sheldon. "Now why would this guy pay *you* a visit?"

"I tried not to tell him anything," Sheldon stammered as tears rolled down his cheeks. "He *tortured* me. He tied this belt around my…"

"Shut the frig up!" Herrera-Sanchez roared, losing his patience. "I asked you a question! Why did he come to you and what did you tell him?"

"Nothing," Sheldon whimpered. "He stole my pocketbook with my list of names in it. All he asked for was a name."

"Oh, all he asked for was a name. And which name might that be?" Herrera-Sanchez asked in a reasonable manner.

Shifting his weight from one foot to another Sheldon was determined not to look at anyone in the room for fear that they would be able to see how terrified he was. Despite his resolve his eyes made contact with Jairo Herrera-Sanchez's cold reptilian gaze. He felt his stomach cramp and the need to urinate overwhelmed him. The eyes seemed to swallow him into their depths.

"Which *name* did you give him?" Herrera-Sanchez demanded.

"I'll tell you. You gotta remember…he tortured me…otherwise I wouldn't have said nothing'. You know that."

Herrera-Sanchez waited, not saying anything as he looked at Sheldon. A trickle of water fell noisily into a bucket from a leaky faucet outside the office door. The sound of the water was amplified in the silence.

Sheldon's labored breathing stopped. He listened briefly as a siren wailed its faint and lonely call somewhere out in the dark. The silence went on until Sheldon finally whispered something that no one could hear.

"What? Speak the frig up!" Sanchez shouted.

"I told him Ruddick's name! I had no choice!" Sheldon shrieked.

"You also told him Neigel's name too, didn't you?" Sanchez enquired as he leaned back and took several long draws on his cigar to get it glowing again. The smoke filled the small room and caused Sheldon to look at the glowing end again.

Sheldon shook his head up and down rapidly but said nothing, afraid to trust his voice to another admission of betrayal. He looked quickly over at Conway and the other man. Conway looked back with a blank expression on his face.

Herrera-Sanchez turned to Conway and waved his cigar back and forth in the air. "How do we find this guy, Haggard?"

Conway straightened himself up and thought quickly. He pointed to Sheldon and nodded in his direction. "He should be able to get it easy enough. It should be on record. He worked on Haggard's motorhome."

Herrera-Sanchez looked slowly back at Sheldon and got to his feet. "I have wasted enough time with you. You have caused me a great deal of grief and a lot of expense. Shit, this guy even has a list of names you gave him! Go with Conway and get the friggin' information I need. I want to know where this Haggard lives and I want to know right away."

Sheldon almost collapsed with relief. He nodded and slid sideways along the wall towards the doorway. "I'll make it up to you. I'll..."

"Just get the frig out of my sight!" Jairo said in disgust, wiping some imaginary lint from the front of his suit.

Sheldon rushed past Conway and out into the darkness of the radiator shop with Conway following closely behind. Herrera-Sanchez looked into the eyes of the driver, the one he had labeled as a 'consultant'. He took a long sensuous puff of his cigar. He nodded once.

The other man nodded back.

* * *

"Where the hell could he be?" Lloyd Quiring asked, raising his eyebrows. "He hasn't shown up at his job and he's not at home." He grunted with disappointment as he pointed to a map of the city. "We've covered just about the whole city looking for him."

"Then he's not in the city is he?" Tony Rosza replied walking back to his desk with a cup of coffee in one hand and a frosted pastry in the other. He took a sip of the hot coffee as he sat down. "You better eat one of these before they're all gone."

"How can you eat that crap?" Quiring asked, pushing his unruly red hair back off his forehead.

"Hey, I need to build up my energy," Rosza shot back.

"Yeah, well you won't run empty for a while. Your energy is sticking out well beyond your belt."

"Funny," Rosza mumbled around a mouthful of food. "Asshole."

Quiring smiled and leaned his forearms onto the desk looking at his partner. "You think he's off on a drunk somewhere or maybe visiting an old hangout where he and his girl used to frequent? He took it real hard when she died."

"He doesn't look like the type to run and lick his wounds to me," Rosza said, licking his fingers. "Look at his record." Getting an interested look from Quiring he settled back with his coffee and continued. "Look, Haggard has to be some type of hard-ass what with his background. He certainly must be able to handle himself. I don't think he's off on some drunk. It doesn't fit."

"If it was me and I was innocent of any knowledge or intent I think I'd be looking for some answers," Quiring remarked.

"Yes you would…and you know what? I think Haggard would too. Maybe that's why we can't locate him. Maybe he isn't the type to just sit back and await his fate. Look at his service records, especially police. He continuously got into trouble because of the way he handled the bastards on the street."

"I suppose," Quiring agreed. "Let's hope that if he does come up with something he's smart enough to share it with us. It won't do him any good otherwise."

The telephone rang on Rosza's desk and he leaned ahead and picked it up; "Agent Rosza speaking."

He listened for half a minute before looking across at Lloyd Quiring, nodding his head up and down slightly. He was about to speak but stopped and listened some more, rubbing his neck and leaning back to look at the ceiling as he did.

"Look, we need to speak to him. I…" Anthony Rosza shook his head in annoyance at the interruption, listened some more and then continued. "Okay…no…no don't detain him. Please let him proceed." Rosza listened again and then nodded unconsciously. "Thanks, thanks for the up-date." He hung up.

"Was that about Dan Haggard?" Quiring inquired.

"Yeah, he just crossed the border at the Peace Arch."

"He's left the country? Shit, he has a court appearance coming up."

Rosza shook his head sideways. "No, he came *into* the country thirty minutes ago. They were detaining him. They'll kick him loose. He's on his way south." Rosza looked across at his partner, a puzzled look on his face as he digested the new information. "You still think he may be innocent?"

Quiring looked back with raised eyebrows. "It doesn't look good. Why did he cross the border? Is it drug contacts?"

"I don't know," Rosza answered.

Quiring got up from his chair. "My minds going blank and I'm bloody bushed. It's after midnight. I suppose *you'll* want to hang around and intercept him at his place," he said as he looked tiredly at the other man. "Yeah I can see that you do. Do you have any idea how much longer that will be?"

"I figure about an hour and a bit. Go get some shut eye in the lunchroom," Rosza pointed with his chin. "I'll call you."

"Piss on that," Quiring answered. "I'd end up with a stiff neck like you and having to walk around in circles just to be able to see anything."

Rosza laughed and rubbed his neck. "My neck's okay now."

"I'm happy for you. Let's leave now. I'll get some shut eye while we wait. I feel like I'm getting older and older with all this lost sleep. For all I know Haggard's as guilty as hell."

"Don't blame that on Haggard. You look old in the morning too."

Quiring looked over at Rosza and smiled tiredly. Now it was his turn to utter a friendly comment: "Asshole."

The sky glowed on the horizon with a strange luminance. Radiant offshoots of orange and white flickered and danced and then raced high against a jet-black background like the Aurora Borealis. Traces of yellow shimmered like a halo, skirting the blackness while miniature suns floated on the wind. The bright blush dwindled and almost disappeared but then burst anew and propelled millions of sparkling diamonds into the night.

Red, blue, and white strobes of light pierced the blackness with an urgency that failed to diminish the display paraded and thrown up against the night sky.

While the light was something that dazzled the eye the heat was something to behold and fear. It sucked the oxygen into the bowels of the house at hurricane speed and roared to the core, spewing out as fire, black smoke, ash…and death to anyone who dared get too close.

The roof collapsed, throwing up a solid barrier of fire and sparks. A wall of heat blew sideways towards the firefighters who were trying to set up their equipment and at the spectators who had quickly gathered. Wires snapped and fell, flinging sideways as electrical charges arced into the roadway.

The house to the north burned also, half engulfed and burning furiously as the owners looked on in anxiety and misery. On the south side the wall of a house blackened and smoldered, on the verge of exploding into flame like the tree in the yard.

"Son-of-a-bitch, will you look at that!" Lloyd Quiring pointed as he turned the steering wheel onto the exit ramp. "That is one mother of a fire."

"You have that right," Rosza replied, watching the colors dance across the sky. As they got closer Rosza looked away from the sky and over at Quiring. "We're heading right towards it."

Lloyd Quiring nodded in agreement. "Why do I have this gut feeling?"

They had to abandon the car and walk. They were a block away from their destination. It was also in the same direction as the fire. Emergency vehicles from several agencies lined and filled the roadway. Uniformed police officers fought a loosing battle trying to keep the crowds back and out of the way. Rosza had to show his identification twice before they could get closer to the scene of the fire.

Fire hoses from pumper-trucks and fire hydrants snaked across the roadway and seemed to wonder off haphazardly between emergency vehicles and running men. A wall of water directed towards the smoldering house to the south of the fire seemed to be having an effect but other crews had little success as they focused their efforts towards saving the house to the north.

A woman screamed at the firefighters as she ran back and forth in front of the north house. A man ran to assist another woman who was trying to restrain her. She fought them both with the strength of two people. "Do something for God's sake! Don't let it burn. Oh please, don't let it burn," she screamed and then suddenly fell to her knees sobbing. The fight seemed to go out of her as she realized the hopelessness of it all.

"Man, what a mess," Quiring said as he came to a stop beside Rosza.

Before Rosza could reply an ambulance omitted several brief yelps from the siren as it worked its way through the crowd and emergency personnel. People moved reluctantly out of its path.

"Do you think someone's been hurt?" Quiring asked.

"I don't know. They could be on stand-by in case of injury."

Rosza surveyed the area, taking in the furiously burning houses and a scene vastly altered from a previous visit. "Well I guess your gut feeling was right. You know whose house that is don't you?" he asked as a wall collapsed inward in a great wall of sparks and swirling heat.

"Yeah, Haggard is going to be some pissed when he shows up. I guess we can write this so-called interview off. He sure as hell won't be in any mood to talk to us."

"Someone sure has it in for him," Rosza watched as another wall of sparks flashed towards the sky.

"This has to be connected to the break-in and the murder of his girl."

"Well it sure as hell doesn't look like it could be an accident to me. He's had more shit happen to him in a short time than most people have in a lifetime.' Rosza hesitated. "You may be wrong, this just might be the time to take him aside and have a chat with him. Or at the very least talk with him early tomorrow."

They went back to their car and settled down comfortably. There was nothing anyone could do until the fire cooled and fire inspection teams arrived to determine the cause of the blaze. That would not be until well after daylight. The actual fire was none of their affair but it involved their principal suspect who was implicated in a drug smuggling scheme and one whom they were thinking more and more of as a victim.

The crowds thinned out and some of the emergency vehicles departed as their need to remain diminished. Quiring moved the car and parked on the boulevard close to the scene of the fire. He then leaned back and shut his eyes as Rosza's eyes continuously swept the street, watching as people arrived and left the area.

Rosza knew that Quiring was not sleeping. He was simply employing the technique of shutting out things that were not essential, an important stakeout practice to stay fresh.

Three quarters of an hour later a vehicle stopped at the far side of the road. Rosza watched as a large man walked up the far sidewalk towards the now smoking fire. The man walked with a sense of urgency and a look of awareness about him. Rosza watched as the figure slowed and then stopped.

The emergency lights had been like a beacon to Dan Haggard. They became brighter and stronger against the blackness of the night as he had neared his street. Turning the corner and looking down the block he knew that whatever had happened he was probably not going to like it.

His pace quickened, his gait measured and steady, his back straight from years of military bearing. His eyes tried to adjust to the scene before him and tried to sort out what he was looking at between the intense flashes from the emergency lights and the darkness beyond. It took another ten steps before he realized there was a huge cavity in the landscape. An eerie blackness filled the place where his house was supposed to be.

Haggard slowed and then stopped. Thin wisps of smoke, steam, and an occasional spark rose from the nearly flat pile of charred rubble that used to be the house. His mind took it in but he felt anesthetized, mostly because it was the last thing he had expected to happen. It was a shock to realize that the place that he had shared with Connie was now gone.

Dan was about to move forward to see what had happened when a hand rested on his shoulder. He had been so absorbed with the scene and his thoughts he had not heard anyone approach.

"It's not very good news for you, Mr. Haggard... Dan. We're sorry you lost your house," Rosza said sincerely.

Haggard looked at the two men standing in the dark before him. It did not register who they were right away. His mind was still on the fire and on memories of Connie. "Is the DEA fighting fires now?" he asked.

Lloyd Quiring stepped beyond Haggard and moved a few steps towards the burnt house. He stood watching the fire crews for a moment and then turned back to face Haggard. "You know, all this stuff that's happening to you, is it because they think you still have their drugs or is it something else? Although you and drugs don't seem to have much in common you aren't making it easy for us. It's hard to come up with anything that makes sense."

"No shit," Haggard said sarcastically.

Rosza shrugged as he started to walk towards the fire scene. "So what we're left with is the impression that maybe their doing this to you because of something else. We do our job. We try to catch bad guys and we are seldom wrong. Are you a bad guy, Haggard?"

Haggard had fallen into step and was nearing the pile of rubble. He came to a spot that would have been opposite the picture window and stopped. "What have you found out about this?"

"Nothing yet," Quiring answered. "I heard the Chief telling one of the uniformed officers that an accelerant has been used on your place. Other than that, well...we'll have to wait until later in the day."

"In other words someone torched my house."

"Look, we need to talk." Rosza turned away from looking at the smoking heap. "You could be in danger. Your place got broken into, your wife was murdered, and now this."

"You forgot one," Haggard said, stone-faced. "I was set up."

"So you keep saying. Talk to us and maybe we'll be convinced," Quiring said as he shrugged his shoulders.

"This may come as a shock to you guys but I just lost everything. I don't even have a clean shirt for the morning. Your timing stinks."

"So does yours, Dan. What were you doing back in Canada?" Rosza asked.

Haggard looked at Rosza and raised his eyebrows. "Wow, I'm impressed."

"Look, let the uniformed cop over there know that you're here. Leave your cell number with him and we'll help you settle this thing," Quiring offered. "We can open a lot of doors and stop a lot of aggravation but we need your input and from what you tell us we may be able to figure out who's behind this. We deal with these drug gangs all the time."

"Okay, I'll be in to see you at one o'clock in the afternoon," Haggard finally relented. "Give me one of your cards. I have a lot of things to do."

Rosza handed Haggard a business card, looking him over as he put the card in his pocket. "One of the things you might like to do is get some clothes, Dan. From the looks of your pants you've been climbing trees and wrestling with cougars or something."

Haggard looked down at his pants. He knew that the torn cloth and muddy pant leg from the farm ditch looked strange. He looked back at Rosza. "I promise to be nice and spiffy for you tomorrow."

Rosza and Quiring left, leaving Haggard standing on the sidewalk with the stink of wet, smoky wood in his nostrils. Haggard knew that this was probably pay-back time from the local hoods and that they had come looking for him because of his visit to the drug house. Who else could it be? If it was the locals—then someone had talked. He thought of Sheldon.

CHAPTER NINE

Vince Rizzo's nose was out of joint and he was in an angry and sulky mood. Sigger had not left with the shipment for Seattle yet and he was giving orders left and right. *He* was supposed to be in charge of the breakdown and the move, not Sigger. Every time he wanted to do something Sigger vetoed it and told him to carry more things out of the barn.

He angrily threw some rolled up wire into the back of the rented three-ton truck and watched it as it landed with a crash on top of the huge reflectors. The role of wire slipped off the pile and landed on the bed of the truck. For a moment Rizzo considered jumping into the back of the truck and throwing it as hard as he could at the interior wall. He turned instead and stomped back into the barn.

Due to the lack of generator power large openings had been knocked out high up on the barn walls to allow light to enter. A huge opening in the side of the barn allowed quick access directly into the rental truck. A tarp hung between the truck and the barn to stop anyone from looking into the interior of the barn. There was not much chance of that while the dogs were tethered on a long rope near the front of the house.

Sigger was surprised at the speed of the dismantling of the equipment and the removal of the items that were needed at the new location. Two men looked after the electrical wiring and the generators while two others packed the timers, bulbs and water hoses into large boxes. The reflectors and fans did not need to be packed but they took up a lot of room. He was glad that he had moved the latest crop of young plants to the new location as it was one less security and transportation problem.

He looked around as Vince Rizzo stormed into the barn and realized that the man could handle the rest without any problem. He needed to think about his trip to Seattle and the problem of getting the shipment into the United States and across a very tight border.

"Rizzo," Sigger yelled, waving the man to come over to him. Rizzo stopped and looked at him in a surly manner before moving in his direction.

As Rizzo walked towards him from the other side of the barn billions of dust particles floated, swirled, and danced in unison on the intense beams of sunlight slanting through the openings. Looking at the crap floating in the air Sigger was glad to be able to turn the move over to Rizzo. The weed was starting to bother him in the same way that it bothered Roy Tully. He found it hard to breathe at times.

"What?" Rizzo said as he stopped in front of him.

Sigger was about to put the man in his place. He thought of wiping the disrespectful look from his face with a cuff to the head but changed his mind. He needed the transfer to run smoothly and no matter what Roy Tully had said it would all fall back on him and not on Rizzo if it went wrong.

"What do you want?" Rizzo asked again.

"I'm leaving. You're doing a great job here and you don't need me here to help anymore."

Rizzo was caught-short by the man's unusual generosity and the compliment. He was in a foul mood and wanted to stay that way but found his spirits lifting at the prospect of Sigger leaving. "For a while there I thought *you* were going to do the whole move yourself," he griped, still not quite mollified by Sigger's sugarcoated words.

"Nah, you know we both work well together," Sigger smiled with false flattery. "I just wanted to make sure we had a good head start. Besides, you remember what Roy said would happen if you screwed up don't you?"

Rizzo remembered the meeting all too well and did not want to think about it. He just wanted Sigger to go so he could do the job and show Frank and Roy that he could look after his own grow.

"Look, you can leave. Everything will be okay. There won't be anything left here and what we don't need I'll have the boys dump in the cornfield."

"No," Sigger commanded. "Leave anything you don't need in the barn. Who gives a shit? You put it in the cornfield all you'll do is piss off the farmer. Who knows maybe the Tully's will put you back here in charge of your own grow after things cool down," Sigger said smoothly.

"You think so?" Rizzo asked eagerly.

What a fucking moron, Sigger thought as he smiled and nodded his encouragement. "You set the new place up the way it's supposed to be and I'll put in a good word for you."

"I appreciate that, Mike. I'll make sure it's up and running even with the cameras and monitors."

"Okay, it's all yours, sport." He turned to leave but then turned back to Rizzo. "Don't be pissing these guys off. You push them too hard and they won't want to work," Sigger said, knowing that the cocky little bastard would be strutting and yelling orders within five minutes of his leaving. "Look after the dogs."

Sigger walked out of the barn and into bright sunlight, punching Frank Tully's number into his phone and waiting for the connection; Roy Tully answered on the second ring.

"It's me; I must have hit the wrong number. I thought I dialed Frank."

"What, you can't talk to me?" Roy Tully snarled in a sarcastic manner.

"Yeah of course, Roy, it's just that I thought I had dialed up Frank."

"Forget it! I'm at Frank's place. You got the move completed?" Roy pushed, knowing it was too soon.

"I left it with Vince. He should do okay. I'm ready to get to work on the Seattle run."

"We wouldn't be moving the operation at all if you had properly managed those pricks who visited the farm. You should have let the dogs do what they were supposed to do."

Sigger's attention increased as he pressed the earpiece closer to his head. "What are you saying? Are you saying one of those guys ran to the cops after I dealt with them? I don't think so!"

"Well our sources say different," Tully stated. "When they showed up with all those injuries the hospital called the cops. The police rattled them. Like I said, you should have let the dogs do a proper job on them. You screwed up. Mark this down as another one of your fucking fantastic jobs!"

"I called it as I saw it," Sigger replied. "It's water under the bridge. I need to get going on Seattle."

"Okay, okay, drop by my place and we'll all go over it. I'm sure you are anxious to get to Seattle to get our goods back." Sigger was about to reply when Roy Tully spoke again. "Oh, I'm sorry. I forgot you may not want to visit the guy. He may be a lot tougher than that woman." Roy Tully laughed, his snicker cut off as he hung up the phone.

Sigger's hand clamped down and he squeezed his phone involuntarily. He was sure that if Roy Tully had been there he wouldn't have been able to stop himself from killing him. He did not take shit from anybody!

His temper was under control however by the time he entered Roy Tully's place. It was a small and sparsely furnished apartment with a large television, comfortable seating, and little else. Liquor Bottles sat on top of a small built in bar, the mirror behind the bottles showed signs of needing a good cleaning. It was supposed to be a hip bachelor pad. Sigger thought the place looked like a cheap dump.

"Nice place," Sigger said with a trace of sarcasm as he accepted the obligatory drink from Roy Tully.

Tully looked at Sigger and tried to determine the meaning of the remark but let it slide. He took a sip of his own drink before sitting down across from his brother, Frank.

"Okay, this is how we have it set up," Frank began. "It's nothing elaborate. We've kept it as simple as possible. It goes by sealed container that will be loaded into a semi-trailer. The shipment inside the container is legitimate. I don't know what the shipment is and I don't care, but the container it's in has a false ceiling that we will pack tightly with our shit after we wrap it in tinfoil. It will look like part of the container."

"Where will the packing be done?"

It's being set aside for us at the docks."

"So what do we do about x-rays?" Sigger asked again. "They check every bloody thing that moves and see terrorists everywhere."

"Like I said, it's packed so solid and so thin it looks like part of the container roof."

"And sniffer dogs?" Sigger prodded.

"We can only do what we can do. That's why we picked the roof. It puts it way up from the road."

"Okay, where is it and what time does it leave?" Sigger asked.

"We'll have it loaded but unfortunately we can't get it out until the day after tomorrow, probably in the afternoon. That's when the driver comes for the container. We don't expect to be able to get our goods out of the container until a day or two after it arrives in Seattle."

"So I follow it. Does the driver know?"

"He doesn't have a clue," Roy Tully contributed. "He has orders to drop the trailer and container at this lot after it is unloaded."

Roy Tully handed Sigger a piece of paper with an address on it. "You can move in after he leaves. The description of the truck is on the top of the page. He'll cross at the Pacific Truck Crossing. We'll phone you when he's pulling out."

Sigger glanced at the information and jammed the paper into his shirt pocket to read later. "Okay, it looks like I'll be away for a week, maybe longer."

"Just so you get the job done," Frank said. "We have expense money for you."

"You want me to check out the new grow-op location before I go?" Sigger asked casually, directing his question to Frank Tully.

"If you want to swing by that's up to you. Just make sure you are ready to move when we tell you the truck is ready to pull out."

They talked and planned for another half hour with Sigger making a few suggestions. His job was to track the shipment, arrange with Seattle for manpower to unload the container, then deliver the goods and make the trade with the Americans. There was also the problem of getting the Cocaine back into Canada once the trade took place. The Americans were going to have it very, very easy on this job.

Sigger did not understand the reluctance on Seattle's part in not doing business as usual but he had another piece of work to think about. He was going to have to visit Haggard at his home again. He thought of his last visit and he was sure that the woman would have talked if there had been more time to deal with her. This time he would just have to stick around and deal with this Haggard guy in person.

"I'll have the expense money ready by the time you leave," Frank Tully said at the door. "Cash as usual and no credit cards are to be used unless you have some newly acquired cards off of the street."

"I'll be in touch," Sigger nodded.

* * *

Sigger pulled to a stop in the driving lane but as near to the side of the paved roadway as possible. The road was narrow with no shoulder except for a foot wide strip of dirt next to a ditch. He shut off the engine and got out into the murky dusk of early night. Crickets greeted him with their nightly chatter as he looked both ways along the country road. A far off streetlight came on and shone dimly at a rural intersection.

On the other side of the shallow ditch another paved road ran in the same direction. Both roads dwindled into the distance and merged as one with Mount Baker forming part of the backdrop. The snowcapped top had just lost its sun-drenched golden crown.

Sigger noticed tire tracks emerging from the ditch behind his vehicle and other tracks crisscrossed and flattened the tall grass in numerous places. Deep gouges indicated that some vehicles had suffered problems between the two roads and had hung up due to low undercarriages. Dirt and mud coated the roads on both sides of the ditch and it was surprising how many tire tracks there actually were.

The small ditch was the only barrier between British Columbia and Washington State. The ditch ran for miles and then disappeared, turning into open countryside where fields from the two countries merged and stood undefended and open. Further on, lakes and mountains offered other opportunities for illegal activities.

Sigger smiled and thought of the trips he and his buddies used to make when he was a kid. They would load up with booze and cigarettes and then throw it all across the border to be picked up after they had entered through the border crossing. They'd have a massive drunk and then sell the rest for a profit at the bars.

Sigger had no false illusions about the ditch now. He knew that Canadian and American authorities routinely apprehended smugglers and border jumpers as they tried to move their drugs, guns, alcohol, tobacco, and human cargo into one country or the other. Visible troops did not defend the border but that did not mean it was unguarded. Roaming patrols and hidden sensors and cameras covered a vast area of the known trouble spots and high traffic areas.

Just how sophisticated became apparent when the newly Integrated Customs and Border Protection Agency discovered the million dollar tunnel running from house to house under the very road that he was standing on. Times had changed.

The landscape along this area of the international border was open and flat, making it difficult to move around without natural cover. Sigger did not like it. The only cover appeared to be raspberry fields and stands of timber around the homes and farms in the area. The lush countryside only turned into rolling hills a few miles to the north.

He looked north across the road towards the newly rented property and barn. The driveway was short and the property was small compared to the other grow-op. It was too open and it was too close to the road. It would be very difficult to protect. People could watch the comings and goings of everyone connected to the operation and people were nosey, especially of new neighbors. He hoped the Tully brothers knew what they were doing.

There was a small house near the road. The front door had a small roof over the entrance way and it appeared to open directly into a living room with a small kitchen to the rear and one large or two small bedrooms. The house had cedar siding, the paint looked like a washed out baby blue in the growing darkness.

Sigger got back into the half-ton pickup and drove up the gravel driveway, kicking up dust as he passed the small abandoned house. He drove to the rear of the property and to the area of the barn. An old Ford truck sat to his left and under a tree. It was an old telephone truck with metal side compartments and had long ago lost any defining color or outstanding features. Sigger knew it belonged to Chuck Snow, the guy who did all their electrical wiring.

Sigger tried the barn door but found it locked. He was not annoyed; it showed that someone was thinking. He pounded on the door and waited. A few minutes later a man walked around the far corner of the barn towards him. He walked slowly and with a limp. Sigger waited for him.

"I thought you were headed south," the middle-aged man said. He was dressed in a yellow short-sleeve shirt, blue jeans, and had a leather tool belt strapped around his waist. He needed a shave and a haircut but his ruffled appearance matched his demeanor. His bulbous nose suited his face, making him look friendly and trustworthy.

"Hi, Chuck. How did you know I was going south?"

"Easy, Roy told me. Said to make sure things were set up properly when you were gone." Chuck chuckled and shook his head. "He said that Vince was in charge but not to listen to him if it fucked anything up."

Sigger laughed in spite of the fact that Roy Tully was giving out information about his movements. "I guess we have to give Rizzo a chance to prove himself. Who knows?

"Yeah, who knows," Chuck Snow smiled back. "So, when are you going?"

"I'll leave when I'm needed. I thought I would see how things are setup here."

"Come and see then," Snow said as he turned and walked towards the back. "If we don't get things operating soon though, you may lose some plants."

"Rizzo will be here soon. Once he's clear of the other place it will go fairly fast here."

They entered the barn. Sigger could see right away that a lot of work was going to have to be done. It was no way near as good as the other place. It was smaller, older, and had too many openings. The low ceiling would provide a bit of an obstacle for setting up a proper operation.

The once white walls and ceilings were covered with cobwebs and dust and defused any light that the feeble and filthy light bulbs tried to produce. Old farm equipment littered the floors and hung from hooks on the walls. Doors hung crookedly on worn hinges and were jammed against the floor.

"Not much to look at, Mike," Snow said as he walked towards the section he was working in. "I figure you could have done better."

"You're telling me," Sigger replied. "Is there any loft or lower area?"

"Yeah, I had to run some wires from above. Go through there and up the ladder at the end of the old cattle stalls."

The wooden ladder was smooth to the touch and well worn from years of use. He could see a large opening above and next to the ladder, probably for throwing feed down to the animals. As he climbed into the darkness the smell of decay and staleness hit him. It was so thick it was like there was a shortage of oxygen. He was unable to venture any further without a flashlight but he knew that if the upper area could be used then there would be more of a growing area than he thought. Sigger climbed down and walked through the barn towards Chuck Snow.

"Did you find anything useful?" Snow asked as he tacked a wire against a wall.

"Yeah, I guess so." He watched the other man at work. "I'm going to miss the generators. I hate these damn bypasses. They screw up more grows than anything else. If it isn't fires it's prying bloody hydro workers."

"Well, I'll try and hide my handiwork as much as possible. I think I can even make the electrical meter churn around at a rate to make it look normal. What Rizzo has to worry about is the water. The pressure is the shits."

"Well I'm sure as hell not going to worry about it. Tell Rizzo to check the pump and if he needs to buy a new one then to go ahead and do it."

Sigger walked around the interior of the barn. The marijuana plants hindered his movement because they had not been stored in any order. He bent and looked at a couple of plants. Chuck was right, they would need attention soon. The move had come too soon and at an awkward time.

Sigger walked out into the darkness and stood listening to the night sounds. A fast car headed west on the American side of the border, the headlights glowing in the black sky as it dwindled into the distance. Although the border was handy he did not like the place at all. A far off dog let the world know it existed. He thought of his dogs and knew it would be a harder place for them to work. There were too many people in the area and the last thing he needed was some neighbor getting chewed upon.

Tam Hy turned off the road and drove towards the barn in his small pick-up. As he drew nearer his slight frame became visible in the glow of the vehicle's lights. He avoided Sigger as he parked and got out, walking quickly towards the barn to look after the plants.

"Damn spooks taking over the world," Sigger muttered. He had to grudgingly admit that Tam Hy knew his job but he sure as hell didn't have to like him.

Tam Hy shuffled into the barn and headed towards the small plants, giving Chuck Snow a small wave as he walked by.

"You see Sigger out there, Tam?"

"Yeah, I see," Tam Hy answered, clearly unhappy at the memory.

Chuck Snow laughed. "Don't let him get to you, Tam. They don't call him Happy for nothing."

Tam Hy looked at the other man and shook his head. "He is not a happy man! I no like! He is mean."

"You just remember that my friend and you'll do just fine."

* * *

Agents Lloyd Quiring and Anthony Rosza watched from their car as Ted Conway slipped out of his apartment building and moved slowly towards his dilapidated Dodge. A spattering of rain marked the windshield as they got out and quietly walked towards him.

"You walk like your high on coke, Conway," Rosza said as he moved to intercept him.

Conway visibly jumped and any thoughts that were in his mind were wrenched out of existence as he whirled towards the two DEA men. His face registered shock and uncertainty as he tried to command his unwilling body to move.

"Yep, I think he's carrying and he's definitely using," Quiring nodded to Rosza. "Look at him. He's stumbling all over the place."

"No! No, I'm not. I'm…I'm just tired. I didn't get much sleep and…"

"You're lying, Conway," Rosza interrupted. "Remember what I said would happen if you didn't come through with some information on the hit on Ruddick and Neigel?

"I…I couldn't find out anything, man. Nobody knows nothing. I tried but…"

Quiring cut him off. "Learn to speak English you little twit. It's 'no one knows anything.' Why are you so fidgety? You're stalling. You've found out something."

"We better take him downtown," Rosza stated, taking his portable radio out and watching as Conway looked desperately for a way out.

"No!" Conway shouted. "I'm not going' man. You can't do that. I didn't do nothing."

"You know who hit that house, Conway. That makes you an accessory after the fact. You involved in murder, Conway?"

Ted Conway did not say anything. He stood looking at the two DEA Agents with a miserable expression on his face as he tried to figure out what to do. If he told them that he knew that Haggard might be the one that had visited Ruddick and Neigel then he would be placing himself in jeopardy. They would figure out his involvement with Sheldon Porter and maybe the Cocaine loading of the motorhome. He could not involve Haggard without involving Herrera-Sanchez either. He was more afraid of Herrera-Sanchez. He had to keep his mouth shut if he wanted to continue living.

"Well, Conway? We haven't got all day here," Rosza instructed.

"I said I would try and find out something. You didn't give me enough time," Conway complained.

"You are a big disappointment," Anthony Rosza sighed. "I don't know about my partner but I'm for taking you in."

Quiring just stood and stared at Conway for a few moments. "Maybe he's right," he finally said. "Maybe we never gave him enough time. I don't want him making stuff up. You *are* going to jail though if you don't come up with something quick. Do you know that, Conway?"

Ted Conway shook his head and agreed immediately. He moved closer to Quiring. "You know I'll try man. I just need time that's all. You gotta give me more time."

Quiring smiled and patted Conway on the shoulder. "I'll tell you this much my friend; if you do not deliver something we'll both come down on you as hard as the law allows. If you do not deliver the next time we meet you had better be squeaky clean or you'll be doing ten years."

Conway moved away, walking backwards away from the two men. "Like I said, I'll find something. Okay?"

"You do that, Conway," Quiring said, glowering at him.

"Well that was a wasted effort," Rosza commented on the way back to the car.

"I don't know about that," Quiring replied as he opened the car door. "Did you read him? That guy was really scared about something. Either something he knows or something he's involved in. He acted guilty as hell. He jumped out of his skin when we pulled up."

"When the hell isn't he?" Rosza said letting out a tired breath. "Let's go, we have an appointment to keep."

* * *

Dan Haggard walked into the Office of the Drug Enforcement Administration at exactly one o'clock in the afternoon. He stood in line behind an older woman at the reception desk for five minutes before finally being directed to a seat.

Rosza walked in ten minutes later followed by Quiring. "Sorry we kept you waiting. We were tied up on another case."

"No problem," Haggard answered although he had a lot to do and very little time in which to do it.

"You find a place to live?" Rosza asked as he led the way down a hallway towards a back office.

"Motel for now," Haggard said quietly, not wanting to give away too much information.

Haggard entered the office as Rosza pointed to an uncomfortable looking chair. Rosza sat in one of the chairs and Haggard moved to sit next to him.

"You must have been shopping," Quiring said as he sat down behind a desk. "You look a hell of a lot better than you did last night."

Haggard smiled and sat down; the new windbreaker rustled as he settled back. "Good an excuse as any to shop I guess. What did you guys want me down here for specifically?"

"Like we said yesterday," Rosza began as he got up and sat on the corner of the desk. "You are in danger. We also think you know more than you are telling us. A little co-operation would go along way towards convincing the prosecutor and getting your property back. That is if you can convince *us* that you were set up."

"God knows you've endured enough. If you *are* innocent I sure as hell feel sorry for you," Quiring added.

Haggard had thought a lot about what he was going to say and what he needed to do long before he had even started the day. He knew he really needed some allies and maybe these two fit the bill but he also needed his freedom to find the vultures that destroyed his life and destroyed Connie. One thing for sure, the law could not do it. Besides, the scum were not going to leave him alone.

Haggard turned towards Lloyd Quiring and looked him directly in the eyes. "You keep saying 'if I'm innocent', so I guess you're not convinced."

"I generally need solid evidence of someone's guilt," Quiring replied. "To be honest, in your case I need evidence of your innocence."

"Well I can't give you any evidence of my innocence!" Haggard said with some heat. "All I can give you is the fact that my motorhome was stuffed with Cocaine without me knowing it. I took it into Canada without knowing it. Then I chased off some bastard who I thought was stealing my car or something but who really wanted the Cocaine. Then I lose my motorhome, my wife, my house, and maybe my freedom. You are right, I *have* no evidence! I don't have anything!"

Rosza got up and walked to a corner table. "You want some coffee?"

"No, I don't," Haggard said, anger still in his voice. He knew he had to co-operate as far as what took place in Canada and what happened up to the point at the border, but that was all. He had to take the chance that they would investigate what he told them.

"So that's why you were back in Canada? Were you up there looking for information?" Quiring asked.

He gave them what he had; the registration, the description of the vehicle, the driver and the location of the farm. He told them of his suspicions and that he thought they were major movers of drugs into the United States. He also told them that he thought a Canadian had killed Connie while he was looking for his lost Cocaine.

Rosza sighed and shook his head. "Looks like our seizure at the border started a lot of trouble for you."

"No, my trouble started when some asshole loaded the shit onto my RV," Haggard answered.

Quiring leaned ahead and placed his elbows onto his knees as he looked at Haggard, seeming to size him up. "That may be, Dan, but you might want to think twice before you visit Canada again. We appreciate anything that you learn about those people but remember you have a court case pending and I don't think you are allowed to leave the State of Washington."

The telephone rang and Rosza leaned over and picked it up. He listened quietly for a few moments and then hung up. He looked at Haggard for a moment and was about to speak when Haggard spoke first.

"What now? I can see by your look that it's not good."

"It isn't getting any better for you, Haggard. It's a good thing we can confirm that you were in Canada. They just found a charred body in the rubble of your burnt house."

CHAPTER TEN

After leaving the DEA office, Haggard telephoned the insurance company and informed them of the loss and of the police involvement. They told him that an agent would be in touch with him as soon as they got a police report. He was full of conflicting emotions about his loses. Losing the house had been a bit of a shock. Even though it was on the market and he had wanted to get rid of it he still never thought it would be this way. He did not know if the insurance company would even cover the loss.

He had also lost everything to do with Connie. All her possessions were gone including all of the photos of her and the times they had together. All the things he was supposed to get rid of but hadn't got around to doing were also gone. All he had now were the memories.

He had not relished going through her belongings because of the emotional pain but it should have been something that he had dealt with in his own time and when he was ready. It would have been a way of gradually saying goodbye. They took that away too.

The police had obviously done their work and were gone but yellow tape warned everyone to steer clear of the wreckage. He stood on the street looking at the cold, charred pile and tried to figure out who the person was that perished in the blaze. He wished he could snoop around because there could be some small thing left of Connie's, something that did not burn and was buried under the rubble. It would be nice to have something.

The Mule

A sudden thought struck Haggard and he was surprised that he had not even thought of it until now. There was a possibility that there was still one hundred and twenty-eight thousand dollars down in the basement under the floorboards of the house where he had put it. The last thing he needed now was to try to explain away all that money. There would be too many questions and not too many answers to fit. It would really nail down the fact that he was involved in drugs. A little chill ran up his spine at that prospect.

Walking around to the back of the lot he searched for the entrance to the basement. Small mounds of charred and blistered wood lay scattered across the yard and pieces of metal poked out of some of the piles in a twisted unrecognizable mass. The stench from the fire was overpowering as he walked nearer and he knew it was seeping into his clothes.

He looked towards the neighbors as he approached the police tape to see if anyone was watching. No one was in sight. He quickly stepped over the tape and walked to the basement steps, moving a piece of lumber before moving quickly down the steps to the doorway. He was surprised to see that the door was missing from the frame.

Haggard stepped inside. The ceiling was a blackened, sodden scar that was riddled with holes, twisted wires, and in places, hanging insulation. The floor was covered in two inches of water and allowed small articles to float about his feet. Strangely, some of the walls were not touched while others had felt the fierce breath of the firestorm.

Two broken windows, blown out by the heat or by structure collapse, provided an almost clear path where the fire had not grabbed a foothold. Haggard could almost visualize the air moving at colossal speed through the windows to feed the hungry inferno burning above.

Sloshing his way towards the blackened stairs created ripples and waves that moved debris this way and that. He walked on by the stairs towards the recess he was looking for in the ceiling. Pieces of wood hung down at odd angles and the floor above sagged in a threatening bulge. The gloomy back area of the basement provided little light but it only took him a moment to realize that the case that he had placed in the recess of the ceiling was not there.

As his eyes adjusted he saw that there was a hole in the ceiling allowing filtered light through the debris above. Haggard looked up at what used to be his and Connie's bedroom.

Kicking aside some insulation Haggard pushed on a soggy cardboard box full of wet clothing. It collapsed under the pressure of his foot revealing the black case half-submerged in the water. He was surprised at the weight until water started to flow out between the lid and the bottom of the case. The case was badly warped from the heat and had wide gaps along the hinge area.

Looking around the basement he could not believe the destruction. He had seen enough fires in his day to know that this had been a very hot fire. An accelerant would certainly have given it a substantial start so that it would burn quickly. *These guys are not going to leave me alone,* he thought.

Turning to walk towards the light he accidentally kicked a small board floating in the water. Tiny shafts of light sparkled up from one end of the board as it slowly drifted away towards the window.

Haggard looked closely at the board but could not tell what it was he was looking at. The wood was black and spongy to the touch as he picked it up. A thin delicate chain suddenly fell and hung from the end of the piece of wood. A double heart-shaped locket glowed wetly back at him. Diamonds glittered from each heart as it spun before his eyes. The look of surprise on Haggard's face was replaced by a sad, warm smile of remembrance.

As much as he did not want to, Haggard went shopping again. He hated shopping but all he had was the clothes on his back. Besides, he needed to make some special purchases. It kept him busy and stopped him from dwelling too much on the mountain of problems that seemed to be land sliding down on top of him.

The local police had not come looking for him yet. There would be a full investigation gearing up in regards to the body the firefighters had found in the house. Although he wanted to know who had perished in the fire he was not about to hang around for hours at a time to answer questions he knew absolutely nothing about.

He had unanswered questions of his own that rumbled around in his mind and he knew that his time was growing shorter by the day. As he stepped harder onto the gas pedal he thought of his court case. He was doomed if he did not move faster. He could not afford to stay in the city to be bogged down by some investigation, not when the answers lay to the north.

Whoever killed Connie was still sitting safely in Canada. They had already dismissed her life from their minds. She was nothing to even think about, just some insignificant thing to be discarded. Well, he had news for them.

Haggard's thoughts were far from pleasant as he neared the Canadian Border again. Crossing the border into Canada did not concern him but having a search carried out at Customs did. In the wheel well under the rear cargo area he had outfitted himself with a better assortment of clothing, equipment, and a few other items he thought he might need, items that would not be welcomed inside of Canada.

Haggard found a place to pull over five miles short of the border. Lifting the rear cargo area he pulled out the small duffle bag and placed it on the passenger seat next to him. It was small and compact, the dark green canvas tough and waterproof.

Three miles east of Canadian Customs, Dan drove slowly along a narrow paved road. The sharp tang of cow manure hung in the air, reminding him of other far away places. Large open fields dwindled to the horizon in all directions with small wooded areas butting up to the border.

Another road ran in the same direction to his right on the other side of a grass and weed choked ditch. The other road was in Canada. He could see that intersecting roads ran northwards.

He lowered the passenger window as he drove westward. The road he was on ended and turned southward close to a wooded area two hundred feet further on. He made note of the name on a mailbox on the American side and quickly tossed the duffle bag out of the passenger window into the grass filled ditch and accelerated slowly away.

The bag rolled down into the ditch, flattening the grass as it came to a stop. By the time Haggard turned around the bend in the road the grass was already regaining its original shape around the bag and as it stretched skyward it provided perfect concealment.

"Where's home and what is your citizenship?" the man asked in a disinterested voice. Dan told him and received a disinterested nod. "Are you in possession of any weapons?"

"No," Haggard answered.

"What's the purpose of your visit?" the man asked sleepily.

He was through customs in less than three minutes and began looking for the road that ran along the border. He found the area with little difficulty but he had to drive back and forth three times to avoid local traffic before he could stop and quickly gather up the duffle bag from the ditch. He kept his eye on a small tattered house, hoping no one would see him in the ditch between the two countries.

Dan drove northward and away from the border and headed inland towards the winding hills surrounding the Fraser River. He managed to get lost and twisted around in his sense of direction but as the late afternoon sun cast long shadows upon the earth he drove slowly by the driveway and the ditch where he had earlier concealed himself from the dogs. There was no sign of activity as he peered up the driveway.

Parked under the cover of low hanging trees, well back off the roadway, he waited for complete darkness. He changed into a pair of dark pants and a sweater. A pair of thick-soled hiking boots followed with a black toque ready to pull onto his head. Filling a small fanny pack with the items he purchased he grabbed a smaller knapsack out of the larger bag and set off at a fast pace towards the farm.

It was a black, moonless night but the low and heavily laden clouds made it even darker. He descended down a deep slope where any hint of a breeze soon disappeared. Other than the occasional sound of his footfalls and the sound of his own breathing there was no sound in the deadness around him.

The night vision goggles were a mixed blessing, they allowed him to move freely and fast but they limited his peripheral vision. With the opposition in possession of the equipment he did not dare be without them. Ghostly lime green bushes, trees, stumps, and tall phosphorous wild oats quickly disappeared to his right and left.

Entering a cornfield, Haggard moved diagonally across the rows of corn until he figured he was beyond the old house that was visible from the street. Turning to his left the going became easier and a few minutes later he came to an abrupt stop at a split rail fence.

Controlling his breathing, Dan stood perfectly still and listened to the night. An owl hooted, sending an uncontrolled chill up his spine for no apparent reason. It reminded him of when he was a kid when he had dared himself to walk home along a lonely stretch of road in the dark just to prove that there was no reason to be afraid.

A brief picture of two Dobermans moving in the darkness flashed through his mind and he was aware that this was a different place, a different time, and sure as hell different circumstances.

He moved his head slowly to the left, moving a drooping cornstalk leaf out of his way. The ghostly green back wall of the farmhouse radiated back, a forlorn picture showing obvious abandonment. The rear door was open and a broken window completed the appearance of a vacant house.

Looking to the right, Haggard looked carefully at the barn and the area in between. There was no light anywhere. That did not mean a thing. He was very conscious of the last time he visited the place and the dogs had materialized silently out of the blackness. Besides the dogs they also probably used surveillance equipment, lights and even booby traps. He could not afford the mistake of blundering in unprepared.

The frogs kept up their communication as Haggard moved carefully along the inside of the fence towards the barn. He noticed that the barn had a large dark hole in the end of the building as well as one on the upper side. Something large loomed ahead by the opening at the end of the barn. As he moved closer he saw the outline of a generator.

Scanning a utility pole and the edges of the barn he looked for cameras through the night vision goggles. None were visible but that did not comfort him as he moved towards the entrance. He expected to hear the rapid drumming of feet and the guttural snarl of the dogs at any time and reached into the small fanny pack.

Looking around the edge of the hole and into the barn he was immediately disappointed. The interior was barren, stripped clean except for hanging wires, broken light bulbs, and old pots. The place reeked of marijuana, the floors and walls fully permeated with that peculiar sharp perfume known the world over.

A quick search turned up nothing. Haggard moved along the edge of the cornfield towards the abandoned house. He moved quickly and silently on his soft-soled boots, stopping to the right of the door and looking inwards.

He stepped inside. The house was filthy. Garbage littered the floor and holes in the walls allowed him to look into other rooms. Stepping over old pizza boxes he quickly checked the last room; a moldy old couch sagged against one wall, the only piece of furniture in the room.

Stairs led downwards from the kitchen area and seeing no sign of life, Haggard quietly descended. A semi-automatic filled his right hand. At the bottom of the stairs he was surprised to find that a wall had been knocked out. A long tunnel led off towards the rear of the property.

The tunnel was creepy and items that hung or were strewn along the tunnel appeared suddenly in green ghoulish shapes that heightened his awareness. Bending uncomfortably low he made his way past a ladder and abruptly ended up in a small square room.

He could see heavy wire running upwards that snuggled against a board that vanished into a hole above his head. An old gas can sat in the corner and he knew where the generator had come from that lay outside.

Climbing the ladder, Haggard pushed on a trap door and looked around the inside of the barn again. He lowered the door quietly to the floor and stepped up and out onto the floor. *What a bloody waste of time*, he thought.

Heading back to the cornfield across the open yard, Haggard had to admit to himself that he was out of options. He had not counted on the place being deserted and abandoned.

Sliding over the top rail of the fence he took two steps into the cornfield when his vision unexpectedly flared in a painful burst of brilliance that seemed to seer all the way to the back of his brain.

Whipping off the night goggles, he froze in place as flashes and dots filled his head. He was unable to see anything even when everything started to turn black.

He became aware of the sound of an approaching car or truck and crouched down in place. His eyesight returned to normal and he could make out the outline of the cornstalks against the approaching headlights.

The Mule

A small pickup truck went by rapidly, dust particles swirling like the inside of a firestorm as the brake lights lit up the blackness. The truck was overrun by its own dusty radiance as it came to a stop.

A small man got out from behind the wheel and left the truck running as he walked into the headlights and bent over the generator. Haggard immediately recognized him from his last visit. He was the same man who had driven the small truck that he had followed to the farm. It was also the same truck from the campsite.

Haggard watched as Rizzo walked quickly to the cab of the truck and drove it forward then reversed and stopped short of the generator. Rizzo stepped out of the cab and walked to the rear, dropping the tailgate down and pulling a wide plank from the bed of the truck. He dropped one end to the ground. He bent over the generator and hooked a cable onto the frame in preparation of winching it onto the ramp and up onto the truck.

"Son-of-a-bitch," Rizzo grunted as he tried to pull the generator straight.

"You want some help?" Haggard said quietly from the darkness directly behind Rizzo.

Rizzo reaction was immediate and he spun around anxiously, trying to see into the blackness and wiping his hands on the sides of his jeans nervously. "Who's there?"

A slight breeze blew across the yard bringing the faint and forlorn howl of a coyote towards the two of them. Haggard lowered the knapsack to the ground and walked towards Rizzo and into the dim circle of red light.

"Man, you scared the shit out of me!" Rizzo looked at the tall man dressed in black and realized he was alone and vulnerable. "Who the hell are you? This is private property."

Haggard just stood there and looked at Rizzo. The sound of his voice played around in his mind. Other things besides the voice zipped across his mind, like running feet, a brief struggle, and a dark campground. It seemed like a lifetime ago, or like it had happened to someone else but the pain was still there, and so was the anger. The guy in front of him had a lot of answers.

Rizzo looked nervously towards the front of the truck where he had left the old revolver. "Uh…yeah. Yeah, I could use a hand. I'll just get my gloves."

Haggard stepped in front of Rizzo and put his arm around his shoulders and squeezed, pulling him towards the heavy piece of equipment. "You don't need gloves, man. What are you, a pussy?"

Rizzo laughed nervously, feeling the power of the other man in the brief contact. "You live around here? I never saw you walk up or anything."

"No," Haggard smiled. "I live south of here."

Rizzo pulled the winch chain tight, keeping his eyes averted and trying to find something to say to the unexpected arriver. "South…where, Aldergrove?"

Haggard moved closer to Rizzo and stood beside him. "No, further south than that. I'm surprised you don't remember me."

Rizzo looked at Haggard, the glow from the red taillight highlighting the puzzled look on his face. Straightening up, he scratched his scalp and shook his head. "I don't remember you. Are you a friend of Sigger?"

A gentle breeze blew across Haggard's face and evaporated some of the sweat that had gathered on his forehead. He looked at Rizzo who was waiting patiently for an answer. The name Sigger did not ring any bells with him but he figured it had to be the other guy who was in the campground that night.

"Maybe if I knew your name I would remember you," Rizzo offered.

"Yeah, Sigger and I go way back. I work the other side of the city. You mean he didn't mention the name of Dan to you?"

"Dan…Dan. No. Not that I remember," Rizzo said, starting to work the winch.

"Where is he now? I have some unfinished business with him," Haggard stated.

"He might be over at the new place along the border or he could be headed into the States already."

"Shit," Haggard said with mock disappointment. "I really wanted to set something up with him. What's he going into the States for?"

Rizzo looked Haggard over, weighing his options before answering. Hell, he finally reasoned, the guy looks like he's been around and he sure as hell knows Sigger. It would piss Sigger off if Haggard complained that he hadn't helped him out. Besides, he knew to look for Sigger here at the farm.

"Look, you don't want to tell me where Sigger is then I'll just find him myself," he said in annoyance.

"No, no. No problem, he's following a shipment down. I don't know if he's left yet though, he might have to wait for the semi to load up."

Haggard needed better intelligence than that. He needed to know where the truck was and where it was headed. "Is that the one he said was going to Seattle?" Haggard asked, guessing.

"Yeah," Rizzo grunted as he pushed the generator onto the bed from the ramp and shut off the winch. "Between you and me and half the world he shouldn't even be going down there but we have to personally deliver the stuff this time.

"Why is that?"

"It's part of the deal. Sigger tell you about the shipment we lost?"

Haggard walked closer and helped Rizzo shut the tailgate. "Scuttlebutt is that Sigger made a visit to some guy down there to try and get it back," Haggard guessed again.

"Yeah, what a waste of time that was. She didn't know a damn thing."

"She?" Haggard asked as a tremor of anger surged through him. "I thought it was a guy."

"We couldn't find the guy. His old woman was home though."

"How do you know that?" he asked as he leaned on the tailgate closer to Rizzo.

"Shit, I was there man. That Sigger is a ruthless prick... Ah, don't go saying nothing to him, okay?...I mean he was just doing his thing. But man did he work her over."

"You must have got in your licks too," Haggard chuckled with suppressed rage, his voice flat and low.

"Just a couple of good belts," Rizzo said walking towards the cab. "She wouldn't shut her bloody mouth. I hate screaming dames."

"Show me where this new place is," Haggard ordered as his eyes bored into the back of Rizzo's head. "I'll follow you. Wait here while I grab my wheels."

He watched as Rizzo pulled off the two lane paved road into a gravel driveway alongside the U.S. Border. He recognized the area having passed the place when he made his pickup from the ditch during the day. He came to a stop to the left of Rizzo's pickup, keeping the truck between him and the other man. He shut off the lights and got out into damp air.

"I don't see his wheels, man. You're too late he's gone."

The small farm was in total blackness. Even the sky was a vacuum, a void that produced no illumination. The trees blended perfectly with the sky and seemed to disappear a quarter of the way up the trunks.

As he moved towards Rizzo his night vision improved and he was able to pick out the outline of the house back near the road. Rizzo was standing and waiting for him to say something.

"He's gone, man."

"Where's the truck?" he demanded.

"What truck?" Rizzo asked, seemingly mystified.

"The semi—the truck that's going into the States—where is it?"

Rizzo became alert, not liking Dan Haggard's tone or demands and feeling more confident now that he was back on the new turf. "Look, you want to know that you phone Sigger on his cell. I got my own problems setting this place up."

Haggard changed the subject, looking towards the blackness of the barn. "Don't go getting uppity on me. What's in the barn?"

"What do you care? Listen, I think maybe you better deal with Mike. Yeah, if Sigger is so anxious to hear from you, you better call him direct. I gotta go. The dogs gotta be fed."

Haggard was fed up with the charade and moved up next to the vague outline of the smaller man. "He's probably at the semi. Where's it located?"

Rizzo turned and walked away. "Piss on that, no way man. You phone Sigger yourself."

Dan Haggard smiled at the receding form and let him go. Sound traveled and the night was too quiet for any kind of outdoor interrogation. The smile faded from his face and was replaced by a look that would put an executioner to shame. The building storm within was too powerful to suppress. He had found one of Connie's killers.

The Mule

Picking up his small knapsack from the Honda he made his way to the barn door and cracked it open. A dirty light bulb glowed back at him on the other side of an open doorway at the other end of a small square room. He could hear a faint voice further back in the barn.

Everything smelled old. He took in the dust covered items hanging from a grimy cinderblock wall as he made his way to the open area beyond. The voice became stronger as he drew nearer. He looked around the opening and saw that Rizzo was feeding the two Doberman Pinchers. A shiver ran up Dan's spine at the thought of facing those powerful jaws.

He quietly retraced his steps and left the barn. He reached into his knapsack and pulled out a rolled-up jacket. The jacket unrolled easily revealing a commando combat crossbow with a light polymer stock and aluminum frame.

Working quickly he assembled the stock and the limb, or bow, attaching the scope with the red dot sight and placed a sixteen-inch arrow or bolt onto the weapon ready for use. Cocking the weapon using the cocking lever he was ready to re-enter the barn.

The dogs must have heard him enter the barn. He had barely reached the inner doorway when he saw one of the dogs moving rapidly in his direction.

The slim, sixteen-inch bolt shot across the forty-foot distance at two hundred and thirty-five feet per second. It entered the dog's head one inch to the left of the red dot and interrupted the dog's nervous system. The dog tumbled onto the rough concrete, dead before it hit the floor but the body continuing to move in un-coordinated movements.

The Doberman had not made a sound but the second dog ran quickly to the fallen animal, bewildered by its actions. He sniffed and whined and then pawed at the head in an effort too gain a response.

It must have been the noise of the cocking mechanism; the second dog wheeled around and charged towards him in an enraged viciousness. The ears were flat against the head and the snout was rolled back in a series of hard ridges allowing the teeth and gums to be bared in preparation for ripping and tearing.

He almost panicked. It was not just the sight of the dog charging towards him it was the total silence of the attack. It came at lightning speed, the sound of the feet muffled by old straw on the floor. The dog's eyes shone a pale blue in the faint light and seemed to bore into Haggard's brain.

He had a hard time lining up the red dot of the infrared sight on the moving animal. He had a second or two at the most before the dog would be on him and he lost his chance. The red and tan colors of the dog blended in so well with the surroundings Haggard had to wait until the last moment.

The bolt left the crossbow and immediately entered the dog's chest cavity. Tearing through the heart and lungs it was deflected down by a rib and shot down through the bowels. The range was so close the bolt left the animal and lodged in a lower wall, burying itself an inch into the cinderblock.

The Doberman crashed into the door jam and fell at Haggard's feet, its tongue hanging out the side of his mouth and the open eyes no longer shining.

"What the hell?" Rizzo yelled, running towards the fallen dogs.

There had not been a sound other than the dogs crashing to the floor and into the wall. He stopped short, looking at the bolt sticking out of the dog's forehead. "What the hell?…

Haggard stepped around the edge of the doorframe and looked at Rizzo. It took a moment for Rizzo to realize that he was being watched but then he exploded in anger. "What the fuck did you do, man? What the hell is that sticking out of his head?"

"Probably the same thing that's going to be sticking out of yours if I don't get answers from you," Haggard said darkly as he advanced towards Rizzo.

Rizzo turned to run but a powerful arm lock prevented him from moving. He felt himself blacking out as a lateral neck restraint application cut off the blood to his brain. He collapsed and Haggard let him thud to the floor.

Rizzo awoke confused, his eyes moving with an unfocused and uncomprehending twitch. He slowly focused on the man standing in front of him, shaking his head and trying to clear his mind. "Wha… What are you doing? Are you crazy? Sigger will kill you, man. He loved those dogs."

The Mule

Bending down he looked at Rizzo, seeing a tiny slug of a man who contributed nothing to life. His whole life would continue to create nothing but misery for anyone he met and for a whole lot of others he would never meet. He set the crossbow down in front of Rizzo and met the man's frightened eyes.

"Why are you doing this?" Rizzo asked trying to sit up but realized both his arms were tied behind him to a beam.

"Do you remember that house in Seattle and that little lady you beat the hell out of down there?"

Rizzo did not answer. He sat very still; wary of what might be coming next, the rapid throbbing pulse just below the skin on his neck betraying his calmness.

Haggard waited for a few seconds and then picked up the crossbow. Rizzo's eyes followed his actions nervously. "That was my house you broke into," he said quietly.

Terror flared in Rizzo's eyes and he turned a sick pasty color. "It wasn't me! I was...just along for...for the ride," Rizzo stammered between gulps of air.

"Were you just along for the ride at the campsite? Huh? Were you just along for the ride when you threw in a couple of punches at my wife? And were you along for the ride when you burned down of my house?"

"Your house? I never burnt your house, man! Nobody burnt your house down," Rizzo said, a sob escaping from his throat.

"You beat the hell out of my lady." He looked into Rizzo's terror-stricken eyes. "She died."

Rizzo reacted violently, trying to loosen his bonds and get up off the floor. He kicked out at Haggard and struggled for several minutes before he finally fell back exhausted and weak.

"You are now going to tell me where and how to find this guy, Sigger. How and when you tell me is up to you but you are going to tell me."

One half hour later, Haggard walked out of the barn and got into his vehicle. A faint glow lit up the area around the barn as he shut the door to the Honda CRV. The whole of the main floor was ablaze and feeding hungrily on the gasoline soaked interior. He was four miles away when the fire burst through the roof and ignited sideways. The fire just loved the old and dry lumber.

Rizzo never suffered at all. He sat upright with his sightless eyes aimed at the dazzling light, a bolt from the crossbow pinning his head to a fiery beam.

He had wanted Rizzo to suffer as Connie had. He had wanted him to feel real pain. But in the end Rizzo just sickened him and he just wanted the man to be gone. He felt no remorse, no anxiety, and no satisfaction. The guy needed to die. It was a more humane way than what he had done to Connie.

When he found Mike Sigger that would be a whole different matter.

CHAPTER ELEVEN

"I'm telling you," Roy Tully said, red in the face and obviously trying to control his temper. "I want you here before you take off. I want to talk to you about the delivery. I want you here in under an hour."

Roy turned to his brother as he slammed down the handset. "Sigger's getting too big for his britches. Son-of-a-bitch said he didn't have time to come by to talk to us."

Frank smiled patiently at is brother, wishing not for the first time that he would cool his temper. Roy always had to be the tough guy, even when they were kids. He had a vicious inner streak that he had always used to bully and torment others until they not only did what he wanted but they paid him the respect and submissiveness that he demanded.

Frank knew it was a contest of personalities and wills between Sigger and his brother. Both were used to running things and giving orders. Both were extremely brutal. He was always on guard to make sure the two men did not upset the daily operation with their hostilities.

"He does have point, Roy. He is busy. But I agree that he has to stop by otherwise we could end up with a problem at the other end when he arrives." Frank got up and walked to the bar. "Have a drink and relax."

"I don't want a bloody drink. I want that semi on the road and safely out of the country. It's due to leave at sunrise and that's not too far from now. I'm tired of worrying about it."

"It'll be okay," Frank offered in a soothing manner, taking a sip of his drink.

"It had better be! We lose this shipment and we are financially...how do they say...stretched? I tell you I will sleep a lot sounder when it crosses into Washington. Did you see those new sensors sticking up everywhere at the border?"

"They're radiation detectors, Roy. We're not shipping atom bombs or plutonium you know."

"Funny." Roy sat back and grabbed a magazine. "When's the wife back?"

Frank looked towards his brother, glad of the change of topic. "Irene's coming home the day after tomorrow. She's helping her sister with the last of the decorating."

"Too bad, I was hoping for a decent meal."

"Come over after the delivery and we'll have a nice evening. Let's go over some of the problems on the East side while we're waiting for Sigger."

Sigger walked through the lower side door and down into the bar area three quarters of an hour later. He nodded to Frank and sat at a barstool. Frank placed a beer in front of him.

"About bloody time," Roy Tully said from behind and across the room.

Mike Sigger looked at Frank, saying nothing but conveying the message that this was not going to go on much longer. He took a sip of the beer and turned around on the stool. Roy was walking towards the bar.

Before Roy Tully could speak, Mike Sigger turned and looked at his brother. "Okay, Frank, time is short. What did you want to pass on?"

Roy Tully felt the snub and his face turned an ugly shade of red. He made as to speak but Frank stepped out from behind the bar in front of him and faced Sigger. "I... We think there could be the possibility of a rip-off when you reach Seattle. A little birdie told me they are having some sort of problem of their own down there. Now we..."

"Why should we get hit? Shit, we're giving them a gift as well as the payment to make sure we maintain a fast and steady supply. We're good customers."

The Mule

"Well obviously," Roy Tully interrupted, "some group or somebody is ripping them off down there. We don't want to be part of any rip-off."

"Did you ask them what's going down?"

"They don't seem to be in a sharing mood for some reason," Roy said in a sarcastic voice.

"Anyway, there has been a change of plans. Roy will follow you to the truck and even help ride escort on the way down. We want to stay with that trailer at all times until it is off-loaded," Frank instructed. "You make your deal as fast as possible. We can't afford to lose this shipment to some other group."

"I don't need him," Sigger said, nodding towards Roy Tully. "He'll just get in the way."

"What did you say?" Roy Tully demanded angrily. "Listen you snot, I was running this operation long before you came along. You had…"

"You both are going to have to work together," Frank said with a raised voice. "You are going to have to move fast once you cross the border. When you get across go to the locker, pick up your weapons, and get back to the truck. Don't let *anyone* near our stuff."

"Yeah." Sigger finished his beer and looked at Roy with dislike, wanting to wipe all signs of life from his face very badly.

"How's the new grow going?" Frank asked. "Is Rizzo pulling his weight?"

"Shit, he's running around like a fucking rooster shot full of Viagra. He's all over the place. Good thing I'm leaving. Drives me crazy he's so eager."

Frank smiled as he walked Sigger towards the door. "He's not like you, eh, Mike? Cool Hand Luke himself."

"Cool Hand Luke my ass," Roy laughed as he grabbed his jacket from across the room. "More like, Luke Warm if you ask me. Yeah, Luke Warm Luke, that's Mike to a tee."

Sigger stopped by the doorway and turned towards Frank Tully, speaking in a quiet whisper. "You better do something about your brother, Frank…before I do."

"I know, Mike, I know. I'll work on him," Frank said, patting Mike's shoulder as he eased him through the door.

Roy stopped beside his brother as he was putting on his jacket and looked at Frank's disgusted look. "What? What's the problem?"

"You are. Can it with Sigger. Concentrate on the fucking job, Roy."

"Ah, I'm just having a little fun with the prick."

"Yeah? That little prick is about shove his shotgun up your nose and clean your sinuses for you."

Roy laughed and as he walked towards the door he called back to Frank. "You worry too much big brother."

Frank heard the car start up and accelerate out of the driveway as he made his way back to the bar. He picked up his glass, drained the last of the scotch and walked out of the bar area towards his office, shutting lights off as he went.

He turned on the small desk lamp. The turmoil between Mike Sigger and his brother was still very much on his mind. He did not know how he was going to deal with the two of them. Maybe he could set it up so the two of them did not cross paths.

Frank Tully forgot about them. A half hour later he was still working on a distribution problem. He did not see the figure of the man standing in the shadows on the other side of the doorframe. He gave a slight start and peered into the darkness. "Is that you, Roy? Did you forget something?"

The dim light from the bar clock provided a vague outline of the man but the desk lamp prevented him from seeing into the darkness beyond. Frank realized that the person standing there was larger than his brother. "Mike?"

The man stepped forward into the glow of the desk lamp. He was difficult to see because he was dressed in black clothing. "Who is it?"

Frank Tully did not recognize the face that appeared in the soft light above him. The face was drawn and looked slightly fatigued. The man's nose was slightly bent in the middle. It took away any chance of him being handsome but it was a good-looking face. The man's eyes were hard and cold and set above a thin mouth that looked like it never moved.

"Who in the hell are you?" Frank exclaimed, starting to stand up from behind the desk.

"Sit down!" Haggard commanded quietly as he moved quickly to

Frank Tully's right side and pushed on Frank's shoulder and sending him back down into the chair.

Frank jumped up and forward instantly. "To hell with you!" he bellowed as he reached towards a desk drawer and pulled it open. He reached inside and was about to remove a small handgun when the drawer slammed against his wrist. Haggard's kick sent a numbing shockwave up Frank's arm.

"Son-of-a-bitch!" Frank screamed, falling back into his chair and holding his injured wrist. "Who the hell *are you?* What do you want?"

Haggard sat on the edge of the desk and removed the small pistol from the drawer before closing it. He nonchalantly pointed his own at Frank Tully while he studied him. "You're the guy who calls all the shots around here, right?"

Tully just sat there looking at Haggard, rubbing his bruised and throbbing wrist and wincing in pain. He let out a long sigh and finally answered. "What do you want?"

"I'll tell you what I want. I want everything that you took from me."

"Took from you? I never took anything from you. I don't even know who the hell you are!"

Leaning forward, Haggard stared into Frank Tully's eyes. His eyes seemed to penetrate deeply into the other man's core and it made Tully sit further back and out of the glow of the small lamp. He noticed that Haggard was wearing black leather driving gloves.

"People like you leave destruction in your wake every day. You create so much misery you can't even keep up with it. Well I'm here to educate you."

Haggard got up off the desk and moved backward from Frank Tully and turned on the lights in the other room so he could see into the bar area. "I'm sure you remember the drugs on that motorhome from Washington State that you wanted so badly," he said moving back towards the desk.

"The motorhome... What's that got to do with you?"

"It was mine, asshole." Haggard's voice was just above a whisper. "You guys set me up."

"That had nothing to do with me! It was all set up across the line, not here. All we were going to do was take the shit off your rig and let you do your thing. We weren't the ones who set you up."

"But you do remember sending one of your men to my house, a guy by the name of Sigger."

"No way, he did that on his own! I…"

"He's your man and your man beat the hell out of my wife."

"Look, we can settle this. Your vacation was messed up a little. I'll look after it. And I understand your anger about your wife and if there are any medical bills I will take care of it plus a little more for your trouble."

"You've proved my point. You have no idea of the chaos and destruction you cause in people's lives."

"It isn't anything that can't be settled," Frank Tully said with more confidence, his usual authority starting to surface.

"Is that a fact?"

"Yeah, it's not my doing but…"

"It's all…your doing. This is your racket. You make the call. You're the big man, the general, and your troops obey your orders. You are going to tell me exactly where Sigger is headed with that semi-trailer."

Frank Tully's face showed a flicker of surprise that the man standing before him knew all about the shipment. His face became neutral. "You're dreaming. It'll never happen,"

Dan sat on the corner of the desk again. His gun was inches from the other man's face as his eyes bored into Tully's. "Let me explain something to you, Tully. Your man, this Sigger…he broke into my house. He killed my wife."

'I didn't know that!" Frank Tully blurted. He…"

"He killed my wife while looking for your drugs. I was arrested for importing your garbage and they seized my motorhome.

"I told you, Sigger acted on his own," Frank Tully snapped belligerently.

Somebody torched my house, Frank. They found a body inside. Things do not look good for me right now. I have nothing to lose. I want you to ask yourself, do I look like I give a shit about you."

Frank Tully sat there saying nothing and not meeting Dan Haggard's eyes.

Haggard leaned towards Tully. "Where is the truck heading to?"

"Fuck you, Pal."

Dan made as to get off the desk but turned back swiftly and slammed the semi-automatic against Tully's right ear. His head snapped to the left and the chair almost tipped over with Tully's weight shift.

The pain was so bad that Tully could only rock back and forth, moaning as he held his ear. He finally felt his ear to see what damage there was and finding it in one piece he looked at Dan Haggard with hatred.

"Why is it that you guys think you are the only ones that can play hardball? You will tell me what I need to know or you will suffer a great deal. After I am finished with you I'll burn this shack to the ground and everything in it."

"No, you can't do that! My wife..."

"I'm playing by your rules now," Haggard said, looking at the change in Frank Tully's facial expression. He had hit a nerve. "Like I said, I have nothing left to lose and if you think I won't do it then you had better think again. To me you are nothing but a slime ball. Now where is the truck going?"

Frank Tully's eyes darted about the room. He needed to come up with something to satisfy the man in front of him. If he told him about the shipment he could be in a great deal of financial trouble if something happened to it. Of course he could always tip off Sigger about this guy. The only thing that worried him was the man's threat to burn the house down. Even though his wife was out of town it would hurt her to lose everything.

"I'm waiting. Time is running out," Haggard stated.

"My... My wife is upstairs," Tully lied. "Are you going to burn her too?"

Haggard just looked back. "So now you get to worry about what's dear to you."

Frank Tully's face took on a defiant look as he stared back. "Yeah, well you can get your information somewhere else."

"But that does not mean I won't torch the house. It'll go up with you in it."

"Bullshit. I think you're full of bullshit," Frank muttered.

"Then why don't you phone your flunky? Phone the guy at the barn along the border who is supposed to set up your new grow-op."

"How do you know about that?" Tully demanded, looking surprised.

"Go ahead and phone. I'm afraid you're not going to get an answer though. The place is smoldering down around ground level by now with the punk in amongst the ashes.

Frank Tully's face took on a pasty appearance and it was evident that he believed what Dan Haggard had told him. "You dirty bastard!"

"You *still* don't get it yet. All your earthly problems are about to disappear if I do not get what I want from you. Where is the tractor-trailer unit heading? I want an address."

"Fuck y..."

The barrel of the pistol rammed its way between Frank Tully's partially open lips and collided with his teeth briefly as it continued all the way into his mouth. Blood and pieces of shattered teeth oozed out from the corner of his mouth as Tully tried to scream around the weapon. The weapon forced his head onto the back of the chair.

Tully started to choke and Haggard pulled the automatic back slightly. "You have about five seconds to live. Do you believe me?"

Tully looked at Haggard with pain filled eyes and he closed them briefly as a wave of pain hit him even harder. He opened his eyes and nodded.

"The address, where is it?" Haggard stepped back and pulled out the gun in a not so gentle manner.

Tully grabbed his mouth as a new cut appeared. "Ahhh! Som-ob-a-biks!" His lips were swelling rapidly and it was obvious that he would not be able to talk soon, if at all.

"The address, either write it down or show me where you have it," Haggard ordered as he placed the gun against Tully's temple.

Frank leaned ahead and pulled open the narrow center drawer of the desk. He pointed to a small, dark green book and fell back in the chair obviously in too much pain to even lift it out.

Picking up the book Haggard scanned the contents. It was all mumbo-jumbo to him. "Where is the address?" he asked angrily as he tossed the book onto Tully's lap.

Frank Tully picked up the book and with violently shaking hands slowly opened it. He rifled through the pages, looking with unfocused eyes for the entry. He stopped near the end of the book and held it for Haggard to see.

A Seattle address had been written in neat handwriting. There was also a license plate and the name of a trucking firm written with the address.

He put the book in his pocket and turned to Frank Tully. "Who is in charge down there? Who set me up and who do you deal with?"

Frank Tully shook his head from side to side as his toothless mouth bled down onto his clothing. "Yuh gobba kill me anyway. Fug yuh," he said.

"I'm glad you understand. You should have known that sooner or later somebody would catch up with you. And you know what? I'm sure they'll catch up with me too. But they are not going to put me away because of you if I can help it. Even you know that if you don't take care of your own problems no one else will. I can't have you coming after me, Tully."

"It's not me yuh wan," Tully said painfully.

You killed my wife. I am not going to sit in some jail for years thinking about you sitting here swilling wine and smoking cigars. You made your own choices, asshole."

"Dun hur mu wuf," Frank Tully said with pleading eyes, worried now that Haggard might come back out of vengeance.

"Nobody is going to hurt your wife, Frank. She probably doesn't even know you deal drugs. She thinks you sell motorcycles, right?"

Frank Tully nodded his head up and down, his shoulders slumping with defeat.

"Well at least you thought about her," he said as he took Frank Tully's small gun out of his pocket. "You know what, Tully? I keep thinking of mine too."

Haggard's hand shot upwards into the center of Frank Tully's mouth and he pulled the trigger. The bullet slammed his head back into the soft leather and then he slumped forward.

He stopped Tully from falling and eased the body back. He placed the weapon in Tully's hand and shoved the gun inside his mouth and let go. His hand fell back down with the gun still wrapped around the trigger guard. *It certainly won't fly as a suicide*, Haggard thought, *but it will baffle a few people for a while*. He looked at the man who was partially responsible for his loss and felt no satisfaction. In fact he was far from satisfied.

Turning from the desk, he saw Tully's cellular phone lying next to a package of cigarettes and placed it in his pocket on impulse. Maybe it had some numbers stored in it.

Dan washed the gloves under the tap in the bar sink and walked away from the house and let things be. He did not feel the least bit sorry for Frank Tully but he had a sad feeling inside for his wife. Did he just do the same thing to her as Tully or Sigger did to him? Did he just take away her life too?

Yeah I did, he admitted to himself. *Which makes me no better than Sigger.* However there was always that picture in his mind of Connie and her radiant smile, her chuckle, and then…her battered and swollen face.

He walked the half-mile to his vehicle in the pre-dawn light and got inside. He was surprised to see his hands shaking when he rested them on the steering wheel.

Why were his hands shaking when he did not *feel* anything? Shouldn't he *feel* something? Shouldn't he feel fright or sorrow or anger, or something to let himself know he was human? *I should*, he thought, but there was nothing there except the mild shaking.

The shakes have to be a sign of something. Guilt maybe, he thought. As he put the Honda into drive and turned out of the bushy area and onto the road towards the border, Haggard had a sneaky feeling he was right. He felt guilty about Tully's wife and what she would go through.

He could hardly wait to put Canada behind him. But this time he had to find a way to get across the border without being seen. From what he had observed earlier it shouldn't be that difficult.

* * *

Mike Sigger watched as the driver finished hooking the black and gray tractor onto the fifty-three foot trailer. The driver was short and wiry and his balding head had a serious case of comb over. Multiple tattoos adorned his shoulders and upper arms in some sort of mural. His movements were quick and precise and as he walked around checking the tires and hoses it was obvious that he knew and liked his job.

The truck was in a compound enclosed by a high chain link fence. It sat next to several other rigs that were backed up to a loading dock on Sigger's right. The low one story structure had seen better days but seemed to serve the purpose of moving freight from one place to another.

The driver disappeared around to the other side of the trailer but a few moments later Sigger and Roy Tully caught a brief glimpse of him entering the building.

"Where the hell is he going now?" Roy Tully asked.

"How the hell should I know? Maybe he needs to take a piss," Sigger answered.

The two men were sitting inside of Sigger's rented four-door Malibu, rented under a well-known company name for the trip south. Sigger was dressed in tan slacks, light blue shirt, and a dark blue sports jacket, while Roy Tully was dressed in jeans and a western shirt. His blue jean jacket was on the seat in his pickup truck.

"He'd need more than a piss if he knew what he was hauling in that trailer," Roy Tully laughed.

"Yeah?" Sigger said sarcastically. "Well who's going to be crapping if that truck doesn't make it across?"

"It'll get across don't you worry your ass about that."

"Well *assuming* we get across, Roy, I'll head to the locker to get the guns. You stay with the driver until I catch up. I won't need you after that and you can take off."

"Don't you start giving me orders, Sigger. I'm going all the way to Seattle with this haul to make sure you don't screw up again."

"Yeah, well then you had better start making up a plan to bring the coke back across. You want to run the show then start doing it right now. If you want to run it you are not going to blame me for any screw up."

Roy gave a light-hearted but phony laugh. He needed Sigger whether he liked it or not. Slapping Sigger on the shoulder he tried to make light of his last remark. "Ease up, Mike. You're the man."

"Fuck you," Sigger said as he shrugged off Tully's hand. "Where the hell is he? He's taking too damn long. We should be moving by now."

"Here he comes now. He's got a fistful of papers in his hand."

The driver jumped into the cab and fired up the engine sending black exhaust upwards and into a stiff breeze from the twin stacks. The exhaust left a long smudge in the air as the truck started to move.

"Okay, Roy. I'll see you on the other side. You cross first and I'll wait until I see the truck moving out of the customs port before I follow."

The big rig moved slowly away from the platform and across the freight yard. Roy Tully waited until the truck turned onto the roadway and was a block away before he opened the door and walked towards his pickup truck. A few moments later he drove away in the same direction.

Sigger started the car and drove towards the Pacific Border Crossing. It was only a few miles from the famed Peace Arch crossing but this crossing dealt primarily with the large commercial trucks.

He was in no rush. It was going to be a slow process for the truck to clear the border. Long lineups, diligent customs officers, immigration checks, drug enforcement patrols, Border Patrol units, and even random searches by an agricultural inspector could be one of the many reasons for the time consuming procedure. They all worked under the Department of Homeland Security and the new Customs and Border Protection Agency. Then there was the screening of the trucks by radiation detectors, mobile gamma-ray scanners, and dogs trained to detect drugs and explosives.

It all sounded like it was very secure, but the United States had to process twenty million commercial trucks or more per year at all their border crossings. The manpower and the equipment was just not available everywhere or all the time. They were also under immense pressure to keep commerce flowing in both directions.

US Customs and Border Protection seized well over two million pounds of marijuana and over ninety thousand pounds of Cocaine yearly. Over nine million shipping containers at thirty-seven hundred passenger and cargo terminals entered the United States along with one hundred and sixteen million vehicles crossing at the borders. They simply could not begin to scratch the surface in their search for illegal drugs. They knew it, the criminal underworld knew it, and that was what Sigger was counting on once again.

Sigger had seen it all, including trailers filled with sand, hollow wooden pallets, phony toolboxes and fuel tanks, and even tires filled with drugs. Although lots of drugs made it through other shipments did not and it was getting harder to come up with new methods.

Sigger watched from a distance as Roy Tully eased into the inspection port and handed a uniformed man something. There was a prolonged conversation with the uniformed man peering into the rear of the truck. A few moments later he watched as the pickup drove away.

It took less time than Mike Sigger thought. The tractor-trailer was clear of the border within twenty minutes. *They didn't find it!* He thought gleefully.

Sigger entered the port just as the truck rolled out of the truck area. He gave the female officer his friendliest smile. "Good morning."

"Identification please," was the reply.

Sigger handed over a Canadian passport, counterfeit in every way except for his photo and guaranteed to provide worry free use and it damn well should for the high price that was demanded and paid out.

He watched as she scanned it quickly with her eyes and then looked him over. She then scanned it into a computer. She was in her forties, a little on the heavy side, and wore her black hair in a style that was very short. *Another butch,* he observed.

"What is the purpose of your visit?"

This one is as cold as ice. "Business, I'm going to Bremerton to see about new fabricated parts."

"How long to you expect to stay in the United States?"

"A couple of days I think." Sigger noticed the wedding ring on her hand. Wedding band or not he could spot them a mile off.

"Are you bringing anything into the U.S. that will remain in the country?"

"No, nothing."

"Okay, go ahead," and handed Sigger the passport.

The tractor-trailer unit was not very far on down the road. Sigger saw that it was stuck in slow moving traffic and Roy Tully's pickup became visible as he drew closer.

He drove with the slow moving traffic, his mind still back in the customs bay. *'Are you bringing anything into the U.S. that will remain in the country?'* he heard her ask again.

Sigger laughed out loud. "Baby if you only knew!"

CHAPTER TWELVE

Jairo Herrera-Sanchez put the cellular phone gently onto the desktop of his expensive teakwood desk and turned towards Ted Conway who was standing just inside the doorway to Jairo's den. Brushing imaginary lint off his tie he stood up and tried to push the perfect knot into an already perfect position. "That was Mike Sigger. The shipment made it safely across. You make sure you are there to welcome him when he phones and tells me the truck is unloaded and on the move."

"The trailer might not be unloaded right away. I..."

"I don't give a frig when the trailer is unloaded, just *be* there when I tell you to be there. When that tractor drops the empty trailer off you had better be in a position to help Sigger bring in the weed. I want extra security. Nobody interferes. I'm not having the friggin' Canadians sayin' we can't handle our own turf."

Conway sighed inwardly, not daring to show Jairo that he was sick of his lectures. "I'll get everything lined up," he said defensively. "When the truck comes into the lot I'll have guys watching. As soon as it starts to move away from the trailer I'll go and meet with Sigger. It'll be okay."

"It'll be okay," Jairo Herrera-Sanchez mimicked. "It had better be."

"No problem," Conway said, shuffling uncomfortably and anxious to be out of Herrera-Sanchez's eyesight. He looked with envy at the expensive teak furniture and the cream colored walls lined with books. "We can rip the stuff out of there in no time and get back to the shop to do the deal."

Jairo walked towards a patio door. The door opened into an enclosed yard that was lushly landscaped with huge rocks, a small waterfall, and large plants and many blooming flowers. He stopped at the patio door and looked out. He was able to see over the back hedge that offered a view of the city and the open water beyond. A small boat was skipping across the open water and it left a continuous white feathery plume that hung in the air against a darkening gray sky.

Conway continued, uncomfortable even when Jairo was quiet. "That guy from Vegas said he would take the whole lot as soon as we are ready. He's anxious to get some of that Bud. All we have to do is…"

Herrera-Sanchez turned from the patio doorway. "All we have to do is get the stuff first. I want it packaged smaller, about a quarter of a pound smaller and the price stays the same. If there are any questions tell him there are high demands and a shortage of the product. Just like friggin' gas and oil."

"You figure they'll line up to pay more for less?" Conway asked.

Jairo laughed. "If the friggin' A-rab bastards can do it why can't I?"

"Let's just hope they don't go somewhere else," Conway said, thinking out loud without realizing it.

"Your friggin' job is to do what you are told. My friggin' job is to do the thinkin'. You keep doin' what you are told and maybe, just maybe mind you, I'll let you do some of the thinkin'. But don't hold your breath."

What an asshole! Conway secretly shouted in his mind. "You're the boss," he said aloud.

"Friggin' right I'm the boss. Now go and set up the meet. Take plenty of help and phone me when you head for the radiator shop with the goods."

Conway nodded and walked out of the house. The place was huge and he knew it was worth more than four million easily. As he got into his old car he looked back and up at the house and the portal at the front driveway. The entrance was protected against the elements by huge pillars and a peaked roof. "Like a damn hotel," Conway grumbled out loud. "Jairo, you and I are going to have to have a talk about my future. You do not pay me enough. Not by far."

Sure he was making a fair to middling buck compared to some of the others but it was not enough when you compared it to the take. All the cream was staying at the top and he was being taken for granted. *I can't sock much away for a rainy day*, he thought. *Shit, it rains all the fucking time.*

He started the old car and swore inwardly as the stench of burnt oil reached his nostrils. *I'm sick of driving this piece of crap!* Although the car was only for show he was tired of having to drive around in it. *I'm like some poor beggar or some prick on welfare*, he thought.

Conway knew he deserved more compensation for the risks he took and for the responsibility he shouldered. His mood was dark and not at all geared towards the task ahead as he gunned the car along the driveway and out towards the quiet neighborhood street.

"To hell with it," Conway said aloud. "I'm going to get myself some new wheels and somehow Mr. Hotshot is going to pay for it. He thinks he knows everything. He knows shit." Conway smiled and relaxed back into the seat as he tried to formulate a plan to brighten up his existence. He was not going to a meet looking like a slob.

* * *

Mike Sigger watched as the truck backed towards the bay door, moving very slowly until the trailer bumped gently against the heavy rubber protectors on the platform. He watched as the driver got out and walked towards the rear of the trailer. There was less than a foot between the trailer and the closed bay doors of the building. The driver, apparently satisfied, walked back and began to unhook the trailer.

Sigger knew the load was safe for the night and that it would not be unloaded until sometime the next day. He had time to kill until the driver dropped the empty unit off at the arranged location.

There was a tap on his driver's side window and Sigger jumped, angry at himself for doing so. He turned to see Roy Tully smirking at him and waiting for him to roll down the window. He pushed the button and the window dropped silently as he looked at Tully.

"Well that's that. What say we go have us a drink?" Tully asked in an enthusiastic manner and all buddy, buddy like they were on a vacation.

"What say you go and have a drink? I'm going to visit a man with a motorhome and see about getting some goods back for us."

"What, all by your lonesome?" Tully asked with raised eyebrows. "What happens if he chases you again?"

"Then he's going to run into a brick wall. You want to come along for the fun or do you just talk the talk."

"One day you may find out, but yeah, let's do it. Let's go get our shit back. I'll leave the pickup here."

Sigger weaved his way expertly through traffic, gradually moving into the area that he remembered from his previous visit. He turned the car onto the quiet street and drove slowly forward as he looked for a familiar landmark.

"You remember which one?" Roy Tully asked.

"Yeah, I think it's a little further on. It should be about mid-block. As far as I remem…"

"What? What's the matter?"

"Look for yourself. The house is gone. It burned to the ground by the looks of it."

Roy Tully leaned ahead and peered out of the left side of the windshield. "How the hell are we going to find him now?"

Sigger stopped the car and looked to his left and out at the spot where the house used to be. He looked around at the neighboring houses and noticed a man looking out of a window of a house to their right. "We're being watched."

"Yeah just another nosey neighbor; they're everywhere," Tully quipped.

"See that busted real estate sign on the front lawn? The guy had the place up for sale before it went up in flames. I'm going to ask the nosey neighbor a few questions. Maybe he knows where the guy is living now."

Sigger knocked on the door and the curtains parted slightly. A moment later the door lock clicked over. A middle-aged guy with a baseball cap perched on his head opened the door slightly.

"Yeah, what can I do for you?" George asked suspiciously.

"Yeah, sorry to bother you, sport. I was looking at the real estate listing for the place across the street but I didn't expect to see it burnt up. Can you tell me where the owner is?"

George shook his head from side to side. "I can't help you. Call the real estate guy."

"Too bad, I was going to make him a good offer."

"You were going to make him a good offer on a burnt down house?" George said with some sarcasm and a raised eyebrow. "You better talk to the insurance company then. Maybe they'll be happy to sell it to you."

"So you don't know where I can find the owner."

George shook his head and looked at the car parked at the curb. "Nope, don't know where he is."

"Thanks," Sigger said and returned to the car.

"Did the guy tell you anything?"

"Not a thing. He probably knows but he isn't about to say. I said I was interested in buying the house but I'm pretty sure he spotted the license plates on the car."

"How the hell are we going to track him down now?" Roy Tully asked.

"I'm not sure but the guy must have a job somewhere and he has to hole up someplace. We'll look around some before we have to head back. We can take a whole week."

"The guy on the sign, the real estate guy, he must know something about how to get a hold of him," Roy suggested.

"Shit and here all the time I thought you couldn't think." Sigger said in a biting manner.

"What say we cut the bullshit until this is over? I want this guy just as much as you. Maybe more," Tully said angrily.

"Then get out and write down the number off of that sign. Let's get the hell out of here."

* * *

Dan Haggard finished washing his hands and opened the door of the restroom. Several customers that were lined up to pay for their fuel prevented him from getting close to a display rack. He pored himself a deep roasted coffee and added half and half cream. Selecting a Danish pastry he stepped into the line-up and waited.

"You're next," the clerk finally said, looking at him.

Dan picked up a map of Seattle from the display rack and put it on the counter next to the coffee and the pastry. "Are you familiar with this area?" he asked the youth.

"What area?"

Haggard sighed. He held up a piece of paper and pointed to the name of the street he had written down earlier. "Do you know where this street is?"

The clerk looked briefly and shook his head. "No, I never heard of it."

Why bother to ask he groaned to himself, thinking that he had yet to find anyone behind a counter who knew directions to anything. He wondered how they found their way to and from work.

Dan pushed the glass door open with his shoulder and juggling the coffee with the pastry sitting on top of the lid, he made his way to the Honda CRV sitting at the end of the line of parked cars.

He put the coffee on the roof, fished out his keys and clicked the electronic keyless entry to open the door. He placed the coffee in the drink holder and was about to close the door when a man filled the opening.

"Are you Daniel Haggard?"

The man was tall, slim, and a bit on the homely side. His face looked like it had been used as an old riverbed and then baked dry. His fluffy, peppery hair moved gently in the breeze as he gazed steadfastly at Haggard from a long narrow face.

"What can I do for you?"

The man reached into his pocket and produced a slim leather wallet. Flipping it open he displayed a police shield. "Police, the name is Edicott. We need to talk."

Damn, what bad timing, Haggard thought. Looking beyond Edicott he could see another man watching his every move. The guy was in his mid-thirties, sported a brush cut, and had stuffed his bodybuilding frame into an ill-fitting suit. "What's this all about? Is this about my house?"

"We'll talk down at headquarters. You coming on your own accord or do we have to arrest you?" Edicott asked in a friendly manner.

The Mule

Dan shrugged and picked up his coffee and the pastry as he exited the car. "Fine, let's go. You don't mind do you?" He said indicating the coffee, "I need a shot."

Edicott pointed to a dark colored vehicle that had pulled sideways behind the Honda and then quickly frisked Haggard. "Get into the back."

He did not bother to ask any questions on the short ride to the police office. He knew they wanted him to stew and if he had asked anything they would have just put him off until he was on their turf. He was not about to give them any satisfaction by asking them anything.

Dan kept thinking about his burnt house and the body the firefighters had found inside the house. He knew he could not avoid the investigators forever. They would have plenty of questions they would want answers to, unless of course it was something else. He didn't want to think of what the something else might be. In any event, he would soon find out.

The car pulled into the back of the building and he walked inside with the two men. Deposited in a small room and left alone he knew this was another tactic to drive up the blood pressure to make the individual fret and worry. There was one small table and three chairs in the room. The only other item was a pad of blank paper on the tabletop.

He did not have long to wait before the two men returned. Edicott sat down at the table with him while the other sat in a corner. "Okay, Mr. Haggard, we need to talk."

"You said that before."

"Yes I did, didn't I? Well we need some answers and we think you can help us out."

Haggard knew it was supposed to be his turn now and that he was supposed to ask how he could help, or help with what, or why did they think he had any answers to their questions, but he just sat and waited for the detective to continue.

Howard Edicott did not keep him wondering for long. "Have you ever heard of the name, Porter?"

He was genuinely puzzled. The name did not mean a thing to him. "No. I don't know that name."

"You don't know the name of Sheldon Porter?" Edicott prodded.

Silent alarm bells started going off inside of his mind. *Sheldon... The*

Puke… He had not bothered to get his last name. *Now what did they want to know about him? He would not have told them about the visit to his basement suite.*

"Sheldon Porter worked at the place where you had your motorhome serviced. He's the guy that might have, from what we are told, and with or without your knowledge, plugged your rig with Cocaine. From what we are told you might have a lot of reasons to be pissed off with him. Are you sure you do not know him?"

The best defense is the truth, Haggard knew. They were looking for answers, sure, but they were waiting for you to lie. If you lied and they knew you should have the answer, they had you. You were hiding something when you had no reason to hide something. That meant you were involved in something, somehow, and were trying to cover your tracks. If you were innocent of any wrong doing then why lie? Tell what you know without hurting yourself.

"Yes, I know who you mean. I remember him working around my motorhome and I didn't like the looks of him. He looks like a shit-rat."

"Looked like a shit-rat," Edicott remarked. "Past tense, he doesn't look like anything now."

"You're kidding. What happened to him?" He knew that anything could have happened to Sheldon—or the Puke as he still thought of him. Someone would be out for answers after his visit to the drug house and it looked like Sheldon had not taken his advice and left town.

"Strange you should ask, Haggard," Edicott said in a bewildered tone. "Why, we were just going to ask you that very same question."

"Me?" Dan chuckled. "You got the wrong guy if you think I know anything about this Sheldon. The only thing I know about him is that he worked on my rig and I didn't like him touching it."

"Oh he did more than work on it from what we are told. In fact you told the DEA boys that you were set up and that it could only have been one guy."

"No," Dan smiled, aware of the trick question. "I told the DEA I was set up by some asshole and whoever he was he caused me a shit-load of problems."

"Well he won't do that anymore. We *do* investigate Dan and Sheldon Porter was involved in the drug trade and he did work around your RV.

Haggard shrugged as Edicott continued. "Tell me, Dan, did you set fire to your house?"

"Yeah, sure. I put it up for sale hoping to make a buck and then I burned it down. Oh and don't bring up the insurance either, they're nothing but a pain in the ass."

"Yeah," Howard Edicott smiled. "They tend to be that way in an arson case. We tend to be pain in the ass too, especially when a body is found in a house."

"I don't get it. Why are you interested in something that is out of your area?"

"You don't show any surprise about someone being burnt up in your house," Edicott countered.

"I already knew."

"That's what we figured. In fact maybe you placed it in there and torched the house."

"You know, I get the feeling that you are going to tell me that this Sheldon guy was the body they found in the fire; right?"

"You win the Coupee Doll. Of course this is a surprise to you, right?" Edicott smirked.

"It is about it being this Sheldon, yes, about the body, no. I was with the DEA when the body was discovered and they told me about it. As far as the fire or the arson, I was in Canada. The DEA can vouch for me. They have a record of me crossing through customs. I still don't understand. Why are you guys interested?"

"Do you happen to know a couple of guys by the name of Neigel and Ruddick?"

Haggard's heart did a couple of double-time beats and he hoped nothing showed. "Never heard of them," he said calmly and looked Edicott straight in the eye.

"Yeah? They had a quick trip out of this world recently too. They were, uh...acquaintances of Sheldon's. Yeah, very strange that this Sheldon ends up dead in your house and these other two end up dead as hell also. Looks sort of like..."

"Looks sort of like you are fishing for some answers that I can't help you with," Haggard interrupted. "Think about it. What kind of nitwit does somebody in and leaves him to be found in his own house?"

"Some people think they can cover up a crime that way, Haggard. Not the first time."

"I'm sure you are aware that I used to be a police officer. You already know that if you've done your background work properly. If you know that then you also know that I would not leave someone in my house to be found by some fireman."

"Yeah, we know all about your police career. From what we are told your file shows heavy-handed arrests, assault charges, civil complaints, internal investigations and more than a few lost court cases because of your involvement. Quite an upstanding file they have on you."

"Still, I would not leave people to burn up in my house to hide evidence." Haggard fumed inwardly. "All it does is bring heat onto you. It's not intelligent."

"What is your style, Haggard? Do you bust them up head on, on their own turf? Take them out in one swoop, what?"

"I have already told you. I was in Canada when the fire was set."

"Where were you when Ruddick and Neigel were done in?" Edicott enquired easily.

"Like I said, I don't know them so how the hell can I tell you where I was when they died."

"Oh I forgot, just like the fire you were probably out of the country when…"

"Someone obviously busted into my house and torched it. Maybe it's the same people that beat up and killed my wife."

"So someone busted into your house and had an argument while they were there and one of them was conveniently killed before the house went up in flames. Is that what you are saying? On the other hand, maybe someone is leaving you a message, Dan. Do you think maybe someone left you a message?"

"Well let me think," Dan offered. "They already busted into my house once. That was a message. Then they killed my wife, and I guess that was a message." Silent fury building, his eyes were hard as he looked back at the other man. "Now they burn the house down, so I guess that's another message. I am getting a lot of messages aren't I, Edicott?"

"It would seem so. More than your share and maybe a guy can get to the point where some of the messages have to be answered. You being an ex-marine and all, maybe you went visiting some of the people who left you messages. For the record though, you are saying that you do not know the names Neigel and Ruddick and never met them.

"You know I've already answered all of this. Here you are accusing me of all sorts of things and you haven't warned me of my rights or anything."

"Dan, Dan, Dan. Easy now, you know how this works. You have not been arrested. We are just getting you to help us out with some questions that are hanging out there. Some of the questions have led us to you. Some of these people may have had a hand in causing you a lot of grief. It is just our job to get to the bottom of a couple of murders, that's all. They were a couple of real winners and deserved everything that came their way but you know how it is, you do what you have to do."

"That's right," Haggard said. "You do what you have to do. You guys had better get me a telephone so I can call a lawyer. I'm tired of sitting here. While you are at it you had better call Agents Rosza and Quiring so they can help answer some of your questions for you. It will make your job a whole lot easier."

"Oh, we've already talked to them, but you know…it sort of opens up a whole lot of unanswered questions for us. I mean you are certainly a victim of a major crime here but this Sheldon guy who works on your rig, he dies in your house? Sheldon is connected to Neigel and Ruddick…and they die too? We think somehow you and Sheldon, and maybe even Neigel and Ruddick, are connected. What do you think?"

"Look, I am about to lose my cool. Did you guys ever think that perhaps this druggy, this…Sheldon, was looking for the same thing that the other guys were looking for? The ones that broke in and killed Connie and that maybe even someone else was looking for the Cocaine at the same time. The drugs were seized from under my motorhome and they don't know it! They think I have it! They kill each other off looking for the stuff and you come after the victim. You are starting to piss me off!"

"Thanks for coming in, Dan. We'll be in touch," Howard Edicott said as he stood up.

"What, aren't you going to give me a ride back to my car? You want my co-operation but I have to walk back to my car?"

He started for the door but Edicott spoke before he was halfway there. "Oh, Mr. Haggard, I forgot to tell you that your friendly local police are waiting for you in the next office to talk to you about the fire. They'll give you a ride."

CHAPTER THIRTEEN

Ted Conway walked briskly into the small office in the radiator shop. He was about to make an announcement when he noticed a feeble old man standing in front of Herrera-Sanchez's desk.

The old man was dressed in clean but well worn brown pants, a heavy plaid shirt that did not go with his pants, and a sweater with missing buttons. The old man held a wallet in a hand that had a steady and continuous tremor.

Herrera-Sanchez turned and looked at Conway then turned back to look up at the old man. Leaning forward he spoke in a loud voice into the old man's ear. "Look, Mr. Asher, I told you we had to put in a new radiator. New hoses, clamps, and anti-freeze are all part of the original estimate but we had to get a special radiator for your car. It cost more. There was more labor and a shippin' charge and…"

"I don't have that kind of money," the old man said in a shaky voice. "You should have asked me first. You'll just have to take it out because I can't give you more than what I have."

"Take it out?" Jairo Herrera-Sanchez laughed in a loud voice. "That will cost you more labor, Mr. Asher. All this cost is mostly extra labor. I will just have to hold your car until you can pay your bill."

Old Mr. Asher looked crestfallen and turned very pale. His shaking increased and he had trouble speaking. "Pl…Please don't…don't do that. My, my wife needs to go to the clinic a lot. I need…need the car."

Conway watched as Jairo worked the older man without any remorse what-so-ever. He knew he would bleed him for every penny he could get and not give a damn for the man's problems or what it would do to him. The scam, used repeatedly, was highly successful on older people who did not know where to turn to for help.

The old man sat down unsteadily and his hands shook as he looked for money that was not there. Conway knew old man Asher from seeing him around the neighborhood. He was always talking to people on the sidewalk and pushing his wife in her wheelchair. Conway remembered that they always seemed to be smiling. Old man Asher reminded him of his own grandfather and it even upset *him* to see the old man suffer because of Herrera-Sanchez.

He walked over to the older man and looked over his shoulder at the bill. The bill was for six hundred and eight dollars. He looked up into Jairo's smiling eyes and his own disapproval must have shown because Herrera-Sanchez's eyes became cold.

"What is your problem, Conway?"

"I, uh…I think maybe I could help this old gent out."

"What does that mean?"

"It means that I'll pay the difference and you can give him his car."

Herrera-Sanchez did not like interference. He had a mark and there was money to be made on the sale of the car. "What is this? Is he a relative of yours or somethin'?" he sneered.

"I know the man. He needs a break that's all."

Herrera-Sanchez glared at Conway then looked at the old man sitting in the chair. Old Asher had not heard the exchange between the two men because of his hearing loss and he was unaware of Conway's offer. "What the hell are you friggin' playin' at, Conway?"

"I told you, I know him. You will really hurt the guy."

"So what do you want me to do, give him the friggin' job for nothin'?" Jairo asked sarcastically.

"No… Yeah, that would be great," Conway changed his mind. "Think of it as helping out the community," he said, not believing he had the courage to speak up.

"Frig the friggin' community!" Herrera-Sanchez said glaring at Conway.

Conway shrugged and crossed his arms over his small chest. "Whatever."

Herrera-Sanchez looked back at the old man, watching him as he fidgeted in the chair. Finally he stood up and walked around the desk to old man Asher. He took the bill out of his hands.

Startled, Asher looked up and looked at Jairo. "What...?"

Herrera-Sanchez ripped the bill in half and spoke in a loud voice. "It's okay Mr. Asher. Forget about it. It's on the house. Go and get your car."

It took ten more minutes of arguing to get old Asher out of the office and into his vehicle because he would not accept charity. Herrera-Sanchez finally sat down in disgust. He looked at Conway through slotted eyes.

"Look, I said I would pay the difference you didn't have to tear up the bill," Conway blurted.

"Shut the frig up!" Conway got up and pored himself two fingers of whiskey, not bothering to ask Conway if he wanted one. He took a swallow and put the glass on the desk as he sat down. "What the hell are you doin' here anyway? You are supposed to be lookin' after settin' up the meet with Mike Sigger."

"Oh," Conway came to life. "Yeah, I was on my way over there and I got some info. The police picked up this Haggard guy and took him downtown in the back of a police car."

Jairo leaned forward and carefully placed his arms on the desk, being careful not to soil his cuffs. "Is that a fact? Where did you get this?"

"I had the word out. I got it from one of the pushers. He heard one of the cops ask the guy if his name was Dan Haggard. They frisked him and took him away."

"What police station did he go to?"

"Local as far as I know," Conway shrugged. "Hell, it could be anywhere. The pusher didn't know the cop and I was lucky to stumble onto this."

Herrera-Sanchez took a sip of his drink then got up and walked out into the shop with Conway in tow. He looked out towards the lot and then turned and walked to a keyboard tacked onto the wall next to the office.

"Take the green Toyota. See what you can find out. I want to know where this Haggard goes when they release him."

"What if they don't release him?" Conway asked.

"They'll release him. Shit, they release everybody now. I want to know where he hangs his hat you got that? I want the bastard."

"I got it," Conway said walking out towards the newer green Toyota. "If he's there I'll find out where he's staying."

"You better! You cost me a lot of money today you little prick!" Conway walked towards the car. "And look after that Canadian shipment!" Herrera-Sanchez yelled after him.

* * *

Dan Haggard gently closed the lid of the cell phone and sat back in thought. His manager had just informed him that they had just lost two employees, one who was moving to another state, and one to a competitor. Hiring competent staff was becoming a problem and it took a long time to train them. He'd asked his manager to try to find out what the competitor did to take one of his people away and to go through the applicants on file. He did not need further business problems now. He just did not have the time.

He looked around the inside of the car and sighed inwardly. He was beginning to hate the sight of it. Lately he felt as if he lived in it. He had changed motels three times, once for convenience and twice because he felt uncomfortable and vulnerable.

It had been a rotten day. He had wanted to sit on the truck and trailer that was on the way down from Canada so he could find out where the drugs went but the police had made it rough for the whole day. The police had grilled him for a long time and on the same subject: the body found in his burnt house.

Feeling his stomach bang against his backbone for about the third time he reached for the ignition. He desperately needed a steak and a stiff drink in a quiet place so he could think. He needed to get set up on the tractor-trailer but there was no way he could do that without something to eat.

He was halfway into turning the ignition key when his cell phone began chirping. He opened the lid and said hello.

"Is that you, Dan? This is George."

"George. How in the hell are you?" he asked in a friendly voice. "Are you keeping an eye on my non-existent house?"

"Believe it or not, Dan, that's why I'm phoning. Some guy knocked on my door looking to buy your place. They were bloody strange looking dudes if you ask me anything."

"Why is that, George," Haggard asked as he turned the key to the off position and sat back against the seat.

"Well any fool can see that your house is gone but this one guy comes to my house and asks me where you are because he wants to buy your house. Any fool could see that he had about as much interest in your house as your insurance company."

Haggard laughed despite the feeling of being trod upon all day. "What did he look like?"

George gave an audible sigh over the phone. "Well he was a big mother, big belly anyways. Ring in his ear and balding. Not your typical house hunter if you ask me anything. Another guy was waiting in the car. Oh…and another thing, they wasn't from Washington neither. The plate was a different color."

"It sounds like I may have more visitors looking for me," Haggard answered.

"Yeah and I saw them look at that real estate sign. They may be trying the guy to see where you are. Does your real estate guy know where you are living or anything?"

"George, even I don't know where I'm living."

George gave a short hoot of laughter. A silence followed.

"Are you there, George?"

"I didn't mean to laugh at your predicament."

Haggard laughed and felt a fondness for his neighbor. "You know, George, Connie always liked you. You have a way of making people feel good."

George was silent for a moment and quickly changed the subject, a slight catch in his voice. "Ah…I'll keep an eye out for those guys but if I was you I'd be careful. They really did look like tough dudes. You know?"

"I know. Thanks for calling. I really appreciate the information."

He clicked off and sat thinking. By the description he had just received from George and from the information he had obtained in Canada, it looked like the Canadian was back looking for him and the missing Cocaine.

He closed his eyes. The image of a balding man with a large beer gut emerged. He stood in the dark with a shotgun while two Dobermans ran around sniffing the night air. Haggard smiled. If the guy was looking for him then that made it a whole lot easier. He just had to make sure that when they met it was on his terms.

It was time to move to another location again, something further out of the city with easy access but out of the clutches of snooping police officers that tied up his day. Time was his enemy and he was running out of it.

Starting the vehicle he headed for a popular steakhouse. He needed a quiet corner to do some thinking. The cell phone chirped again and in annoyance he flipped it open without looking at the call display. "Yeah."

"Hello, Dan. It's Amber," the low voice said softly into his ear.

He was not prepared to hear from Amber and was momentarily at a loss for words. His mind had been in a completely different world from the happy one that Amber used to be a part of.

"Are you there, Dan? Am I calling at the wrong time?"

"No…not at all. It's… It's just that I never expected to hear your voice. My world has been a little topsy-turvy."

"Dan I'm so sorry for all that you have gone through. I would like to get together when you are able. I…I'm having a hard time about Connie and I never really have had a chance to talk to you about the whole thing."

Haggard thought about that and realized that she was right and that they needed to talk. She had been a great and longtime friend to Connie and must find it extremely difficult having lost her. But he also knew that the timing was wrong. He needed to find that truck and anyone connected with it, especially the Canadian.

"You're not a great talker, Dan," Amber insisted. "I get the feeling I am intruding."

Haggard realized he was being rude. "You could never intrude, Amber. Connie really loved you." He hesitated briefly. "Look…I don't know if you are aware that the house was torched by someone. I am…"

"Yes. I heard, Dan."

Steering carefully around a dump truck he eased back into the curb lane and drove at a moderate speed. "I'm being charged for importing drugs. I have a court case coming up soon and very little time to try to clear my name. I had nothing to do with it but that won't matter if I am behind bars. You know why Connie was killed; they were looking for their drugs. I'm trying to track down those who did this to me…and to Connie."

"I know you must have a lot on your mind. I'm sorry I called, it's just that…"

"I'm glad you called," Haggard interrupted her. "You need to talk and to tell you the truth I need a friend myself. It can't be today however. Can you give me your cell phone number and I'll get back to you."

"Sure, that's no problem," Amber answered.

Haggard copied her number down and promised to call her the next day. He said goodbye and dropped the cell phone into the cup holder. He was about to turn his attention to his driving when he noticed a second cell phone he had tucked away in the vehicle's cubbyhole area in the dash.

The phone was the one he had taken from Frank Tully. What with everything happening, he had not had a chance to look at it or to see what was stored on it. It was something he could do over a glass of wine.

* * *

The green Toyota sat at the far end of the parking lot. Ted Conway was hunched down behind the wheel in a miserable mood. He'd sat outside the police station for what had seemed like forever, waiting for Dan Haggard to show up.

He almost missed him when he did finally appear because he was in the back of a police car. He had followed at a distance and watched as the cops delivered Haggard back to his vehicle at the gas station. He had high hopes that Haggard would head straight to the place where he was staying so that he could report to Herrera-Sanchez and hightail it. Haggard had not done that.

Here he was still sitting in the stinking car while the guy was in a restaurant filling his face. The smell of food blowing out of a vent was driving him crazy. *How can this be taking for ever!* Conway asked himself.

Conway lit another cigarette from the end of the one he already had going and considered what he should do. If he waited too long he would catch hell from Herrera-Sanchez and if he left before knowing where Haggard was staying then he would still get it.

Asshole's too cheap to hire more help, he thought. *I have to do every fucking thing myself. Screw it, if he's not out in another half hour I'm gone.*

Inside the restaurant Haggard sat sipping a scotch on the rocks while he scrolled through the phonebook of Frank Tully's cell phone. It mostly had names of people associated with telephone numbers in Canada but there were area codes for cities like Seattle, Bellevue, Tacoma, Spokane, and Bellingham. Dan knew many of the area codes because of his business contacts but a couple he did not recognize and they looked like they were out of state.

He started by concentrating on the names. It did not take long before the names of Roy Tully and Mike Sigger appeared. The names were not listed as such but the names were sufficient. Tully had to be the other brother that Vince Rizzo had mentioned before he went up in smoke in the barn and he did not need to guess who Sigger was.

Just looking at the names and the cell numbers of the two men made him feel like he was close. They were just the push of a button away. If he could find a good use for the phone and the information it would be a valuable tool.

His food arrived and he placed the cell phone onto the table. The smell of the sizzling steak made his mouth water as the waitress poured his wine. He had to force himself to eat slowly.

Twenty-five minutes later he walked out into a light breeze and a darkening sky. He headed for his motel to freshen up and to plan his next move. He had a feeling that most of what he needed to do would occur under the cover of darkness and he needed a change of clothing.

The one story motel was set off the highway and built in the shape of a horseshoe. Pulling passed the office he turned left and parked three units in. He then walked back across the driveway in the opposite direction from where he had parked towards the room where he was staying.

He opened the door, turned on a light and locked the door behind him. The place was depressing to say the least. It was about a homey as a bus station. It gave you a place to sleep and a place to get out of the rain and that was about it. The closed blinds did not make it any cozier and he had to force himself not to start to feel sorry for himself.

Looking at the neat but sterile room he decided to follow his own earlier advice and to pack up and get out. He did not feel comfortable closing his eyes in the place. He felt vulnerable, but then again he could not think of a place that he would feel at ease. He just needed to keep moving.

Outside, Ted Conway noted the name of the motel and where the Honda CRV was located. He punched in a phone number and waited for Herrera-Sanchez to answer. He turned the Toyota around and headed back to the street.

"Yeah," Herrera-Sanchez answered.

"I got him," Conway said as he turned the wheel, watching for traffic before entering the roadway.

"About friggin' time, where is he?"

"He's at a motel." He gave Herrera-Sanchez the name and location. "I'm heading to see the guys about setting up the meet now. The police had this guy forever and then he filled his face before he went home. I'm bloody well starving' myself."

"You're always starvin'!" Herrera-Sanchez said dryly. "Don't worry too much about the meet yet. I'll let you know. Go get somethin' to eat."

"Wha... What the hell? What's going on? I thought I was to meet them for the transfer?"

"Keep you britches on," Sanchez barked. "The load arrived but it looks like it's goin' to sit there all night. It won't be unloaded until tomorrow, maybe even the day after. We will have to keep an eye on the trailer until we can get to it."

"Okay. Are you going to pay a visit to this Haggard guy?"

"I have a couple of people who are interested in him. It shouldn't be too difficult to let them handle it. What number is he in?"

"Uh, I forgot to look. I…"

"What a friggin' idiot you are! How many rooms they got there— twenty, thirty? How the hell are we supposed to find him?"

"His SUV is parked in front of the door. It's a brown Honda. Go in and turn to the left. The place is built in a U-shape.

"Okay, stay by the phone." As Herrera-Sanchez began to hang up Conway heard him talking to someone that was in the room with him at the other end of the line. "That friggin' idiot…"

The phone went dead and Conway began to fume again. "Bastard, I deserve better treatment than this bullshit!"

Conway slowed down as he looked for a fast food restaurant. He was relieved that he could take some time off. *I need to find another outfit to work for*, he thought. There was no way he was going anywhere with Herrera-Sanchez and he knew he wouldn't make any real money working for him either.

* * *

Lloyd Quiring and Anthony Rosza entered the office and began their usual checks for messages and interoffice memos. Rosza sat behind his desk while Quiring stood by the window looking at a piece of paper.

"Got some Intel here," Quiring said almost to himself.

"Oh? Who's it from?" Tony Rosza asked with genuine interest.

"It's from the RCMP. Two guys crossed the border into Washington earlier today and they think we would be interested in them. They are active in importing and distributing in the Vancouver area. The targets were observed together in Canada just before they crossed the border but they apparently crossed over in different vehicles."

"That sounds like they are shadowing a load," Rosza remarked.

Quiring handed a sheet of paper to Rosza. "Here are their names and descriptions along with the vehicles they were in."

Rosza quickly scanned the information making a note to run the names through their own databank. "You know, I keep thinking about Dan Haggard." He leaned back and put his hands behind his head. "I can't help but think about him every time someone mentions the

Canadian Border. You think maybe his not-so-good friends are on the way down again?"

"Who the hell knows? There are a lot of active people out there. If they are shadowing a load then that narrows the field down as to who is capable of accepting it."

"You got Haggard's phone number?" Rosza asked Quiring.

Quiring took out his notebook and flipped through the pages. "I have his home number but somehow I don't think it will work anymore. His...here it is, it's the one his office gave us. You want to call him?"

"I think we need to remind him he's running out of time. We need to know if he comes up with anything, especially if he has any knowledge of a load coming south. You never know. It wasn't that long ago that Haggard was up there."

"Give him a call," Quiring agreed. "Maybe you'll make his day."

"Shit, I need somebody to make mine," Rosza sighed.

* * *

Sigger walked quietly alongside the entranceway to the motel followed by Roy Tully. He glanced towards the office and saw the night clerk watching a program on a small television. He quickly continued on by and stopped at the corner of the building.

Tully stopped beside him and looked around the end of the building. "Where the hell is the vehicle? I don't see any Honda."

Sigger was busy scanning the whole of the courtyard and quietly muttered to himself. "Why can't anything be simple?"

Sigger turned and walked directly towards the office, catching Tully unawares and left standing outside alone. He opened the door roughly and walked to the counter as the young man behind the counter let his chair fall forward.

"Can I help you, Sir?"

"Yeah, there was a guy in a Honda SUV staying here. His name is Haggard—a friend of mine. Is he still here?"

The clerk looked at Sigger a little apprehensively then consulted a box

with some index cards inside. "Uh… Uh, yeah, I think he checked out."
He lifted a card and nodded. "Yeah, he checked out about an hour ago."

Did he say where he was going?" Sigger asked without expecting an answer.

"No, Sir. People come and go. We don't ask and they don't say."

Sigger turned and walked out without thanking the clerk. The night air was heavy with the fumes of the city and the noise of traffic. He walked to the car and Tully followed and got inside.

"What the hell? Is he here or not?"

"No. He checked out an hour ago."

"Now what?" Tully asked.

"How the hell should I know? You're the big hotshot why don't you come up with an idea for once?" Sigger bristled.

Roy Tully's cellular erupted into a cheerful tune and he scrambled to get it out of his pocket. He finally pulled it free and looked at the call display. "It's from B.C."

"Don't answer it," Sigger said sarcastically. "You may have to pay long distance."

"Yeah," Roy Tully said into the phone.

Sigger watched Tully's face as he sat listening to the caller, trying to see if it was anything important. He could tell right away that something else had gone wrong.

"That's bullshit! Tully said. "No, no way! That's bullshit you bastard!" Tully began to scream into the phone. "What the hell are you saying? Where? What the fuck happened?"

Sigger sat and watched. It always fascinated him when Tully's eyes bulged out of his face. They bulged when he got angry and they bulged when he had trouble dealing with something or someone. It had always amused Sigger but this time he was looking at something different and he did not quite know what it was.

Several minutes passed and Sigger heard Roy Tully finally mutter in a small voice: "I'll be in touch."

"What was that all about?"

"Frank. They found… They found Frank. They say he committed suicide and blew his head off with his pistol."

The Mule

Sigger was shocked. "Now that *is* bullshit!" He finally agreed with something Roy Tully had said. He actually felt as shocked as Roy Tully. He knew that Frank Tully would never do himself in. "When did it happen?"

"They're not sure. Shit—we just left him!"

"Roy, there is no way your brother would do that! Who found him?"

"A cleaning woman...shit! Frank's wife will not even know about this. She's away."

Sigger sat and thought quietly. The better of the two brothers had just died and he knew his future was at stake now that there was only Roy. The future did not look very rosy.

"I hope Frank was careful," Sigger noted aloud. "The cops will be all over that place. They'll be sticking their nose into every cubbyhole they can while they have the chance."

"Why would he *do* that?" Roy Tully asked with a bewildered look on his face. "There's no *reason* for it."

"I'm telling you he did not..." Sigger's phone went off. "What?" He snarled.

He listened and said nothing for a full two minutes. "Okay, I'll call you back."

"Was that about my brother?" Roy Tully asked, lighting a cigarette with shaking hands.

"No. You won't believe this. You won't like it either. The new location, the barn—it burnt to the ground with Rizzo inside. He was done in by somebody."

"What the *fuck* is happening here?" Roy Tully screamed.

CHAPTER FOURTEEN

The motor-inn sat well off I-90 in the Issaquah area. After checking in, Haggard threw his meager items onto the bed and dresser and quickly showered. He pocketed the key and left immediately, leaving a light on and the blinds closed.

Driving west on the freeway he hit pockets of traffic that backed up for no reason at all before bursting out into open lanes with hardly anyone on the road. He worked his way to the other side of 405, crossing Mercer Island and then I-5, continuing into the industrial area just before Alaskan Way South.

The trucking terminal was a little difficult to find even with the map because it was screened from the roadway by older growth trees and a chain link fence covered in red berry-filled Pyracantha bushes. Finding the entrance on a side street he got out of the vehicle to a locked gate. He had the description of the tractor-trailer unit but the place was in darkness except for a dim light on a loading dock and he could not see anything from where he was.

Dan walked the fence to his left and followed it to the end on a weed-choked path. He allowed himself a small chuckle as he realized the fence ended without any intersecting fence. He stepped around the end of the fence into the shipping yard. Haggard was unable to see into the darkness to his left, it was either a field or some other area under development.

Walking to his right he angled towards the building and the parked tractor-trailer units. A dim security light on the building now gave off enough light that he did not have to worry about finding what he was looking for. It also gave off enough light to allow others to see him. He would have a lot of explaining to do if a police patrol showed up.

He walked behind the nearest trailer and kept to the dark areas and out of sight from the roadway, hoping there wasn't a night watchman walking around.

A cat ran rapidly towards him across the platform on his left and started mewing. Dan stopped and rubbed his hand down the length of the cat a couple of times as it stood next to him at chest level. The cat followed him, starved for attention and probably food.

It took two more minutes before he realized he was actually looking at the truck and trailer that fit the description he had obtained. He walked around to the front of the cab and looked at the license plate. It had Washington plates on it. He double-checked the number and the name of the trucking firm. Satisfied, he retraced his steps and walked back onto the street and his parked Honda.

Leaning back against the seat and settling himself behind the steering wheel he tried to figure out what to do next. It was a long way to daylight and he had no idea what time the truck would be unloaded. He started the vehicle and drove slowly around the area until he located a spot that gave him a view of the trucking firm and would allow him to sit in one spot without being too obvious to anyone passing by.

It was going to be a bit of a wait. He locked the car doors and settled back for a nap. He tried to get comfortable but couldn't. He lowered the back of the driver's seat until his head was an inch or so below the window edge and closed his eyes. Muttering, he still found it uncomfortable until he realized he was sitting on something. He reached behind him and found something sticking out between the seat cushions. He pulled out Frank Tully's cell phone. It must have fallen out of his pocket.

He hefted the phone a few times wondering what good it was. It was useless if he couldn't use the information it contained. He knew that Sigger and Roy Tully were in Seattle somewhere and probably looking for him. He needed to find them too. But he also knew that they would show up soon to pick up their drugs.

Opening the phone he thumbed the phonebook until the name Tully showed in the little window. Could he gain anything by phoning him? If they wanted him so bad maybe it was time to be on the offensive with these guys. He could rattle a few cages and shake them up while they were away from their home turf and in Seattle.

He was about to push the button when the cellular erupted in his hand. He jumped involuntarily, feeling immediately foolish and somewhat relieved at the same time. It took him a few moments to realize that it was not the one in his hand but his own cell phone in his inside jacket pocket.

While reaching for the phone Dan looked outside to check the immediate area. Nothing was moving in the darkness that he could see. "Hello", he said quietly.

"You *are* still up. I thought you kept decent hours, Mr. Haggard," a familiar voice said.

"And who might this be?" Haggard responded.

"Now you have hurt my feelings," Agent Rosza said.

"Okay, I've got you pegged. It's the whine of a Federal Officer." Rosza laughed into Haggard's ear. "What can I do for you?"

Rosza turned all business and Haggard sensed with the first few words that he had better pay attention. He placed the seat in an upward position for comfort and concentration.

"You have a court case coming up, Dan. You are running out of time. We need information if we are going to be able help you. Do you have anything for us? I mean something we can move on to help us back up your story?"

Haggard looked out through the windshield in the direction of the truck terminal and the darkened area of the trailers. A car drove by passing from right to left, his eyes automatically followed the car.

Telling the DEA about the trailer parked across the street was not going to do anything to clear him. It meant absolutely nothing except that he had information on the movement of some drugs. "I may have something for you later. Not now."

"Come on, Dan. Time is running out on you. Give us something! At least we will have a heads up and know which direction we are looking and what resources we will need."

"I'll tell you this much, a large shipment of BC Bud has already entered

Seattle and there is going to be a meet so the guys delivering it can pick up a load of Cocaine."

"Usual stuff," Rosza commented. "Where is it taking place?"

"I'm still working on it."

"You know, you're moving around in some dangerous territory. You need…"

"I need my space to find out who is behind this," Haggard cut in.

"You need back-up is what I was going to say. Remember that before you go busting in somewhere. Being dead is a hell of a lot worse than being in jail."

"Is it?" Haggard scoffed. "Easy to say when it isn't you."

"I really hope you can find what you are looking for. I really do. Don't get your hopes too high though, Dan. It takes us months and months to sketch the framework and organizational charts of these people. You do not have months and months."

"I am also not you. I have my own guidelines," Haggard said as he eyed another passing vehicle.

"Okay," Rosza sighed. "When will we hear from you?"

"As soon as I have something you will be the first one I call. You can bet on it."

"I'll say it again, Dan. Bring us something we can use and we will go to bat for you. Make sure you stay alive."

"I'll do my best."

Haggard closed the lid of the cellular phone and put the seat back into the rest mode that he had before. He knew that Rosza's offer was genuine but like Rosza said, he needed evidence that he was not involved. How he was going to do that he did not know. With Sheldon Porter having been found toasted in his house he now did not have a witness to say he had been set up. He needed the other half of the equation. Sheldon packed it under the motorhome but some other guy delivered it and some other guy provided it. He needed to find them.

Picking up Frank Tully's cell phone he again deliberated on what he should do with it. *What the hell, they already know I'm in Seattle. Maybe I can make their life miserable.*

Looking through the list of numbers, he came to the one he wanted and punched the send button and waited. The phone rang three times before being answered by an angry voice.

"What!"

"Tully," Dan said.

'What, who the hell is this?"

Haggard changed his mind about identifying himself and decided to wing it. "I hear you have arrived in town."

"Yeah, who is this?"

"Who do you think? No names on the phone, just say I'm part of the reception committee. You ready to make the meet?"

"The rigs not unloaded yet. I said we would call when it was ready. It will probably be midmorning. We already phoned on this. I won't be able to be there. I have to head back up."

"Why? I do not like last minute changes. What am I dealing with here?" Haggard demanded.

"I... My brother got killed. I... I have to get back."

"What, are you talking about Frank? Frank's dead?"

"Yeah..."

"How did it happen?" Dan asked, waiting for the answer.

"Some schmuck says he got shot. I don't have all the details. I have to get back to see what happened. If somebody did this to Frank I may have me a war on my hands," Roy Tully stated.

"So who makes the deal with us?" Haggard asked, already knowing the answer.

"Same as always, Sigger will do the meet and the exchange."

"We were not going to mention names," Haggard said, giving a little dig at Tully. The last thing he wanted now was for Roy Tully to leave and return to Canada.

"Well you fucking asked, didn't you? What the fuck, nothing has changed. We make the meet and do the deal then carry on. You just have..." Roy Tully covered the mouthpiece for a moment as he talked to someone else. "You just have this Conway meet us so we can get this over with."

Conway, Dan thought. Another name and someone else to look for, maybe before any meet tomorrow. "Everything will be in place but it won't go through unless you are there. We have other business to discuss."

"I *told you*," Tully seethed. "I have to get back to see about my brother. What, are you some heartless son-of-a-bitch or what?"

"I can appreciate your loss, Tully, but it is only one more day or maybe two and then everything will be wrapped up. Like you said, he has passed on. You cannot help him now. Phone and give your condolences and get your men to do what is necessary while you are away and let's get this business out of the way."

"Fuck you!" Roy Tully screamed. "Where do you get off telling me to ignore my brother? Where do you get off…?"

"It's your choice, Tully. I am only offering my help. If you go home we will do a deal maybe in six months or so."

"What? We have a truck sitting there waiting! We need to unload it and move it. You *know* that you son-of-a-bitch!"

"You be at the meet. The deal goes through as fast as possible and then we will carry on as usual. It's your choice."

The line was quiet for a good ten seconds as Haggard waited to see what Roy Tully would decide. He hoped it was to stay and finish the job. If he had Tully figured right he would look after himself and say to hell with the dead, brother or not.

"Okay, you prick. I will be there. I want to see you face to face."

"That's a wise choice. Do you feel comfortable with the meeting place or do you want somewhere else?"

Roy Tully hesitated before answering. "Keep it the same. We'll do the switch at the trailer then follow Conway to do the deal."

"Okay," Dan said and quickly disconnected.

Roy Tully thumped his hand down onto the top of the mini-bar in a fit of rage and sent a glass flying towards the door of the upscale hotel room. Several miniature liquor bottles remained standing and he swept them off with the back of his arm.

"Take it easy, Roy," Sigger said as he stepped forward. "What happened, what did the guy want?"

"He said if I went home because of Frank then the deal won't go through. He wants me there to discuss other business as he calls it; the heartless bastard!"

Sigger almost laughed aloud. If any heartless bastards were around he was looking at one. Roy Tully would bury a roomful of kids if there was a buck to be made. Sigger liked to think of himself as tough as well, and you had to be in this business, but only in your business dealings. Sigger did not see himself as being from the same mold as Roy Tully.

"That son-of-a-bitch," Tully continued to rant as he walked over and picked up and opened a miniature whiskey bottle, drinking it straight from the bottle.

'I don't get it," Sigger said almost to himself. "I mean I was the one who was doing this deal anyway. You were an afterthought."

"Fuck you, you asshole," Tully snarled as he whirled around, his mood ugly and dangerous.

Sigger held up his hands and waved them back and forth. "No, no, that's not what I meant. I mean you never decided to come on this trip until we ran into problems. Why the sudden worry about you leaving? The deal would have gone down if I had come alone. Who the hell were you talking to anyway?"

"How the hell should I know?" Tully said as he opened another miniature bottle from the bar. "He said no names on the phone."

"Yeah, I noticed you used mine enough," Sigger said. "Let me see your cell phone. See if the guy is on the call display."

Roy Tully reached into his pocket looking for the phone then turned and found it on the floor by the bed. He picked up the phone and went to incoming calls received. The first one that showed was Frank Tully's number.

Roy looked over at Sigger with a bewildered look on his face. Sigger walked over and took the phone out of his hands. Sigger stood there looking at the number in front of him.

"That's Frank's cell phone," Roy said.

"It sure the hell is," Sigger nodded. "I don't know who you were talking to but he was using Frank's cell."

"Who the hell is using Frank's phone?" Roy asked, the unfinished whiskey forgotten in his hands.

"Better yet, how did he get the damn thing?" Sigger wanted to know.

Tully looked at Sigger and slowly set his drink down. "Whoever that was, he must have been with Frank. I mean...how else would he get it?"

"Someone is playing head games with you," Mike Sigger continued. "They either want you in Seattle so they know where you are or they want to keep you away from Vancouver."

Tully shook his head in the negative. "This guy knew everything about the deal. He knew about the load, he knew about the meet, he knew about you and he talked like he was *in* Seattle, not Vancouver."

"Well then, you don't have a choice do you? You have to stay here for the exchange. We can't afford any more problems and with Frank gone it is going to be one big mess to clean up."

"Oh, I'll stay alright. Whoever this guy is, he and I have to meet."

* * *

Haggard decided to leave the area. There was nothing to accomplish by sitting on the trailer all night. He figured that he would need to be back by early to midmorning in order to see what happened with the trailer. He punched in another number as he drove away.

"Hello?"

"Hello, Amber. It's Dan. I know it's late but if you need company I am not far away."

"What happened? Are you okay? You said you couldn't make it."

"I'm fine. I...to tell you the truth I need a place close by and I need to be out of sight until morning. It will give us a chance to talk."

There was a slight hesitation on the phone before Amber replied. "Have you eaten?"

"Yes, I have. Thanks."

"Okay, I'll have a glass of wine ready for you."

He knocked on Amber's door and waited for her to open the door. She peeked out from behind some blinds at the side window then opened the door. Her smile was genuine but a tad on the tired side. She stepped back so he could enter the small but comfortable house. She wore tan slacks that tumbled onto cozy looking slippers and a medium blue pullover that was too large for her.

"Hi there," Dan said awkwardly, giving her a small hug and a kiss on the cheek. "Now that I'm here I feel stupid. It is pretty late."

Amber shook her head. "Not at all, make yourself at home.

She led him into a comfortable family style room that held a television, a large mirror, several overly stuffed chairs that did not match and a huge coffee table in the center of it all. It wasn't until he walked by it that he recognized that the table was a door, cleverly converted and finished.

"Hey, what a great idea," he said pointing to the table.

Amber smiled and gave a little wave as if to shrug off the compliment. "I made it when times were really tough. Now I can't part with it. Have a seat."

He picked a comfortable looking chair facing the television as Amber left the room. An old cowboy movie with Burt Lancaster came on as a commercial ended. As he looked around the room he liked what he saw. Soft colored walls, tastefully displayed artwork, and some photos completed the homey atmosphere.

A picture of Amber and Connie hung on one of the walls. Connie had one arm draped around Amber's shoulders as they sat in the darkness behind a robust bonfire. The camera had caught the flames at just the right moment and Connie's dark tan and Amber's natural tone were highlighted and made even darker. It made both their smiles even whiter in the night.

He looked at Connie's happy face in the photo and his heart felt like it was just too heavy to go on beating any longer. *She was so full of life*, he thought. *She was…*

"We were at a cottage that belonged to a friend of my dad," Amber said as she set some wine down on the table along with the cheese and crackers. She straightened and looked at the picture. "God, it seems like so long ago."

"How long ago was it?"

"Oh, I guess about nine years ago. We had so many good times together. I lay awake at night and the good times play across my mind like a movie. It helps to bring her back…but the movie runs out and I realize

I cannot just pick up the telephone and call her. I know what you are going through, Dan, but it is hell for me all over again."

"Yeah, you went through this when you lost your husband. Grant was a great guy. You are a very lucky person to have those memories. I have very few because she went too early. They took our future when they took her and they left nothing at all when they burnt the house down."

Amber poured the red wine into a glass and then sat down across from Haggard. "Yes I am lucky, but to tell you the truth those memories hurt like hell even while I am lost in the past thinking about them. The memories of my husband are fond memories but it still hurts to think of the loss and what we could have had. And now with Connie…sometimes it's just too much."

"I have something to show you," Haggard said as he pulled a delicate chain out of his wallet towing a gold locket that dangled and shimmered with small diamonds. "I guess I have one thing of hers. I found this in the basement of the house after the fire."

Amber leaned ahead and took it gently out of Dan's hand. "Oh I remember when you gave her this. She was thrilled. She wore it every day and kept patting it to make sure it was still around her neck."

"Yeah, well it's all I have left."

Amber had a sip of wine. "I may have some photos you can look at and a few you can have when you get time to look at them."

"That is very thoughtful of you. Yes, I'll take you up on that."

"You know one of the things that still upsets me? They would not let me in to see her at the hospital. That hurts me so much and I so much wanted to be there for her."

"You were there for her, Amber. We are all helpless in situations like this. We put our trust in doctors and nurses and machines and God and…sometimes none of them work."

Amber was quiet for several moments as she rubbed the cool glass back and forth across her forehead. "It seems so *strange* sitting here with you without Connie being here. I feel like I'm cheating on her or something."

"Don't feel that way. Connie was your friend and…she always will be. Are you feeling guilty because you are alive and she isn't?"

"Something like that… No not really guilt, but I guess it's as if I'm trespassing as I walk through the day. Like…why am I here and she isn't? It isn't fair. I see her so vividly in my mind but when I turn around, where *is she*? She was my best friend and I feel so empty without her."

Her eyes glistened and filled to the breaking point and then tears ran in shallow streams and flowed over her cheeks. She sat up straighter and gave a small shake of her head. "I thought I was all cried out."

"Don't be so tough on yourself. It isn't wrong to let it out."

"Oh?" Amber asked, looking into his eyes. "When does Dan Haggard let his feelings out?"

"I've let out a few."

"But not really," Amber stated. "You need to do more of that too."

"I can't afford to do that right now. I'll do that when I have a little peace inside my head. All that's in there right now is…is…"

"Hate?" Amber asked, "Maybe revenge and payback?"

"I'd call it justice. But if I do not find these people I will spend a lot of time in prison for something I did not do. The cops are bloody useless and helpless. I cannot imagine myself in some prison, but worse, I cannot imagine being in prison while those bastards are outside and enjoying life."

"You haven't touched your wine."

Haggard smiled and lifted his glass. "To Connie," he said in a husky voice and drained half the glass.

Amber took a drink and offered to refill his glass but he shook his head from side to side. "No thanks. It's funny that I haven't been here before, visiting you with Connie."

"We were all too busy doing are thing."

"I guess," Dan smiled back.

"You look beat. I have a spare bedroom and a hot shower will make you sleep like a baby."

Being here with you and being able to talk has taken the edge off. But yeah, I'm bushed." He smiled and stood up. "The bed sounds fantastic, are you sure?"

"Follow me," Amber ordered and showed him the small but clean room. "I don't get many guests so the bed doesn't get used much, there are no lumps anyway. The bathroom's just down the hallway."

Dan smiled and thanked her, feeling awkward standing in the hallway. "Now I know what you meant earlier about feeling strange. Somehow this is not real."

Amber came into his arms and laid her head on his shoulder, the smell of shampoo still in her hair. He could feel the quiet shaking of her shoulders as she sobbed without a sound. It was all he could do not to join her. She suddenly stepped back and turned away. "What time do you want to get up in the morning?"

"Is seven okay? I don't know what you have planned or what time you need to get up."

"Seven will be okay. I'll be up a little earlier but you won't be a bother."

After a quick shower, Dan climbed into the bed and lay back and closed his eyes. He was shocked when Amber called from the doorway that it was time to get up. She had a hot breakfast ready for him and said that she had to leave within the hour.

He sat down to the kitchen table a few minutes later. "I really needed that break. Thanks, Amber."

"I want you to come back, Dan. I couldn't do anything for Connie but I can damn well help you. You have probably been staying in motels all this time, am I right?"

"I can't do that, Amber. I have some very nasty people looking for me and if they knew I was staying here you would be in serious danger. You know what they did to Connie. I can't worry about that happening to you also."

"Well, you can remember the offer if you get in a jam and have no place to go."

"That I will," he smiled in reply.

Twenty minutes later he put on his jacket and gave Amber a light kiss on the cheek and a hug. "You are a special gal. Thank you."

"Nothing special about me," Amber smiled.

"Hey, any girl who watches cowboy movies with Burt Lancaster is special in my book."

He closed the door on her smile and scanned the neighborhood, thinking how quickly life and circumstances change. A short while back this would not be happening. He would not be leaving Amber's home early in the morning. He would have been with Connie.

As he turned the motor on his mood turned ugly with the thought of the forced changes in his life. He thought of Amber and Eleanor and all the pain that everyone suffered.

He reached under the passenger's seat and pulled the storage box out. Removing the heavy automatic, he placed it in the small of his back and behind his belt.

Was it really hate and revenge that drove him like Amber had said earlier. He sat and thought for a second before dropping the gearshift into drive. It was self-preservation for sure because he needed to clear himself. But, he asked himself, was it really payback time also? His mind flashed an angry answer. *You damn well better believe it!*

CHAPTER FIFTEEN

Howard Edicott stood in front of his desk leafing through the printouts that someone had put into his in-basket. The early morning sun played little tricks with the color of the fonts on the paper, changing the ink from black to deep shiny blue in places. Dust motes floated in and around his desk in the intense stream of light coming through the window. The third printout from the Drug Enforcement Administration caught his attention as he walked around his desk to read the communications.

It was shared intelligence related to his recent homicide victims, Neigel and Ruddick. Solving a murder case involving drug traffickers was difficult and especially homicides mixed in with turf wars between gangs. Edicott welcomed any information that came his way.

The information was from the data banks of the DEA and was sent over by Agents Rosza and Quiring as they had promised. It outlined the activities and connections between various and well known participants in the drug trade in and around the Seattle area. It also contained a list of arrests and convictions for the names on the list. The list showed many arrests but far too few convictions. Edicott was familiar with much of the information.

Names like Herrera-Sanchez, Neigel, Conway, Ruddick, were prominent along with many other well known users, pushers and major players. The name Porter also came up. Past surveillance had linked Sheldon Porter (deceased), with Ted Conway, Ruddick (deceased), and Neigel (deceased), and as such, with the Herrera-Sanchez organization.

The Intel was clear on the fact that the Sheldon Porter link was not solid and only guessed at as part of the organizational chart. It did however tie Ruddick and Neigel with Herrera-Sanchez. Edicott read further:

Sheldon Porter (his body recently found in a burnt house belonging to a Daniel Haggard of Kirkland) was believed to be a conduit in the movement of drugs to Canada. It is believed that the drugs were supplied by courier, Ted Conway, a street lieutenant for Herrera-Sanchez of Seattle.

It is pure conjecture that Porter had a falling out with someone in the organization but if so, the reason for any falling out is not known. It is felt that Sheldon Porter was probably killed because he was a security risk and that he was silenced to keep him from leaking information to authorities or anyone else.

As to why he was found in the home of Daniel Haggard, a suspected drug offender now before the courts, this is also unknown but Agents of the DEA believe Haggard was being paid back for the lost shipment of drugs, drugs seized by the Border Protection Agency while Haggard was entering the country from Canada.

Reading the printout, Howard Edicott tried to gather insight into the why and the how. He wanted some tidbit that might tie someone to the murders of Neigel and Ruddick. He thought of Dan Haggard, a picture formed in his mind of the man sitting in a chair during the interview. He wasn't sure, now that he thought back to the interview, if he had interviewed a victim, a con-artist, a drug trafficker, or a hit man. Edicott shook his head as he leaned back and massaged his tired eyes. He knew that it could be one, the other, or all of them together. "What the hell," he muttered to himself.

He knew that Haggard was a victim in the extreme and that he was facing serious charges. What he did not know was how Haggard was tied in with the whole scheme of things. Was it gang related? Edicott did not think Haggard belonged to any organized crime ring from what he had been able to dig up. But again, was he just a victim or was he the man he wanted? There were just too many unknown variables in the case. So far he was unable to find anyone on the street who even knew Haggard.

The telephone jangled on Edicott's desk and he picked it up; "Edicott here."

"It's Rosza, did you get our info?"

"Yes, I did. Thanks for sending it over."

"Well it probably won't help much but that isn't why I'm calling. We may need your services in the near future."

"Okay, what's up?"

"We received some Intel. A large shipment of BC Bud just hit the city and it's being tracked."

"So how can I help?"

"We may need local back-up on short notice. If this goes as planned we won't have much time."

"Okay," Edicott said into the phone, nodding his head in agreement. "I'll notify Special Weapons and the area supervisors."

"How's your investigation going?" Rosza asked.

"I'm struggling. I...I was just thinking about this guy Dan Haggard when you called and you know, I am really confused about this guy. Is he clean? Is he a victim? Or is he really involved in the drug business?"

"You want our opinion?"

"Absolutely," Edicott replied.

"Well, my partner and I have had many conversations about our friend, Haggard. We do not always agree by the way but I think we pretty well see eye to eye now on the fact that this guy is fighting for his survival. We think he was an unwilling mule and we think his house was torched and his girlfriend was murdered during a home invasion because he pissed some people off or they think he has the drugs stashed. Yeah, he's definitely trying to come up with some answers. The fact is, he is probably heading to jail for a long time. Trouble is we can't *prove* he is involved with unknowns or if he is just caught in the middle. He did have the Cocaine."

"I'm trying to figure out if he was involved with my two victims and as you just said, did he get hit because he pissed someone off? If he did, what did he do, did he hit my two victims? That would certainly call for retaliation from the guys around here."

Rosza gave a short laugh in Edicott's ear. "Could be, but to tell you the truth I don't know when he had the time. He's been back and forth to Canada a lot. He was there when his house went up in flames and he was in our custody when his house got broken into."

"So I keep hearing from Haggard," Edicott replied.

"He certainly was surprised to hear that they had found a body in his house. I was there and saw the reaction on his face. We've dug into Haggard's past quite a bit and since arriving in this area he has built quite a legitimate business. He just does not fit the profile that we have been trying to put together. He has just not been in any trouble that we…"

"I still have a gut feeling about him," Edicott interrupted. "He strikes me as the type with enough drive to go after these guys. He has the training, and like you say he's fighting to survive. I think any of us would have a hate on for these guys if they whacked our wife."

"Absolutely," Rosza agreed. "But I think you'll have a hard time putting this together if Haggard is involved. There isn't too much sympathy out there and there sure won't be much with a jury."

Okay, getting back to you request, do you have any idea what vicinity we are talking about? Where do you want back-up?"

"Not a clue," Rosza responded. "You can be sure that you won't be too disappointed. It will be in your backyard."

"Thanks," Edicott smiled.

* * *

Ted Conway drove the new Chrysler off of the car lot and accelerated swiftly, the transmission shifting smoothly through the gears. The dark metallic grey car sparkled even in the dark morning clouds that had moved in.

He felt like a new man. No more crummy vehicles for him. He was going to dress the part and he was going to move around in style. It was for damn sure he was not going to meet the Canadians looking like some poor second cousin to Herrera-Sanchez. Image counted in this business and you had to look successful to be successful. You had to demand respect. Nobody gives any respect to some twit driving some ten year old Dodge. *To hell with that noise,* he thought.

And another thing, Conway insisted in his mind, *an increase in my status and income won't hurt none either.* He was not looking forward to confronting Herrera-Sanchez about the matter however and his mood was soured slightly as he drove onto the freeway and pressed his foot further into the pedal. Anyway he had other plans if Sanchez didn't want to elevate his income and his place in the organization.

He had a lot of contacts and there were other ways of making a buck. He had put a bit more money into the car than he had expected. He needed to make more money. "Shit," he said aloud, his voice sounding muted in the car. "I should own three or four of these things by now."

Conway looked at his watch and turned on the radio, bouncing around in the seat and synchronizing his movements to the music as it boomed and pulsated with ear-splitting power through the open windows.

He had timed it just right. He would hit the truck terminal well before the Canadians arrived and he would make sure the driver didn't screw up as to where the trailer was to be dropped off. He would then escort the Canadians to the site for the transfer. A smaller truck with several men was already on its way to the lot for off-loading. Herrera-Sanchez didn't need to tell *him* how to run things.

Conway left the freeway ramp well above the posted speed limit and felt pure exhilaration as he dropped the automatic transmission down a gear and maneuvered around a stopped car at the intersection like it didn't exist.

The traffic thinned out and as he worked his way into the industrial area. The twin tailpipes gave a throaty bark and a rumble that sent a sense of pride surging through him. *This has got to impress,* Conway thought.

A few spatters of rain hit the windshield and Conway felt a surge of disappointment course through him. He hit each electric window one at a time, watching as it rose smoothly into the frame. He turned the volume on the radio up another notch as a Honda CRV turned onto the roadway a block behind him from a connecting street.

Ted Conway slowed as he neared the terminal and strained to see into the area behind the fence and bushes. Failing to see much he turned left and followed the fence until his visibility improved. He noticed the truck and trailer almost instantly and swerved into the entranceway and drove straight for the unit. Stopping by the driver's door he got out just as the driver was about to get inside. "Finished unloading so soon?"

"No, I have to move to another loading dock. Who are you?"

"Oh...sorry," Conway smiled. "I'm expecting the trailer and the container after you've finished unloading and wanted to see how soon you can drop it off at our location."

"You are a little early," the driver nodded as he climbed up onto the step and opened the door. It will probably be another hour and then the driving time to your location. Say an hour and a half."

Both men did not notice the Honda as it went slowly by the truck lot on the other side of the fence. They did not notice the driver observing their conversation nor did they see the attention that was directed towards Conway and his new car.

"Okay, I'll get out of your way," Conway smiled. "You know the way to the lot?"

"Yep, I have the address and I have a GPS system to direct me there."

"Cool," Conway acknowledged as he waved and got inside the Chrysler and moved it ahead and out of the way.

On the other side of the fence the Honda CRV turned around in the narrow street and disappeared before Conway exited the truck lot. Dan Haggard parked between two buildings and in the same location he had the previous night and watched as Conway stopped his car on the street and parked at the curb.

The driver was moving around in the car and Dan could not figure out what he was doing until he opened the window and heard the explosion of music.

The truck moved within the area of the terminal and Haggard could just make out the color of the cab through the hedges. He thought the truck was leaving until he saw it backing up again. So that meant that the guy across the street, who was probably Conway, was waiting for the truck to be unloaded. If he was correct, he knew he was also waiting to meet Sigger and the other Tully brother.

He started the vehicle and slowly reversed so that Conway was barely visible as he looked passed the edge of the building and between two parked cars on the lot.

The drizzle increased. It fell in a fine mist with heavier drops occasionally landing heavily on the already obscured windshield. Trucks passing by on the roadway looked as if they had a swarm of bees following them as the water was kicked up and then sucked along behind.

Haggard sat quietly listening to the radio as he waited and watched. A car pulled up exactly forty-eight minutes later and stopped next to the dark grey car facing in the opposite direction, driver's door to driver's door. He had a difficult time seeing the color, never mind the make or who was inside. He took a chance and flicked the wipers once. The wipers quickly cleared the window and he could see that the car was a light colored Malibu. The brake lights were shining through the rainy mist and the exhaust, creating intricate designs between the brake lights of the other car and the running water on his windshield.

Two men, the back of their heads just visible within the car, were talking to the guy in the large dark gray car. It appeared that Conway was doing most of the talking as his hands kept moving as he talked. The passenger in the right font seat of the Malibu was leaning to the left and appeared to be gesturing in an angry manner.

Looking across the short distance that he could easily walk in a few moments, Haggard knew he was looking at the guy who was Connie's killer. He had a powerful urge to simply walk across the street and end this guy's life right there and then. He let the feeling pass and sat back to watch.

Conway sat looking into the cold eyes of the two men seated in the car parked next to him. The driver had parked so close he could reach out and touch him. *Man, they're worse looking than Herrera fucking Sanchez,* he thought. The one in the passenger seat looked like he was ready to erupt.

"Looks like a new machine you have there," Sigger remarked through the open window. "I can smell it from here."

Ted Conway sat up a little straighter and beamed with pride and at the fact that they had noticed not only his car but recognized his success. "Yeah, I just picked it up."

"You sure it's yours? It looks a little too much for you," Tully said with a smirk.

"What do you mean? It's mine," Conway said defensively.

"Then why is it you look like a damn chauffeur sitting there?" Sigger laughed sarcastically.

"What the hell…" Conway started to say with a trace of anger.

"Never mind this crap! We brought the load," Tully cut in. "What's the holdup?"

"No holdup," Conway managed to say without displaying any of his inner nervousness to the two men. "I… The truck isn't unloaded yet. As soon as it starts to move we can get started. Everything will be fine."

"It had better be," Roy Tully muttered loud enough for Conway to hear.

"Yeah, we're in kind of a hurry to wrap this up," Sigger said as he looked at Conway with renewed interest. "You boys got us down here when there is no need. We could have done this in the usual way. My friend sitting beside me is very upset as it is."

"Hey," Conway said as he held up his hands in protest, "I'm just here to help you in the final leg of the shipment and to take you to the meet. It isn't up to me, you know?"

Tully leaned ahead and partially in front of Sigger. "I don't give a rat's ass. You guys never know what the other guy's doing. You all have your own separate little jobs, and I can understand security, but someone up top has called the shots on this and made me feel like an errand boy, jeopardizing *my* security by making us come down here with the load. I want to get this thing settled and over with as quickly as possible. You understand what I am saying here?"

Conway nodded and looked nervously over his shoulder, willing the truck to pull out from the lot. "Like I said, everything will be fine. Herrera-Sanchez will be there and we can do the usual exchange."

"Yeah," Tully growled. "Except now we have to figure out a way to take the coke back across the line."

"You notice anybody looking you over?" Sigger asked.

Ted Conway shrugged and looked bewildered. "What do you mean looking me over?"

"Strange guys, people following you, suspicious cars, you know? Did you notice anyone watching you or following you? We've had a hit back home and we think the guy's keeping tabs on us and this load," Sigger explained.

"No, I watch all the time. The fucking cops are always trying to follow me and I watch all the time. No way, I would see it right away if they were following me."

"Not the cops, you dope. Did I say anything about the cops? I said strangers or someone nosing around your business. Have you had any problems?"

"Not really. Except…well we had a hit on two of our guys and…hey you know what? You know the guy…we loaded the coke onto his motorhome for delivery up to you, well he went nosing around asking questions. One of the guys we had loading for us, he uh, he told us the guy came and did a job on him."

"Which means your man must have told him things." Tully remarked quietly.

"We think he did," Conway nodded.

"So maybe we can talk to your guy too," Sigger suggested.

"Can't, he's deader than shit."

"Do I ask how?" Sigger prodded.

"He… He got caught in a house fire. Must have been asleep or something and couldn't get out."

Sigger looked over at Tully; both men thought of the burnt out remains of Haggard's house and both men realizing that maybe the problems on both sides of the border were from the same source.

"Yeah," Sigger smiled. "Fire can be a real bastard. If I were you, Conway, I would really watch my back. Whether you did it or not the guy who owns that motorhome just may be after you now for torching his house."

Conway felt an involuntary shiver and just gave a weak nod in reply, not sure if he should have mentioned Haggard to these people. Herrera-Sanchez told him on many occasions to keep his mouth shut about his business but these two seemed to already know that it was Haggard's house that Porter died in. Not good.

"The guy's name is Haggard, right?" Sigger asked, jerking Conway away from his own private thoughts.

"Yeah, yeah, that's the name."

"Are you still having problems?" Roy Tully asked. "I sure as hell hope not because you need to have tight security for us while we are down here. Why haven't you taken care of this guy, Haggard?"

"He's like a butterfly, flitting here and flitting there, never in the same place," Conway said in an agitated manner. "We got a lot of people out looking for him though and believe me we have made his life miserable."

Tully's eyes seemed to bulge within his head, triggered by the thought of his brother and the man by the name of Haggard. "You don't know the meaning of the word miserable. I'll peel his bloody skin off of him when I find him. You and your boss remember that! He's mine."

"Well I am not about to get involved in any of that shit," Conway said as he shifted about in his new car. "I mean that is up to Sanchez. He lost a whole shit-load of coke and two of his best men were taken out. I don't think he will just hand Haggard over to you if he finds him, although he told you he was at the motel, didn't he?"

"He skipped before we got there," Sigger said as he wiped condensation off of the inside of his window.

"See, like I said, a butterfly."

The wind increased along with the rain and Conway and his new car were starting to get wet. He wanted to shut the window but was afraid of offending the two other men. He was going to suggest that he move to the other car when he heard the deep rattle of a diesel engine.

"The truck and trailer are moving away from the dock," Roy Tully said, briefly pointing towards the terminal.

Thank you, momma, Conway thought and zipped his window part way up as the other two men looked the other way. "You want to follow me?" he asked Sigger.

"You want to follow me?" Sigger mocked sarcastically. "I thought we were following the bloody truck!"

Conway shrunk back into his seat and quietly waited for the truck and trailer to appear on the street. *What miserable bastards. The sooner they leave the better.*

The tractor unit appeared at the gate to the truck lot and Conway watched in his rearview mirror as it made the slow turn out of the narrow entranceway. He glanced at Sigger as the man put his car in reverse and backed up and stopped facing him on the same side of the street. The truck and trailer passed both vehicles a few moments later.

Sigger allowed Conway to follow the truck and he fell in behind a full block to the rear. He did not want to appear to be part of anything Conway was involved in because he had no idea how much, if any, surveillance was going on in the city involving Conway and his group. He also wanted to keep an eye to his rear to see if anyone was tailing the little convoy to the trailer drop.

"Anyone back there," Tully asked, having watched as Sigger glanced in the mirror several times.

"Not that I can tell. It all looks normal."

"What are we going to do about getting the goods back across the border?" Roy Tully asked. He seemed subdued towards Sigger since he had received the news about his brother.

"It is a bit of a problem," Sigger admitted. "We'll have quite a load and I do not want to do the semi-trailer bit. It's too risky. Oh, we left your pick-up back there. When do you want to grab it?"

"Yeah, I'll get it later. Do you want to split it up and do different routes? That way we won't risk losing it all at the same time."

"I have an idea. Give me a couple of hours to think on it. Maybe this Sanchez guy has some resources we can use."

"Okay, I..." Tully's cell phone interrupted what he was going to say. He opened the phone and answered quietly. "Yes."

Sigger took his eyes off of Conway's car and the truck and glanced over at Tully. He was shaking his head back and forth as he listened. It looked like more bad news.

"I already know about it, Irene. I'm sorry that I can't be there."

Tully listened for a long while before speaking again. "I'm in Seattle and I will be back soon. No... No it was not that way. He did not *do that*, Irene. You know Frank would never do that. It must have been a...a robbery or something."

Tully was rubbing his forehead as he listened to his sister-in-law trying to deal with the death of his brother, Frank. It was another ten minutes before he was able to convince her that everything would be okay and that he would be there to look after things. The rain was pounding the windshield by the time he said goodbye to her.

"Is she doing okay?" Sigger did really want to know. Over time he'd had his problems with the Tully brothers but he had always liked and respected Irene Tully because she had always kept herself out of her husband's business. Although, he thought, maybe she played dumb on purpose.

"She's taking it very hard. It's like a bomb hit her. She doesn't understand why Frank would take his own life. I think I've convinced her that he didn't and if she believes me I know she would feel better about that."

"Yeah, because she doesn't want to think that Frank abandoned her on purpose."

"That rotten son-of-a-bitch," Tully yelled, spittle running out of the corner of his mouth as he pounded his fist into his right leg. "I'll kill him. I'll kill the bastard."

"We have to find him first," Sigger said.

The man they wanted to kill so badly was following them a block and a half to their rear. His eyes were riveted onto the truck, the Chrysler, and the rented vehicle with Canadian plates.

Haggard had his goals also, goals that had to be met if his life was to have any meaning at all. He knew the two men in front of him were searching for him and that they wanted very badly to meet him in person. Thankfully, Haggard had the advantage and didn't need to do any searching. He had already found *them* and there would be no question about them meeting. He definitely would meet them when it was time. His survival...not theirs, depended on it.

CHAPTER SIXTEEN

"Do you think he has anything yet?" Quiring asked as he spun the wheel of the older green van.

"I say let him alone for a while," Rosza said through a stifled yawn. "He's the one under pressure not us. When he gets desperate enough or when he needs our help, I think he'll call."

Quiring took his eyes off of the road and looked over at his partner, his eyebrows raised in a questioning manner. He looked back towards the road and the constantly stirring traffic and moved to a different driving lane. The van they were in had a landscaping company's logo on the side with just the right amount of abuse to make it look well used. Some of the telephone numbers were obscured with mud and it drew little or no attention.

"What? You think I am wrong? You think he won't call," Rosza asked.

"I didn't say a thing!" Quiring shrugged in reply.

"Yeah, well by the look on your face I gather you think we should call him."

"The danger in not talking to Haggard and not offering him assistance or an alternative is that he may just not want us around. You know what I mean? We may end up with nothing. What if he figures he can handle everything himself and just wants to get back at these guys?"

"That won't help him in court will it? He needs us whether he knows it or not. He needs information to clear himself or at the very least enough to cut a strong deal and a way out of the mess he is in."

"Okay," Quiring relented. "Give him a little more time and see what happens."

"Let's go around to Herrera-Sanchez's place."

Quiring looked in the rearview mirror and changed lanes again. "You want the house or the radiator shop?"

Rosza looked at his watch and thought about the man's known habits. He was not known to be an early riser. He let the guys on the lower end of the ladder open and maintain the radiator shop as a business front in case any legitimate customers came through the doorway. He kept late hours and was known to like long 'business' dinners and meetings.

"Go by the house first. See if anything is happening."

"You think he's entertaining the Canadian gang at his house?" Quiring asked as he rummaged around the filthy counsel.

"What the hell are you looking for?" Rosza said in an irritated manner.

"I thought I had a candy bar here someplace. I'm getting the pangs."

"I ate it," Rosza said, looking out his side window to hide his smile.

"You ate it! My candy bar and you ate it! I'm getting hungry. Being my partner doesn't mean you eat my food," Quiring fumed.

"I'm your savior. I'm stopping you from killing yourself."

"Yeah, well I don't need to be saved or for you to commit suicide on my behalf."

"Quit your bitchin', I'll get you a nice fresh apple. Anyway I don't think the guys from Canada are going to be showing up at Sanchez's house. The last thing he wants is a business deal out of that place. No, he keeps everything in one place."

"You remember last year the local cops hit that place with a warrant? They never found a damn thing."

"Herrera-Sanchez is not stupid. He may be uneducated, but he isn't stupid. If he is doing business out of that shop then the drugs have to be there somewhere."

"We should have taken Conway in and hit him hard," Quiring remarked as he turned onto the freeway entrance. "That little shit would never take a fall of ten years if he thought he could cut a deal."

"I'm sure Conway is well paid to keep quiet. He may be a tough nut to crack. We'd find him in the gutter the next morning if he did open his mouth. These people spend a fortune paying people to transport and hide their goods *and* to keep their mouth shut; you know that."

Quiring shook his head in agreement. "Yeah, million dollar tunnels, high-tech communication gear and a distribution network to rival Wal-Mart." He shook his head again and looked out the driver's side window in disgust. "And yeah, like you say, all those paid flunkeys to run interference".

Rosza smiled in sympathy. "Yeah, and they've got nothing but time."

"I still say we should take a crack at Conway," Quiring insisted.

"We will, we will." Anthony Rosza smiled, looking at the clearing sky on the horizon.

It took another twenty-five minutes to get to Herrera-Sanchez's neighborhood. It would have been sooner if Quiring hadn't decided to stop at a gas bar to pick up a couple of sandwiches. He pulled parallel to the curb a hundred feet short of the driveway. The huge house was visible through well-tended shrubbery and trees.

"Look at that place," Rosza muttered almost to himself.

"Makes you want to weep, doesn't it? How do they get away with owning all this stuff without any visible signs of a huge income?"

"Out of my league," Rosza smiled as he settled back in the seat. "Are you going to share one of those sandwiches?"

Quiring looked over at Rosza and gave him a withering look. "I should share my food with a thief?"

"It was only a candy bar for crying-out-loud and not a very good one at that," Rosza sniffed.

"Here," Lloyd Quiring smiled, tossing a wrapped sandwich at him. "You owe me big time."

"Thanks. What am I eating?"

"It's called roast beef."

Rosza sniffed at the sandwich and looked back at Quiring. "Is this lettuce or is the beef a green color?"

"Funny. If you don't want it, just say so and..." Quiring swallowed part of his sandwich and pointed out the windshield of the old van. "A car just pulled into Herrera-Sanchez's driveway."

"So I see. You recognize the vehicle at all?"

"No." Quiring opened the driver's door and stepped out onto the pavement, grabbing a clipboard from between the seats. "I'll go see if I can get a look at the plate."

Rosza watched as the tall redhead sauntered up the street, munching on his sandwich as he crossed over to the other side. He watched as Quiring reached the end of the driveway, looked to his left, and then disappeared out of sight towards the house. "Shit, stay the hell where I can see you."

A full minute went by and Rosza was getting concerned. He was about to get out of the van when his partner walked into view and slowly walked back towards the truck. He opened the door, tossed the clipboard between the seats and got in. "Nobody in sight. The plate number is on the clipboard if you want to radio it in. It's a tan colored Lexus."

"Okay. I never got a look at the driver. Is it a man or a woman?"

"I didn't see either. The windows on the car are pretty dark."

Rosza picked up the under-dash microphone and requested the registered owner for the plate. "What's it look like up by the house?" he asked as he took a bite of his own sandwich.

"There are a lot of shrubs. You drive under an entrance way and the driveway has a big turn around with a pond in the middle on the other side of the main entrance. The place reeks of money. The Lexus is parked by the front door under the roof. No sign of anyone outside or in."

The radio came to life, static briefly crackling through the speakers before the voice became clear. "I have your R.O. for you when you are ready to copy."

"Go ahead," Rosza said quietly into the microphone.

"The vehicle is registered as a 2007 Lexus, brown in color, to DZ Enterprises, Seattle. I have the address and VIN number if you require it. You want it saved?"

"Roger," Rosza replied and replaced the microphone.

"Another player," Quiring guessed. "Who the hell is DZ Enterprises?"

"Is it the initials DZ do you think? Maybe its deezy and the guy's Spanish," Rosza laughed. "You know, as in dizzy?"

"You're dizzy. You want my guess I say he's a buyer. If he is it's a little unusual for these people to show up at Sanchez's place to do business. He doesn't like the exposure."

"We have some digging to do. I want to know who this DZ Enterprises is and what they do. I also want to know what possible business they have with our friend over there."

"It can't be good if it has anything to do with Herrera-Sanchez. Man I hate hyphenated names," Quiring said as he started the vehicle. "Where to now, the office?"

"Are there other cars up at the house?"

"None that I could see, just the Lexus, but there's a three car garage."

"Let's get back to the office and do some digging. Then maybe we can find that monkey, Conway."

"Now you're talking," Quiring smiled, putting the van in gear.

* * *

Herrera-Sanchez paced nervously in front of the huge fireplace, fidgeting with his cuffs one moment and his tie the next. The gaping and cold black hole of the fireplace matched his inner feelings of anxiety. He took nervous glances at his visitor.

The other man sat in front of an enormous picture window. His body was in silhouette and the outside glare made it almost impossible to see his face never mind read his thoughts.

Herrera-Sanchez knew he was at a disadvantage and moved to the side to avoid the gleam and to ease his headache. Bright lights would bring on a migraine if he wasn't careful.

"Why don't you sit down, Jairo?" the visitor asked.

"Can I get you a drink?" Herrera-Sanchez countered.

"Yeah, sure. A scotch if you have one, on the rocks."

Sanchez almost ran to the hidden bar in the corner of the room. He touched a button and two mirrors slid apart revealing a fully stocked wet-bar with the appropriate glasses and a small ice-maker built into the wall.

Placing some ice in a glass he quickly surveyed the bottles and selected the best scotch he could find. His hands shook as he splashed the liquid over the ice. Selecting another glass he filled it half way with Canadian whiskey and not bothering with ice or mix. He took a quick swallow of his drink and the liquid slowly burned a path on the way to his stomach.

He glanced quickly over at the dark silhouette by the window and carried the glasses over. "Here you are. Let me know if it's not to your likin'," he gushed, his face blooming with a slight reddening. He was far from his arrogant and cocky self.

"That is just fine, thank you. Now sit down," the silhouette commanded.

Herrera-Sanchez moved off to the other man's right and found a comfortable chair that lessened the effects of the shadowy profile before him. He took another large swallow of his drink and waited for his guest to speak. He started to adjust his tie but quickly stopped the movement, recognizing the fact that it made him appear very nervous.

"Here's to you," Sanchez muttered as he raised his glass and lowered the contents again. He noticed that his guest had not touched his drink and only sipped at it in reply to his toast.

"Let's get down to business," the other man said in a brusque manner. "I am very concerned about some events that have taken place, events that are under your control."

"Uh, uh… What events in particular?" Jairo managed to ask.

"Now don't you go getting sly on me, Jairo. You have lost a great deal of our…no that is not true, you have lost a great deal of *my* product. No product available for my customers represents a loss of income. I have paid for something you have lost. I was depending on you to look after my interests."

"I, I ah, I'm on top of this. I have Conway meetin' with the Canadians right now as we speak. We are gettin' a better price on the next deal. I have a buyer…"

"I am not talking about the Canadians. I don't give a shit about the Canadians! They paid for their order and it was delivered. If they lost it, it's too bad. I am talking about the loss of two good men and a whole shipment of big C. Plus—plus mind you, a big pocketful of change."

"Yes, yes, I know who did this," Sanchez stammered.

"Then why is he still walking and talking? Where is my money?"

"It is…he is hard to find. We had a canary who talked too much and that is why we lost everythin' on the hit at the house. The canary is out of the picture but the guy responsible is all over the place."

"I *know* all this already and I know who the *guy* is, Jairo," the other man said with a sigh. He hesitated then asked quietly: "What is your job, Jairo?" He took a sip of his scotch as he waited for a reply.

"To run the deal here," Herrera-Sanchez shrugged. "To make sure everythin' is in place and the stuff comes in and goes out when it should."

"No, it is not. Your *job* is to make sure that I don't have *any* problems and I don't lose *any* of my shipments. Especially to some local dimwit who makes me look bad in the eyes of my business associates. I am not pleased at your performance."

"With all due respect, this came at us out of the blue. I am workin' on findin' this guy and when I do he will wish…"

"I don't want to hear it," the visitor announced. "Do you have any idea how much I have exposed myself by coming to see you here? I have spent years setting up this network that has no outward connection to each other. You are jeopardizing this network by your sloppy work."

"It will be handled," Herrera-Sanchez said somewhat forcefully. "I do not like this either. I do not like some…some…jackal makin' me look bad. As soon as I wrap up this deal and the transfer with the Canadians, I will put everyone to dealin' with the matter."

"Good. I want you to be very clear in what I am saying here today, Jairo. You are paid exceptionally well. If I have any more losses I will be forced to take a very serious look at your ability to run things for me. You have to perform just as well as the others. None of the others seem to have problems with their teams."

"I have always performed and delivered," Jairo Herrera-Sanchez stated in a huffy manner. "You have no reason to complain of my past performances. This is only an isolated incidence."

"One isolated incidence too many," the other man said quietly. "When I lose that much money in a single day…I get very annoyed."

"Like I said," Herrera-Sanchez mumbled, "I will deal with it."

"Enough! I have to leave. You will fix everything and we will not have to have this conversation again. Is that correct?"

"Yeah, just like always," Sanchez said as he stood up to escort his guest to the door.

"Good, good, I expect to see everything back to normal with no further problems. Goodbye."

As the door closed on the other man Herrera-Sanchez walked quickly back to his chair and finished off the remaining alcohol in his glass. He walked to the bar and refilled his glass, his hands shaking with anger at being humiliated and treated like a street soldier.

He had no delusions about being *fired* from his job. If something went wrong again he would be placed in a lower position and his status would suffer immensely. Besides no one was ever fired, you were buried.

His thoughts drifted towards those responsible for making him look bad and for jeopardizing his position. It sure as hell wasn't *his* fault that the Canadians screwed up in the pick-up of the shipment. It wasn't *his* fault that they invaded his territory and hit Haggard's house without his blessing. It wasn't *his* fault that Sheldon shot his mouth off to Haggard and it sure as hell wasn't *his* fault that he was robbed. Conway should have been on top of all that stuff out on the street.

Conway! Herrera-Sanchez screeched in his mind. *You are the one not doin' your friggin' job, not me.* He hurried over to a corner table and picked up a cordless telephone. He punched in one number and almost threw his glass at the wall in his impatience and anger. He stopped doing so only because he remembered his surroundings.

The phone was answered on the third ring; "Yeah."

"Where the frig are you?" Herrera-Sanchez half sputtered and half screamed into the mouthpiece. "Get your friggin' ass back here right now!"

"I'm with the Canucks. I can't leave *now*! I was supposed to get them to the transfer and then down to the shop later to see you," Conway answered in bewilderment.

"I changed my mind. I'll meet you down at the shop. I am totally pissed at you and you have made me look like an amateur. The Canadians can wait until it gets dark for the transfer. Put a couple of men on the trailer and tell them to come back when it is dark."

Conway was silent for a moment, astounded at the turn of events and at the venom directed towards him for no reason at all. He was silent for a moment too long.

"Are you there you friggin' snake? I am talkin' to you!"

"I don't understand the problem, Jairo. You have not seen these Canadians. They are two mean looking bastards and they will not like being kept waiting."

"I have met them before. What, I should worry about this Mike person? You tell him we will do business after dark. Tell them to go sightseein' or somethin'."

"It's not Mike, it's the other guy. He looks like he wants to kill someone...anyone, just to make himself feel better. He is pissed off at the whole world."

"You get your ass back down to the shop now!" Herrera-Sanchez snarled and slammed down the phone. He drained his glass, belched, and inhaled the alcoholic fumes. "Things are damned well goin' to change around here," he said aloud. "Jairo Herrera-Sanchez is not goin' to pussyfoot around any friggin' more."

Conway walked slowly towards the two waiting men and made a show of being busy with the phone as he desperately tried to think of what to say to them. He put the cell away in his pocket as he became aware of their movement towards him. As he looked up they stopped in front of him. They just stood there, waiting for him to say something.

"I just got a call." He shrugged his shoulders in way of an explanation. "There's been a change. We have to do this after dark."

Roy Tully took a step forward, his eyes piercing and dangerous. "Are you trying to set us up for something, Conway?"

"No, no! Look, I'm just doing what I am told. You guys...we want things to go right. If we have to do this after dark it is because we are worried about security of the shipment and want the transfer to go smoothly. Man, we want you out of here with your goods."

Mike Sigger stepped up next to Roy Tully and looked closely at Conway before he turned to Tully and spoke quietly into Roy Tully's ear. "They haven't jerked me around in the past, Roy. Maybe it would be better after dark."

"I don't think so," Tully countered. "During the day we look like a bunch of guys working. At night we attract attention. I want to know what the hell is happening here."

Ted Conway decided to tell them the truth. He knew that Mike Sigger might understand the situation he was in as Mike essentially did the same job as he did. Besides, Sigger had seen Herrera-Sanchez and his outbursts in the past.

"You look a little pasty around the gills, Conway," Sigger said, his head at a thoughtful angle as he studied Conway. "Are you playing at something?"

"Mike, Sanchez is pissed off at me for something and wants to see me right away. It has nothing to do with you guys. He is constantly on my back. He said that you guys should go sightseeing until it gets dark."

"Sightseeing," Tully repeated, his eyes starting to bulge. "He wants us to go sightseeing?"

"I'm just repeating what he said. I'll secure the load until later."

"I'll remember his hospitality, you tell him that for me," Tully answered. "I will remember how poorly we have been treated."

Mike Sigger stepped forward and placed his hand on Conway's shoulder, turning him away from Roy Tully as he walked away a few steps. "Okay, Ted, we'll go away for a while." Sigger pointed towards the trailer. "We'll do it your way but if we loose that load over there before the trade takes place I will hold you personally responsible." He tightened his grip on Conway's shoulder and squeezed to the point of pain. He whispered in Conway's right ear. "If we lose that load I'll slit your throat my friend, make no mistake about that."

Conway felt as if a cold hand had touched his soul and he quickly stepped away from Sigger. "I wouldn't screw you around, Mike. I'll have several guys watching it. Nobody touches that load. I can't help what the cops do, but anyone else, no way."

Sigger looked at Conway for any sign of treachery. "We'll be back after dusk." Sigger turned and walked away.

Ted Conway let out a very slow breath and moved towards the trailer. He spoke quietly for a few moments with the four men that were parked close by in a large cube van. He set up instructions for guarding the shipment and made arrangements for a gofer for meals. He made sure they all had his cellular and that they were all armed.

This was going to cost him extra out of his own pocket to keep these guys happy. Again he was being screwed over by Herrera-Sanchez. Sanchez just didn't get it when it came to looking after his crew and keeping their loyalty.

Getting into the new car altered his mood somewhat. As he heard the throaty response to the engine he momentarily put other thoughts from his mind. He was just not going to let Herrera-Sanchez spoil everything he did.

As he shifted into gear he thought of his need for more funds. He needed more money but it didn't sound like the high and mighty Mr. Jairo Herrera-Sanchez was in the mood to talk about it. He knew there never would be a *right time* to talk to Sanchez but he would just have to see about that.

Dan Haggard had a problem. The trailer had been backed and dropped onto a small lot by a railway track. It was partially hidden from the road by a concrete wall and other large containers but he had his targets in plain view as they stood talking by the roadway. It looked like everyone was splitting up for some unknown reason. He watched as Sigger and Tully got into their vehicle and it looked as if they were preparing to leave. The little guy from the Chrysler walked further onto the lot and was giving instructions to a group of men and it looked like he was going to leave as well.

If he followed Mike Sigger and Roy Tully he was sure they would have to eventually return to the location of the trailer and their goods. As much as he hated to leave them, he needed intelligence.

Haggard got a good look at Sigger as his head poked briefly out of the driver's window as he looked back prior to pulling away. He looked over to his left just as Conway dropped into his car. *No, this is the one*, he thought. *This is the guy with the answers.*

He waited until both vehicles were out of the immediate area before he trailed along behind Conway. Sigger's light colored vehicle turned right at a stop sign but the Chrysler burnt rubber as he left the stop sign and drove straight ahead.

He closed the distance as the traffic got heavier but he could see that the driver was paying absolutely no attention to his surroundings. The blast of music and the deep thump of a boom box reverberated back upon him as the driver continually thumped the steering wheel in an uncoordinated rhythm.

Dan needed to divert the guy from his intended route and get him somewhere isolated, and soon. But the question was how and where? He would need the other vehicle to stop otherwise he would attract too much attention by forcing him off of the road.

Moving in closer, Haggard got a closer look at the Chrysler. It was obviously new. The driver was still bouncing around in the interior of the car in semi-synchronization to the horrible noise that he seemed addicted to. He jotted down the plate number in case he lost him and continued to follow close behind. It looked like Conway was headed for the freeway.

Haggard knew that if he followed and did not try to intercept there was a good chance the other man might lead him to another and good source of information. On the other hand the guy could just be going to a crowded bar for lunch or to visit one of his customers. He needed the information now.

Conway turned his radio up even louder as he approached a yellow light, listening to the rewarding blast of the deep throbbing base. The Chrysler glided smoothly to a stop and Conway took the opportunity to glance around the interior of the car. He was about to congratulate himself on his purchase again when his head snapped viciously to the rear and into the headrest. "What the hell…"

Conway was momentarily disoriented, unable to comprehend what had happened. He looked to his left, then out the windshield and then into the rearview mirror. From his position in the car, the top part of a grill stared back at him. It finally dawned on him that he had been hit by someone. Then it really struck him that his new car had been hit.

Getting out of the car he turned towards the vehicle behind him, anger and disbelief playing across his face at the same time. Other cars rolled forward as the light turned green while other drivers pounded on their horns in an angry unison behind the accident. "What the fuck are you doing, man?"

The Mule

Haggard opened the driver's door and got out from behind the steering wheel in a calm and sheepish manner. He approached the Conway who was now bending to look at the damage to the rear of his car. "Sorry about that. I mean it happened so fast. You made such a sudden stop."

Haggard watched as the other man went from being angry to absolute fury. He watched as the man tried to control himself. He turned and moved to look at the damage on his car and moved back to look into his eyes again. He saw Conway size him up and saw the subtle change in the other man's eyes when he new he could not take him on.

"Look what the hell you did, man! Two or three hours out of the showroom and you trash my new car. Shit, man, look at the damage. The rear decks crimped and the bumpers bent in and shit, look at the taillight." Conway smashed his closed fist down onto the damaged car in frustration and turned away. He immediately turned back to face Haggard. "What the hell do you mean I made a sudden stop? I was sitting still when you smucked into me!"

"Hey, calm down," Haggard answered. "I'll look after the whole thing, okay? It was my fault. I don't want the police or the insurance involved. I'll make it up to you."

"How are you going to make up a new car? The whole thing is devalued. I'm going to lose big money here. It's brand new. *I just got it!*"

Haggard walked back towards the Honda CRV, the smaller Conway following him. He saw that the Honda had sustained damage to the bumper and grill. "Pull off the road and we'll exchange names and talk," Haggard suggested.

"We'll do more than talk," Conway yelled as he walked back to his car. "I want some serious money here."

Haggard pulled out and drove around Conway as he was getting into his car. He smiled as he looked at Conway's face, knowing that the other man thought he was going to drive away. *If he only knew,* he thought.

* * *

"Nothing, absolutely nothing but more blind alleys," Rosza muttered. "This is getting monotonous."

Lloyd Quiring looked up from an overdue file he was working on. "What did you find out?"

"DZ Enterprises is a subsidiary of a company called MCMXCIX Holdings of Greater Seattle. This in turn is an annex or auxiliary to another company called Big Little Ocean Enterprises which is listed as an import and freight forwarding service. I'm afraid to look up and see if Big Little Ocean Enterprises is connected to something else."

"I don't mind telling you, I am bagged," Quiring said around a large yawn. "Nothing is ever simple is it?"

"Yeah, tell me about it. Just try and dig up who the principle parties are without a lot of bullshit. All I want to know is who the hell is driving the Lexus. It's a simple thing, right? My ass it is. Let's go and get something to eat. We can't afford to be in the wrong place at the wrong time with this."

Quiring stood up slowly. He produced another massive yawn and then shook his head and shoulders from side to side in an effort to wake up. "Why is it that lately I feel like I'm *always* in the wrong place at the wrong time?"

CHAPTER SEVENTEEN

"Where the friggin' hell is Conway?" Herrera-Sanchez yelled as he violently drove the door against the inner wall of the radiator shop. "Where is he? I told him to friggin' *be here!*

A youth, hired to run errands and clean the shop, looked up in surprise and shock, quickly taking his crossed feet off of the desk and thumping the chair forward. He tried to stand but a pocket of his filthy coveralls got caught on the arm of the chair. "I…I don't…"

"What the hell are you doin' in my chair you little bastard? I don't pay you to sit around lookin' like you own the place. Where the hell is Conway?"

"He isn't here. I…I haven't seen him," the youth said as he quickly scampered away from behind the desk. "I was just going to make a call to one of the customers and…"

"Don't you bullshit me you little punk. Get your ass out to the shop and do somethin'."

Herrera-Sanchez sat down at his desk and pushed some papers around as the youth hurried out of the office. Not having any interest he shoved the papers out of his way. He carefully laid his wrists onto the edge of the desk, his cuffs set at a forty-five degree angle. Through the dirty window to the shop he could see one car being serviced. A pick-up truck was parked with the hood up, the front end sticking partially through the bay door.

He sat and fumed, still feeling humiliated because of the reprimand he had received. He thought again of how his position in the organization would be in jeopardy if his people did not do their job. Conway was a key player in that he relied on him to be at his beck and call and to handle many issues that kept him—Herrera-Sanchez—separate and out of the eyes of the law.

Herrera-Sanchez gradually felt himself calming down. He knew he had acted stupidly. He should not have demanded that Conway return to the radiator shop while he was handling a transaction but what he had been told at his house was actually correct. He had to get to the bottom of these problems. Shit, not water, ran down hill and Conway was going to get his fair share of it.

Herrera-Sanchez picked up his phone and punched in Conway's cell number. It rang numerous times before a recorded message said that the cellular customer was not available or was away from the phone.

"Where the hell is Conway?" Herrera-Sanchez bellowed to no one in particular. Out in the shop the youth walked around to the other side of the vehicle being serviced and out of the view from the office. There was no way he wanted any part of the vicious temper that could spring without warning from such as vicious little man.

* * *

Conway watched in frustration as the Honda CRV moved rapidly away from him. Traffic kept going around him and back into his lane, cutting him off from any forward movement. He laid on the horn and punched the accelerator and cut off a young woman who gave him a hostile look and the middle finger in an upper movement of her hand.

"The hell with you, bitch," Conway muttered to himself, carefully closing the gap between himself and Dan Haggard. He watched and was somewhat relieved as the other vehicle pulled off of the main roadway and appeared to be looking for a place to stop. "Okay asshole, stop already."

Haggard eased the CRV onto the back of a lot behind a deserted and boarded up gas station. He shut the vehicle off and watched as the other car stopped behind him. He watched as the other driver got out and walked towards him, a superior look replacing the look of anger on the man's face.

"Okay, what are you going to do for me?" Conway said at Haggard's window.

"Get in." He pointed to the empty front passenger seat. "We'll exchange names and we'll talk cash."

Conway hesitated, looking at his watch. He looked back at his car then back again at Haggard as if he was unsure of what to do. "Look, maybe we should call the cops. Your insurance will pay for it and I want a new car. Shit it's only a few hours off of the car lot."

"No." Haggard shook his head and indicated for Conway to get in. "I don't want any cops or any insurance. I said I would make it good. Are you going to get in and listen or what?"

Conway stood for a moment then walked around the front of the Honda and got in beside Haggard. "Okay, what's the deal? I figure I got three maybe four thousand dollars damage to my new car plus the depreciation."

"How would you like fifty thousand dollars for your trouble?"

Conway's head snapped around and looked at Haggard. "How much...how much did you say?"

"I said how would you like fifty thousand dollars?"

"Yeah, right. Quit jerking me around," Conway replied as he wiped his nose vigorously back and forth with his right sleeve. "Let's talk some sense here. I haven't got all day."

"How long do you have to work to make fifty grand?" Haggard asked. "Probably a year or more but maybe you don't make that much. That looks like a new car. Is it paid for? I'm telling you I've got fifty grand and it's yours for your trouble plus a little information."

"What information? Who the hell are you?" Conway turned towards Haggard as his hand drifted towards his inner jacket.

"Sit back and relax," Haggard instructed as he forced Conway's head back with his forearm and swiftly relieved him of a small nickel plated 9 mm automatic pistol before he could re-act.

"Hey," Conway said, trying to reach for the weapon. "Who the hell are you? Are you a cop?"

I need information and I'm willing to pay you for your trouble. You give me what I want and you walk away a lot richer. You refuse and you may not walk away."

Conway grabbed the handle of the passenger door as he looked at Haggard. "What is it you want? Who are you?"

"Who am I? I'll tell you who I am. Do you remember a large motorhome and a guy by the name of Sheldon? How about a burnt down house, do you remember that?"

Conway opened the passenger door and was halfway out when a huge hand grabbed the back of his neck and a second hand grabbed an ear and yanked him back inside with savage force. Conway screamed in pain as Haggard held him against the door frame with his right forearm jammed against his neck.

"Now that you know who I am, I want you to think real hard about your future. Make no mistake scumbag, I will kill you if I don't get the information that I want. I have absolutely nothing to lose and I doubt that you will be missed very much. Your name is Conway, am I right?" Conway didn't answer and Haggard pressed harder against his neck, cutting off circulation.

"Okay… Okay, it's Conway, Ted Conway."

"I'm going to ease off on your neck, Conway and we are going to talk." He eased back from Conway and pulled the door shut, watching as he sat up straighter. "You give me everything I want and I'll give you the benefit of the doubt. You don't look like the big decision maker anyway. You can make fifty thousand dollars or you can erase any doubt that I have that you are one stupid asshole and I will still get my information. You won't see another new day."

Conway sat and looked straight ahead out of the windshield of the Honda, rubbing his neck and saying nothing. Haggard reached over and flicked his finger at Conway's already red and sore ear. "Ouch, son-of-a-bitch—that hurt! I'm thinking for crying out loud."

"Yeah?" Dan smiled. "You are actually thinking? If you think that little flick on the ear is painful then just wait. I have a lot of anger built up in me just waiting for someone like you to come along. Someone who had something to do with killing my wife, or burning my house, or…"

The Mule

"Okay, okay, ease off a moment will you?" Conway yelled. "I'm not getting killed for some asshole that couldn't care less about me." Conway took a deep breath and looked out through the closed passenger window to his right. "I was thinking of moving anyhow," he said almost to himself. "I'm sick of this shit and...let me see the money."

Haggard back handed Conway across the face with a closed fist and watched as blood streamed out of his nose and down his jacket front. "I'm not in the mood for games. I'll decide if you deserve the money, not you. If you want out of this then you had better earn it. If you try and con me it will be a big mistake."

Conway sat still for a few moments. His eyes watered and tears ran down a face that was smeared with blood. He didn't look as smug as he had when he had entered the car. He looked over at Haggard and he knew he wasn't going to be able to bullshit him like he did with the police. "You ran your car into me on purpose."

"Give the man a cigar," Dan answered. "Who's your boss?"

Conway sat back and let a long sigh escape from his body. He shoved the hair off of his forehead and looked behind him towards his car. "I knew this would happen one day. If not the cops then some other group would come along and I would be caught in the middle. This guy I work for, he really doesn't give a shit about me or anyone else who works for him. He gets all the cream and we get the skim milk. You have no idea what I do for him...and for what? His table scraps."

"What is his name?" Haggard prompted.

"I get the money, right? I mean once I talk to you I'll have to move to someplace. You might as well kill me because if I don't get the money to get away from here and make a new start they'll kill me for sure."

"As much as it will bother me you'll get your money and a chance to get out of the city. Here's the other part of the deal though. If I ever see you again you are a dead man." Haggard placed the pistol against Conway's temple. "No one will be able to protect you, remember that."

"Okay, okay. An hour, one hour and I'm gone, man." Conway paused briefly before continuing. "His name is Jairo Herrera-Sanchez. He's a real mean bastard. He thinks he's the Godfather or something, dressing up in thousand dollar suits all the time."

229

"Where do I find this Herrera-Sanchez?" Haggard enquired softly.

Conway told him. He told him about the radiator shop and the house and their locations. He told him about the Cocaine stash behind the radiator hoses and down in the basement of the shop. He told him about how Sanchez fixed it so Sheldon Porter was found dead in his house and how he had burnt it down and how it was Herrera-Sanchez who set it up so that the Cocaine was put under his motorhome.

"This Herrera-Sanchez is a pretty busy guy." Haggard remarked. "You of course had nothing to do with this, right?"

"Yeah, I did," Conway answered truthfully. "I was paid to do what I had to do. It had nothing to do with you personally. I just did what I was told to do."

"What did Herrera-Sanchez have to do with the beating of my wife and the break-in at my place?"

"Nothing actually; he was a bit pissed because he didn't like anyone bringing problems into his area. He…"

Conway's cell phone beeped and burbled with what Conway thought was a neat sound. He looked at it and put it back in his pocket. "That's Sanchez. He phoned me and he expects me at the shop by now. I was supposed to look after the shipment coming in but he is really pissed with all the problems he has been having lately. He blames me for everything. He lost a shipment of coke and a bundle of cash…but you know about that. Is that the cash you are trying to pawn off on me?"

"Money is money, Conway. It was one hundred and thirty grand but I have expenses. Fifty thousand will take you a long way and set you up until you find what you want. My guess it will me more of the same crap you are involved with here."

Conway looked away, not answering Haggard. He turned back, hesitating before he spoke. "Maybe, but maybe you are not right about everything."

"Give me your cell phone."

"What for, Man? I need it. It's got all my contact numbers on…oh, I guess I won't need it will I?"

"You use that cell phone and they will find you in no time flat. I have a much better use for it than you do right now anyway. Its part of the package, hand it over."

Conway gave the cell to him and sat back waiting. Haggard got out of the CRV and opened the rear tailgate. He lifted out the dried and crusted old case and handed it to Conway. "If I were you I would get moving."

"You still owe me for the car," Conway remarked.

"Don't push your luck, Conway. Remember what I said. I had better not see you ever again. Remember, I know you are the guy involved in doing Sheldon in."

Conway walked towards his car. Before he got in he turned to Haggard. "You had better not push *your* luck. If they find you, you are one dead mother. *My guess* is you are already dead, dead as hell."

Ted Conway started the car and without looking at Haggard he backed up and left the lot. He felt a cold hand grab his heart and felt a deep dread for what he had just done. Herrera-Sanchez would not forget, ever. But there was no way he was going to *die* for the asshole.

He entered the open freeway and a new feeling came over him. A sense of euphoria and freedom encased him like he had never experienced before. He had money. He had a new car. He had the open road. He also had the sweet taste of revenge for all that Herrera-Sanchez had put him through.

A picture of Sheldon Porter popped into his mind, the beaten and tortured body that had suffered an agonizing slow death before being tossed onto a burning heap inside Haggard's house. Conway shuddered and stepped on the gas pedal. A half hour and he would be out of the city and on the open road and he would be ancient history as far as Herrera-Sanchez was concerned.

* * *

Agent Lloyd Quiring's cell phone rang as he was about to take a sip of his second cup of coffee. He put the cup down onto the table top and looked at the call display. "What the hell?"

"Who is it?" Anthony Rosza asked, his mouth half full of a thick and spicy meat Samosa.

"It says Ted Conway. The idiot allows his name to be displayed?"

"How would he get your number? Answer it, this should be good."

"Yeah," Quiring barked into the cell.

"Now that is not a very professional way to answer your phone. What I think you meant to say was, 'Agent Quiring speaking, may I be of service.'"

"You are not very smart, Conway. You are not very funny either. We want to talk to you and right now."

"It's not Conway. Conway's gone on a trip and probably won't be back. It's Dan Haggard. Conway loaned me his cell phone."

"You do get around, Haggard. For your sake I sure hope Conway doesn't turn up dead."

"I couldn't care less about Conway. I want to make a meet with you guys."

"Why? Tell us what you have," Quiring countered.

"I've got more than enough intelligence to keep you guys busy for a while. We need to meet and fairly fast."

"Hold on," Quiring punched the mute button on his phone. "It's Dan Haggard. He's got Conway's cell phone. I don't know what's gone down but he wants to make an urgent meet."

Rosza looked at his watch and back at his partner. "Make it for three quarters of an hour from now. Tell him we'll meet him at 8th and Olive. There's a parking lot there."

Quiring passed on the information and closed the cell phone lid. "It sounds like he has something big."

"For some reason I don't think Haggard would call us unless he did," Rosza said as he stood up from the table and brushed crumbs off of his clothes. "Let's alert Howard Edicott that something might be going down in his area. I don't know how much time we'll have to act on any info Haggard gives us. I'm going to pass it on upstairs in case they need to prepare for more manpower."

"Haggard should be a cop," Quiring said as he got up from the table.

"He was, remember? He's getting results because he isn't a cop. He doesn't have to worry about Miranda."

"Yeah, well screw Miranda."

The Mule

* * *

Mike Sigger followed Roy Tully out of the tavern. They walked slowly towards the rental car that was parked at the other end of the lot under a tree. Sigger could tell by the look on Tully's face that he may have a hard time controlling him if things didn't go right. "Not a bad lunch," he offered conversationally.

"Like eating dog shit," Tully scowled as he opened the passenger door of the car.

"Yeah? I've never eaten dog shit. What's it taste like?" Sigger smiled over the roof towards Tully.

"Just like the crap I had in that place, that's what it tastes like."

Dropping behind the wheel, Sigger sat back without starting the car. "Well anyway your beer must have been good. You managed to wash the shit down fast enough." Before Tully could reply Sigger continued. "I don't know about you but I feel totally pissed. We're wasting time here. You need to get back to see about Frank and I need to make arrangements to get the Cocaine back across the border.

"You know what I feel? I feel like I would like to kill the dirty son-of-a-bitch that is screwing me around. I feel like I want this deal over with. This prick, Jairo, he doesn't give a shit about our operation. You want to know how I feel? I feel like I'm being treated like someone who phones customer service. You're sent round and round in circles because no one's there and no one gives a shit."

"Glad I asked," Sigger said as he started the car. "I know where Herrera-Sanchez operates out of. Maybe we should pay him a visit and shake things up."

Roy Tully looked over at Mike Sigger with renewed interest. "Why the hell didn't you say so? Let's go, I'm not sitting around on my ass all day. He can stick his sightseeing into his darkest regions."

"Put on your seatbelt," Sigger smirked as he pulled out of the lot into heavy traffic.

Twenty minutes later Sigger pulled to the curb and cut the engine. The two men sat looking at the front entrance to the radiator shop. Traffic on the street was light and there was zero pedestrian movement.

"Not much to look at," Tully remarked, watching as a piece of paper lifted and twirled in the street.

Sigger looked over at Roy Tully and then nodded towards the radiator shop. "Don't be fooled by appearances. More junk flows in and out of that place in three months than we see all year. I've been in there a couple of times but I'll be damned if I know if he warehouses it there. He sets up the deals but you always have to go someplace else to take delivery."

"I thought this was where we were to do the trade tonight," Roy Tully remarked.

"It is and I think it's highly unusual for him to do that. Maybe he doesn't want to move around in the open. I don't know if he stashes it there or not but he sure does the business."

"That may be but it looks dead as hell right now. Let's go and see if the jerk's there."

Sigger got out of the car but did not follow Tully as he started towards the building. Sigger leaned against the vehicle and did a scan of the other buildings and the vehicles parked along the street. He'd been in the business too long to just blunder into a place that could well be under surveillance by local police or federal enforcement agencies.

"What the hell is the problem now? Are you coming or not, Sigger?" Tully called back. Sigger did not answer and Roy Tully walked back towards him. "What's the problem?"

"No problem, Roy. How well do *you* know this place? Do *you* know if it's ready to be busted? It doesn't hurt to look around a bit and besides maybe this guy Haggard is in the area some where."

"Oh, wouldn't that be nice," Tully replied in a low and hard voice. "Oh please, let him be here."

"Let's go and scout around before we go in," Sigger said and headed down the street.

* * *

Dan Haggard watched as the two men from the Drug Enforcement Administration drove onto the parking lot. He could see that they had spotted him right away but he did not make a move to get out of his vehicle. They pulled up alongside and Rosza rolled his window down.

"Come on over," Dan invited.

The two men got out as a blast of wind whipped up dust and debris and moved it around in a miniature twister. Rosza opened the front passenger door and got in. He shut the door as Quiring hopped into the rear behind him. "Looks like a storm coming," Rosza noted.

The car rocked slightly. Haggard turned from looking out the windshield at the strengthening wind. "Yeah, well a storm may help you guys. You could have your hands full and it will probably be tonight."

"What have you got, Dan?" Rosza asked.

"Quite a bit and I could have a lot more by the time I am finished. But let's be candid here. I am not doing this as good and outstanding citizen."

"You're not?" Quiring chuckled.

"These are the people that set me up with that load of coke that was taken from under my motorhome. I have no way to actually prove it. As far as the United States Government is concerned I am a drug importer and dealer. But I think you know differently. Come on, importing Cocaine *from* Canada? That isn't exactly the route that it takes and I think you know I innocently took it into Canada. I told you both what happened up there."

"Yeah we've heard this all before, Dan. So what is it you want?" Rosza asked.

"I can hand you a large shipment of marijuana and the approximate time and location of a trade off for Cocaine along with all the principal participants. It's happening later today or tonight but you guys can't have it for nothing. I want my charges dropped and my name cleared."

Quiring leaned ahead so that he could look into Haggard's face and get his attention. "Listen, Haggard... Dan, we can only make recommendations and we certainly can't make deals to drop everything if it appears that you are just ratting on your buddies to save your own skin."

Haggard felt the hair at the back of his neck rise and his face flush with anger. "You listen to me..."

Rosza held up his hand and stopped him from continuing. "Hold it! Look, Dan, my partner has a point. We have to look at this the way the prosecutor will look at it. Sure you are giving us good information but we still need something that will turn this around for you. A witness or some other intelligence that points us in a different direction and to the people that actually set you up."

Haggard laughed slightly as another blast of wind shook the vehicle. "I guess I outfoxed myself then. I just gave Conway a free ticket to get out of town in exchange for what he knew. He was one of the ones involved in setting me up. So was the guy that they found in my burnt down house." He chuckled again. "I guess I sent my only witness packing."

"We didn't say we wouldn't go to bat for you, Dan," Quiring said. "I just said that we would have a pretty hard time convincing others that you are totally innocent. You drove into the United States with one shit load of coke."

"Yeah, well it sounds like you would like everything delivered to you all gift wrapped and yet there's no guarantee of anything to help me out. Maybe I'll have to think about this and look after things myself to see what other information I can come up with to clear myself."

"You can't handle all this yourself!" Rosza said, genuinely flabbergasted. "How are you going to take down a drug deal by yourself?"

"You are thinking like a cop," Haggard answered. "I don't give a damn about your drug shipment or the deal they are setting up. I'm looking for the people responsible for doing this to me. Believe me I am not going to be hampered by your set of rules when my life is on the line."

"You need our help just like we need your information," Rosza countered as he turned towards Haggard and spoke earnestly. "Look at me, Dan. I'm telling you we will do everything we can to set this right for you but the last thing we want is to see you either end up dead or in deeper water because of your actions. Tell us what you have and we will keep you in the loop. We can work together on this."

Haggard turned his head away and looked out the side driver's window. People were leaning into the wind and battling their way towards their cars. He knew he really did not have much of a choice. He needed their help. He needed it now and he would probably need it in the future. Besides, he was the one that called the meeting.

"Come on, Haggard," Quiring coached. "I'm really not against you."

Dan turned back and looked at the two men. He saw an open and honest request and offer of help. "You had better alert your surveillance teams. I'll show you where a large trailer is being guarded until the transfer takes place. My guess is they are going to offload the shipment and transfer it to another location to do the deal after it gets dark. It could be sooner but that's what I was told. The principal participants are from Canada and some decision makers in Seattle will be there."

"How many are guarding the trailer?" Quiring asked.

"I don't know—four maybe five guys."

Rosza turned around to look at his partner. "I don't think we want to take them down at the trailer, Lloyd. We need them all together."

"No, I wasn't thinking of doing that. I just want to know what manpower we should have in case something goes wrong."

Rosza smiled easily at Haggard. "What else? We already know the why, but we need the who, what, where and the when; we need it all."

"You'll get what I have, except for one thing for now. I have to go and make a visit someplace to see what else I can come up with. Stay by your cell phones." He started the engine of the CRV. "Follow me and I'll take you to the location of the trailer."

As they left the lot the sky seemed to close in on them. Black clouds rolled and tumbled in choreographed unison, bulging into puffed up silvery balloons while lower down, light-gray clouds dashed by on the racing wind. As the sky darkened, lights began to appear almost reluctantly. Huge drops started to hit the windshield. It didn't do much to brighten Haggard's mood.

CHAPTER EIGHTEEN

They approached the open bay door of the radiator shop. A sudden gust of wind brought the dank smell of the radiator shop to their nostrils. Several old hubcaps hung limply on the side of the building, banging back and forth and fighting to keep their perch. A strong gust sent one sideways along the wall until it clattered to the ground and rolled along amongst paper, dust and other debris. The temperature dropped drastically as the storm moved in.

Mike Sigger led the way. He ignored the office door and skirted a dirty yellow pick-up truck parked in the open bay door. He stopped and looked around the dismal interior.

"Not exactly franchise material," Roy Tully said behind him.

Sigger stepped around an unknown pool of guck on the floor being careful not splash any on his shoes or clothes. He headed for the small office, ignoring the two males that were busy under the hood of a car. He saw Herrera-Sanchez sitting at his desk and talking on the telephone.

"Is this guy for real?" Roy Tully asked quietly with raised eyebrows. "He looks like he works on Wall Street."

"He thinks he's a mob boss. He likes to swagger and play the part," Sigger chuckled as he stepped towards the office.

Herrera-Sanchez looked up and spoke quickly into the phone. "I got to go, I have customers."

"Yeah, you got customers," Tully said as Sanchez hung up and before

Sigger could open his mouth. "Good customers that you are treating like dog shit! What's with this bullshit of keeping me waiting here, eh?"

"You must be the other Tully," Herrera-Sanchez said and then turned to Sigger. "Hi, Mike. Good to see you again," he said smoothly as he stretched his arm across the desk and offered his hand to Sigger.

Sigger took the hand and quickly dropped it. "You don't look too busy, Jairo. Why are you keeping us waiting?"

"I've had problems," Sanchez shrugged.

"We all have problems," Tully shot back. "You don't know what problems are! I lose my shipment, my barns burn down, I got men dying, my brother is dead, and you sit here talking crap on the phone while I'm left to wait. Because of you we still have to arrange for the crack to be shipped back north. This is bad business," Tully said, his eyes beginning to bulge out.

"Your brother's dead? You're not talkin' about Frank are you?" Sanchez asked with a shocked look on his face. "Not Frank!"

"Yeah, Frank," Sigger answered. "We figure it's the guy that took off with our goods. He paid us a little visit up our way and Frank ended up dead."

"That's Haggard," Herrera-Sanchez said looking at Mike Sigger. You busted his house up and did a good number on his wife. She died in the hospital,"

"I didn't know that," Sigger said with little interest.

"Yeah, well this has brought a lot of problems and attention from the locals and the Feds. You guys moved into my area and pissed a lot of people off includin' this guy, Haggard. I think this Haggard took out two of my men and took one hundred and thirty grand and ten times as much coke from me. What you guys did has caused me major losses. Don't talk your problems to me either."

"It looks like we both have things to iron out," Sigger cut in. "We still need to get this business over with and get back. At least Roy does and I need to set up the return route."

"This thing with your brother, how did it happen?" Sanchez asked, trying to appear genuinely interested.

"Cops say he blew his own brains out but that is a load of crap. We figure Haggard did it because he phoned Roy using Frank's cell phone," Sigger said as he looked around the depressing office. "Where are we doing the transaction?"

"I'm sorry to hear about Frank. We talked a lot over the phone. It looks like maybe Haggard is not the patsy you thought he was."

"He won't be anything when I meet him," Tully boasted.

"To answer your other question," Herrera-Sanchez said as he got up from behind the desk, "I'll make an exception. We'll do it here after dark with everythin' sealed up from the outside. You can leave with your stuff and I'll give you some of my men as an escort to wherever you want to go."

"This is taking too long," Tully objected.

Mike Sigger stepped forward and looked at Tully. "Roy, the bud isn't even unloaded. The stuff has to be moved and we don't need any further complications."

Tully capitulated. "Fine, fine, do your thing." He turned to Sanchez. "One of us will meet your men at the trailer after dark and follow it in. I may come here and wait with you until it arrives. I've got calls to make anyway."

"Good, I'll have Conway handle it. That's if I can find the bastard."

"He said he was coming to see you. He broke off our business because *you* called him back," Sigger said.

"Yeah...well he isn't here. Another problem I have to handle. Incompetence everywhere I look. These guys are somethin' else."

Sigger thought of Vince Rizzo and how his ambitions went to hell when he and the barn went up in a ball of fire. He wondered if Conway was that ambitious or whether Herrera-Sanchez had managed to choke any and all ambition out of him.

"Just so someone is there for the transfer," Roy Tully said with meaning.

"I will look after everythin', don't you friggin' worry. When Jairo says somethin' it is already done. You two come back later and I will take you out for somethin' to eat before we move on this."

The two men walked out into driving rain, bent over against the wind as they hurried to the car. Shutting the door with relief, Tully turned to

Sigger. "How can you deal with that pompous prick? *When Jairo say something, it is already done!*" Tully mimicked. "The guy's been watching too much TV."

"Jerk or not, he had better not screw this up, Roy. If he does you are in serious trouble. You need this shipment."

The use of the word you, instead of we, was not lost on Roy Tully.

* * *

The cell phone jerked Haggard back from his far away thoughts of Connie. He had been looking out at the driving rain, waiting for his food as he nursed a cup of coffee. Washington State was the only name listed in the call display. "Hello," he said tiredly.

"I was worried about you. I hope I'm not interrupting anything."

"Amber," he replied, smiling into the telephone. "No, I was just going to have something to eat. How are you making out?"

"Not bad I guess. After you left I said to hell with it and stayed home. I owe it to myself. I got to thinking of Connie all over again and I just wasn't up to going in."

"I was just doing the same thing when you called. I haven't had much of an opportunity to do that."

"Like I said, you need time for yourself. You need to get rid of some of those bottled up feelings," Connie reminded him.

"I don't have much room for feelings right now, Amber. I can't let it catch up with me yet."

"Yes I did that for a long time too. I just wanted to tell you, it... It helped being around you, Dan. Thank you."

"We'll talk some more when this is over," he answered as he moved back to allow the waitress to place his food on the table, nodding his thanks.

"You may need a place to stay. If you get in a jam please phone me."

"Most people wouldn't want to get involved with a guy that has been accused of drug smuggling."

"Give me a break," Amber said in his ear. "You've let it be known, I don't know how many times, what you think of drug pushers. I know what you are trying to do, Dan. The question is would Connie want you to do this?"

"I don't know. I just know I have to do it, if not only for Connie then for myself."

"You are not invincible. Please be careful and remember my offer."

He thanked her and disconnected. Looking at the food he began to force it down, fuel for a tired soul.

* * *

The task force was made up of members of the DEA, the County Sheriff, Seattle Anti-Crime Teams and the Narcotics Unit. The task force was backed by the Seattle Chief of Police, the DEA Special Agent in Charge of the Seattle Field Division, and the United States Attorney for the Western Judicial District of Washington. Also included was Howard Edicott because his murder investigation tied in closely with the other investigations.

The combined intelligence sharing and the allocation of specialized manpower had made a difference in the past and Rosza and Quiring were both confident that they had what was needed to nail this particular target down.

"Quite an impressive group on such short notice," Edicott smiled as he shook Tony Rosza's hand, turning to shake Quiring's as well.

"We're geared up for this but not usually this quick. A lot of these people had to drop some important stuff to be here. I hope to hell it will be worth the effort. Grab a coffee and we'll fill you in."

Edicott sat down with the two agents, placing his coffee cup in front of him and stretching his long legs out in front of him as he looked at the other two men. "I appreciate you calling me in on this. I haven't made one bit of headway on the Niegel and Ruddick murders."

"Do you really expect to get anywhere with it?" Lloyd Quiring asked.

Edicott sighed, taking a sip of his coffee before leaning back in the chair. "I don't think I've got a hope in hell if you really want to know. These slugs kill each other off everyday. They aren't about to call me up or call the *America's Most Wanted* hotline."

Rosza chuckled and took a sip of his coffee. "That's why we wanted you in on this. You may have a chance to talk to some of the guys we scoop later on. Your two victims all worked together with these people. Maybe one or two will have something."

"Yeah rumors travel fast with these guys. The scuttlebutt that these guys pass onto each other usually has quite a bit of truth to it and sometimes a slip-up will go a long way to solving a case."

Rosza nodded his head in agreement. "We've got men sitting on a tractor-trailer loaded with BC Bud. They've spotted five known faces that are there to keep people away from the load. We think it will be unloaded as soon as it's dark. Two men, a Mike Sigger and a Roy Tully are down from Canada and are supposed to meet up with Herrera-Sanchez and his group for a Cocaine trade-off sometime tonight. We intend to take them down."

"You guys must have a good source."

Quiring and Rosza exchanged looks, both seeming to come to an agreement. Quiring spoke first. "Yes, we do. It's Dan Haggard."

"You've got to be kidding! I have him pegged as suspect number one for hitting Niegel and Ruddick. Is he protecting his own butt in exchange for giving you this?"

Rosza sighed and took a small drink from his cup, taking his time to phrase what he wanted to say. "Howard this will not come as a surprise to you. Lloyd and I think Haggard was made a fall guy and that he had no idea that the drugs were under his motorhome. We don't think he had the knowledge or the intention to smuggle drugs into the country. In other words, from what we have seen, we don't think he should go to court on this."

"He still brought the drugs across the border, isn't that the charge he is facing?" Edicott asked.

"Yep, and his lawyer is going to have one hell of a time convincing the prosecutor or the court that he was an innocent stooge unless he can come up with something," Rosza answered.

"It doesn't mean he didn't blow away two dealers looking for answers or in a fit of rage or for revenge. I have trouble writing him off. I think that he's connected someway to the victims. Sheldon Porter and…"

"And he wasn't even here when the house went up in flames. Believe me we checked," Quiring cut in. "You can also believe that it took a lot to convince *me* that this guy Haggard has been had, and big time."

"Haggard is the biggest victim I have ever come across," Rosza added. "The trouble is he won't accept that he is a victim. He wants answers— and we don't blame him. He gave us information because he was able to get it where and when we couldn't. He sort of screwed himself in the process by letting a witness get away that could have cleared him."

"A witness? Who is it? I'd be interested in talking to him," Edicott said as he sat straighter and took out his notebook.

"Ted Conway, Herrera-Sanchez's flunky. But Haggard said he left town in a big hurry after he had a talk with him," Rosza answered.

Quickly swallowing a mouthful of coffee, Edicott looked back and forth between the two men. "Yeah, I know the guy. What does Conway know that would clear Haggard?"

"Probably who placed the Cocaine on Haggard's motorhome without his knowledge and who's behind it all. Maybe even who trashed his house and murdered his girl," Quiring answered.

"I sure as hell wouldn't have let something like that just walk away," Edicott grunted in disbelief.

"Maybe Haggard wants the sharks instead of the leeches," Rosza offered. "Maybe he isn't thinking straight at this point."

"You know what? I think I will get back to you guys in a while. I'm going to see what I can do to collar and round up Conway. He sounds just too good to let him get away. If he helps Haggard, fine...but if he helps my case all the better."

* * *

Haggard sat as far down behind the steering wheel as he could without interfering with his forward vision. His eyes were riveted on the building one hundred yards down the road on the other side of the street. The radiator shop was a misty and watery mirage through the windshield. The rain had not let up. If anything it had increased in volume and strength, driven to a wild frenzy on a south west wind.

His view of the building began to deteriorate as the settling darkness moved in swiftly with the storm. He was about to move a bit closer when a vehicle approached from the rear and stopped a moment later in front of the radiator shop. It was the same vehicle that had parked next to Conway by the trucking terminal. Sigger and Tully had arrived.

He briefly flicked the wipers and watched as the vehicle sat idling. The exhaust curled momentarily up behind the car before being blasted away on the wind. The right front passenger door opened and a man ran behind the car towards the radiator shop. He made a mental note of the other man as he dashed in the rain towards the building and disappeared inside. He did not fit Mike Sigger's profile and that meant that the driver was probably Sigger. The brake lights on the car flashed briefly before moving forward again.

Haggard put the SUV in gear and followed at a steady distance. He waited a block behind as the vehicle sat at red light, watching as the traffic light did a dance on a taut wire in the wind. He moved forward rapidly when the light turned green and maintained his distance. The car made a turn and he knew it was heading back towards the trailer for the drugs.

He needed Sigger. He needed Sigger very, very badly. He owed it to Connie and he needed it for himself. No excuses, no talking it over, no nothing. The man had brutally beaten and stabbed Connie without the least bit of remorse and with about as much thought as squishing a bug. He knew the man would never face any criminal court for his actions. Right or wrong, Sigger had to pay and Dan Haggard had to be the one to collect.

Federal agents and local police would be watching the trailer when Sigger arrived. That meant he would be under surveillance from then on. It could mean that he would be arrested shortly thereafter and from there to possible detention time. He needed to act fast, but how? He drove another block trying to think of how he could isolate him.

Haggard pulled out the cell phone he had removed from Frank Tully's body in Canada and fumbled in the darkness as he looked through Tully's phonebook. He found Sigger's cell phone number and memorized it.

Closing the phone, he picked up Conway's cell and punched in Sigger's number as he watched the car ahead of him pull up to another red light.

"Yeah, who's this?" Sigger answered.

"Mike, it's Ted," he said with a restricted voice, squeezing his own neck and vocal cords.

"Ted who…who the fuck is this?" Sigger asked belligerently.

"Conway, its Ted Conway. Shit, Mike I just left you."

"It doesn't sound like you, what the hell's wrong with you?"

"It's my new car, it broke down. It flooded out or something in a huge puddle and I've been standing in the rain. I need you to pick me up for the meet. Sanchez will kill me if I don't get there."

Silence followed. He visualized Mike Sigger as he either thought about the request or was checking his call display for verification. He gave it a few moments longer before speaking. "Shit, man I'm soaking wet out here. Are you going to help me or what? We need to move that load."

"Where are you?"

"Not far from the trailer, man." Haggard looked at a sign that gave advanced notice of street names along the arterial roadway and mentally ticked off the streets. "Keep your eye out for Forest Street, South. Turn right and I'm right there."

If it hadn't been for Haggard's business and his reputation for delivering parts on an as needed basis he would not have a clue about the area. This, in a way, was his turf.

"You're a bloody pain in the ass, Conway. How am I supposed to find that street?"

"If you are heading towards the trailer it isn't far from there. You'll see it man," Dan croaked. He quickly ended the call and watched as Sigger hit the brakes briefly as he came to each new intersection. At Forest Street, South, Sigger stopped and then turned right and disappeared from Haggard's view.

Haggard accelerated, turning his headlamps off as he turned left in the opposite direction from Sigger and into a dead end area. Making a U-turn he sat and watched as Sigger searched the area on the other side of the main road. He turned on his headlamps, put them on high beam, and activated his four-way flashers.

The reaction was immediate. Sigger reversed his car and began to turn around to drive to his location. Haggard slipped out from behind the wheel into a cold driving rain that turned his hair into a sopping mess within seconds. He walked to the rear of the SUV and off into the night before Sigger's headlamps locked onto him.

Sigger moved rapidly across the intersection and then slowed as he approached the blinding lights from the SUV. He stopped the car twenty feet away, holding his hand up in front of his face trying to see Conway. He finally opened his window and leaned out into the downpour. "Conway. What the hell are you doing? Get in the fucking car!

There was no response and Sigger pounded the steering wheel in disgust. He was getting soaking wet and there was no way he was going to get any wetter for the likes of Conway. He leaned out and looked towards the headlamps, the bright flashing orange lights from the Honda turning his complexion a sickly pallor. Taking a closer look beyond the brilliant lights of the Honda CRV Sigger began to realize it wasn't Conway's lower car.

He was about to close the window when pain rippled up his neck and across the top of his head as the hard metal of a pistol was rammed against a nerve between his ear and his spine. Sigger knew instinctively that it was the barrel of a gun. He began to move but a fist pounded his head down onto the window ledge.

"Reach over and shut the car off," a voice commanded. "Do it now!"

Sigger stretched and fumbled with the ignition. The motor stopped. The noise of the engine was replaced by the hammering of rain drops on the roof and hood. He dropped his hand casually from the ignition and was instantly engulfed in pain about his right ear. The driver's door was yanked open and Sigger found himself lying face down on the wet and oily surface of the cracked and potholed road. Hands frisked his body and he was relieved of a knife, an automatic and another small pistol from an ankle holster.

"Okay get up," Haggard demanded as he stepped back from the prone Sigger.

Sigger moved slowly, buying time as he tried to figure out who and what he was dealing with. "Take it easy, buddy. You got the wrong guy."

Haggard watched as Sigger swayed to his feet in the glare of the headlamps, the driving rain making it difficult for Sigger to see. He stepped forward and gave Sigger a violent shove. Sigger didn't move easily and Haggard became wary of the other man's strength. "Move, walk to the right and behind the other vehicle."

Sigger began to move but he had the gait of a man who was ready to spring at any moment, a predator in unfamiliar circumstances. "You move the wrong way, even a little, and you are a dead man," Haggard warned as he reached into the car and switched off the lights with gloved hands.

Haggard led Sigger off to the right and away from a street lamp. He reached in and shut down the lights of the Honda SUV as he kept Sigger in sight. A gray and shadowy area loomed ahead and Haggard halted Sigger at the edge of the shadow and the darkness beyond.

"Who the hell are you?" Sigger asked rubbing his neck as the water pored down his face.

Haggard just stood there. He looked into the dark eyes of the man that had caused so much grief in such a short time. He wondered how one man could have ruined so much of what mattered to him.

"Who the hell are you? What do you want?" Sigger repeated.

"Who am I? I'm the last human being you are going to see on earth, Sigger. I want you to remember this moment before you take your tour in hell."

Sigger looked at the face in front of him and the eyes showed some interest. "You're Haggard."

"Who put the Cocaine under my rig, Sigger?"

"Go screw yourself."

'Who's running things here in Seattle?"

"Go screw yourself," Sigger repeated, squinting through the rain.

"It doesn't matter. I already know. You made a big mistake, Sigger. You killed my girl."

Sigger just stood and tried to look at Haggard beyond the flashlight beam. The rain washed across his features as his mind tried to figure a way out. He shrugged, a slight smirk coming to his lips out of habit. It was the wrong thing to do.

The Mule

Haggard hefted Sigger's gun, holding it loosely in his left hand. "I'm sorry I had to kill your dogs, Sigger. They had more moral character than you."

Mike Sigger's eyes darted to the right and then to the left. People he knew would be surprised at the nervousness and uncertainty displayed there.

"You made another mistake and picked on the wrong guy. But do you know your biggest mistake, Sigger? It was being born as a complete asshole."

In one swift motion he placed the automatic against Sigger's temple and pulled the trigger. The shot cracked sharply but the sound was lost just as quickly in the rain. Sigger dropped where he stood, his feet and legs twitching in an uncoordinated dance as his unseeing eyes looked up at the torrential rainfall in disbelief.

He wiped the weapon down with his gloves and placed it in Sigger's right hand. He stood there for several moments and looked at what remained of the man that had taken Connie from him.

There was a brief feeling of satisfaction of having eliminated the piece of scum at his feet. There was another feeling of having dealt a blow for Connie. It was called street justice and the only kind of justice that Sigger understood. But it wasn't enough. He wished he could kill Sigger again.

CHAPTER NINETEEN

Roy Tully sat with a chair tilted back into the corner of the small office, listening to the rain as it hammered the windows and roof. The furious onslaught never seemed to end. He had just talked to Frank's wife. She was holding her own and had her side of the family with her. He had promised her he would return the next day and that he would look after everything.

The problem was, could he? He knew the business was going to hell. Frank was not there to keep things running and the loss of a barn and a lot of equipment was a major blow. The other locations were not due to be harvested any time soon either. Sigger was right; he needed this deal to go down so the cash would keep coming in.

"You want more coffee?" Herrera-Sanchez asked from behind his desk. He still looked like he had stepped out of fashion magazine.

Tully made a face and moved his head from side to side without opening his eyes. His stomach was still rebelling from the thick black ooze they all seemed to love in Seattle. The phone rang and the sound reverberated from a bell out in the shop area. He listened as Sanchez answered, not opening his eyes.

"Yeah," Sanchez answered, listening for quite a while to the caller. "What the hell? Hold on." Herrera-Sanchez turned to Roy Tully and out of habit covered the mouthpiece. "Hey, Roy, one of my men is on the line. He wants to know where Mike is. Sigger didn't show up for the transfer."

Tully opened his eyes and let the chair fall forward onto the front legs.

He looked at his watch and knew that Sigger should have been almost finished with the transfer. "What's the status of the transfer?"

"They haven't started. I told them not to touch anythin' unless you or Mike was there." Sanchez answered.

"Where the hell is he?" Tully bristled in anger. "He knows how to get there. He should have been there long ago!"

"Could be the storm," Sanchez answered helpfully.

"He has a cell phone doesn't he?" Tully snapped. "I'm so sick of these problems!" Tully reached into his pocket and pulled out his phone. He waited and listened as Sigger's phone rang and rang and rang. Sighing, he placed it back in his pocket. "You have a car and another man to go with me? I'll need to do this myself."

"Sure, take that one just inside the door. I'll get the kid to go with you. You want me to have my men start on rippin' the container apart?"

Tully looked at Herrera-Sanchez and came to a quick decision. "Yeah, do that. I know exactly how many bricks we have anyway," he said with meaning. "I hope one of your boys doesn't get an itch or anything."

"If they do, they will answer to Herrera-Sanchez," was the reply.

Tully walked out to the shop area and got into the car as the young kid opened the large bay door. "If they do, they will answer to Herrera-Sanchez. What a jerk." Tully muttered.

* * *

The task force was well hidden. Snipers sat in ponchos and watched from roof tops, insurance against anything going wrong. Others sat in darkened buildings a block away, waiting for the word to move. Lloyd Quiring and Tony Rosza were fortunate to have a command post of sorts on the inside of an old boxcar sitting on the railway siding.

The trailer they were watching was parked behind a low concrete wall. They had an unobstructed view and they were partially hidden by a stack of barrels and pallets along the tracks. Absolutely nothing moved in the area except for light traffic on 4th Avenue, south. Cigarettes glowed from inside a van as the guys guarding the shipment waited for someone to show.

"This is taking a lot longer than I envisioned," Rosza said as he shifted his body armor to a more comfortable position. "Haggard said they were going to move on this as soon as it got dark."

Quiring nodded in agreement. The dark interior of the boxcar smelled of something he couldn't place. "At least we're not up on one of those roofs."

"They're probably as snug as a bug," Rosza answered. "They have hot coffee and..."

They both heard the door of the van sliding open. Four men got out and opened the back of the trailer and then got in and shut the doors. A sliver of light was visible around the edges of the rear doors. The glow of a single cigarette was still visible from the van.

"Finally," Quiring said in a low voice. "Whatever they were waiting for it looks like they got the word."

Both men sat in silence but nothing changed. The sound of construction noises continued from inside the trailer for fifteen minutes. Quiring walked back to the door after relieving himself in the corner of the boxcar. "What's that smell in here?"

"You, you just relieved yourself," Rosza said quietly.

"Funny. No there's a smell in here I just can't place. It's not unpleasant; I just don't know what it is."

"Cotton," Rosza replied. "Its raw cotton and was most likely bound and shipped in this thing. These things move all over."

"What do you know about cotton?" Quiring asked.

"I'm full of informa..."

Both men heard it at the same time in their earpieces. *Heads up, there's a vehicle pulling into your location.*

Rosza and Quiring moved to their left, Quiring watching over Rosza's shoulder through the crack in the door as a car drove onto the lot and doused its lights. It continued on slowly until it reached the parked van. Two males emerged. Unheard words were exchanged with the man from the van. They watched as the rear doors were opened and then closed once more. The guard remained outside in the rain; he threw his soggy cigarette away in disgust.

The Mule

* * *

Haggard drove slowly, working his way back towards the radiator shop. He needed answers and it didn't look like he was getting any. There was absolutely nothing substantial for the DEA to take to the prosecutor. It was going to become exceedingly difficult to find the answers to his questions now that he had involved the DEA. They or some other agency could pop up anywhere and make arrests. He could quite easily find himself with nowhere to go.

He pulled into the parking lot of a restaurant and went in and signaled the waitress that he wanted a coffee. He dropped a coin into the slot of a pay phone and three rings later the call was picked up.

"Yes?" her voice said sleepily.

"I woke you," he apologized.

Amber relieved him of any guilt immediately. "No, I'm glad you phoned. I fell asleep in front of the TV. I wouldn't have slept all night if you hadn't called."

"Not another cowboy movie," Haggard asked and smiled to himself.

"No, some stupid sitcom. What's up, Dan?"

"I need a favor. In case you are asked sometime down the road. You have to know that I'm putting you on the spot and you can say no with no problem at all."

"Go ahead, what is it you need?"

"After I talked to you the last time on the phone I came to your place for supper and had a delicious meatloaf. I left fifteen minutes ago."

There was silence on the line for a few seconds as Amber seemed to digest what he was asking. "Should I expect to be asked?"

"Probably not, but you may."

"Is this about the people who hurt Connie?"

"Yes it is," he answered almost in a whisper.

"Then we had a great meatloaf and you had two glasses of red wine. And no dessert," she continued.

"Thanks, Amber. I have to go. I'll call you soon."

"Yes, call me soon, Dan. Please be careful."

He hung up and walked back to the counter. His coffee was waiting for him along with a piece of pie. He looked up questioningly at the waitress, a well-groomed middle aged woman with no ring on her finger.

"You look like you could use a little cheering up," she smiled.

He pulled the pie closer and smiled back. "Fill a man's belly and he's happy, right?"

"Among other things," she said with a slight smile.

He chuckled and then sat in silence. He noticed that the wind had died down slightly and that the rain was now falling in a normal pattern. He finished off the coffee and pie. It was time to move. He got up and left a generous tip for the woman. "Thanks for brightening my day. Someone's going to be a lucky guy one day."

She stopped what she was doing and smiled her thanks. "I sure as heck hope it's soon. The good ones keep walking out the door."

Haggard rummaged around in the back of the SUV. He threw a small flashlight forward onto the rear passenger seat. He noticed a small digital recorder he'd forgotten about and put it in his pocket along with an extra ammo clip. He got in and started the vehicle, moving off into traffic. Ten minutes later he parked in the same location as he had when Sigger had pulled up and dropped Tully off.

Dan didn't really know what he was looking for. He assumed the delivery of the drugs would happen soon, followed by the DEA and maybe the take down. It all wasn't going to help him very much even though he had assisted them in a major bust.

He also didn't know what he had done to their stakeout by confronting and taking out Sigger. It was a disruption for the DEA as well as the bad guys and one they would not have expected.

It most likely wouldn't take long for local investigators to identify Sigger's body but it could take longer for them to connect it to the DEA drug investigation. The only question to be asked was who would the investigators think did it? He didn't want to know the answer.

He didn't know if Tully was still inside the radiator shop or not and he didn't know how many armed men were inside. He decided his only option was to wait it out.

Haggard sat up in surprise, jolted out of a deep sleep by an unknown sound. A black van was facing towards him further on down the street. It started to back away from him towards the open door of the radiator shop and as it did the lights from the van played across the interior roof of the Honda CRV. Haggard looked at his watch. He had slept for almost three quarters of an hour.

A car door slammed shut. He had not noticed the vehicle parked on the far side of the van. Roy Tully and a younger man walked through the drizzle and followed the van into the shop. He watched as an unknown male looked up and down the street before closing the heavy bay door.

It took exactly four minutes before a nondescript little car approached and quietly coasted by in front of the building. Two men were visible in the front seat as they passed his location. The car kept going and disappeared around a corner. *Let the games begin,* Haggard thought.

Actually it was another ten minutes before any signs of life took place. He was just beginning to wonder if the DEA would even show up when a man stuck his head out from the edge of a building and then disappeared from view. A few moments later six men ran across the street towards the front of the shop and flattened themselves against the wall.

They were all carrying short weapons suspended from slings. He suspected it was the 9mm Heckler & Koch MP5. The submachine gun spat out rounds at eight hundred rounds per minute, a deadly tool that was needed against the firepower of the drug gangs.

Four more men appeared and aligned themselves with the small front pedestrian door to the shop. One man was carrying a metal battering ram and another either a shotgun or a teargas gun, Haggard couldn't see which in the darkness. An additional four ran to the rear of the building and out of sight.

It appeared to Haggard that the team would have their work cut out for them. It looked like entry would gained only be to a front office and that would give anyone inside a lot of time to re-act.

A large and heavy truck rumbled out of the darkness with no running lights. Painted a flat black, it displayed a massive steel structure in front of the grill. It approached rapidly. It gained speed and turned without warning towards the large bay door of the radiator shop.

The collision was impressive. The thud from the crash echoed off the buildings up and down the street, the sound amplified by the quiet of the night. The bay door left its support rails and draped over the front hood and over part of the roof of the huge truck. A secondary thump could be heard as the truck collided with a vehicle inside.

Haggard watched the coordinated assault on the building with great interest. The moment the huge vehicle struck the bay door the smaller assault team rammed the small office door and was inside while the truck was still rocking on its springs. The six men who had lined the wall sprang through the crumbled door opening on each side of the now stopped truck. Whoever was inside would still be trying to recover from the shock.

Stun grenades rocked the building. Haggard watched as a window literally bent with the brief force of the concussion. Shots rang out and then there was silence. Dust and smoke billowed out of the entrance followed by the stink of explosive residue.

Very well done, Haggard thought to himself. He knew the risk in this type of operation and the planning that was involved to avoid injuries.

He was about to drive a little closer for a better view when a door he hadn't noticed burst open on the side of the building. A man was briefly silhouetted in the opening as he dashed frantically towards the sidewalk. He slipped and slid in some mud before turning and running down the street behind the Honda SUV. Haggard wouldn't have thought much of it, some joker doing his best to get away, but this guy was dressed like he was the best man at someone's wedding.

* * *

Herrera-Sanchez had everything laid out under a tarp on the big table that was usually used at night to sort, weigh and package the drugs. During the day it was covered with tools and radiator hoses and parts. He sat patiently in his office even though he was tired. It had been a long day. Fifteen minutes, that's all the time he had set for the deal. In, unload, check the quality and quantity, and out the door before anyone started to snoop around.

He was in the middle of a long drawn out yawn when he heard the bay door begin to rise. Getting up he walked to the office door and out into the shop as the rear end of the dripping wet van drove into the opening.

He moved aside and waited until the vehicle was all the way in and the motor was cut before moving down the passenger side of the van towards the rear. He rubbed his hands in anticipation.

"Finally," Roy Tully said as he got out and slammed the passenger door and followed Herrera-Sanchez towards the rear. "Have you heard from Sigger?"

"Not a friggin' peep," Sanchez said, shrugging his shoulders and being careful not to brush up against the van. "Where the hell do you think he's at?"

"*I* don't know," Tully said, frustration written all over his face. "I need him to move the stuff north. I don't have the time and I don't have any experienced people down here to replace him."

The large bay door began to rattle downward, the racket partially cutting off Herrera-Sanchez's reply. "…Escort you out of the area but you have to know where you are goin'."

"Let's unload the bud," Roy Tully said impatiently. "I'll move my car inside and get it loaded as soon as we are both satisfied."

Three men started to off-load the van, carrying the packages towards the large table where Sanchez was now standing. As Tully approached he flung the tarp back with a display of bravado. Cocaine bricks covered the top.

"Shit. Sigger said he had an idea for getting this stuff back across the line and I don't have a clue what he had in mind," Tully remarked as he looked at the full load involved.

"I hate to say this, my friend," Herrera-Sanchez said, hefting a brick of Cocaine. "I think somethin' has happened to Sigger. He has been gone too long."

"Yeah, like what?" Tully asked suspiciously, thinking maybe Sanchez might be setting things up to fall his own way.

"Around here it could be anythin'. Maybe he had an accident or maybe the police got him," he said as he randomly picked up another of the brick sized packages and walked over towards his office. He dropped them on the floor by his office door and started to walk back. "You can run your test on those two packages after we unload." He looked at Tully. "Maybe Sigger simply took off."

"That's a crock of shi..."

Tully and Herrera-Sanchez both jumped in different directions as the large bay door crashed inwards, collapsed from the frame and fell with a large bang. They moved automatically, their reflexes sharpen by nerves and suspicion. Something unknown smashed into the van sending it towards the table.

"What the fuck..." Sanchez yelled as he rolled towards a far wall, for once all thoughts of his dapper clothing erased from his mind. He crashed into some large empty cartons stacked against the wall. They tumbled down about him as he came to a stop by a seldom-used side doorway.

Tully was not so fortunate, he spun so fast in his haste to see what was happening his heel caught on a parcel of BC Bud. When he tried to gain his balance his other foot slipped in a pool of greasy slime. He went down on his left elbow and pain shot up his arm as a ball of fire rocked the interior. The concussion completely disorientated him, the energy from the detonation seeming to drive him into the floor. It would have been worse if he had not already fallen.

Rip-off, he thought. He felt cornered and vulnerable. It was not uncommon for word to get out that a deal was going down. He was in a strange city alone now that Sigger was missing. Alone or not, nobody was going to just waltz in and rip him off.

He reached for his weapon as he got to his knees then to his feet. He saw two men running in a cloud of smoke and dust towards the table and his goods. "Fuck you, assholes!" he yelled, eyes bulging as he fired towards the nearest man.

Roy Tully made a bad decision by turning and firing his weapon. It was the last decision he would ever make. There was no pain, no standing with a look of bewilderment on his face, and no falling to his knees and gradually fading away. One moment he was standing in the middle of smoke and floating debris, and the next moment he ceased to exist.

Herrera-Sanchez watched as the scene seemed to unfold in slow motion in front of him. He lay partially hidden under the fallen boxes, stunned by the explosion and numb and confused from the aftermath. He watched as Tully got up slowly and turned and fired a pistol. At least it looked like he fired his gun because he couldn't hear a thing. Roy Tully

disappeared abruptly from his line of vision, an unknown force yanking
him away.

Survival instincts rapidly returned. Herrera-Sanchez crawled towards
the wall hidden behind the fallen boxes. He looked up and saw the
crossbar on the fire door and knew he only had to jump up and push
down to open it. Turning his head towards the shop he saw the heavily
armed men in their paramilitary garb. *Cops!* They were moving slowly
towards the fallen Tully, others giving them cover.

With fear racing through his chest, Sanchez jumped up quickly and
rammed the bar down on the door, expecting it not to open but if it did
to find someone blocking his way. The cool, wet air hit him suddenly and
surprise registered on his face as he dashed from the building. He could
see the street and freedom only a dozen steps away.

Slipping, sliding and cursing, Herrera-Sanchez finally made contact
with the hard wet sidewalk and he broke into a full run. He panted and
wheezed with the unaccustomed exertion. Pain registered on his face and
he winced at the thought of a bullet slamming into his back.

"Cover all the exits," a voice commanded, too late.

Two men ran out of the side door as the rear door to the shop burst
open and three men came in low, a forth bringing his weapon to bear
around the edge of the doorway.

A quick search revealed no further combatants. The four men who
had entered the small front door had quickly taken the other hostiles
down as they floundered around at the rear of the van.

"Okay, stand down," Rosza ordered. "Let's get some more light in
here."

The lights came on as two members from Special Weapons and
Tactics entered the building from the emergency fire door. "That must
have been Sanchez. He ran like he had a fire up his ass," one of them said.
"By the time we hit the sidewalk there was no sign of him."

Quiring nodded at the two then looked around the interior. Men were
being handcuffed and led away as others were searched for loose weapons
or other dangerous items. Two men stood over Roy Tully and Quiring
walked up to them. "Leave everything as it is, forensic will be here shortly.
We'll get everything photographed before we do a thing."

"Yeah, well this one isn't going anywhere," one of the men remarked.

"Who took this one out?" another man asked as he walked up to Quiring and the other two men. He was the team leader.

"I did, Paul. He didn't give me a choice. Started blasting away," the shorter of the two replied.

"I saw him," Paul nodded. "My vision was cut off by the van though and I didn't know who responded. Good job." The team leader turned around and raised his voice. "Sound off! Everybody accounted for?" One by one all of the assault team reported in. There were no injuries.

"Well it went fairly well although we certainly can't call it perfect," Paul remarked as he extended his hand and took the weapon from the police shooter for forensic evidence.

"I'd call it damn good, if you ask me," Rosza said as he walked up to the group.

"No, damn good is when we don't have casualties on either side."

"Come on," Quiring cut in. "You guys couldn't have been better."

"Look, we get second-guessed all the time and we have to be better than perfect or answer for it. If it isn't the media and some of our good liberty-minded citizens it's an inquest or a departmental investigation. No, we'll have an immediate debriefing when we get back. You can bet that we're a lot harder on ourselves when it comes to something like this. We'll go over this point by point to see where or if we went wrong and where we could have done better."

"The only thing *wrong* is lying right there on the floor," Rosza said.

The forensic team was just about finished when Quiring and Rosza managed to figure out the location and unearthed the stairway to the underground cellar. They were met by a locked and massive door.

Quiring stood and scanned the locked door. "We'll have to call someone in on this. The large padlock and bar isn't a problem but that deadbolt is some heavy duty. The steel door is flush with the frame."

"It looks like our Mr. Dan Haggard had some good information," Anthony Rosza smiled. "Think this will slow the organization down some?"

"Yeah," Quiring laughed. "For about five minutes."

The Mule

* * *

Haggard watched in the mirror as the small overly-dressed man raced down the street as fast as his feet could carry him. He rounded a corner and disappeared from sight.

A picture of Conway jumped into mind. *"His name is Jairo Herrera-Sanchez. He's a real mean bastard. He thinks he's the Godfather or something, dressing up in thousand dollar suits all the time."*

He was about to start the SUV when two uniformed men ran out onto the sidewalk and looked in both directions for any movement. They stood watching for a moment but then turned and went back inside. Dan started the SUV and made a quick U-turn. He turned the corner a few seconds later.

Further on up the street the man could be seen running diagonally across the street, his form faintly outlined against the city lights on the uphill grade. He moved the vehicle ahead slowly, not wanting to lose him when he topped the hill. As the man disappeared from sight he accelerated to the top of the grade and watched as the running figure turned to the left at another intersection.

It was like he was in a different city. Run down apartment buildings with shabby store fronts of yesteryear were replaced by upscale shops, restaurants and nightspots. People moved about in a vibrant atmosphere, replacing the dark and deserted streets he had just left.

He watched as Herrera-Sanchez ran to a taxi stand where a cab was keeping a lonely vigil at the doorway to an upscale hotel. A moment later the cab pulled away from the curb with Haggard following at a discreet distance. He blended in with the traffic and timed his approach to the intersections to match that of the cab.

Haggard had a feeling that the key to his future was riding in that taxi and he desperately needed that key. Hell, he needed to find the lock first!

CHAPTER TWENTY

Agents Rosza and Quiring sat on the top step and watched as the man manipulated the cordless drill like he was performing brain surgery. His balding head had a low sheen of perspiration despite the cooler temperature at the bottom of the stairs. His khaki colored shirt was damp at the armpits and across parts of his back. He had been at it for ten minutes.

"How's it going?" Tony Rosza queried.

The man looked back and up, a look of frustration and tension creasing his features. "This is a good one. It's well put together. I should have it in a few more minutes I think."

Quiring looked at his watch and decided to see how long it actually took before the door was finally opened. True to his word, it took exactly three and a half minutes. The click could be heard from the top of the stairs as the bolt slipped back and the door opened slightly on its own.

"That's it; we'll take it from here. Don't open the door please," Lloyd Quiring said as he jumped up. "Good job and thanks for getting here so fast."

The man nodded and stepped back from the door. He quickly gathered up his tools turning sideways at the top of the stairs as Quiring and Rosza started down.

Quiring took out a small pocket flashlight and shone it all around the edge of the partially opened door. Except for the magnetic contact on the upper side of the door for the alarm he could not see any other signs of an attached device.

"Look okay to you," Rosza asked from behind.

"Yeah, no sign of any booby-trap. I'm going to inch it open a bit further."

Quiring moved the door enough to shine the flashlight further into the interior and along the other side of the door. Rows of shelves leaped into view from the darkness, visible behind pinpoints of floating particles of dust as they swirled in front of the flashlight beam. He moved the door open all the way. The air was stale and motionless.

"Well, well, well," Rosza smiled as he looked into the dimly lit room. "I think we've hit the mother load."

Quiring looked around the edge of the doorway and felt the wall on his left. He flicked a wall switch and a large bulb lit the room in a brilliance that momentarily hurt the eyes. Both men walked into the vault followed by the team leader and one other uniformed officer.

They all stood there in silence as they took in the row after row of bundles. They knew they had a lot of work ahead of them, a lot of work.

"There's millions here," Quiring said softly.

"I'm glad I took that fucker out."

They all turned and looked at the man who had shot Roy Tully in self-defense. He looked back defiantly but they all knew what he meant. It was his way of saying that if the guy had to go then he was glad he was the one who got to do it. His comment would not leave the room, ever.

* * *

Jairo Herrera-Sanchez felt like puking. His mind pictured Roy Tully as he was jerked violently out of his line of vision and he felt another wave of nausea as he realized how close he had come to the same fate. *I have to get hold of myself,* he thought. Tully was yanked away in his mind again and he suddenly realized that with both the Tully brothers gone he had lost a valuable buyer and a huge geographical area that he hadn't had to worry about.

His mind pictured the table with all the Cocaine laid out and ready to go. *Laid out for them like it was a friggin' banquet,* he thought. *Fifteen more minutes and I would have been free and clear. How could this happen! Cops everywhere!* His mind went to the table full of Cocaine and then to the loaded van. *Shit, friggin' shit!*

His mind raced as he discarded the image and tried to calculate his losses. He couldn't count the loaded van as his loss. It would have been sweet to have but it really wasn't his. The Cocaine was another matter. He'd already had to try and explain the other heavy losses, and now this!

Herrera-Sanchez knew that it was a good thing that he had the main supply well hidden in the vault or it would be a complete disaster...a shudder rocked him as he thought of the underground being lost. Blood seemed to drain from his head as his head fell against the window of the taxi. He tried to convince himself that it was safe. *No! They'll never find the underground room!*

"Hey, are you okay, fella?"

Herrera-Sanchez pressed the window button and wet, night air buffeted over his face. He looked at the driver and then turned away and ignored him. He would be dog meat if the stash was found. It was his responsibility! But he doubted they would find it...not unless somebody had shot their mouth off.

Sanchez flipped open his phone and dialed a number from memory. He had instructed all of his men to have no numbers stored in their phones and to erase all numbers that were received and sent at the completion of a call. It was good advice and a good practice to get into but then, Herrera-Sanchez seldom followed his own advice.

"It's me," he said when the call was answered.

"Why are you phoning me at this time of night?"

Herrera-Sanchez shivered again at the thought of having to report what had just taken place. "There was a hit," he said quietly. "The shop was raided by the cops right in the middle of the transaction."

"What are the losses?" the voice asked in his ear.

"We lost everythin' that we laid out and everythin' that we were waitin' for. The whole thing is gone."

"Where are you now?"

"I'm in a cab. I was lucky to get out of there. We have to talk. They've made arrests and took out a major player. I need to come over. I'm on the way now."

"What about the, ah…items in storage, did they get that too?"

"I don't friggin' know. I'm worried friggin' sick here."

"Then find out," the voice ordered.

"How am I supposed to do that? You should have seen the place. They came through the buildin' with a friggin' tank! The whole side caved in. They threw friggin' *grenades* at us. They're still there! How am I supposed to find that out?"

"I really don't care. Find out then we will set up a meet." The phone went dead.

"Son-of-a-whore," Sanchez said in amazement to no one in particular. "How am I supposed to do this?"

"You need help with something there, partner?" the cab driver asked.

Herrera-Sanchez looked up at the smiling eyes in the mirror, weighing his reply before answering. "I might. I might also pay a lot of money for the right kind of help."

"Heh heh, that's me. They call me, *Mr.* Helpful. How can I help you?"

"You can start by turnin' the cab around and headin' back where we came from. I'll fill you in on the way."

"You bet," the cabby answered as he quickly made a u-turn.

"You have to understand, driver…what's your name?"

"Len, my friends call me Len," the eyes smiled again into the rearview mirror.

"You have to understand that I am willin' to pay you under-the-table hard cash for your help but you need to have a very bad memory of it all. You know what I mean? If you can get me some simple information I will pay you well. If you can't you get the taxi fare and that's all."

"Look, I've been around, okay? You don't need to worry. I've done a couple of stretches and I need to connect up with something. I'm sick of this crap of driving assholes around all night."

"So…I'm an asshole?" Herrera-Sanchez taunted, narrowing his eyes.

The driver laughed easily, not in the least bit concerned about offending his passenger. He looked into the mirror. A pair of black eyes looked back, the passing street lights flitted across a face that displayed no emotion. "I like you man, you got a sense of humor."

Herrera-Sanchez didn't feel the least bit humorous. He felt terror taking over and it was burrowing deeper and deeper into his chest.

Haggard was taken by surprise. One moment the taxi was cruising slightly above the speed limit and the next moment it made a wide and fast U-turn and came towards him. He fought his first reaction to step on the brake and to make a u-turn as well. He watched as the cab drove back in the opposite direction. Both occupants appeared unaware of him.

Making a right turn into a vacant lot he doused the lights and turned quickly and faced back towards the other direction. He waited as two cars whipped by before entering the roadway. The taxi was at an intersection two blocks away and starting to leave on a green light.

Accelerating to sixty miles per hour he closed the gap rapidly with his lights still turned off. Several on-coming vehicles flashed their lights at him. Taking a chance, he ran a red light at a T-intersection, turning his lights back on as he did so. The cab seemed to be retracing the same route.

The cab stopped at the entrance of the hotel a few minutes later and the passenger got out quickly. Haggard came to a stop on the lot of a closed business and watched as Herrera-Sanchez walked to the doorway of the hotel. *What was this guy playing at?* The taxi drove away but Sanchez just remained in the shelter of the doorway. Dan had no choice. He sat back, curious as to what was happening.

* * *

The cab driver let the taxi coast quietly to the left curb, angling in and only coming to a complete stop when the left front wheel gently bumped and rubbed along the edge of the sidewalk. He got out of the car and looked up and down the street and then at the large truck that seemed to be imbedded in the front of the building.

Yellow police tape was strung everywhere, the usual warning for honest citizens to keep out. But there was just too much money involved for the cab driver to be worried about a little bit of police tape. He had brazened his way through a lot of things in his life and he knew that the trick was to appear confident, like you had permission to be there and like you belonged.

He had learned that in prison, bullshitting the guards. When you were questioned you had to have the answers ready. Even cops could think that you were somebody that was supposed to be there if they all didn't know each other.

He quickly stepped to the small entrance and the shattered doorway. Stepping across pieces of wood he found himself in a vacant and small office. A large and filthy window looked out towards a shop where uniformed men and women were moving about. He saw a small door to the right of the window but kept clear of it.

Standing to one side he watched as a group of men kept themselves busy around a large table covered with white bundles. He took a couple of steps to get a closer look but his attention was diverted as two men in plain clothes popped out of the floor beneath some hanging hoses in a far corner. They were carrying more of the bundles in their arms. Hell, he had the information he needed without even having to go inside. It was that easy.

He turned to leave and he saw something out of the corner of his eye. He was surprised. Two wrapped bundles sat on the floor just outside the office. He knew exactly what they were. He immediately started to fidget, his mind tumbling from one thought to another as his eyes darted everywhere. If he made a move for those bricks he could be walking the tiers of some prison for a long time.

He looked around quickly. Everybody was busy in the other part of the shop, especially around the stairs that dropped into the floor. He quickly ran to the doorway and bent down before peering around the door jam. Reaching out he picked up the bricks one at a time and then turned and moved towards the exit in a bent over run.

He closed the door of the cab quietly before placing the two parcels onto the passenger side floor and sliding them under the seat. Placing the car in reverse he quietly backed up the street before turning around and leaving the area.

Right from under their nose, he thought, bouncing around in the seat in quiet delight. He knew he had a small fortune sitting right next to him and he experienced a giddy feeling of euphoria. He sobered quickly however at the sight of the hotel. The guy was still standing there. He had to make a decision, and quickly.

Herrera-Sanchez pulled open the front passenger door as the car was still rolling forward and briefly waited as it stopped before getting in. "What did you find out?"

"You need to go someplace. I wouldn't hang around here if I was you. I can talk while I drive."

Sanchez nodded his agreement. "Okay, okay, go out the same way. What did you find out?"

"Bad news for you I'm afraid," the cabby replied as the car left the curb rapidly. "I waltzed into this small office and I could see cops out in the other area. Most of them were gathered around a table. But then these two guys just popped up out of the floor in the corner. They were carrying a shitload of bricks, man."

Herrera-Sanchez tilted his head back and moaned, wave after wave of anxiety rushed up from his stomach and something was crushing his chest. He couldn't think for the agony of it all.

"I'm sorry I had to bring you the bad news, man. Look under your seat."

Herrera-Sanchez didn't hear what was said. He was lost in his own thoughts. Although losing a shipment was generally considered a business risk, literally millions of dollars had just disappeared. He wasn't fooling himself. He was going to pay the price for having lost it.

"Did you hear me, man? Look under your seat," the driver repeated.

Herrera-Sanchez looked around, his mind not seeming to register what was said or even where he was. Looking at the driver and then out the window at the other traffic he gradually came out of his fog. "What, what did you say?"

"I said look under your seat. A little surprise for you, man."

Sanchez bent forward and rummaged between his legs until his fingers gripped the familiar bags. He pulled and both bags slid out from under the seat at the same time. "What's this?"

The driver laughed, ready to let Sanchez in on the joke. "I took it right from under the noses of the cops. Right from under their noses," he laughed. "They don't even know it's gone. What dorks! Maybe I earned a bonus on top of what you promised, right?"

Sanchez sat there looking puzzled. *Why is this clown babblin' about two lousy bags?* "You'll forgive me if I don't get friggin' excited over two bags. I just lost shelves that were friggin' full of them."

The cab driver's face lost its smile. He turned and concentrated on the road ahead, taking one hand off of the wheel as he scratched his head above his ear. He sighed and looked back at his passenger. "It was just a thought, man. You know, getting a little of it back for you."

Herrera-Sanchez nodded but said nothing. He watched as the car moved closer to his destination. Taking out his cell phone he punched the redial button.

"Yes," the same voice said somewhat tiredly.

"I've checked. They found it all."

Silence filled the line. It was a vacuum that Sanchez couldn't hang up on, a stillness that condemned him without anything being said. It was awkward and he knew he would have to be the first to break the emptiness of the connection. "We need to talk."

"Yes we do," a quiet reply came back. "Get over here now."

Len stopped the cab in what appeared to be the middle of nowhere. He knew there were houses in the immediate area but they were all behind high gates and large hedges. "You sure you want out here?"

Sanchez reached into pocket and pulled out a wad of bills. "This is just fine. Here, this is for your help." Peeling off five one hundred dollar bills he placed them in the other man's hand. He was about to get out and stopped himself. "If this works out I'll need a good right hand. Are you interested?"

"You bet. You know where I am."

Sanchez dropped the bags into his lap momentarily. "This is for retrieving the stuff for me." Herrera-Sanchez peeled off another five bills and gave it to the cabby. It wasn't that he was a generous man; he never parted with money if he could help it. The Cocaine was worth a lot more than that though and the guy had earned it. What the hell, the doomed didn't have any need for money anyway, did they?

* * *

Haggard sat and watched from a distance. The figure moved about with little nervous spurts of energy in and around the hotel doorway. It looked as if Herrera-Sanchez was planning on standing in the doorway forever. He was either waiting for someone or for something to happen, but what? If it was the return of the taxi why didn't he just stay in the car and wait? Haggard didn't have much choice; he would just have to wait to see what the guy was up to.

As much as he hated to admit it, he needed a breather. He was mentally drained and physically exhausted from all that had taken place. He didn't have the luxury of back-up or a partner to call upon. Extracting information from Conway and then trying to make use of it all was taking its toll. He had pushed himself hard to find the answers but the answers were always just out of his reach.

Since Connie's death he had pushed himself non-stop. He hadn't been able to think of her in a normal way without thinking about the men responsible for her death. He needed time to heal and he needed time to rest his soul. *Maybe sometime soon,* he thought.

He thought of Mike Sigger. He saw him standing there in the rain and squinting as water ran down his face; the smug little smile in place like he was untouchable. He saw Sigger twitching on the ground. He felt nothing as he remembered the dead eyes seemingly caught in surprise. They all seemed to think that no one could reach them and that they could make and live by their own set of rules. *Well, buddy, you weren't untouchable. You're not the only one who can make rules.*

Dan looked out at the rain, watching as a man and a woman ran across the street and into the hotel entranceway. The man stopped to shake the raindrops from his jacket. An image of another time came without warning.

He stood shaking his coat free of raindrops as he came into the house. It had been a very busy day. All he had wanted was a drink, something to eat, and to vegetate the rest of the night. Connie was having none of it. They were going out for the evening. She had practically dragged him to the bathroom shower, ordering him to hurry up as she placed a drink in his hand.

He had been rushed out to the car. He saw himself sitting next to her as she started the car. "What the hell is the hurry? Are you that hungry?"

"No," that smile on her face, the one he had fallen in love with. "But I made a reservation and we will be late."

She had lied to him of course. They walked into a small Greek restaurant. The warmth of the interior and the aroma of garlic and other spices had immediately made him glad that she had dragged him along. The tables were lit with small candles that flickered inside gold colored glass globes. He looked around at the near deserted interior, puzzled.

He was about to ask her why they needed a reservation when the waiter had interrupted and led them towards the back. The sliding doors opened onto a sea of smiling faces. "Surprise, surprise," they had all yelled.

He had been stupefied, not understanding what it was all about. Recognizing every one of his friends and employees but not understanding why they were there. He turned and looked into Connie's moist eyes, her smile quivering slightly. "I love you," she mouthed.

"I love you too, but what's this all about?" he yelled over the noise.

"This is an anniversary."

"What anniversary?" he laughed.

"It's the anniversary of our fifth date and the very first day that I realized that I loved you," she said with a tear on her cheek. "I wanted to share it with everyone."

He hugged her and gave her a kiss as his own eyes grew moist. She continued to hold onto him as their friends surrounded them. They moved around the room, shaking hands, hugging, and of course laughing.

"You are a nut case and I love you," he said, kissing her as they sat quietly with a drink and watching as their friends had a good time. "I've never had anyone do something like this for me. Thank you."

"You are welcome. I love you too." She smiled that unique little smile that crinkled her nose sometimes. And then the smile started to fade. It went away, replaced by an irregular trickle of water as it ran down the outside of the driver's window on the Honda.

The tears ran down his cheeks. He tried to wipe them away but they wouldn't stop. They just kept flowing on their own accord. It had all been a dream, a memory instead of reality. He was positive he could feel her touch and he could still smell the fragrance in her hair.

His chest heaved. He tried to muffle his cries of anguish with his arm but holding back made it worse. The memory of her smile made an unbearable void within and it seemed like it would never go away. *Why now? Why did you appear here in the middle of the night out of nowhere?*

Haggard sat up suddenly. He realized that he had actually thought of Connie and remembered her as she was in life, not as she was when she had died. It was a wonderful memory and one that he was glad that he had experienced.

His thoughts were cut short however as car headlights lit up the window and he turned to see that the taxi had returned. He watched as Herrera-Sanchez pulled open the door and got in. The car sat for a few moments and then moved away from the curb in the same direction as before.

He had a hard time shaking off the memory of Connie as he left the lot and followed the taxi at a fast clip. A steady rain fell on the near empty streets but the sparse traffic allowed Dan to gradually draw his mind away from the past and move to the present.

The speedometer registered forty-five miles an hour and he was not gaining on the other car. He still did not know why the cab had left and then returned but Sanchez now seemed to be moving somewhere with a purpose. He intended to find out what that purpose was.

He opened the window and let the cool air blow over his moist cheeks and into his eyes. He needed a clear head and he needed to be aware. From what he had been told, Herrera-Sanchez was a cruel bastard and cared little about others.

A different man surfaced and an icy little smile formed on Haggard's face. He looked beyond the slow moving wipers, out towards the taxi, the guy who had set him up and had started all this was just ahead.

CHAPTER TWENTY-ONE

Haggard took note of the name of the tree-lined street as he crossed at an intersection. There was no other traffic in the blackness of the night. Twice he had taken a chance and pulled towards a driveway, dousing his lights as if he had turned off the road and out of sight.

They left the built-up area and the street turned into a country road devoid of road markings or shoulders. He almost drove into a deep ditch twice while following with no headlights. The only bearing he had was the taillights of the taxi.

He turned on his lights as the taxi pulled off of the main road and onto a secondary street and headed towards the water. He slid up to the intersection quietly and watched before following slowly.

The brake lights from the taxi created two long red rivulets on the wet and slick road surface as it came to a stop ahead of him. Haggard put on his right signal light and turned into a driveway. He shut off his lights as he sat watching the other car. The interior of the taxi lit up as the passenger door opened. Haggard could see the dim outline of Herrera-Sanchez as he sat talking with the driver.

If Sanchez got out at the intersection in the dark of night, Haggard reasoned, there was a good chance he would lose him. He turned on the headlights, backed up, and then drove slowly towards the taxi. Sanchez got out and shut the door against the weather and walked forward of the taxi and into the headlights. He was immediately lost in the blackness as the cab did a reverse u-turn.

Accelerating quickly, Haggard drove by the oncoming car and hit his high beams as he did so. Herrera-Sanchez was just walking up to an ornamental wrought iron gate on his left. As he drove by he could see the man leaning towards a speaker set into a stone wall. Dan drove around a bend in the road and stopped. He waited for a full minute and then drove back to the driveway. Herrera-Sanchez was gone and the gate was closed.

Large brass numbers were set in the stone wall and illuminated above the speaker, insurance that emergency personnel could find the owner in the dark countryside. Haggard made note of the numbers as he dialed on his cell phone.

"Agent Rosza," the voice answered crisply, the sound of activity in the background.

"How did you make out?" Haggard asked without identifying himself.

"Haggard, we were wondering if we would hear from you. Boy did you hit the nail on the old head! It's going to keep us busy all tonight and into most of the day. We uncovered that underground stash. It's worth millions on the street."

"I'm happy for you but you let the main guy get away," Haggard reprimanded in a light tone of voice.

"Sanchez? We'll pick him up and tie him in. He won't get far. How do you know we missed him?"

"I followed him from his shop. I have an address for you. It's my guess he's reporting to the big man himself. That means you have an opportunity to identify who that is and clamp a lid down on all of Seattle and stop a lot of people."

"Just a moment while I get a pen," Rosza muttered. Haggard could hear unidentifiable noises as Rosza fumbled around on the other end of the phone. "Okay, go ahead with the address."

Haggard gave him the numbers and the name of the street and the general area outside of the city. "It's pretty high end out this way. My guess is you won't find any place under three million."

"So, is Herrera-Sanchez in there now?"

Haggard nodded to himself and then spoke. "Yeah, it's gated with an inter-com. You need to move on this right away before you lose this guy. If he is with the major player you have a real opportunity here."

"I can't do that, Dan. I'm up to my ass with this crime scene. I've got…"

"You've got other people that can take over. You owe me and this is all part of your take down."

"We don't have a warrant for that address, Dan. We can't just waltz up there and walk in."

Haggard sat for a moment, knowing that the chance to clear his name was going to slip by. There was something on the other side of that wall that he could use to prove his innocence.

"Did you hear me, Dan?"

"You don't need a warrant if there is a threat to life. Get some local backup. I'm not letting this scumbag walk away when he has evidence that will clear me of your charges."

"Now listen, Dan, don't go and…"

"You owe me, Agent Rosza. You had better get a move on or you're going to lose big time."

Haggard closed the connection knowing it would be a while before he could expect any support even if Rosza and his partner made arrangements to leave right away. That's if they left.

He put the vehicle into gear and drove off the road towards the wall. Backing up and parking alongside the stonework to the right of the entrance with the passenger side close to the wall, he shut off the lights and the engine. He sat there with the window down and listened for the sound of voices. The engine began to tick as it cooled but it soon lost out to other sounds of the night. Haggard wasn't interested in other sounds however, he was interested in men, and roaming dogs in the dark.

Opening the door he used it as leverage and a foothold, climbing onto the roof and using the roof rack to pull himself up. He found that the top of the wall only came to his waist. A large house sat back at the other end of a grayish expanse of lawn that was glowing with dew. Trees filtered some of the light coming from a small window.

Haggard stood in place and scanned the grounds for a solid five minutes, looking for movement from a guard or from a dog. Nothing moved as he dropped quietly to the ground and froze in place on the other side. Removing the automatic from the small of his back he ran quickly to an older tree and stopped; still nothing.

This is too easy, Dan thought to himself as he crouched low and ran. He flattened himself against the wall below the window as his feet sank into deep rich soil. His breath erupted from him in short and nervous spurts and a little hazy cloud drifted sideways in the glow from the window before fading away.

The edge of the window came into view as he eased himself upwards, the roughness of the bricks were not unpleasant to the touch. A dark leather easy chair could be seen in a corner of the room opposite the window. He leaned further. It looked like a den. There was a lamp, a small end-table with an open pocketbook face-down, an oil painting, and finally an open and dark doorway. There was no one in the room.

Walking quickly along the front of the house, Haggard stopped at the front entranceway. There was a better than average chance the owner hadn't bothered to lock it after Herrera-Sanchez arrived, especially if the he was the bearer of urgent and bad news.

Haggard grabbed the ornamental brass handle and pressed down slowly on the latch with his thumb. There was a slight click and then the door moved quietly inwards towards total blackness. He moved out of the open doorway, hoping he didn't bump into anything in the darkness as he let his eyes adjust to the lack of light.

His heart began to thump in his chest as adrenaline rushed through his body, pumping him up and making him aware of every sound. He just stood and listened, holding his breath momentarily to try and catch any faint sound. He couldn't detect anything.

It took a few minutes longer than he had anticipated but he started to make out the various objects around him and the general layout of the entranceway. A stairway on his right led upwards but halfway up it disappeared into the darkness as if by magic.

Taking a couple of steps to his left he was aware of the hard ceramic tile underfoot. He didn't even know he had stopped breathing until he stepped onto the softness of a carpet and let out his breath. He checked his watch. Fifteen minutes had elapsed since climbing over the fence.

A thin band of light peeped under a door at the end of a hallway. The light wasn't from the den he had looked into from outside, this light was deeper inside the house. Dan mentally kicked himself for not bringing the small flashlight out of the SUV. He moved slowly, placing each foot in front of him with exaggerated care as he neared the door. He placed an ear next to the door hoping to hear voices but he couldn't hear anything.

Running his hand very slowly and lightly over the door he searched for the doorknob. His palm hit metal and kept going before he stopped and went back. His fingers told him it was a recessed latch and clasp. That meant it was a sliding door and that also meant wheels that moved on a rail, sometimes very noisy and un-oiled wheels.

Haggard felt the latch with his finger tips; it was perpendicular. He applied pressure and watched as a soft sliver of light radiated up the side of the door. Pulling it back further he saw that he was looking into the continuation of the hallway and that the light came from a room at the other end. It was either a kitchen or a nook.

A large family room opened up on his right, lit up from the kitchen area by another entryway. He scanned the room and then stepped down two carpeted stairs into the family room and made his way towards the light. He was passing a large screen television when a voice stopped him cold.

"Do you realize what this means? Do you?"

Another voice replied in a hesitant and fearful manner. "It...it was a raid. I can't friggin' control that!"

"You can't control much of anything, Jairo!" the voice said in controlled fury. "You are not controlling your people. Someone has to have talked. Do you think they found the underground area by accident?"

Dan Haggard cocked his head and listened. *I know that voice! I know the voice...but from where?* He moved towards the voices and stopped in the shadow of a wall, able to watch both entrances to the family room.

As he leaned against the wall something dug into his body. He reached into his pocket and pulled it out. It was the tape recorder. He pressed firmly on the switch hoping it wouldn't make a sound and placed it next to a throw cushion on a chair to his left.

"Of course they friggin' knew, but how am I supposed to stop people from shootin' their friggin' mouth off? I lost about one hundred and thirty thousand and a shipment. I can handle that. I'll make it up to you because it was under my control. But I can't control the police for friggin' sake!"

"You lost millions of dollars tonight. The product was paid for with yesterday's dollars. They've arrested a lot of our people. Are those men going to reveal anything else?"

"No, they are all tight-lipped. Besides, they only know what I want them to know."

"Well they must have known about the vault. Who all knows about it?"

"Just me, you, Conway, Niegel and Ruddick, but Niegel and Ruddick are dead."

"Did Conway get busted?" Haggard heard the familiar voice ask, and listened with interest to the answer.

There was a long hesitation and Haggard wondered what answer Herrera-Sanchez was going to come up with since he couldn't know that Conway had made different choices for himself.

"I don't know where Conway is," Sanchez quietly admitted. "I told him to get his ass back to the shop late this afternoon and I haven't seen him since."

"Are you are sitting there telling me one of your men disappeared and then we had a raid and you can't figure out how it happened?"

"Look, I am not goin' to be made a fall guy here!" Herrera-Sanchez said in a very loud voice. A chair scraped on the floor. "All this trouble started when you said to load that motorhome for the trip north."

And then Dan Haggard knew. He easily matched the voice to a face and wondered what had taken him so long. He used to think the big blustery and friendly voice sounded like the movie actor, Andy Devine. But it wasn't Andy Divine. It was the voice of Richard Zeron. The friendly neighborhood dealer that sold you a vehicle, serviced it, or loaded it down with Cocaine for you.

"It was the Canadians that screwed up, not us," Zeron interjected. "I also should not have to remind you that it was your operation."

"Maybe so, but it was you who told me about Haggard goin' into Canada and you also said, and let me quote: 'The schmuck won't know the difference.' It turns out 'the schmuck' wasn't so much of a schmuck.

The Mule

He's screwed things up pretty well and I'm not takin' the friggin' fall for it."

"Do you think that just because you got away tonight they won't be coming for you? Is that what you think?" Zeron laughed. "I bet you think you can go home and just shut the door and go to bed."

"They don't have anythin'… Somebody was usin' the place without my knowledge," Herrera-Sanchez offered weakly.

A loud and abrasive laugh boomed out of Richard Zeron, a slap in the face to Herrera-Sanchez. "Fine," Sanchez yelled. "Get me out of the country for a while. You…"

"You are of no further use to me, Jairo! You are a liability and you have made enough money off of me to take care of yourself. If I were you I would draw your cash out before they freeze your accounts."

"You are abandoning me! After all this time you offer no loyalty," Sanchez shouted.

There was a moment of silence and Haggard heard someone move in the other room. He brought up the automatic in case Zeron decided to enter the family room. He watched the doorway.

Herrera-Sanchez broke the silence. "Who are you callin'?"

"Carlo is sleeping above the garage. I'll have him take you back to the city. You can't stay here, you are endangering everyone."

"Frig you, you friggin' bastard! I ain't goin' anywhere! Put the phone down!"

Haggard crouched down at the sound of Zeron's next words. "Stay back, Jairo. You won't get my help by threatening me. Let Carlo take you into Seattle. You can find a place for the night then make your plans to leave. You can't function here anymore."

"Carlo? You think I am goin' anywhere with Carlo? I happen to know that you used him two months ago to take out that stealin' little faggot, Reggie. You caught him dealin' on the side and the last anyone saw of him he was goin' someplace with Carlo. Is this goin' to be my little trip with Carlo?"

"Don't be ridiculous! I'm calling Carlo."

The gunshot was unexpected. The detonation in the small room was greatly magnified and jolted Haggard into jumping to a position of cover.

He leveled his gun on the doorway as a piece of furniture toppled over and crashed to the floor with a loud thud.

Silence followed the shot. Haggard listened and tried to fathom what was taking place. Ragged and heavy breathing could be heard in the other room. It was either Herrera-Sanchez breathing heavily as he looked down at the now dead Zeron or it was Zeron moving feebly on the floor in severe trauma. It was time to find out.

* * *

Quiring closed the cell phone and turned to his partner. "The house is listed to a Richard Zeron. NCIC has nothing."

Quiring was referring to the National Crime Information Center and the computerized index of criminal justice information from the FBI. It was available to Federal, state, and local law enforcement agencies.

"Does the name ring a bell with you?" Quiring continued.

"Nope," Rosza replied as he drove around two slower moving cars and pressed the car to move even faster into the night. "Zeron... What is that, South American? It's different."

"With a name like Rosza, you think Zeron is different?" Quiring chuckled.

"Funny. So is it South American do you think?"

Got me, I think it...well, well, well, guess what?"

"What?" Tony Rosza turned and looked over at Quiring with a questioning look on his face then back at the lines as they blurred as one on the road surface.

"A light just came on. Think about it. Richard, Rick, Rich, Ricky or as some like to say... Dick. Dickey Zeron is DZ. We just found our DZ Enterprises and the owner of the car that visited Herrera-Sanchez at his house."

"What a load off of my mind that is. And Haggard has him pegged as the head guy in charge of all the cells in the Seattle area or most of the northwest. I'm glad we turned the radiator shop over to the others."

"Who's coming in with us as back-up?" Quiring asked.

"Mercer Island Police Department is supposed to have a team waiting for us two blocks from the address. They're also working on a warrant based on our intelligence."

"If Haggard has gone in then we may have an emergency situation on our hands," Quiring said as he looked at his watch. "Not far now, is it?"

"Not at this speed," Rosza smiled as he concentrated on the slippery road ahead. "We have a problem if Haggard has gone onto the property. Break and enter, trespassing at night, home invasion, or whatever else he does once he is inside. I shudder to think of the consequences. Who do *we* back up, the owner or Haggard?"

"Let's just play this by ear. So far, Haggard has been right on the button."

"Maybe so, but illegal evidence is still illegal evidence and the big shot will walk on this if we don't do it right," Rosza noted as the vehicle dropped onto Mercer Island and then onto a forested loop. The road turned into a black and twisting snake and Rosza was forced to slow the vehicle down.

"This is unbelievable," Quiring thought out loud as he peered ahead in the darkness. "How is anyone supposed to find an address out here?"

"I have a general idea where… There they are," Rosza pointed as the headlights reflected back off of a couple of patrol cars parked at the next intersection."

"It looks like they take things seriously out here," Quiring commented as he saw the impressive array of equipment and men that had assembled on such short notice.

Getting out, Rosza and Quiring flashed their identification and then shook hands with the men that stepped forward in the glow of the headlights. They were geared for action and looked like they knew their business.

"Martin Scott, Special Operations," a deep voice pronounced as his hand reached out. "We've set up a couple of men on the perimeter of the address and all is quiet for now."

"How did you guys move on this so fast?" Rosza asked Scott.

Martin Scott chuckled. "It's your lucky night. You picked our monthly training night."

"Any sign of a Honda CRV at the house?" Quiring asked.

"Yeah, there's one parked right at the entrance. It's parked against a wall."

"The guy that drives it may have gone onto the property. His name is Daniel Haggard. He's a big mother and the one who provided us with the Intel tonight. He is not on the property with any authority and is acting independently to try and clear his name. He could be capable of taking someone out in the house if need be and although he has called us for back-up you should know that he could be an armed aggressor," Quiring said as he got confirmation from Rosza.

"Yeah, we don't want any injuries here. We think Haggard has been set up. It's a long story. He's desperate to straighten things out. Your people need be careful."

"Just so you know, we did a quick scout of the residence," Martin Scott said. "It has high walls running around three sides and has lots and lots of trees. The land runs down to the water and there is a dock with a small boat and a seaplane moored alongside."

"Do you have the shore covered?" Rosza asked.

"No, our marine patrol isn't running and it's… Hold it a moment," Scott said as he held up his hand and pressed his other palm against a radio receiver in his ear.

Rosza and Quiring checked their weapons and donned their soft body-armor while Scott was busy on the radio. They waited, watching Martin Scott and expecting a report.

"One of our men just heard a shot from within the house."

"Shit!" Rosza exclaimed. "Why do I get the feeling Haggard is stomping around inside."

"That's our in," Martin Scott remarked. "Shots fired life in danger."

"Now where did I hear that before?" Rosza said to Quiring as they turned and quickly headed for their vehicle. "I can hear Haggard's exact words. 'You don't need a warrant if there is a threat to life' he said to me over the phone. It looks like he provided an in for us."

"How very thoughtful of him," Quiring said as he grabbed a police assault shotgun from the trunk and started ramming shells into the weapon. "Remind me to thank him."

CHAPTER TWENTY-TWO

Haggard brought the semi-automatic up and assumed the combat position. He moved towards the wide entrance to the kitchen area that led in from the family room because it would afford an element of surprise and because the room was darker behind him.

Two hardwood steps led up to the other room. The steps were about five or six feet wide and were partially covered in carpet. The image of a table was mirrored in a wide patio door in the nook area as Haggard rounded the bottom of the stairs. A large decorative plant on top of the table blotted out everything else. The voice of Richard Zeron stopped Haggard halfway up the stairs.

"Okay, okay, I can get up."

A piece of furniture scraped along the floor again and the sound of someone moving came back to Haggard. Looking quickly around the edge of the wall he saw Zeron pulling himself up with the help of a bar stool. Herrera-Sanchez lay on the floor in a pool of spreading blood; his feet were kicking in a frenzied and staccato movement.

Haggard moved back quickly, surprised to see Herrera-Sanchez lying on the floor. He had expected it to be Zeron. *Where had the shot come from?* A new voice momentarily froze Haggard in place.

"Are you okay, Boss?"

Haggard cut back through the family room and headed for the other door to the kitchen.

"Yes…thank you, Carlo. I hit my shoulder when I fell back off of the stool." Zeron chuckled and then looked at the body on the floor. "You scared the living hell out of me. You fired that thing off right next to me."

"The asshole was making a move on you. I couldn't let him get close."

Zeron let out a loud sigh. "We need to clean this up. He'll need to go for a boat ride."

Haggard stepped into the hallway. A narrow door stood open on the left between the kitchen and the family room and stairs ascended to what was probably the apartment over the garage.

Haggard looked around the corner and into the kitchen. Both men were turned away from him and looking towards Herrera-Sanchez. Carlo was a huge man, six-five or six-six and weighing well over two hundred and fifty pounds. *Bodyguard,* Haggard thought, knowing he was probably a bit of everything including chauffer, handyman, errand boy…and hit man.

Leaning around the corner of the kitchen, Haggard leveled his weapon and pointed at the big man's back. "Don't move! Drop your weapon!" Both men looked as if they had stop breathing. Carlo hunched his shoulders slightly as if he was going to move and he ordered him again. "You *will* die if you do not drop that gun."

Carlo let the old 357 cal. revolver slide from his hand. It thumped onto the floor at his feet. Carlo turned around and stood looking at Haggard, his eyes hungry to close the distance.

Seeing Carlo turn, Zeron followed suit. A look of amazement registered on his face briefly before he recovered. "Mr. Haggard. Dan my friend, what are you doing?"

"Guess," Haggard said in a cold voice.

"I…I know what you are thinking, Dan, but you must believe me when I say I had nothing to do with any of the unfortunate decisions that this man made." Zeron indicated Herrera-Sanchez on the floor. "He…he acted through one of my employees and I didn't know that he was using my place for illegal activities or…"

"Save it," Haggard said, his eyes matching his voice. He looked over at Carlo. "You, Goliath, kick that weapon towards me."

Carlo looked down and gave the handgun a halfhearted kick, a smirk creasing his mouth as he looked up and focused on Haggard. "So now what, are you planning on making a citizen's arrest?"

"I plan on putting a bullet in your forehead if you don't do what I say," Haggard answered. "Get on the floor, now."

Carlo stood in place for several seconds and looked like he was not going to obey but he finally lowered himself to a sitting position. Haggard walked forward and retrieved the gun off of the floor. As he started to retreat Zeron unexpectedly walked forward and in front of Carlo, his open hands displayed in a sign of friendship.

"Haggard… Dan…look this can be worked out. There's no need for all this…"

Zeron came hurtling into Haggard without warning, pushed from behind by Carlo who kept pushing Zeron forward. It didn't give him a chance to back off. Zeron was now also trying to grab Haggard but he was too close and his large stomach interfered with his actions.

A fist flew by Zeron's head and landed solidly on Dan's right cheek, hurling him backwards with the force of the blow. He collided with a kitchen cupboard, his head banged hard enough to make his ears ring. A second fist entered his vision and he turned to the side in time to hear the cupboard door splinter next to his ear.

He tried to get his bearings but an elbow smashed into his nose making his eyes water as pain shot across his face and up behind his eyes. Flinging his right arm out in desperation he felt the solid impact of the automatic he still held in his hand. Something came down hard on his wrist and he dropped the gun.

Rolling to his left Haggard looked quickly towards Carlo. A little rivulet of blood ran down the left side of Carlo's head and into his ear. Zeron was off to the side holding what looked like a broom-handle, a triumphant smile spreading across his face.

Watching through a cloudy pain-filled mist, Haggard watched as the huge man advanced towards him. *Wait for him to make his move,"* he thought. *Remember the counter move and stay clear of him. Use his weight and strength against him.*

Carlo took a straight-on but powerful jab with his right fist and his intention was well telegraphed. His weight shifted as he leaned all of his power into the forward position. Haggard pivoted onto his left foot and allowed the fist to continue as it moved from left to right in front of his face. He grabbed Carlo's wrist with his right hand and pulled him forward and downward while his left elbow came up and slammed with force into Carlo's face. The big man grunted with pain and his knees buckled beneath him.

Haggard caught movement from the corner of his eye. Excruciating pain erupted across his left ear and then traveled across his head and into his neck. Turning, he saw that Zeron was beginning another swing with the wooden pole. Zeron's eyes were wild with panic and excitement. He waited until the round shaft was on its forward arc and he moved forward and inside the swing, catching the pole under his arm and reefing it away from the other man. Zeron stood there dumbfounded for the few seconds it took Haggard to pound the end of the shaft into his chest. Zeron collapsed, holding his chest in agony.

Dan whirled as Carlo regained his feet. He brought the wooden dowel around in a hard baseball swing. The center of the shaft broke in two as it connected with the side of Carlo's neck. Carlo dropped stone-like onto the hard cold tile of the kitchen floor, his head making an awful sound upon impact.

Haggard picked up his semi-automatic and walked over towards Richard Zeron where he had fallen next to the dead body of Herrera-Sanchez. A broken package of Cocaine that Herrera-Sanchez had carried lay spilled between the two of them. The man was starting to regain his breath. He looked up as Haggard stood over him. He looked at the black hole in the end of the semi-automatic, the one that was pointed at his forehead and his eyes registered disbelief at the way things had turned around.

"This has been…this has been blown all out of proportion," Zeron puffed. "I'll, I'll make it up to you. It was supposed to be a one-time trip across the border. You wouldn't have even known about the shipment. It was a mistake, okay?"

"Yeah," Haggard replied, watching as Zeron's terrified eyes focused on the small black hole. "And one you are going to pay for."

"No, no!" Zeron screamed, scuttling backwards on the floor through the spilt Cocaine.

"Police, drop the gun, Haggard!" a voice commanded.

The Mule

Dan turned his head slowly. Two very steady eyes looked back at him at the far end of a shotgun. One other officer was crouched on one knee, his pistol leveled at Dan's chest. Turning back, he looked beyond Zeron and two more uniforms took aim from the other doorway.

"Dan, its Tony Rosza," a voice said again on his right.

Turning back towards the shotgun, Haggard saw the outline of the DEA Agent as he appeared out of the gloomy hallway. The agent held up an empty hand and signaled him to lower his weapon. "Okay, Dan, you can relax. It's over buddy. We'll take over from here okay?"

Haggard stood with the pistol leveled at Zeron, watching the terrified face as he lined up the sites on his face. Zeron rolled onto the bag of Cocaine and pressed his weight firmly onto the bag as he tried desperately to move away. Air in the busted bag caused the bag to burst further, sending a white cloud floating in the air in and around Zeron.

"Come on, Dan, it's over! Lower your weapon," Rosza commanded quietly.

Haggard felt the gun dropping slowly towards the floor, moving on its own volition. He really wanted to raise it and send the piece of garbage to the dump but the gun wouldn't obey him. He let it slide from his hand.

They were on him in an instant. He was pinned to a wall, frisked and handcuffed as he watched the police team check out Sanchez and then Zeron. He listened bitterly as Zeron started his chant. He should have finished him.

"These two guys broke into my house," Zeron screamed with indignation as he got up off the floor, fear turning to bluster as he pointed to Herrera-Sanchez and then at Haggard. "Look what they did to my gardener! They killed him"

"This gorilla's a gardener?" Quiring laughed as he searched Carlo and propped him up against a cabinet before standing up. "He's just out cold. He's sleeping like a baby."

"Can't say the same for this one," Martin Scott said over his shoulder as he examined Herrera-Sanchez. "He got it in the throat, a bad way to go."

No wonder he was dancing around on the floor, Haggard thought. He spoke for the first time since dropping his weapon. "Check the gorilla's gun. He shot Herrera-Sanchez point blank."

"I want this man arrested!" Zeron continued. I…"

"Here it is, Agent Rosza," a uniformed officer interrupted, handing Rosza a folded piece of paper.

Tony Rosza smiled and turned to Zeron. "Richard Zeron, is that you?"

Zeron nodded, looking at the paper in Rosza's hand and unsure what Rosza was up to.

"Richard Zeron this is a search warrant to search these premises and the land they are situated on for the purpose of preserving evidence on the charge of importing a controlled substance into the United States of America for the purpose trafficking." Rosza smiled without humor and completed the legal chant. He then turned towards Martin Scott. "He's all yours."

"Richard Zeron you are under arrest on suspicion of murder and for the possession of Cocaine," Scott said as another uniformed man handcuffed him.

"This is preposterous! This is *my* house! I didn't shoot Sanchez, Carlo did!"

"You have the right to remain silent. Anything you do say may be used against you in a court of law. You have a right…"

Haggard tuned out the droning voice of Martin Scott. He was weary to the bone and ached and throbbed in places he couldn't identify. He leaned against the wall and suddenly realized that it was all over. There was nothing more he could do about any of it. Whatever happened would just have to happen.

* * *

"How are you feeling?" the doctor asked. He was about forty-five years old, was tall, slim and had tiny, tiny glasses perched on the end of his nose. He was the picture of health.

"I've been worse," Haggard smiled as he gingerly got up off of the bed. He had been admitted into the hospital for overnight observation. He had only agreed to being admitted because he was just too damned tired to argue with the doctor. Besides it would have meant time at the police station if he hadn't.

"Good, glad to hear of it. Slight concussion, a bruised rib area and minor bruising and abrasions seem to be the sum of it. You will be hurting. Here is a prescription for pain relief. Its almost noon, you can leave."

"Thanks for your help, doctor. At least I got some sleep."

The doctor turned at the door and looked back at Haggard. "You got some sleep while you were in here? That's an extra fifty bucks!"

Haggard laughed and then groaned as the numbing pain throbbed across his head and down his stiff neck. Almost an hour later he had signed all the papers required of him and was almost dressed when there was a knock on the door.

"Hi there," a soft female voice called.

He looked up and was pleasantly surprised to see that it was Amber. "Hi yourself, how did you know that I was here?"

"Gee, I'm not sure who it was that told me. It might have been the radio, no...maybe the morning television news, but then again..."

"Am I that famous?" Haggard shook his head, not liking the fact that his name was spread all over the media.

"That you are," Amber said as she picked up his jacket and helped him into it.

"That's just what I needed. Charged drug trafficker re-arrested in Cocaine bust. That's really good for business."

"I don't think you..." Amber didn't get to finish.

"Excuse me I'm looking for a Dan Haggard," a female somewhere in her late twenties said from the doorway. She had a clip board in one hand and a microphone in the other.

"What can I do for you?" Haggard asked

She gave Dan a radiant smile and stepped into the room, moving the microphone on top of the clipboard and offering her hand as she did so. "I'm Lori. I'm with City-Wide News. I wanted to get your story on camera as to the outcome of last nights drug bust by the DEA and local police."

Haggard held up his hand in protest and started to move to around her.

"I'm sorry, Lori. I'm not up to it. I've had a bit of a brutal night and I don't need any further publicity. I have enough problems."

"But this would make such a great story," the woman said with enthusiasm. "This is your opportunity to…"

Haggard brushed by her with Amber in tow. "Sorry, maybe later." He walked rapidly passed the nurses station and ignored the protests of the nurse as she hurried after him pushing a wheelchair.

Taking the stairs he found himself standing next to Amber on the sidewalk a few minutes later. A warm breeze ruffled his hair and as he looked up he saw that the sun was trying to push some small clouds out of the way.

"Great day, isn't it?" Amber smiled up at him.

"What in the world are you looking so contented about?"

"I'm happy for you, that's all," she smiled bashfully. "And I'm glad you weren't seriously hurt."

Haggard moved towards a taxi sitting at the curb. "Yeah, well tell that to my body right now. I need to sit in a hot spa for a month."

"I don't have one of those I'm afraid. I…" Haggard's cell phone bleeped cutting off Amber's reply.

"Yeah," Haggard barked impatiently.

"Mr. Haggard, its Lloyd Quiring, DEA. We need you down at our office."

"Jeez, man, I just walked out of the hospital. Give me a break!" Haggard replied, his head pounding in protest for having to talk.

"You had a busy time yesterday and you can't just walk away from it. I'll send a car around for you. This won't take long. Where are you?"

Haggard sighed and looked at Amber. "You better go ahead. The DEA wants to talk to me. They'll send a car."

"You're not standing out here in your condition waiting on them! I'll take you," Amber scolded as she grabbed his arm and led him towards the parking lot.

Haggard placed the phone against his ear. "Forget the ride, Agent Quiring, I'm on the way."

They rode in silence most of the way, Amber glancing at Haggard every so often as he rested his head against the door post with his eyes closed. She knew he wasn't sleeping, but needed the time to deal with the pain and to put it all the events together. It was probably too soon for him to be dealing with problems when he just got out of the hospital.

They were about a block from the office of the Drug Enforcement Administration when Haggard spoke, his eyes still closed. "I'm not sleeping."

Amber smiled and looked over at him. "I know."

"I'm not being rude I hope. I'm trying to convince my body to go away."

Amber laughed softly and watched as the lines around Dan Haggard's face seemed to ease. The tension and tightness seemed to evaporate, from the set of his lips to the taunt skin of his forehead. "They give you anything for the pain?"

Haggard sat up as Amber pulled to the curb and shut off the engine. "Yeah, they gave me a shot and a prescription. It's finally working a bit. Being the tough guy that I am I said I didn't need a shot. Mind you that was when they were coming at me with a needle."

"Now I know you are not afraid of a little needle," Amber said as they got out of the car.

"Oh, it wasn't the needle," Haggard smiled. "It was where they were going to put it. I can't be showing my ass off to just anybody."

Amber chuckled as she pushed the key fob. The car chirped as she joined Haggard on the sidewalk. "What do they want to see you for?"

"Not a clue. Probably want me to sign a written statement. They'll want me to fill in some of the blanks. Who knows?" Haggard pulled on the outer glass doors and walked towards the elevators. "At any rate, it's over for me. I can't do another thing. I'll be in court in a couple of days. Man do I ever have a lot to explain to my lawyer."

"But, you helped them…"

The doors to the elevator opened and several people joined them as they rode up in silence. Haggard opened the door to the office and saw Rosza gesturing for him to come forward.

"You look worse than I saw you last time," Rosza remarked as Lloyd Quiring walked into the office from another doorway.

"Thanks a heap." He turned towards Amber and smiled. "Amber this is Agents Rosza and Quiring. Meet Amber Lafreniere, a good friend of mine."

Rosza and Quiring shook hands briefly with Quiring being the one to speak to her. "Glad to meet you. Are you from a French background?"

"No, my late husband was from New Orleans. His ancestors picked up the name somewhere along the way."

"I hope you don't mind, Amber, but we need to speak privately with Dan. You are welcome to stay. There's coffee and a few donuts in the outer office in the corner."

"Not at all, I'll make myself busy," Amber smiled as she moved away from the men.

Haggard followed the two men into a different office and flopped into a chair. He looked from one to the other as they settled into the other chairs. "Okay, I'm here. What's so important?"

Anthony Rosza pushed a cup of coffee towards Haggard. "You did well with that information you passed on to us."

Haggard just nodded and waited to see where the interview was heading. There would be a lot of unanswered questions and they would want to keep at it until they were satisfied.

Rosza continued. "I'm glad we stepped in at Zeron's house when we did, Dan. We may not be sitting here like this otherwise."

"I called you for backup didn't I?" Haggard asked.

Lloyd Quiring answered and his face was not unfriendly. "All we're saying is we are glad we arrived when we did." Quiring paused. "Out of curiosity would you have put that prick away?"

Haggard smiled briefly at the choice of words Quiring had used. It was supposed to be a subtle hint, a man to man agreement that Zeron needed to be blown away. "To satisfy your curiosity, I don't know."

"You know that we had to take out one of the Canadians at the raid?"
Haggard shook his head. "No, who was it?"

"His name was Roy Tully. He started firing his weapon instead of doing what he was told," Rosza answered.

"Now *that* was a dangerous individual," Haggard said. "No loss to this world."

"Maybe so but the other Canuck, a Mike Sigger, was found on a dead end street not far from the drug trailer. It looks like the poor lost soul took his own life. He shot himself in the head."

Haggard wasn't about to engage in any conversation about Sigger. Even the slightest slip-up would be deadly. "You believe that?"

Quiring chuckled. "Not likely. He was done in but the motive isn't clear as yet. Can you think of a motive, Dan?"

"Oh, I think people in his line of work are bound to make enemies, don't you?"

"That they do," Quiring agreed. "As far as the dead Canadians are concerned though, our only interest is in their drug dealings. They were big players."

"I'm sure his death is tied into his drug dealings," Haggard offered. "These guys rip each other off and bump each other off all the time."

"It's really nothing to do with us but we wanted you to know that a Seattle Investigator wants to talk to you. His name is Howard Edicott. He's waiting down the hall to talk to you when we are finished."

Haggard felt his pulse quicken involuntarily. He wondered if he betrayed himself in any manner. "We've met. Now why would he want to talk to me?"

Rosza shrugged his shoulders. "You'll have to ask him. He's using our facilities as a convenience to you. We told him of your, ah…input and assistance in the drug take-down. He knows you just got out of the hospital so he's making an allowance."

"Okay, but what is it that you want? Didn't some of the information pan out for you or what?"

"It is sort of a good news bad news thing, Dan," Rosza smiled.

"Well since all I've had is bad news, it would be kind of nice to hear something good for a change."

Rosza leaned closer to Haggard and leaned both forearms onto his knees as he spoke. "The prosecutor listened to that tape you planted at Zeron's house. The good news is that you can forget about your trial. All the charges against you have been dropped."

Haggard just sat and looked at the two men. He could feel a weight lifting off of his shoulders and a great relief flood through him. He managed a slight smile and let out a loud breath of air. "The tape, I forgot about the damn tape I left on the chair."

"It picked up every damn thing that Zeron said," Quiring said as he got up and moved towards a desk. "This is the full transcript of the tape."

"I'm a little fuzzy on some of the things that were said," Haggard said truthfully.

"Then listen to this part," Quiring said with pleasure. *"This has been...this has been blown all out of proportion. I'll, I'll make it up to you. It was supposed to be a one-time trip across the border. You wouldn't have even known about the shipment. It was a mistake, okay?"*

Haggard remembered every word as it was read out to him. He also remembered Zeron talking to Herrera-Sanchez about loading up the motorhome.

"That was Zeron speaking as you stuck a gun in his face," Rosza offered. "It may not be good enough to use on Zeron in a court of law but apparently good enough for the prosecutor. You're free and the Administration will place a large news release out by tomorrow to help ease things for you."

"Thanks for coming to my rescue last night," Haggard said, knowing that he hadn't needed any rescuing from anything but himself. Haggard knew that they understood what he meant as well.

"Then there is the bad news," Rosza stated.

Haggard braced himself, not knowing what to expect after all the things he had been through. It could only mean that new and different charges were going to be laid on a different matter. God knew he had been free and easy with any laws. It could stem from his actions when he broke into Zeron's home armed with a weapon and threatening Zeron. He was sure Zeron would have laid a complaint.

"It's about your motorhome. We may not be able to get it back for you," Rosza explained.

Haggard sat there with a puzzled expression on his face. He had been expecting reality to come crashing down on him and he had a hard time grasping the fact that Rosza was only talking about his motorhome.

Rosza continued upon seeing Haggard's expression. "It's a long drawn out procedure. It's now considered federal government property and they just do not hand property back. I'm not saying this is a certainty but at least you won't have to ask for the return by court and appeal procedures. We'll work on this for you, Dan. You have been heavily shafted enough."

Haggard began to chuckle. It started low in his chest and rumbled up and across his throat until it became a solid and unexpected laugh. It startled the other two men and they sat back bewildered. Haggard shook his head and knew he had to explain. "It's not funny I know, but after all I've been through I was expecting the news to be much worse. Of course I want my motorhome back and I will appreciate all you can do but right now all I want is one or two normal days in a row."

Quiring smiled as he dropped the transcript back onto the desk and walked back towards Haggard. "You'll have it, Dan, but first we need your written statement. You saw and heard things that could carry a lot of weight in a court of law. We need it to help nail Richard Zeron. We want to see if we can confiscate every damn thing he owns. We're calling in the IRS as well."

Dan Haggard sat back and did some serious thinking as to what his next step should be. Any statements he gave to help the DEA prosecute Zeron and any of the others involved would seriously implicate him in other illegal activities. Busting into Zeron's house was not a legal activity, and carrying a weapon while doing so could have serious consequences. Zeron was not stupid and he would be waiting for any opening.

"Well, Dan?" Rosza said with a raised eyebrow.

"I appreciate all that you have done," Haggard said honestly. "But think of what you are asking. It's up to you guys to use what I dug up for you and it's up to the prosecutor to make it stick."

"We dug up some very incriminating papers as well as some very sophisticated communication equipment," Rosza stated with some enthusiasm. "But it may not be enough. It's up to us to make the evidence stick but the court will still want to know how we obtained the evidence. You actually saw and heard Zeron do things in that house when he didn't know you were there. You saw and heard things that were not obtained by the police and therefore may be admissible. You might have a lot of evidence that won't be thrown out. You come under different criteria. We need your co-operation here."

"I want full protection against prosecution no matter what comes to light. We are talking about bringing down a major drug ring and you know it. I know you are going to investigate Zeron's every move and his every connection but I don't take another step without that protection and you can't blame me."

Quiring sat back and let out a long verbal sigh. "We kind of thought that's what you would say, so we had a long talk with the DA and he's working on it right now. The defense will have a field day about your evidence but we'll get back to you when we have an answer. Then we'll want that statement."

"In the meantime," Rosza added, "you need to walk next door and talk to Howard Edicott."

Haggard nodded and got up slowly. He was suddenly tired and ached just about everywhere he could imagine. Muscles that he had built to perfection in the past were reminding him of his neglect. He nodded to the two agents and shook their hands and then walked towards the closed door. The day had just begun but he wished it was bedtime so he could just lay back and blot everything out. His emotions were in a whirlwind. Relief, apprehension, satisfaction, sadness, and even regret were unable to come to the surface so he could deal with them.

"Haggard," Quiring called quietly.

Haggard turned and looked at Quiring questioningly, wondering what was coming next.

"You be careful in there."

Haggard was unsure of what Quiring had said. "What was that?"

"I said be careful in there". Quiring just stood and looked into Haggard's eyes. His face offered nothing but his eyes said it all. *We know what you did*, his eyes seemed to say. *We know you did it to survive, but we still know what you did.*

CHAPTER TWENTY-THREE

Howard Edicott sat behind a desk; the top was neat and almost barren. The light from the window broke over his shoulder and spread like golden butter over the few papers that he did have fanned out in front of him. The sun highlighted the whitish strands in his salt and pepper hair when he turned his head and looked up as the door opened.

Haggard moved slowly into the room and stopped. His eyes came to rest on Howard Edicott sitting along the right side of the room. "We meet again."

Edicott stood as Haggard approached the desk. He offered his hand and motioned for him to have a seat. He watched as the big man lowered himself slowly onto the chair. "You look like you're hurting."

Haggard shrugged and gave off a slight smile. "Let's just say that David met Goliath and Goliath was a mean son-of-a-bitch."

Edicott laughed quietly and sat back down. "From what I heard, Goliath lost. So maybe David is the mean son-of-a-bitch."

"I'm just a lost shepherd," Haggard quipped.

"I also hear that you made high marks with the DEA. They say that if it wasn't for you they wouldn't have come close to closing down the kingpin in this area. That's pretty good work, don't you think?"

Haggard shrugged his shoulders and didn't reply. Edicott's manner, although pleasant and complimentary, was leading up to something. The only thing he could do was wait and find out what Edicott had or wanted.

"You don't need to be humble, Dan. From what I am told you came up with some extremely valuable information, information that takes law enforcement years to dig up. Mind you, you weren't inhibited by any legal guidelines like we are so I guess you could pretty well go and get what you needed."

"What I needed was to prove my innocence before I was locked away. I was lucky I guess."

Edicott shook his head. "No, luck has nothing to do with it. You're a guy who knows what he needs and goes after it.

"Nobody else seemed interested," Haggard said.

"Here's my question, Dan. What happens if you need something and the person doesn't want to give it to you?"

"Free country I guess," Haggard replied.

"Like I said, you don't have the legal restraints like we do. I was thinking that, well…maybe a person such as yourself might be tempted to apply a little pressure seeing that you had a lot to lose. If that happened and the other people involved pushed back, well things could happen that you may not have counted on or wished for."

"Things like what?" Haggard asked.

"Things like the deaths of Niegel and Ruddick."

"We have been over this before, I think," Haggard responded.

"Yes, and you said you'd never met them."

"I'm glad you keep good records," Haggard replied in a quiet but not sarcastic manner.

Edicott sat back against the chair and looked at Haggard, seeming to measure what he saw. "I picked up Ted Conway," he said suddenly.

"Good, the DEA will want to talk to him," Haggard countered while keeping his feelings hidden.

"I had an interesting conversation with him about Sheldon Porter, the guy they found burnt up in your house. Also we talked about Niegel and Ruddick."

"I'm glad for you," Haggard said with a little sarcasm. "Quit beating around the bush, I'm not some punk off of the street. If you have something to say then say it, because I'm certainly not going to sit here and make your day."

Edicott looked at Haggard for several moments and then sighed.

"Okay, no more bullshit." Edicott leaned forward and placed his forearms onto the desk top. "I don't know what you have on this Conway. He either likes you or he is deathly afraid of you. I called you in here to give it one more shot, but what the hell…I'm wrapping it up."

"What do you mean?" Haggard asked.

"I mean the cases involving Niegel and Ruddick are going into the pending and unsolved category until new evidence surfaces. Conway told us that he knows nothing about how Sheldon Porter got in your house. We don't believe him. He knows for certain that you had nothing to do with Niegel and Ruddick. He says he thinks it was the late Herrera-Sanchez who did it because they were ripping him off. *I* think he heard on the news that your out and walking around."

Haggard sat still and analyzed the information he had just been given. Was it too good to be true? "Do you believe him?"

Edicott smiled and looked Haggard directly in the eye. "No. But I'm wrapping it up because even if Conway had implicated you and ended up testifying against you I don't think a jury would buy Conway's story. Not against a decorated Marine, a local businessman that supports charities and was the victim of numerous crimes in which Conway was involved and certainly not after you found evidence that cleared you of any wrong doing. My bosses don't think so either."

"Where is Conway now?"

"We turned him over to the DEA, but my guess is he'll walk. After he provides some information against Zeron is my guess."

"Did you find anything on him?"

"If you mean the money you gave him to blow town after he gave you what you wanted—no. He had nothing on him."

"So, now what," Haggard asked.

"Now we talk about a man named, Sigger. Mike Sigger."

Haggard's forehead rippled in a frown and he felt the skin around his face tighten slightly as he looked back at Edicott. "You're talking about the guy that brought the shipment of marijuana down from Canada."

"He's dead."

"I know, what a terrible loss," Haggard replied.

"You know, this may seem like a coincidence but everybody that seems to have tried to screw you around ends up dead. This leaves me with one hell of a lot of paper work."

"How did he die?" Haggard said returning his stare. "What, did he strangle himself?"

"Just in case you don't know, he shot himself in the temple with a pistol that had the serial numbers removed. It fit perfectly into an ankle holster he was wearing."

"Well there you go," Haggard smiled. "Case solved."

"No, they all remain pending, Dan. They stay that way until new evidence surfaces. But don't worry; I won't be talking to you anymore until it does."

"Then I guess this is goodbye?" Dan asked.

Edicott stood up and walked towards the door. He opened it and waited for Haggard as he walked towards him. "Don't push it, Haggard. You are very lucky that you aren't in a cell for assault and battery, break and enter, carrying a concealed weapon or half a dozen other charges stemming from stomping into Zeron's house."

"So why aren't I?" Haggard asked, really wanting to know.

Edicott shook his head sideways and sighed. "Because a federal law enforcement agency put a lot of pressure onto the Mercer Island Police and they also got the word from the State Capital. Someone must be grateful to get rid of the likes of Zeron."

Haggard took in the information and knew he owed Rosza and Quiring big time. "But if you had your way?" Haggard said looking at Edicott.

"You have my sympathies, but just barely. Go and pick up the pieces."

Haggard walked out into the main office and looked over towards the corner where Amber was sitting. He watched as she looked up and saw him standing there. She put a magazine down, picked up her purse and walked towards him. She was looking at his face to try and gauge if it was good news or bad. She stopped in front of him.

"Hi," he said.

"Is everything okay?"

"According to the DEA I'm going to be very busy helping them out with their case against Zeron. They've dropped the charges and they are going to try and get the motorhome back for me."

Amber flung herself against Haggard and hugged him, squealing with delight. "Oh, I'm so happy for you," she said as she wiped a tear away. Moving back she looked at Haggard. "You did good, Dan. You did real good."

"I was going to ask if I can catch a ride home," Haggard smiled. "But I just realized... I'm a homeless person."

"You're coming to my place," Amber said with some authority.

"No, Amber. Thank you—but no. Give me a lift across town and I'll set myself up in a better hotel until I can find an apartment. I really need a lot of time to myself."

"Yes, I guess you do. I'm sorry; I was just trying to be helpful."

"You are, believe me. When you lost your husband you needed time didn't you?"

"Yes, of course," Amber nodded. "In a way I still do."

"Then give me some time and then I'll call you. I think we... I don't know, I think we have..."

"I think we have a good friend in each other," Amber finished for him. "I think Connie would like that."

"I know she would. Yes," he smiled, "I know she would." Haggard put his arm around her shoulder and the two of them walked slowly towards the exit. He didn't know where the future would lead him and he didn't dare think that it might lead back to a normal life, but his soul was just too weighed down at the moment to care.

THE END